ECLIPSO'S HAPPY QUEST

BOOK IV:MURDER MOST SAURIAN?

Extra special thanks to Russell Weaver for his brilliant cover painting. And endless appreciation to Maria and Don for their editorial input!
In Memoriam to Peter George

Other novels in the Four Planet series by David Taylor
(all published by Virtual Bookworm):

A Tale of Four Planets trilogy:
Book One: Sessions with the Seer
Book Two: The Rejected Counsel of Oomb
Book Three: Centers of the Universe

Eclipso's Happy Quest:
Book One: Goosed By An Iguanodon?
Book Two: Eau De Diplodocus?
Book Three: The Saurient Express?

Eclipso's Happy Quest
Book Four: Murder Most Saurian
A Novel by David Taylor
ISBN: 978-1-63868-230-1 (softcover)
ISBN 978-1-63868231-8 (hardcover)
ISBN: 978-1-63868-232-5 (ebook)
Library of Congress Number on file with publisher.

ECLIPSO'S HAPPY QUEST

a Post-Planets Prequel by David
Taylor

Book Four:
Murder Most Saurian?

Dedicated to Maria

"The most beautiful thing we can experience is the mysterious..."

Albert Einstein

Prologue: Scape Ore Swamp, South Carolina, March 1980

Slosh!

Slosh!

Paul Smith, Aaron Levy, and Ruth Schenker waded slowly up to their waists into the brackish water. But they couldn't wade slowly enough to do it quietly.

"Cripes!" complained Paul, coming to a halt. "We've made enough racket to wake a fossilized dino from its sandstone tomb! If our quarry *is* out and about, we might have chased it off!"

"But remember," pushed back Aaron. "Lizard Man, or whatever, can't hear us on our intercom between sound-proofed helmets. And it can't detect our spoor quarantined inside our waterproof suits. It's probably going to assume the splashing about is from some fellow monster such as a black bear simply passing through."

"Point well taken," Paul conceded while suddenly realizing, to his great surprise, how notably non-claustrophobic, non-stuffy he found his helmeted attire. "Still can't get over this hazmat suit. Fits loosely enough, feels like I could go jogging in it. Yet it's so protective, I could walk on the moon."

"But you don't have to beware of cottonmouths on the moon," spilled from Aaron's mouth into his helmet mike while he anxiously scanned the moonlit swamp water for telltale squiggles.

True, Ruth Schenker did give them assurances earlier. Not even a gator could tear through their outfits, let alone a small-mouthed snake. And yet...

"Less banter, more what we're here for, gents," lectured Ruth Schenker. That was her signature demand back at

Ruth's Primeval Good-For-You, her chain of health food stores spread across North and South Carolina.

Aaron and Paul first met when they were hired at the Raleigh Good-For-You branch to work the stock room, on break from studies at the University of North Carolina. That was the same place they also met Ruth.

They'd been at it for weeks, and built a friendship on such common interests as backpacking, and railing against water pollution from pork farms. Also didn't hurt, their discovery they both were from Philadelphia.

Then one afternoon, Aaron paused from organizing a display of local produce, to muse over an heirloom tomato's butt cheeks. And Paul seized that moment to say, "I know we've talked about hiking the Appalachian Trail one of these weekends. However, I have a proposal for something more adventurous."

"Oh?" reacted Aaron. *I'm open to that.*

"Less banter, more what we're here for," Ruth broke in from where she stood at the storage room entrance.

"Who the hell are you?" Paul bristled. But he softened after checking out Ruth's diminutive figure clothed in a green and yellow flower-print dress. He could easily imagine her offering a tray full of fresh-baked chocolate chip cookies.

"I'm Ruth. *That* Ruth." She pointed over her head at the store's logo sign, featuring a fanciful Tyrannosaurus Rex contentedly patting its rotund belly.

"You're this store's namesake? Wow," wowed Aaron, too wowed to fear what might ensue from his new friend's testy reaction to Ruth.

"I tour my stores time to time, just checking," said Ruth nonchalantly, whether affected or sincere. "As you were...before your banter set in." With that, she spun around on oversized-looking running sneakers, and pranced off.

After they completed the bulk of their work for that day, Paul asked Aaron into the restroom to resume making his pitch. He figured they'd be safe there from any additional random scrutiny by the grocery outlet's head honcho.

"Okay," said Aaron apprehensively, standing beside Paul at the urinals. What did this guy have in mind? "Like hitting the Appalachian Trail isn't adventurous enough, what's your proposal?"

"You see that report last night from South Carolina? A teenager saying he was chased into his car by something akin to *The Creature From The Black Lagoon*?"

"Oh jeez," moaned Aaron, wishing he could zip shut his new buddy's mouth like he was zipping shut his own pants. "You're talking about Lizard Man? You want us to drive down to South Carolina to investigate a kid's made-up excuse for his parents' car getting scratched up?"

"So, what was it exactly that left two sets of three parallel scrapes in the rooftop?!" Paul demanded more than asked. "That had to be either some gi-normous bird, or reptilian," he went on. "Bears have five claws on each foot, not three."

"Okay," Aaron sighed. Against his better judgment, investigating the Lizard Man story did appeal to him.

"Think of it, my man!" enthused Paul all the more, sensing headway made. "A large reptile standing upright, we could be talking about a dinosaur!"

"A dinosaur?!"

"I know," acknowledged Paul, holding a palm in Aaron's face. "Anything like that still romping about, people assume it has to be in an unexplored swamp, some far-flung corner of the globe."

"If at all."

"If at all," Paul nodded reluctantly. "But say some small-scale version of a Tyrannosaurus Rex hibernates the middle of a Carolina marsh or a Louisiana bayou. It only emerges from under blankets of peaty mud once or twice a year, to gobble down a hapless snapping turtle or gator. And this has gone on for millions of years. But now, gas stations and Boogie Burger joints and grocery stores, not to mention new housing developments, are encroaching on its habitat. Might that force it into an occasional foray outside its comfort zone?"

"Oh, so we introduce ourselves as bait? And while one of us is being disemboweled, the other reports out the find of the century?"

"Maybe the creature mistook the car for a fellow beastie," Paul continued, undeterred. "Thinking the headlights were eyes, it attacked."

"Just like sharks attack people when mistaking them for seals."

"Exactly!" Paul pounded thin air with his fist.

"There's still a considerable risk that while we're on our Lizard Man slash dinky dino stakeout, we are bitten by a copperhead snake. Or a black bear takes a disemboweling claw swipe at us."

As though to punctuate Aaron's warning with an exclamation mark, a loud flush issued unexpectedly from a toilet stall, directly across from where they stood at the bathroom sinks. Primeval Good-For-You Ruth Schenker emerged, admitting, "I just did that for effect, guys. But if you can hold off your search for two weeks, I'll join you. *And* put at your disposal specially adapted Hazmat suits fitted with micro surveillance cams."

Paul and Aaron wouldn't have been much more surprised, had a baby T-Rex just revealed itself.

"FYI, I hide in toilets all the time, men's as well as women's. That way I get to hear what people really say about me and the business," Ruth explained. "I consider it a bonus, though, to listen in on such exciting plans. Would love to throw my considerable resources behind them, if you're serious. Just think of the new logo Primeval Good-For-You could concoct from photos of a still-thriving dinosaur!"

So there Aaron and Paul were two weeks later, accompanied by a grocery store entrepreneur, up to their waists in moonlit swamp water... Aaron freaked out, stumbling his boot against a hard bulge. To endless relief, he quickly ascertained it was merely one of the submerged nobs encircling a tall cypress.

There were numerous cypresses to hide amidst. That is, once Aaron and company judged themselves deep enough into the South Carolina bog for their stakeout.

All well and good, if they got to spy on their prospective prehistoric throwback oblivious to their presence. However, what if it did become aware of them, especially before they became aware of it? Would they be able to outrun it, trudging through swampland? And avoid getting mauled?

"That squiggle," Aaron pointed anxiously at a sideways-moving water ripple. "That has to be a snake of considerable length. But which one?"

"I'll grab it and find out," offered Paul, reaching down.

Ruth swiped Paul's hand away from the undulating snake. "Gents!" her reprimanding if creaky voice shouted in both their protective helmets. "Less banter,-"

A loud, moaning hiss suddenly spewed from the cypress-enshrouded darkness up ahead, silencing Ruth.

Water streamed off something enormous rising out of the swamp, accompanied by the persisting hiss.

Aided by the infrared lens retrofitted to their hazmat suits, Ruth, Aaron and Paul spotted a gray, scaly something. It took the classic shape of a theropod dinosaur, complete with a dripping-wet tail lifted stiffly straight behind it. Turning its parrot-beaked head towards the humans, webbed spines down its back opened like an umbrella to form a bell-shape-curved sail.

Or not?

Ruth, Aaron and Paul let out a collective gasp. No sooner that, though, than they found themselves focused on a cypress with its top broken off. Was the tail in fact a disproportionately long branch near the base of its trunk?

But what about the head?

The head suddenly lifted off from the cypress, apparently an osprey carrying a wriggling fish in its talons. Did that raptor surgically snatch its hapless prey out of the swamp? Causing the racket that Ruth and company mistook for water streaming off a monstrous creature's back?

But what about that bell-shape-curved sail back?

Aaron realized a proliferation of Spanish moss favored one side only of the cypress tree. Too much sunlight on the other side during the day? Yet how could Spanish moss be confused for a sail back opening like an umbrella?

We shouldn't be here filled the three searchers' minds with unspeakable dread.

Coincidentally, the osprey turned their direction mid-flight, and held their attention with its unusually large eyes.

We need to protect the Earth by protecting THAT.

Whatever THAT was, the swamp water started churning like it had become boiling hot. And the apparent osprey's outsized-looking, parrot-type beak finished squeezing the life out of the hapless fish. Hovering lower and lower, this grim spectacle sank below the surface of the roiled swamp water.

That's when Aaron, Paul and Ruth realized the supposed cypress tree with the broken-off top had vanished.

Ruth felt like she might as well have been woken from a too-deep slumber, with no time to waste. There used to be mutual respect between her and the fellow who sprang to mind. She was one of the few outsiders he trusted not to divulge his whereabouts, nor his odd commitment. He followed the directives of a strange little creature his tragically lost wife discovered on a small South-Pacific atoll. No matter whether those directives were intuited, mentally telepathed, or wishful-thinking fantasized to distract him from his grief.

Ruth suddenly felt possessed by grim determination he must be stopped. She would bankroll the ambition of these two young men, nicely balanced temperamentally between cautious and adventurous.

Like a curse, she whispered under her breath, "Eclipso!"

Chapter 1

"What's this Scott told me, about you hearing someone go, 'Buk-buk-buk' on your phone, middle of the night?" asked Irene McDowell, folklore researcher.

"No; it was 'Buk-buk-buk-buk-BUK!'" corrected Dr. Augustine "Augie" Matias, former paleontologist at the Smithsonian Museum of Natural History. "And yes, it did sound exactly like Houdini Chicken."

"I didn't think you were going to give her your phone number. Once she ran off with that rooster...Sorry, Augie," Irene chortled in her deep voice, unable to keep a straight face any longer.

"Quite alright," Augie chuckled affably. "I know how absurd the whole thing sounds."

Irene raised the issue for want of anything better to mention while she, Augie, Scott, Sherman, and Sherman's artificial intelligence entity named Charly awaited someone else's arrival at Drunk In The Wool.

Drunk In The Wool was a pub in Kelpyguard, South Wales. The sign hung outside featured a tipsy sheep holding a can of Toohey's Beer, a favored local brew.

"Did you ever ask Sergeant Frankly, or even our belovedly notorious skeptic-in-residence, Stephen, if that was a prank?" inquired Sherman, his chin once again scrunched firmly against his neck.

So firmly, Irene figured he might as well be addressing his belly button rather than Augie. And about to offer it a sip of his hot chocolate before bringing the cup to his lips again for another loud slurp.

"I can't see Stephen indulging such nonsense," Augie shook his head dismissively. "As for Sergeant Frankly, he told me he did clown around on the phone. But only a bit, and the timing's all wrong anyway."

"Oh?" Sherman delayed his next slurp to utter, his curiosity piqued.

"Yeah, he tried calling me early that evening to ask a small favor. When nobody picked up, he left a message that started with a 'Buk-buk-BUK!' But he immediately followed up with his request. Only, I never heard the phone ring, and the message didn't record."

Click...whirr... "Would you like a message from me on your phone?" Charly suddenly stirred alive to ask in his robotically cadenced voice.

"Charly, please disable your empathy program," said Sherman into his cup of hot chocolate.

Click...click...whirr... "Done." Click...whirr... "What I meant to say, Augustine, was: I don't care." With that, Charly whirred back to statuesquely still.

"Maybe Fred Frankly's message did get through," suggested Scott, too focused on Augie's puzzling experience to be distracted by Charly's behavior. "But due to a glitch, your phone rang several hours later with only the clucking part."

"If Stephen were here, he'd likely applaud your hypothesis, Scott," Augie had to admit. "One big prob, though. Fred insists he did a 'Buk-buk-BUK!' Yet I clearly heard a 'Buk-buk-buk-buk-BUK!' Five buks instead of three."

"Maybe someone was passing the buks," quipped Irene. "Okay," she continued on a marginally more serious note. "What was this small favor the sergeant wanted? Permission to cuss freely, next time your wife's class eavesdrops?"

"Oh, you really don't know?" Augie asked, genuinely startled. "Fred ended up asking Laura for permission to leave a homing beacon at her condo. He said that otherwise, his crew could have trouble tracking it from their starship, umm..."

"The Smoke and Mirrors," Irene reminded Augie. "Hard to forget that name, once they told us it's a time-travel spacecraft."

"Thanks, um, well anyway," stumbled Augie. "It's no news to any of us, that Fred and company believe the Smoke and Mirrors is currently caught inside a black hole."

"Yes," nodded Irene, Scott nodding along. "And that there's no telling when it will escape from there to pick up 'Fred and company.'"

"Wherefore the issue. Our professed time travelers have this homing beacon."

"We also know about that," nodded Scott, Irene nodding along this time. "They said their crew uses it to locate them after they trade out guns for solar panels and the like."

"Exactly," nodded Augie, whole lot of nodding going on. "Well, Fred told me that he, Ali, and Kevin agreed they should leave it at a fixed location. That is, if they're going to continue tagging along on our search instead of just cooling their heels for who knows how long. And so, when he didn't hear back from me, he got in touch with Laura. Her condo, like our house, isn't going anywhere."

"I don't understand," said Irene. "Why can't they just continue to take the homing beacon wherever they go? Wouldn't that be more direct than their crew having to detour through Laura's condo?"

"That's where it gets a little too complicated for me to wrap my head around," Augie confessed. "Something about a quantum wave, and what if they arrive even one second early, into our future, or one second late, into our past, let alone hours or days."

Only at this juncture did Augie realize the attention he'd drawn from Drunk-In-The-Wool patrons. They couldn't help listening in, for how bizarre his remarks struck them.

The more the pub regulars listened, the quieter they became. So much for Augie's hope that he and his team would remain inconspicuous for their meeting with a certain local. *I know Sherman should have left Charly back aboard Cloud Nine*, Augie told himself ruefully. *The second he made his robotic whirs and clicks, that alone probably turned lots of heads.*

Nevertheless, Augie soldiered on, "Fred said they have this thing called a firefly donut. It can access the homing beacon signal even if their starship doesn't make an exact return to our split-second present. But the problem is..." he trailed off finally. His discomfort had grown too pronounced over Drunk-In-The-Wool regulars hanging on his every word. And so, in place of how he was originally going to conclude, he said, "The problem is, it can't help us find the best fish and chips in Wales."

That was it. That was all the hunched-over man at the counter could take, with his unkempt, greasy-looking, gray-streaked hair persistently straying across his eyes, no matter how often he brushed it aside. Up to then, he'd been nursing his third pint of Toohey's Beer. And unlike other regulars, he hadn't yet stolen even a glimpse at Augie and company. But the crazy remarks just kept piling up. Buk-buk-buks over a telephone, a starship, time travelers, a quantum wave, and now a firefly donut...Nigel Morgan finally couldn't help himself. He swung his head Augie's direction...

...which prompted barkeep Gerwyn Davies to set down a pint glass only half filled from the tap, and spring into action. Before Nigel could finish staggering drunkenly off his bar stool, Gerwyn was over beside Augie's table, saying, "Excuse me, I'm not being funny, right? Are you the blokes...and bloke-ess," he awkwardly acknowledged Irene, "who have come here to ask Kay about her student's dinosaur sighting at Strumblehead?"

"Oh, so is it a living dinosaur as well?" Nigel complained in his plastered voice. "Time travel and spaceships are not enough for you bloody bastards, are they?"

Beer sloshed from Nigel's pint glass held at so shallow an angle, Augie wouldn't have been surprised to see every last drop spill out. Plus, he imagined Nigel a fully clothed gorilla scrapping for a fight.

"My great grandfather grew up around here," said Augie. He lifted a paper-clipped photocopy of his great grandfather's autobiographical pamphlet before him as a nervously wielded shield from Nigel. "Nobody knows whether he was being serious, or just clowning around. But he wrote about seeing a dragon near a cavern down on the shore below the Strumblehead lighthouse. That's in the same place, coincidentally, a dinosaur was supposedly observed by a schoolboy, headed out to sea."

"You'd think the schoolboy would have stayed ashore, and sent the dinosaur out to sea instead! Cheers!" said one of the patrons seated on a barstool, lifting high his can of Toohey's.

"Wait," said Gerwyn loudly enough to be heard above laughter accompanied by shoes stomping the floor. "Is that-" pointing at Augie's photocopy "-where he wrote what he did as a child? For example, scooping up what he believed was dragon dung? Then smearing it all over a certain railing his school master was in the habit of gripping when he addressed his class?"

"*Lesu Mawr (My God)!*" exclaimed one of the many eavesdroppers nursing a pint. "I had me own copy of that pamphlet, I did! Lost it in a pile of hay, but that's another story."

Chuckles from his companions were promptly tamped down by Nigel. With a dumbstruck, mouth-hanging-open regard, he raged, "*Ach-y-fi!* What the bloody hell are you blokes on about?!?! As for *YOU!!*" he abruptly turned to

Augie, and gave him the uncomfortable feeling that if he could have, he would have hung his mouth wide enough open to swallow him whole. "You really want to see your dragonsaur?! You're goin' to need special equipment!"

"What equipment might that be?" asked Sherman. He lifted his chin off his neck to give Nigel his full attention, only to find the drunkard perilously close to falling over flat on his face.

"Two things you need, to see your dinosaur roamin' near Strumblehead!" staggering-about Nigel spat out. He sprayed so much phlegm at Augie and his crew, Irene lifted her arms in self-defense. "You need your *mouth...*" His additional phlegm sent Sherman scrunching his chin back into his neck. "...and a sixpack of *this!*" He raised his pint glass so quickly, half its remaining contents sloshed ceilingward, drenching his scraggly gray hair.

"Now see here, Nigel!" bristled Gerwyn, loud enough again to be heard clearly above patron reactions ranging from disgust to amusement. "You're not being fair to old Toohey's!" In an aside to the dinosaur searchers, he added, "Unless you fancy hot chocolate like your friend there, you might want to give this tidy brew a wee sip.

"Incidentally," Gerwyn proceeded for more general consumption, "I also happen to have seen this booklet before, same as old Smitty. Which is to say, before some lass in the hay distracted him."

"Oh yeah?!" literally spat out Nigel as he staggered closer to the bartender, and beer buddies lifted their pint glasses to salute Smitty. "Well then, have you seen *these* before?"

Nigel raised his fists in Gerwyn's face, thereby carelessly letting go his pint glass. It crashed to pieces, spilling beer across the dark-wood floor. Then Nigel spilled himself across the dark-wood floor, as well. "My point is this," he lifted his head to add groggily. "I'm wasted, and yet I still can't believe a dinosaur is wanderin' about Strumblehead...or anywhere else!"

"But you just said one requires a six-pack of beer to see a dinosaur roaming about," Sherman couldn't help noting. "How do you reconcile the contradiction?"

Mouth hung open anew, Nigel gave Sherman a what-are-you-saying? long stare. And with a prolonged belch, he wobbled his head into a floorward lunge.

Waitress Robin Pugh's quick reflexes, and her prior experience, saved Nigel from knocking himself senseless on the polished hard-wood. Just in the nick of time, she shoved a green-cushioned pillow between his head and the floor.

Click...whirr... "The conversation about what one requires to view a surviving non-avian dinosaur has yielded no useful information," stiffly stated Sherman's artificial intelligence entity, Charly.

"Deeply appreciated, that is, Robin," said Gerwyn. He adjusted his green-and-red-patterned tartan bowtie on the way to grabbing a broom for the shattered pint glass. "Saved me dealing with a blood-stained floor, you did. Don't suppose you'd fancy a meal later? My treat?"

"That's the whole problem, Gerwyn." Robin shook her head NO while she finished assuring that passed-out Nigel's head was centered comfortably on the old pillow. "A treat for you, treatin' me, while ych a fi where I'm concerned! I know you'd be fancyin' a cuddle for dessert that is definitely NOT on my menu!"

"I hear ya," said Gerwyn resignedly, bent into sweeping his broom.

Robin resolved she better pin up her long auburn hair in a bun before the next time she reported to work. She needed to mute at least that part of her allure for the ever-creepy bartender, as she regarded him. Although...

"I'm not bein' funny, right?" pub regular John Jones

addressed Sherman. "Is that your pet robot?" He pointed at Charly, seated stiff as a board after his latest, emotionlessly intoned declaration.

"Heavens no! He's his own man, every bit the full human being," Sherman lied while heartily clapping Charly on the back, which afforded him the concealed chance to reactivate Charly's empathy program. "For some people he does come off a bit rigid, though. Isn't that right, Charly?"

Click...whirr... "Playing along, that's absolutely right. In fact," ...click...whirr... "I do rather fancy a pint, but am afraid of short-circuiting."

"Well there you go!" John Jones waggled an accusing forefinger at Charly. "Short-circuitin' is somethin' a robot does! And what's all that mechanical noise I hear?! And 'playing along'?! What the bloody hell did he mean by *that*?!"

"No, no," Sherman waved his hand dismissively. "Short-circuiting is Charly's way of expressing how easily drunk he becomes on the smallest sip of anything. Isn't it, Charly? As for that mechanical noise,-"

"*Yaki da (Cheers)*, mate, I want to hear your bloody stiff-as-an-eight-iron friend tell me directly, himself, without you interpolatin' for him!"

Click...whirr...

"There it is again!" John Jones exclaimed, pointing anew.

"My joints have been making that noise ever since my..." ...whirr...click... "knee surgery."

Sherman sighed with relief; as expected and hoped for, Charly's retooled empathy program allowed him to generate little white lies.

Eclipso's team heartily agreed with Sherman. It would be better if the general public didn't figure out Charly's true nature, even at the cost of dishonesty.

"Knee surgery, was it?" huffed John Jones. But on a

calmer note, he went on, "Look, I'm not wantin' to be chopsy with you, mate. 'Specially since your friend here," he waved towards Augie, "has local roots. You do know what I mean, though, don't you? Seems you'd be more tampin' upset than you are, over my accusin' you of bein' a robot."

Grumbles of agreement echoed throughout the pub. They drowned out Charly's newest clicks and whirs prior to his saying, "I become very detached when I avoid getting..." ...click...whirr... "...wasted. I had an aunt like this."

"You did, did you?" said John, for once not so certain Charly was spewing total nonsense. "Tell me more, if you have a mind to."

"I can't..." ...click...whirr... "...because she doesn't exist."

I suppose that's a good thing, my empathy program modification doesn't enable Charly to embroider his little white lies.

"Ach, sorry to hear that, I am," John waved away Charly as he turned his back on him to rejoin his buddies. *"Fel rhech mewn pot jam,"* he grumbled not so quietly that Augie couldn't hear him.

"If I'm not confusing what little Welsh I learned way back when," Augie whispered to his cohorts, "he just compared Charly's remarks to a fart in a jam jar."

"Charly becomes rather catatonic when he goes for too very long in the presence of strangers," Sherman said to no one in particular. After shutting down Charly, his artificial intelligence entity slumped forward in its chair.

"Kay! I'm glad you've finally arrived," Gerwyn rushed to greet grade school teacher Kay Jones at the door, even though he still had a broom and a dust pan in hand. "I'm not being funny, right? Your visitors have caused quite the stir. Maybe was not the best time for you to be here now in a minute."

"You can blame those bloody sensationalist rags for putting our lad's story out there worldwide in the first place! Whether it was a seal or a dinosaur, I'm not saying! Oh, well isn't *he golygus!*" Kay gushed. She preened herself on taking in Augie's lingering smile over the fart in a jam jar bit.

Irene was struck by just how effusively Kay gushed…and at the same time cast a fleeting glance about the pub until it landed on Nigel sprawled out semi-conscious on the floor. *Trying to make him jealous?*

"Fancy a *cwtch (cuddle)* with him, do you? I'd be careful with that whole lot."

"If they're dragons, they're well disguised," said Kay to brush off Gerwyn's concern as she approached Augie's table. She steered a wide path round Nigel, his being too large for Gerwyn to broom into a dust pan, as much as he might have wanted to. Kay gave the hapless fellow what was supposed to be a perfunctory nod from seeing him drunk senseless, countless times before. But Irene thought her glance lasted a bit too long to be simply of the so-what variety.

"Sorry I'm late, cheers and all that," said Kay in a breathless rush. She gripped the backrest of Augie's chair while yet again, her additional glance Nigel's way did not escape Irene's notice. "I intended to be here in a flea's poo. But at our staff meetings, one of my illustrious colleagues likes to listen to herself speak forever and a day, even though what she has to say is not worth a sheep's fart. Wait," Kay caught herself up short. "You really are that crowd from the states, doing a follow-up on me wee lad who thought he saw a dinosaur? And truth be told, got me to wondering what I saw, meself?"

"Guilty as charged," said Sherman raising a hand. "You are Kay Jones?"

"Not so loud; the paparazzi might hear," Kay whispered

light-heartedly. "Now where's the lad with that fine Welsh last name of Matias, who I spoke with on the phone?"

No sooner did Augie sheepishly raise his forefinger than Kay gushed, with a lightning-fast glance anew at sprawled-out Nigel, "Oh that's proper, that is!" Then she craned her head around to eyeball Augie kissably close. "But listen," she frowned abruptly. "Sorry not to be dragging along David Taylor beside me. That's the fine young lad's name. His parents were not at all keen on bringing him to this pub."

"Understandable," said Scott, nodding towards drunken Nigel. "Could we meet somewhere else more to their liking?"

"The fact of the matter is, they wanted me to check you out first, assure you're on the up and up."

"I don't blame them," said Stephen, ever ready to cast deadpan aspersions on Eclipso's crew, Augie well knew.

"Will that be cash or credit card?" Gerwyn meanwhile asked two gentlemen impeccably attired in ties and sweater vests at a nearby table.

Stephen's remark having silenced Augie's table, they heard every word, as well as the lankier man's response, "Neither."

"Excuse me?"

"I have a coupon for two free meals," Lanky Guy explained, unfolding a paper from inside his vest.

"Huh," huh-ed Gerwyn, puzzled over how to handle the situation delicately, diplomatically. "I'm not being funny, right? But I don't ever remember our having distributed coupons before."

"But there it is. It exists."

"It does indeed. Listen, give me two ticks to share this with the general manager."

"He can't but be impressed."

Kay took advantage of Augie's curiosity, over what was

developing at the nearby table, to point towards him while asking Stephen, "Far as you know, is he attached?"

"Not since his umbilical cord was cut."

Snapping himself out of his entrancement by the meal coupon situation, Augie pressed on, "Well I do hope, Ms. Jones, those parents can be persuaded to allow us an audience with their son."

"I'm fully confident that once I report what you lot have to say for yourselves…"

"It's a serendipitous circumstance, you see," Augie explained. "We've been crossing the globe these past four months, in search of a surviving dinosaur, under the generous auspices of someone who remains behind the scenes."

"Someone who might eventually wish to walk away anonymous," Stephen deadpanned.

"That someone is totally committed," observed Irene, where she'd actually have rather knocked Stephen about the head.

"Maybe he should be committed," mused Stephen with a grin.

Before Irene could retort, *What does that tell us about your participation?*, Kay said, "I'm sorry, you do have me all rabbit ears. But does your friend over there feel okay?" She indicated Charly sitting bent over, perfectly still.

"We're used to him being not quite himself after a sleepless night," Sherman quickly responded, affecting nonchalance.

Stephen had to stifle himself from adding, *He's not anyone else, either.* The same as on other occasions, he sensed definite limits to how much smug disdain his associates could take.

"I can assure you he's okay," said Augie emphatically, impatient to proceed. "Anyway, it seems there's someone anxious to sabotage our search with the most ambitious hoaxes imaginable. Among other gems, we've had to deal with an inflated dinosaur balloon, and a balsam wood replica of a Pteranodon that could actually fly, though engineered to crumble apart while air borne."

"Well isn't that enough to make anyone tamping furious!" Kay exclaimed empathetically, while giving the statuesquely immobile Charly yet another worried regard.

"It is," agreed Sherman, nodding his chin into his neck. "And our behind-the-scenes benefactor to whom Dr. Matias referred wanted to do something about it. That's what brings us here, tracking down a possible lead. We hope that meanwhile, our saboteurs are left hopelessly befuddled as to our location."

"*Dr. Matias, that's quite proper, that is!*" gushed Kay for the umpteenth time, suggestive in her extra-loud voice that she was still putting on a show.

"Doctor of vertebrate paleontology, um, yes," Augie awkwardly confirmed, clearing his throat. "About a possible lead, this is my great grandfather's little booklet." Augie held up his photocopy and turned it from side to side. Anyone curious could see the title: *Farewell To Dragon Caves: My Little Friend's Journey To Adulthood*.

"That was the title of me own copy, that was," piped up the pub patron who recognized it from Augie's description, alone.

"You mean, don't you, Smitty, before it sank out of sight in your hay loft during a cuddle storm?" snarked one of Smitty's buddies, to uproarious laughter.

"Truth be told," Smitty said, taking the hilarity at his expense in stride, "I still get a wee bit seasick, recollecting how much I was rocked about in me barn that evening."

The laughter surged to a new level until Stephen shouted to be heard above it, "Are you sure there wasn't a surviving non-avian dinosaur stirring up the hay?! That went ahead and ate your pamphlet?!"

A chorus of "Huh?" introduced an awkward silence.

Augie took advantage of that to say, "I shared my great grandfather's pamphlet with Ecli- Errr, our benefactor. Thought the dragon stuff might be of mild interest in the context of our search. But I never dreamed it would lead to anything. Apart from maybe the Loch Ness Monster, the United Kingdom doesn't look to hold much promise of harboring any such prehistoric relics."

"After John Jones over there has three or four pints, he becomes a prehistoric relic, himself!" chortled a buddy, to additional uproarious effect.

Augie couldn't help forlorn frustration playing out, all across his face, over so much humor at the search's expense. That produced a breakout of quieting-down sympathy so Augie felt he could proceed, "This is where serendipity came into play. Mere hours after sharing the pamphlet with our benefactor – at my wife's behest I might add – he came into receipt of news from your fair corner of the globe. Old hat for you by now, I suppose, that one of your students believed he saw a dinosaur-looking creature with a long neck and a big body. And that it descended into the surf near your Strumblehead Lighthouse. But now you're saying he misidentified a seal?" Augie asked Kay.

"Caught a glimpse of it, meself, I did! Awful large for any seal I've ever seen before, must admit. However, not sure I can believe it was what me young David Taylor thought it was, without losing me own mind!"

"*Lesu Mawr (My God)!*" John Jones exclaimed breathlessly, accompanied by a dissonant chorus of "huh"s and dismissive grunts.

"There's a detail in my great grandfather's pamphlet that I didn't really notice until our benefactor pointed it out. Owen, as he called himself, described seeing the dragon-like creature with its head topped by a rooster-type coxcomb. Only, the coxcomb was dull purple rather than bright red."

"A chicken monster was it then, mate?"

"That's the thing," reacted Augie quickly and loudly enough to short-circuit the next wave of laughter. "As I mentioned before, we are searching for a non-avian, in other words non-bird, dinosaur. Only recently have we discovered dinosaur fossils that included feather imprints. That, alongside other lines of evidence, has led paleontologists – scientists who study prehistoric life through fossils – to strongly suspect birds descended from dinosaurs. But again, my great grandfather wrote this pamphlet decades earlier, well before anyone knew this. And yet he describes a dinosaur-type creature sporting a bird's feature, the coxcomb."

"People were already familiar with dinosaurs in the early forties, when your great grandfather's book was published. At least I think you said it was around then," Stephen added. "Who's to say he didn't embellish his already fanciful report with that particular detail, because it sounded like a neat-looking feature for a dinosaur?"

"Okay, an embellishment that happens to coincide with the latest findings forty years later," huffed Augie with no little amount of exasperation.

"Far as I recall, David said nothing about a coxcomb on the beast's head. And what wee look I did get me peepers on, nothing like that stood out," said Kay after bowing her head in deep concentration. "But the *niwl (fog)* that rolled in was so thick, our dino-dragon beastie could have been holding an oil-drum-sized can of Toohey's, and we might have missed it!"

"*Yaki da!* I'll drink to that!" announced John Jones, clinking his pint glass against a table mate's. Then he took such a big sloppy swig, beer dribbled down his chin.

"Okay, right. My point is, maybe it is mere meaningless

coincidence, that your dino-dragon sighting took place where my great grandfather wrote he spotted something. We still figure it's a good place to continue our search, in hiding from the hoaxers."

"We've taken extreme measures to remain well-hidden," Sherman added. "They include, but are not limited to, a hi-tech block-out of any tracking devices that someone might have planted on us. The hi-tech aspect was made possible by, well, a bit of amazing ingenuity." He thought better of mentioning the time travelers along for Eclipso's ride while waiting to be raptured eighty years back into the future. That they were responsible for the ingenuity.

Before any of the locals could pester Sherman for more specifics, Gerwyn caught everyone's attention. From a back room, he'd returned to the table of two formally dressed gentlemen, the lankier of whom proffered a special coupon to cover their meal tab.

"I'm exceedingly sorry about this," said Gerwyn, handing back the coupon. "The manager said he knows nothing about this, and really can't accept it."

"Are you positive?" asked Lanky Guy in plain disbelief.

"Beyond a shadow of a doubt."

"But look here, fellow, at the exquisite artistry of this calligraphy."

Lanky Guy pointed at Gothic lettering across the top of the paper. The "c" in "coupon" was flanked by a fanciful rendering of a long-haired maiden. Her reddish-brown locks hung so low, they encircled the flowery-lettered phrase, *Free Meal for two, at Drunk In The Wool.*

"Even though it's paint," Lanky Guy went on, "wouldn't you swear these letters are gold-plated?"

"If you didn't tell me, I might well have committed that error."

"And look further down: This coupon states it is for your particular establishment, Drunk In The Wool, confusing it for no other! You can't deny that!"

"Indeed I can't. But I'm afraid I still have to say NO."

"'NO.' You're really saying 'no' to such an impressively rendered document?"

"Nobody, certainly not I, can deny the exquisite artistry that must have gone into producing- Might I ask from where you obtained this?"

"'From where you obtained this'?!" Lanky Guy repeated most indignantly. "'From where you obtained this'?!?! Sir, I'll have you know I spent long hours in my art studio meticulously bringing this piece to life! Only to have you and your so-called manager take a piss on it! Had I, Elwin Kneath, any least inkling my efforts would be so disparaged, then I certainly would have thought twice, more than twice, about patronizing your establishment!"

"You're admitting you manufactured this coupon yourself? You didn't receive it from somewhere else?"

Elwin gave Gerwyn a long look by turns dumb-founded and enraged, before he finally burst out, "What, you would rather I lied, and been dishonest about it?!"

"Well, um, if we're talking about dishonesty, when you shared this, um, artwork with me, there was rather the implication-"

"'Rather the implication'?!" Elwin rose from his chair to his full six-and-a-half-foot height, causing Gerwyn to flinch. "Just what are you suggesting?!"

"I'm- I'm not suggesting anything," insisted Gerwyn, doing a gut check to look up boldly at Elwin grimacing down at him. He figured if the fellow was going to take a fist to him, he might as well face it like a man. "I'm simply saying we can't accept such a coupon not officially printed by ourselves. Pretty soon, we'd go broke honoring counterfeit coupons from everyone and his brother."

"But no other coupon, not one, could sport anywhere near the sheer artistry of this one! Will you at least admit *that?!*"

"It cannot be denied," Gerwyn shook his head.

Elwin's shoulders suddenly slumped, in tandem with his grimace melting into an exaggerated frown. "So," he mumbled, "not even a partial discount?"

Grimly tight-lipped, Gerwyn shook his head, "No."

"We seem to have reached an impasse, then."

"Are you saying you can't pay?" Gerwyn asked in an admonishing tone.

"I could pay, if only you would accept this coupon which by your own admission achieves an unsurpassed level of artistry," lamented Elwin, his voice cracking like he was about to sob. He held his faked coupon limp, like it was the only thing he had to offer of himself to the world, and knew it wasn't much, for all his bravado.

"You're saying you can't pay for your meal by any other means than that coupon? No credit card? No cash? Not even a bank check?"

With a weary sigh, Elwin's companion pulled out his wallet, extracted a credit card, and said, "No need to become like a dog with two willies over this. I've got us covered, Elwin."

"Such gallantry!" Elwin pepped up. "Then it is only fair you should receive the coupon that could have been someone else's." He stared down Gerwyn as in, *Hint hint.*

"My loss," Gerwyn shrugged his shoulders.

"Great," reacted Elwin's friend to receiving the coupon as in, *Not great.* "I can add it to the pile."

Chapter 2

"On the one hand, we have our beloved Karen Kowalski. Nothing fancy; she simply follows the script. Certainly nothing wrong with that," added curriculum adviser Diane Mueller, flashing a glare at Vicky Copplestone.

I've never said there was anything wrong with that, Vicky had to restrain herself from erupting at the meeting of fourth and fifth grade teachers in Green Pastures Elementary School.

Karen puffed out her chest to nearly remonstrate more than boast, "I consider 'nothing fancy' a badge of honor."

"As well you should," agreed Diane, speaking at an emphatically slow pace, quite pompous where Vicky was concerned. Then she elaborated more speedily, "I've had the pleasure to observe your tireless implementation of grammatical drills. But in case there was any question, you do keep your classroom library well-stocked with an impressive variety of approved books your students are always excited to explore. Nobody can say you neglect the motivation piece of student literacy acquisition." On this, Diane gave Karen the biggest possible, positively gleaming grin...

...followed by a shadow crossing her face as she turned Vick's way to continue, "On the other hand, we have integrated skills specialist, Vicky Copplestone. Had to carve out a special position for her."

"In this corner of the ring," boomed English-as-a-second-language teacher Mark Waltzer, as though he were an emcee for the World Wrestling Federation.

Vicky clenched her hands together high over her head, and shook them side to side as though she were a prize fighter.

Scattered howls of laughter ensued.

"No brass knuckles will be allowed!" shouted school principal Marsha Klondike. She hoped that going with the irreverent flow would bring the gathering back to quietly respectful order, which it did.

"Yes, that's very funny," said Diane with a nails-on-the-chalkboard level of insincerity Vicky found as irritating as Diane found Vicky's play-along with the prizefight comparison. "Well, it should be news to no one that Vicky takes a more unorthodox approach to elementary school instruction. She weaves her husband's dinosaur hunt into her lessons. I guess she hopes it's not only little, first-grade boys interested in prehistoric-"

"Actually, Augie calls it more of a search than a hunt," Vicky interrupted, irritated by Diane's condescending reference to male first-graders.

"Full disclosure," Diane raised her voice a harsh smidge. "Our Ms. Copplestone does appear to have succeeded in, um..."

In pulling the wool over people's eyes? Out with it, Diane, Vicky thought bitterly to herself. *It won't kill you to admit my instruction might be having a positive impact.*

"...that is to say, she has garnered a degree of approval in certain circles. However, we are all about whatever pedagogical approaches do the very best to forge strong minds out of our precious raw materials. After all, children are our greatest natural resource," Diane sighed, blown away by what she regarded as her own special eloquence.

Oh my God, you're really going to talk about children like they're so many rocks and minerals? Vicky asked herself, beyond appalled.

A discomfiting silence met Diane's rapturously wrought analogy. So it was with pretend nonchalance that she went on, "In plainer language, there might be more than one way to skin a cat. But we're asking the question: Which way is best? Karen?" Diane called on Karen expectantly, buoyed by Karen's effervescing grin that accompanied her raised hand.

"I just want to say, Vicky, about that amazing integration of your husband's unusual hobby with your lessons: It's not something I could ever pull off. And it seems there are things I do in my classroom not exactly your cup of tea, either. But like you said, Diane, it is all about the kids, isn't it? Discovering what's best for them? I dare say that's a quest every bit as exciting as a hunt for living dinosaurs, if not more so!"

"So well put, Karen!" gushed Diane, clapping her hands together delightedly. "As for what *is* best for children, I'm completely neutered- Neutral! I'm neutral! Completely neutral! May the best pedagogies win!"

"Does that mean we're doing something else to that cat besides skinning it?" quipped Mark Waltzer to scattered chuckles plus one alarmed-sounding, "Oh my God!"

"We will be conducting a special assessment of fourth grade writing skills," explained principal Marsha Klondike, stepping in for Diane. "It was by intent that all fourth graders *not* enrolled in Vicky's integrated studies elective were grouped together in Karen's class. That way, we hope to learn the comparative strengths and weaknesses of our two colleagues' starkly different approaches. Some of you already know this isn't a top-secret instructional version of the Manhattan Project. The fifth-grade team has devised the test items as an objective third party. This aligns with research that purportedly shows teacher-made assessments give the most valuable data." *There, Vicky; are you satisfied?*

Vicky so wanted to push back, *That's only the case when the assessments are based on what was taught, and prepared by those doing the teaching.* But she suspected that would open one front too many. Instead, she asked, "Will students be able to write on a preferred subject from a varied menu?"

"Evaluating such an anything-goes approach becomes way too subjective, way too qualitative, Vicky," admonished Diane. "Multiple choice items and fill-in-the-blanks that steer clear of anything you guys might have covered in class: That's the formula for making an objective, quantitative analysis regarding best practices."

"How do you propose to avoid overlap with subjects my class is exploring?" Vicky asked without bothering to raise her hand. "We are very wide-ranging."

Diane wore confusion, befuddlement on her face as she asked, "But isn't your class all about dinosaurs? Think we'll have an easy time avoiding that subject."

"The search for surviving non-avian dinosaurs is an interdisciplinary challenge. As a result, my students poke around a variety of topics: the impact of climate change on wildlife habitats; fruit and vegetation that dinosaurs depend on for their diet; local politics that make dinosaur searches difficult...I could go on and on."

"No problem. We should be able to keep at arm's length from anything of interest to students. Wait..."

Too late; Diane's unfortunate word choice left teachers gasping. She saw nothing else but to spin round on her high heels and make for the nearest exit. Click-click-click-click, SLAM!

"Not sure about some of these characters," Mark Waltzer whispered confidentially to Vicky, leaning towards her. "But do know I'm in your corner."

Yeah, you're still trying to get in my corner.

Chapter 3

"Gave up me choir practice for you lot, I did," Wilfrid Taylor grumbled at Augie and company.

They were bunched together on bar stools at the Drunk In The Wool pub.

Looking down at son David seated beside him, Wilfrid added, "You better have really seen a dinosaur, that's all I can say!"

Ethel Taylor reached across David to affectionately pat Wilfrid's hand as she said, "You practice plenty in the shower, you do, Old Bull. I'm confident you'll still drown out everyone else this Sunday. Maybe even wake a sleeping dragon into the bargain."

"Well," Wilfrid reacted, ears red; Ethel's flattery still disarmed him every bit as much as the first day they met. "But there really are this many of you takin' me son's report seriously?" he went on, struck by the size of Augie's group. He had no way of knowing that three of them claimed to be time travelers. But friends did tell him of overhearing talk about a starship, a chicken making a phone call, plus other bizarre curios. One of which he couldn't help asking about. "While we're at it, which one of you might be the robot?"

Click...whirr... "Please don't call me 'the robot,'" Charly pushed back, albeit in stiffly wrought monotone.

Dr. Roberta Quiñones gave Sherman a severe regard he read as, *You should have left Charly aboard Cloud Nine!*

Sherman wished he could bury the rest of his head in his neck along with his chin.

"That hurts my..." ...click...whirr... "...feelings," Charly elaborated. "And far more importantly, yields zero useful data on surviving non-avian dinosaurs."

"Charly has been rather under the weather," explained

Sherman untruthfully, his chin pressed ever more fervently into his neck. "I should have insisted he remain behind, on our, um, our tour vehicle. To finish recuperating."

"Tour vehicle, is it?" bartender Gerwyn asked dubiously, looking up from a toweled-off pint mug. "I'm not being funny, right? Your 'tour vehicle' has to be no small thing to hold you whole bloody lot. Where did you park it? Anyone else here seen it?"

"I have noticed a square cloud hangin' still over the Irish Sea," offered John Jones, raising his forefinger. "Didn't want to get everyone like a dog with two willies over it. But it's been sittin' there, not budgin' a blessed inch, even while other clouds scurry past."

"Then it's not just me!" Gerwyn exclaimed with an air of vindication.

"Never thought you looked anything like a square cloud, mate! *Yaki-da!*" John Jones toasted his buddies with clinking pint glasses. "Yesterday, we did overhear them go on about starships and the like. Maybe they've also found how to travel by cloud."

Augie sighed, and said, "We don't travel by cloud. But our flight vehicle does generate an enveloping mist, because it is steam powered. And true, we have left it hovering over the Irish Sea."

Click...whirr... "Down here on the ground, everyone is under the weather," Charly finally remarked. His politeness program prevented him from speaking any earlier, at risk of interrupting someone.

"I like him!" giggled David, pointing at Charly. "He's funny!"

"You really shouldn't be wasting their time, me son. What you wanted to believe was a dinosaur, wasn't that really only a seal lifting his bonnie head out of a heavy fog?"

"Must I repeat meself, Daddy?" David asked imperiously, swelling out his wee little chest to confront his father. "I've seen more than me share of seals in all manner of weather. This time it *wasn't* a seal, was it, Ms. Jones? A seal with a rooster's crown? Sorry I didn't mention that before, Mum. But you saw yourself how large it was, didn't you? Plus those big tracks..." David spread his hands wide enough to carry a baby lamb, his mother Ethel imagined. "Rather be reading me comic books than making up this stuff, I would."

"Can't be sure whether those were mere rain puddles. Or people's footsteps worn large by the surf. Or a monster's heavy marks in the sand, as our David supposes," said Kay. Rising to David's defense, she stepped behind him to place hands protectively on his shoulders. "But whatever we saw appeared much bigger than a seal, it did, as it headed into the surf."

"David, can you tell us about your favorite comic book?" inquired Stephen with a gently encouraging tone.

"Oh, that would have to be *The Adventures of Boo-Boo Banana!*" David's smile just thinking about it could have glowed in the dark, Augie mused.

"*The Adventures of Boo-Boo Banana*; never heard of that one," Stephen shook his head, continuing in his gentle voice. "Does Boo-Boo Banana ever search for dinosaurs?"

Irene McDowell rolled her eyes and shook her head; she knew where this was going.

"Mostly he searches for buried treasure," responded David after obviously thinking very hard. "But there was one time he, Happy Apple, and Poo-Poo Potato fought off a monster octopus, they did. It was guarding the world's largest emerald at the bottom of the ocean!" he pepped up from recalling.

"Well, isn't that silly," remarked Stephen, his tone turning less gentle.

Irene figured David thwarted Stephen's line of attack, that maybe a dinosaur encounter in one of the lad's comic books led to over-wrought wishful thinking.

"Okay, David," Stephen went on, obviously about to remount his effort, "what do you know about a booklet entitled: *Farewell To Dragon Caves; My Little Friend's Journey to Adulthood*?"

In answer to David's puzzlement, Augie once again held up a photocopy of his great grandfather's booklet.

"I am very sorry I know nothing about that book," said David meekly. "But I should very much like to see a dragon cave."

"No reasonable person would expect you to recognize this," said Augie pointedly.

Before Augie could proceed, an older fellow finished making his way forward, wading past customers and Augie's crew alike. He dressed every bit as dapperly as Elwin Kneath the previous day, a tartan wool vest with a tartan bow tie to match. At the front counter, he said, "If I might weigh in, well weigh in lightly, as I don't expect my remarks to carry that much heft: That photocopied cover does look familiar to me. Well, not overly familiar, but of enough passing acquaintance to not confuse it for anything else. I believe it originated from before me time, though I sincerely doubt from too much before. But not so close to me time that there's any danger it was from ahead of me time. And also, maybe not danger, as I don't believe anyone has ever been seriously imperiled by sheets of paper, whatever the age. Save for a paper cut, which actually can prove quite painful while nothing compared to a broken bone. Not that I would know personally, where the broken-"

"And you are," Irene interrupted forcefully, otherwise fearful what eons might pass before this guy came up for air.

"Oh," he spasmed like he'd just been snapped out of a trance. Facing Irene, with a salute he said, "Rupert

Hamster Holmes, at your service. And might I be so bold as to inquire- Well perhaps boldness is beside the point; I don't expect anyone here to knock me about me head for it."

"It's a f-n' temptation, if he keeps yappin' like that," time-traveling Sergeant, Fred Frankly, mumbled to journalist Laura Gómez.

"Bloody hell, man!" roared Nigel from one of the booths far from the front counter. "Get to the point, will you? Before all the leaves finish turnin' color?!?!"

"Back from the dead are we, Nigel?" Gerwyn called out, uncertain where Nigel sat. "I'll appreciate you tidying up your foul language in the presence of our wee lad here."

"There's nothin' more foul than that tosser makin' Hamlet sound like the most decisive bloke who ever strode the planet! Wherever you're sittin' up there, David, I'd stick to your comic books!" Klunk! "Bloody hell!" Nigel cursed anew, having banged his knee against a table leg as he stood up. "Excuse me," he slobbered drunkenly. "I meant to say, rose-colored hell! Burp!"

"Hamlet?!?! Me, Hamlet?!?!" bristled Rupert Hamster Holmes. "I'll have you know, sir, it is my solemn intent – well perhaps not so much intent as predisposition – to get to the point with all due haste, or maybe not so much haste as a certain economy of verbosity."

"Hate breakin' it to you, but you're too late for any such 'economy of verbosity,' you are! Burp! That ship has already left harbor and sailed halfway round the world!

"I'm comin'! I'm comin'!" Nigel shouted after Robin, the pub assistant who rebuffed Gerwyn asking her on a date. And Elwin Kneath, the guy with the artfully rendered yet still totally bogus meal coupon.

After letting Nigel stagger ahead of them, Robin and Elwin followed him outside, through an exit held open by Elwin. Augie figured they wanted to keep him from tumbling into the gutter.

"I have seen that booklet you waved about, well maybe not so much waved about as shown all around," Rupert continued, heedless of Nigel's departure. "That is, unless you were fanning yourself. Which seems a fair bit unlikely as it's not like we're roasting in here. Though it's not an icebox either, if I'm being honest."

"You already told us you'd seen the booklet before," David's teacher Kay couldn't help observing impatiently. She also glanced towards the pub exit with a brief thought given over to Nigel's well-being, if Augie didn't know better. "Something else you need to add?"

"'Need' might be too strong a – Anyway," Rupert shifted gears abruptly, reading the room grown hostile. "If it's about that dragon, or dinosaur, that your great grandfather Matias, and now our brilliant young lad here, have gone on about, well! I'm not so sure I didn't observe it meself early one morning, a decade ago. Well maybe not early early, but certainly-"

"Your sighting was also on the Strumblehead coast below the lighthouse?" Augie hastened to ask before Rupert could mire himself in another swamp of endless not-so-sures.

Rupert stared at him, stunned. "Well that does cut directly to the bone, doesn't it?"

"What exactly did you see there, Mr. Holmes?" asked journalist Laura Gómez, notepad at the ready.

"I must say, fair maiden, that reporter's pen of yours might as well be the saw slicing right through the aforementioned bone!" Rupert exclaimed. "Very well, then, let's get sawing, or in my case tiptoe ever so gingerly forward, ready to beat a hasty retreat at the slightest hint of any threat. What our young lad there told the local press, I could have been telling them, meself. My odd creature also sported a long, snake-like neck, not so much mounted on an elephantine body as part-and-parcel extending from it, like the sprout from a tulip bulb. Wait, though! There's more! Not a whole lot more, but more enough. From the creature's rear extended a wrinkly thick tail like an alligator's tail. Taken all together, those features suggested not so much a dragon as a dinosaur, of the sauropod variety."

"You thought you saw a dinosaur," drily summarized Stephen Feldman, dripping with derision like blood dripping from a feeding scavenger's teeth, Augie imagined.

"Well, not so much an actual dinosaur as an apparent dinosaur, though that might well be a distinction without a difference."

"Anybody was with you who could corroborate?" Stephen followed up, ever dubious.

"No, no, I was alone with me thoughts, not in fact feeling alone even though me thoughts are not always the best company."

"Any tracks, photos, or other physical evidence?" Scott couldn't help asking out of sheer delight over a new report of a possible dinosaur sighting, the highly eccentric source notwithstanding.

Scott's colleagues cringed visibly, fearing he opened the way for another endless stream of heartily self-amended remarks by Rupert.

"Depressions in the sand, for example? No two, three, or even four ways about it! The answer is yes! Beyond dispute! And moreover, they were spaced far enough apart to suggest the four heavy feet of a lumbering beast!"

"That rules out Nigel, as he only has two heavy feet! Cheers, mates!" John Jones toasted his gang again. But he labored under a cruel delusion, if he thought his irreverent comment would be enough to derail Rupert Hamster Holmes from the rest of what he had to say.

"Not to put too fine a point on it," Holmes went on

relentlessly, "one time I watched the surf erode dog tracks to the size of holes large enough for planting the root balls of evergreens. In other words, they did bear a close resemblance to those depressions I just mentioned. But they were spaced too close together where your typical dinosaur is concerned. It would have been tripping over itself!"

"One has to take a deep breath," advised Gerwyn, while continuing to towel off rinsed pint glasses. His level of skepticism approached Stephen's, Augie gathered.

Nevertheless, Scott questioned Rupert further. "Where were those depressions in relation to Strumblehead lighthouse?"

"Don't think lighthouses are in the habit of leavin' tracks in the sand, or anywhere else! Just sayin', mates! Cheers!"

As the riotous uproar over John Jones's latest nonsensical snark subsided, Rupert quieted it altogether save for a lone "*Ych a fi*!" of disgust. He said, "A detail I neglected, not meaning to neglect it. And my pre-emptive apologies, or rather not so much apologies as an acknowledgement I might well have unwittingly left out other details...By God, me memory's not worth a sheep's fart; seem to have derailed meself..."

"There's a detail you neglected. We were talking about where the tracks were located relative to Strumblehead Lighthouse," said Scott in aid of jarring Rupert's memory.

"Yes! Those are proper spurs against me mind, they are, to send me memory into a brisk gallop again! That is to say, the long-necked beast so frightened me, next thing I knew I was half way up the hill to the parking lot. That's when I got me wits enough about me to return to the beach. By then, though, wouldn't you know it! It was gone! I have no idea whether it went for a swim, or sought shelter in the cave. But one thing I can tell you for absolute sure: Those depressions, tracks or otherwise, they were down directly below the lighthouse, they were! Say someone atop the lighthouse, looking out upon the grand Irish Sea, were chewing gum. And then say they decided - well maybe not so much decided as simply did, because it really would have constituted a thoughtless act. Say they simply spit out their gum with a proper projection forward, like the whole world was their spittoon, while I stood down below. Well! I would not have liked the odds it would not have landed in me hair, leading me to suspect a seagull used me as target practice for its poo! But-"

"Wait!" Augie held up a hand as in, *Please stop*, which he reckoned he might have done even had he nothing to say. As it turned out, though, "My great grandpa mentioned a cave. You mentioned a cave, Mr. Holmes."

"Maybe not so much mentioned as, well, yes, okay, mentioned."

"Ms. Jones, didn't you and David notice a cave close by to your creature?"

David tugged on the sleeve of Kay Jones's forest-green wool sweater.

"There's a good lad, David," Kay Jones said encouragingly. "You tell everyone what you have to say, yourself."

With a clipped nod, David lifted his head high to share, "When I first laid me eyes on the dinosaur, looked like he just exited a cave."

Click...whirr... "Maybe it is the same cave of the other sighting."

"There we go," said Stephen with a certain swagger. "Artificial Intelligence makes a meaningful connection. Which is part of why I have a tough time believing you guys really came here from decades into the future," he addressed Kevin, Fred, and Ali. "By 2050 or whenever it was, something like Charly should have advanced to the point of being totally indispensable. You wouldn't have travelled anywhere without him, especially into the past. In fact, I'm expecting that by 2050, us humans will no longer be necessary. Charly and his kind will have already kicked people to the extinction wayside. He won't travel anywhere *with* you."

Click...whirr... "I would not kick anyone anywhere unless that provided useful information on non-avian dinosaur survival."

"Yeah, such a freakin' miracle, what Charly said," muttered time traveler Fred Frankly sarcastically. "It's a wonder that artificial intelligence entities haven't already taken over, back here in 1982. I was about to say the same thing Charly did, about the cave. But glory freakin' alleluia, he must have saved us an entire two seconds waiting on me to speak. Which we've more than wasted now, yappin' on about it!"

"I have one other question, Rupert," said Augie, declining to weigh in on artificial intelligence. "David mentioned a crown on the creature's head, like a rooster's crown. Did you see anything like that? Or that?"

After much thought, brewing suspense for his audience, Rupert said, "I did see a rooster one time, maybe six years ago, or close to- Okay," Rupert shifted gears. He noticed out the corner of his eye that John Jones was ready to hurl the remainder of a pint in his face. "The rooster was born with no cockscomb whatsoever, although-"

"No, Rupert, he's talking about the creature at the beach," said Gerwyn wearily.

"Yes, of course! Well no, can't say I saw the beast sporting any sort of crown, or wattle for that matter. Though I must point out that from my particular viewpoint, perspective, however you should like to frame it, the beastie had its head reared back very far. Its mama could have been about to feed it a snake, like a mama bird feeding a worm to her chick. But that's not the point. The point is, he reared his head so far back, I was left in no position to either confirm or deny the presence of a cockscomb."

"If it was anything like me wife," chortled John, lifting his Toohey's high for yet another rollicking toast, "it raised its head like that to say, 'You're not good enough for me!' Cheers, mates!"

Augie and company made quick consultation while John Jones's gang guffawed to their drunken heart's content. As a result, by the time they settled down, Augie was ready to make a request of Kay, David's parents, and to a much lesser extent Rupert as in, he wished the fellow would come up with an excuse for being unavailable. "Any chance we could reconvene on the beach by that cave, about ninety minutes from now? That should give us the better part of an hour or so of remaining sunlight, yes?"

"Don't know, mate!" chortled John Jones again. "Depends on whether good ole' Gerwyn here can haul a cooler full of Toohey's out there by then!"

"I doubt Toohey's makes good dinosaur bait," said Gerwyn, finding himself in a lighter mood over the whole ridiculous business.

"What, you think it's more of a Guinness-saur from spendin' too much time roamin' the Irish Sea? Cheers, mates!"

Clink-clink-clink went the pint glasses again.

"Sorry we didn't get to hear more from you, David," Irene made a point of telling the little school boy under cover of the latest riotous din provoked by John Jones.

David shrugged his shoulders to say, "Don't like to hear meself speak that much." He nodded Rupert's direction, and went on, "Also don't want to see me face on *The South Wales Echo*." Pursuant to which he re-donned his little tartan cap, and adjusted it for exiting Drunk In The Wool. And he looked up earnestly into Irene's friendly regard to gently yet firmly conclude, "But I know what I saw, Mum."

Stephen was going to ask about the possibility the crown was a clue that David's dinosaur was really nothing more than a rooster, its proportions distorted by the fog. However, the child's plain earnestness spooked him silent.

Chapter 4

"My Mom remembers my great grandma, Nana, complaining my great grandpa had multiple names for himself. So many, in fact, she would sometimes say, 'Wonder what he'll call himself today?'" Augie reminisced, riding with Scott up front in Kay Jones's mini-van. On his lap, he'd opened his photocopy of *Farewell to Dragon Caves* to the first page.

"Oh, that's proper, that is!" giggled David, seated between his parents in back. "I quite fancy having several names to call meself besides 'David'!" He uttered his own name quite derisively.

"Maybe *Sion Corn* will put a dozen names under the Christmas tree for you," chuckled David's mother, Ethel. "It would certainly be a lot cheaper than all those action figures you ask for!"

"Keep talkin' like that, me son," spat out his father, Wilfrid, tottering between amusement and bitterness, "and I might be callin' you a name or two, meself, on the rude end of the spectrum!"

"Wilfrid!" Ethel reached round back of her son to give her husband a painfully twisting ear tug.

"Ow! I might have a name for that as well!"

"One big mystery is why Trevasaur," Augie went on, hoping to defuse the tension in the back seat before it got really out of hand. "Here's from page one:

> 'Before I knew his name, I had mentally called him
> Owen, Owen Trevasaur. But he was to have many
> different names down the years, discarding each
> one like a meadow brook butterfly were to shed
> more than one chrysalis, flitting about from
> metamorphosis to metamorphosis.'

"Given the title of his booklet, I always assumed the 'saur' part of his name had something to do with dragons. But the 'Treva' part…"

"Hold on tight, Mr. Matias," Kay advised Augie, slapping him on his knee. "You might be in for a wee bit of a shocker round this next bend."

Augie almost quipped, *What, it's devoid of sheep?*

Sheep covered hillsides nearly every direction Augie looked. He could imagine them sprouting from the ground like mushrooms. But round the next bend, instead, a very plain and simple sign read: TREFASAUR.

Before Augie or Scott, for that matter, could recover enough from their shock for either one to open his mouth, Kay pulled off the road onto a gravel lot.

The parking area barely accommodated the caravan that followed behind Kay from Drunk In The Wool.

Cloud Nine hovered overhead. A drone in sheep's clothing, Irene mused. Save for its square-ish form, it might have been just another of several fluffy cumulus dotting the azure sky, as much as sheep dotted nearby hillsides.

Anyhow, Eclipso's crew, their time-travel hangers-on, plus numerous curious locals disembarked to gather round the TREFASAUR sign.

Replete in bright lemon-yellow pants and jacket with no tie, prospective golf course developer Alistair Frump hastily took long strides over beside Augie. "What exactly are we thinking here?" he asked.

Alistair had joined Eclipso Sunray Smith as a co-investor. He planned to open the world's most unique golf course, winding through areas where one could hope to glimpse a wandering dinosaur while putting for par.

"A short carry over this road to the first green?" Alistair elaborated. "With one never knowing when a Tyrannosaur Rex float might come motoring round that bend? Thought we were going for something, errr, more Sea World real, less Disney World animatronic!"

"We are," Augie assured him. "We've stopped for that sign. It features an 'f' instead of a 'v,' but close enough. It still solves the mystery of where my great grandfather got the name, Trevasaur."

"TREFASAUR; oh, I see," Alistair nodded. "Dare we hope that's a heads-up about something more interesting than a chicken or a sheep crossing the road here at fog-enshrouded times of the day?"

"'Tref' is the Welsh word for town," explained Robin. Her boldness stepping forward belied the timidity in her voice.

"Dinosaur town!" Alistair snapped his fingers. "Brilliant! How about we go behind that big gorse bush for a more in-depth discussion?" he asked Robin, smoothly snaking his arm round her shoulders to usher her off.

Robin just-as-smoothly pirouetted away from him, the other side of Augie, Scott, Kay and David.

"Actually," Robin then lifted a correcting forefinger to say, glancing everyone else's direction but Alistair's, "it's far more likely the 'saur' part of that word is Welsh for 'cowhouse urine.'"

"Town of pee!" giggled David.

"David Taylor!" said Ethel admonishingly, while twist-pinching her husband's ear again.

"Ouch! I wasn't the one who said that!"

"But you enjoyed it too much!"

"Think a baby Stegosaurus might be hiding there?" Stephen meanwhile asked Laura Gómez bent down behind the TREFASAUR sign.

"Don't know what I was thinking," Laura shook her head with a passing chuckle. "Just my reporter's instinct to snoop around everything, no good reason necessary."

But the reality was, Laura thought she noticed a narrow, diamond-shaped stone nearly a foot tall underneath the sign. No trace of it to be found on closer inspection, though. *Must have been my imagination.*

"Would have thought it was sheep-house urine," said time traveler Fred to Robin. "Sheep are every f-n'-where you look," he added with a flamboyant arm sweep calling attention to the innumerable fluffs of white dotting the verdant Welsh vista.

"They're obviously not intimidated by the non-avian dinosaurs prowling about," snarked Stephen.

"Maybe those dinos have pulled the wool over their eyes."

Stephen started at Irene's suggestion. Something in her tone didn't sound entirely flippant.

*

> "'Coming to chapel in our horse-drawn carriage,
> little Owen used to always want to face forward
> going, and backward leaving,'"

Augie resumed reading from his great grandfather's pamphlet once the drive resumed out to Strumblehead.

> "'Facing backward to leave gave him a splendid
> view of Garn Fawr (High Rock), rising like the
> volcano Vesuvius over Pompeii, soaring above the
> hedgerows. He wasn't a particular fan of the
> hedgerows themselves. Quite the opposite, as they
> grew too high and too close to the road, on both
> sides, to see much else.'"

"Well isn't this a fine bit of synchronicity," Augie remarked as he set down the photocopied pamphlet in his lap and looked out the window. "The hedgerows are awful high, aren't they? And tell us, Kay, is that Garn Fawr over there?" he pointed.

"It is," she confirmed, patting Augie's knee again.

"These hedgerows do make one claustrophobic," said Scott. He clutched the passenger door handle in a death grip. "This road is so narrow; what do you do if another car comes at you, going the opposite direction?"

"There are these wide clearings called roundabouts, that do allow two vehicles to squeeze past each other," explained Kay. "We passed one already."

"If I might add, Ms. Jones," said Augie.

"Add away," Kay gushed, fantasizing Augie was someone else about whom she couldn't stop thinking. *I'd like to squeeze past you some time, Nigel, if you ever sobered up, you infuriatingly inebriated bloke!*

"The hedgerows make me nervous also, Scott," Augie went on. "But listen to what else my great grandpa aka Owen Trevasaur said about them:

> 'His father, Donald, was always telling our wee lad Owen that the restricted views afforded by hedgerows serve an especially profound purpose. "Suppose we enjoyed unrestricted views of our passed-on friends and relatives in their new existences," he used to say. "Not to mention our future after we are off this particular stage, and our past before we were ever born here. Those distractions would surely drive us clear around the bend crazy! We wear clothes for the same reason. But Garn Fawr rises above it all, to remind us there is a lot more, God's business for only God to know until our rejoining."'"

"What a haunting perspective on life," marveled Scott. "I wonder whether he would lump in living dinosaurs as more crazy-making distraction from what we should really be focused on."

*

"This is so amazing," remarked Augie. While descending a dirt path to the shore below Strumblehead Lighthouse, he had his photocopied pamphlet open to yet another page. This, even as he strained not to stumble, or tear his pants on the long, needle-sharp thorns of orange-blossomed gorse branches. "It's like he's our personal tour guide! Listen:

> 'On a warm Saturday afternoon, Owen's brothers
> and three other boys took him for a swim. The tide
> would be out, and should be nice for bathing. But
> on the steep path down the cliffside to the sea, one
> of his brothers called out excitedly, "Look at the
> fog!" Yet that was only half the excitement! And
> some would argue, far less than half.'"

"They spotted something white and furry on the hillside that wasn't a sheep?" snarked Stephen loudly enough to be heard above the rhythmic din of surf.

"Can you grab his ear, Ms. Taylor?" Irene asked David's mom. "Please continue, Augie."

"Yes, here we are:

> 'Like a white woolen blanket it concealed the
> coastline cave. That epic sight alone was enough for
> him to tell his mother for days thereafter, and
> become a complete nuisance over when he might
> go there again.'"

The sea's ebb and flow scraped countless small pebbles together. This made for a most pleasant tinkling ambience, where everyone was concerned who gathered round Augie to hear more from his great grandfather's pamphlet, published early 1940s.

"'But the real adventure came when a snake-like head, crested as by a rooster's coxcomb, rose on a serpentine neck, punching a sizeable hole in the fog bank and rising well above it.'"

"Mine had the rooster's coxcomb as well! *Yaki da!*" David pumped both his little fists excitedly. "That must be the same dinosaur!"

"There's more, David," said Augie.

"'The fog bank moved off fast enough for our timid young lad to see the neck was attached to a whale-sized belly. The beast was headed from the cave out to sea, leaving a voice in his head that solemnly advised young Owen, "The dragon is going to Bath, and you must never speak of it to anyone."'"

Augie pronounced "Bath" as "bathe," taking for granted a rare typo plus improper capitalization.

"'He assumed his brothers and friends never spoke of it to anyone, neither, as he never heard them mention the subject going on decades thereafter, not even to their parents on their death beds.'"

"Well!" growled Nigel, in a rare moment of sobriety, irritable from having gone hours without a sip of Toohey's. "Isn't that bloody cheek of him, puttin' what he was warned to never speak of in that story of his?!"

"Makes him quite the mischief-maker, for sure," agreed Irene.

"Wait," said Stephen. He held out his hand as he was infamously wont to do, to caution against jumping to any conclusions the least bit amazing. "According to your

Nana, Augie, your great grandfather made up names for himself. Who's to say he didn't make up a lot else as well?"

"Including a creature that happened to look like a sauropod dinosaur..."

"Again, they would have heard all about sauropod dinosaurs well before the 1940s."

"And his sauropod happened to sport a rooster's coxcomb on its head like David here reported?" Augie asked testily.

"That's a proper point, that is," gushed Kay anew, giving Augie a congratulatory slap on the back while also giving Nigel a sideways, hope-you're-seeing-this glance. "By the by," she went on with calculated offhandedness, "does your significant other share your interest in discovering dinosaurs that are not so extinct, after all?"

"Very much; she even features our expeditions in her elementary school classroom. She folds them into her lesson plans."

"Oh, right, but that's back in the states?"

"Yes," confirmed Augie. *What are you getting at, exactly?*

"She doesn't actually accompany you on any of your trips?"

"Unfortunately, that wouldn't be practical; we have a daughter..."

"For the record," said Stephen, barging in between Augie and Kay, "I'm unattached."

"Of course you are," said Kay, peeved enough at Stephen that she threw a bit of his dry wit back in his face, adding, "Very early on, you successfully freed yourself from your mother's umbilical cord."

"This is the beach where you saw the giant creature?" Augie asked David, crouching down beside him.

David's eyes were riveted on the restless Irish Sea. They darted from white cap to white cap, unsuccessfully willing one of them to yield a long serpentine neck rising from the depths. "I know it is, because of the cave behind us," he confirmed while relishing the bracing sea breeze, the lack of a serpentine neck notwithstanding. "The dinosaur – I believe that dragons are really dinosaurs, mate. They are very lonely dinosaurs because the giant asteroid knocked off most of their family. But I saw him move that direction, until I lost him in the fog. Maybe he snuck back to shore down the coast where nobody was around. I don't blame him, really," remarked David, turning away from the sea to look Augie straight in the eye. "I'd be shy of people, too, if I had to go everywhere with no clothes on!" he giggled infectiously, his ears turning bright red.

"David Taylor! I heard that!" bellowed Ethel from nearby.

"It might not be coincidental, that a fog bank was present for your great grandfather's sighting, as well as David's," noted Sherman. Down on his knees close to the surf, he was turning a dark-brown, squarish skate egg from side to side. "Fish are more prone to surface-feed in the fog, when the sun can't blind them. And let's suppose it is the more typical, herbivorous sauropod, not meat-eating. Stands to reason it feels more comfortable feeding on seaweed while cloaked in heavy mists. Its inherited instinct would still have it fearful of prowling Allosaurs and the like."

"Wow!" exclaimed David. "I didn't think about that!"

"Ridiculous," scoffed Stephen, hurrying over to, as he saw it, rescue the young boy from extreme gullibility to the power of suggestion. "Look, say a population of sauropod dinosaurs, such as the Diplodocus or the Brachiosaurus, really is feeding on seaweed along the coastline here. Why are there so few sightings of them? Yours, David? And Mr. Matias's great grandpa's several decades ago? And maybe Rupert's? That's all we're aware of, correct?"

"But if they're hiding in fog banks..." protested David.

"I'm sure people hike along this coastline in all sorts of

weather," said Stephen with growing confidence in his skeptical assessment. "At least some of them should have also caught a glimpse of the creature. Enough for there to be more than three sightings in, what, eighty years?"

"I *wanted* to see a dinosaur!" said David angrily, stamping his little shoe on the pebbly sand. "Maybe those hikers were not so interested."

"Ah, you see there, David," said Stephen as in *Gotcha!* "Exactly! You *wanted* to see a dinosaur. So when a seal, maybe a little larger than usual, lifted his head out of the fog..."

"I would think those hikers you referenced, a good number of them, keep their eyes peeled for dolphins, or a breaching whale or whatever," Irene McDowell interjected, chin lifted regally high. She was intent on defending the little boy's honor. "On more than a few occasions, the thought must surely cross their minds how wonderful it would be to glimpse a sea serpent on holiday from Loch Ness or some such. Why don't any of them wishful-think themselves into seeing Prince Plesiosaur?"

"That's a right proper point, that is!" enthused David, initiating a high-five with Irene.

"A question also occurs to me," said Scott. "How many people have seen what David saw, but are afraid to admit it? Over the risk of being laughed at and ridiculed?"

"Moreover," chimed in Laura, "how many people who saw the creature were of too skeptical a bent? In other words, how many people didn't believe their own eyes, and told themselves they must have merely seen an oversized seal?"

"Okay, you've made your point," conceded Stephen, batting his hands at thin air like he could bat away the words by which his colleagues barraged him. "However, if it's true there's a family of monster-sized plant-eating dinosaurs living along this coast, shouldn't they be virtually vacuuming all the seaweed off the shoreline? How come there's so much kelp washed up here? Paleontologists estimate that the Brachiosaurus, for example, needed to eat at least one ton of plant material each and every day."

"There is an element of the unknowable we're dealing with," said Sherman, stroking his chin thoughtfully, an amazing sight in its own right for Augie to behold. Usually, Sherman scrunched his chin so far into his neck, nothing was left to be stroked, thoughtfully or otherwise. "Long before we arrived, I wondered what quantities of seaweed are available to sustain a population of ancient relic sea reptiles. Turns out that thousands and thousands of tons are harvested each year in nearby Ireland and Scotland. In fact, seaweed helped Ireland through its historically tragic famine of the 1800s, preventing it from getting even worse, as horrific as it did get."

"What's the unknowable part, Sherman?" Laura paused from her manic note-taking to look up and ask.

"Oh, that. Well," Sherman once more bowed his chin into his neck; Augie wondered how he didn't ever leave a saddle-type indentation there. "What we don't know, what we can't know is how much seaweed would be filling the North Irish Sea. That is, were there not a pod of aquatic sauropods surviving on a diet of it, assuming such a population of creatures exist. For all we know, there otherwise might have been a second Sargasso Sea nearby, positively clogged with kelp and the like."

"The same as we don't know what would have happened in a world of no anti-war interventions by time travelers, errr..."

Irene gave Augie a severe regard, to remind him they'd agreed it wouldn't be at all helpful to reveal the identity of their three history-altering hangers-on.

"...or space aliens or whoever they turn out to be. In such

a presumably more polluted, war-faring world, maybe the few surviving non-avian dinosaurs would have already gone extinct for good. If there were any left in the first place."

"What did he say, Mum?" asked David, tugging at his teacher's wool sweater.

"I'll explain later, lad; maybe our gallant young dinosaur searcher there can help."

Augie pretended not to hear Kay while Sherman resumed, "Woe be it for me to detract the least tiny bit from David and his teacher's intriguing testimonials. However, there is an indirect clue that could add considerable heft to the notion of such a creature afoot as they have described. That would be finding distinctly less seaweed by that cave than elsewhere, up and down this coastline."

It occurred to Sherman the wisdom of leaving his artificial intelligence entity, Charly, switched off back aboard Cloud Nine, for the time being at least. Hearing Sherman expound on the "indirect clue," heaven knew what Charly might have done. Would he have thrown caution to the wind, leaping into the North Irish Sea before anyone could stop him? Instantly, obsessively intent on collecting seaweed abundance data, if not actually sneaking up on a submerged, feeding sauropod? And going at it until saltwater rusted him immobile?

"Don't know about that, mate!" Nigel blurted out, stumbling forward. He sprayed spit in nearly the profusion of sea spray, fellow pub-goers would have joked. And he staggered drunkenly on the momentum of his prior imbibing, even though he was as sober as he ever got. "Want me to swim along the coast for a look-see?"

"Spare yourself, Nigel," said Rupert Hamster Holmes stepping up smartly as ever behind him. "Or maybe it's not so much spare yourself as spare us. That is to say,-"

"You have something to contribute to this conversation, Mr. Holmes?" Irene asked to try getting him to the point, on the perhaps-too-generous assumption there was a point to be gotten to.

"Ah, yes, cutting to the bone again, are we? Very well. I have hiked this shoreline on many an occasion, although the path be too smooth and level at times for that endeavor to be labelled a 'hike,' with all the strenuous activity that word implies. Nevertheless, if we are about cutting away all possible embroidery of this account, there would appear to be, at least to my admittedly not always perfect perception, if perfect be it at all, or anything crouching towards that...Where was I?"

"Hiking the coast, your humanly flawed perception..." Irene sighed resignedly.

"'Humanly flawed perception,' exactly! Well put, I say! Keeping that caveat in mind, there appeared to me distinctly less seaweed washed ashore here, before that deep dark cave, than at any point either north or south. Hmm, or rather should I say northeast or southwest..."

"Oh?" Sherman perked up.

"I say, mate, let's not get carried away about it!" cautioned Rupert, holding up one hand as in, *Hold on there!* "The washed-ashore seaweed is not in so much less abundance here than at points northeast and southwest, that one would normally feel compelled to comment on it. But the prospect of a living, breathing reptile of the dinosaur nomenclature is far from normal, so that neither would it have felt proper not to mention it."

"Oh, here we go again with your indecisive straddlin' every line there is, Rupert! Bloody hell!" complained Nigel, increasingly irritated the longer he went without a beer, and staggering back and forth drunken-like before Rupert. "You best not ever try the tender art of seduction, burp! Because the target of your affections – or would target be too strong a word for it, sir? Let's hem and haw over that 'til the sheep are all sheared, shall we? Point is, she- or he, though you're never goin' to persuade me to leer at a fellow bloke's bum, good grief!" Nigel suddenly stopped dead in his tracks, wavering like he might be about to topple over, face first, in the sand. "Now you've got me addin' all the qualifiers too! Let's try this: You test that rhetoric of yours on your sweetie-pie, and she's likely to fall right off to sleep before you've ever even held her bloody hand! Burp!"

"That's quite enough, Nigel!" remonstrated Elwin Kneath stepping forward. Then to Augie and his gang, "Please do accept my sincerest apology for our associate's rudeness. He really is quite a good chap, as is amply evidenced by his joining me in lending courage to our dear Robin, here, in need of a special favor from you."

Robin stepped forward, and nervously worked her long straight auburn hair round her shoulders. Augie sensed she would have wrapped it round her face to talk incognito, if she could have gotten away with that. As it was, in fact, she scrunched her chin into her neck a la Sherman, to soft-spokenly report, "Back in the pub, you probably heard we give our poor, dear bartender, Gerwyn, a bit of a hard time, each in our own cheeky way. But the plain fact is, I do rather fancy him, and well, um…"

Nigel jested, "What Robin is tryin' to say is that I'd be too much of a good thing for her, so she wants to see if any sparks ignite, rubbin' together with Gerwyn instead."

"I wish the best for you, Robin," said Augie. "But I'm not sure I see what any of this has to do with us."

"Well, here's the thing. I was wondering if it would be okay for me to invite Gerwyn on a wee bit of your dinosaur search. That is, supposing you were going to stake out this location of an evening, or some such."

"I've already prepared the most elegant invite

conceivable for her to hand Gerwyn," boasted Elwin, puffing out his chest. "I dare say it puts my free dinner coupon to shame."

There's another reason for shame over that dinner coupon, was the snark Irene kept to herself.

"We are looking at all-night surveillance of this cave and its surroundings," Augie acknowledged. "Shortly, in fact, before the tide rolls in, we do plan a preliminary snoop around here. Anyway, I don't see why we can't accommodate a first date." He looked to Scott, Irene, and Sherman for agreeing nods. "Of course, you must keep in mind that everyone needs to maintain the strictest quiet. If there is any such large creature about as David and his teacher reported, we don't want to scare it off."

"In other words, dearie," tipsily slobbered John Jones stumbling forward with a can of Toohey's in tow, "you'll have to save the canoodlin' 'til later! Cheers, mates!" He lifted his can high, then collapsed into a heap on the pebbly sand.

"Naw, man!" railed Nigel, doing a swaying, staggering hover over the pile of inebriated John Jones. "The date will be perfect for them! Perfect! Burp! I can see them smilin' nervously at one another for hours on end, nary a peep, while they wait for some bloody what-the-f—k-o-don – sorry, David - to poke his head out of there! Or else, show us his business end to give everyone a prehistoric-monster-sized fart! Burp!"

"Eww!" David held his nose and giggled.

"Hey?! Where did you get that can from?!" Nigel asked John Jones.

John Jones was slowly sitting up, if only to take another swig of his Toohey's.

"Where do you think I got it from, mate?" asked John, looking at the label on his can as in, *Oh, this?* "I sat on a nest, cluckin' like a bloody chicken, when all the sudden I felt somethin' exceedin' strange. So I stood up and looked down, only to see the can had exited me bum like an egg! Want me to lay one for you?"

Before Nigel could respond, he heard a distinct downbeat above the soft lapping of the surf, and then a reggae version of the Beatles song, "Good Day, Sunshine." Looking all around, he realized Sherman had set up a large flat-screen television monitor on a tripod, where everyone could watch.

On the TV screen, a closeup of an alligator prevailed. Said gator swung his long snout side to side in a rapturous-seeming dance, by turns boogied and swayed. The camera pulling away revealed he was no bigger than a pencil. And that he danced on a conference table appointed with what Nigel could only describe as a miniature tropical swamp.

The view also encompassed a rotund fellow seated at the table. His grin matched the alligator's reptilian visage. And a toothpick-slim elderly lady stood behind him. Her hair done up in a bun, she sported the most seriously demure expression Nigel had ever seen.

Despite that, Nigel soon found his attention drawn to a half-eaten pretzel. The rotund fellow was gesturing with it like Nigel imagined some king waving about his royal scepter.

"Very good, there," Eclipso motioned at the TV screen with his humus-slathered pretzel, while Nigel realized the elderly lady who stood guard behind him was grinding her jaws. "Looks like you are staking out a most intriguing seaside landscape, indeed. I trust that's where our schoolboy caught a glimpse through the fog of something dinosaurian."

"What's more, it's also where my great grandpa described seeing his Welsh dragon," noted Augie.

"Brilliant, as the English say," reacted Eclipso. Squinting at the screen, leaning his head forward, he added, "I see other people your end, Dr. Matias, besides yourself and our regulars. They are certainly welcome to participate. But we don't want to frighten away the object of our quest. Worldwide, we've seen how reticent it is to show itself, even when Sherman's pungent sprays mask human pheromones."

"I doubt that figments of the imagination scare off easily," snarked Stephen Feldman.

"I'll be providing the participants in tonight's stakeout with a seaweed-based spray," Sherman Peabody assured Eclipso. Although as usual, with his chin bowed into his neck, he looked to Augie like he was confiding in his belly button instead. "However, I would also venture to suggest this particular creature, if creature indeed it is, must have some small tolerance, at least, for human presence. After all, it did come out into the open despite a school field trip nearby."

"Well that certainly is of potentially great noteworthiness, wouldn't you agree, Bonsai Gator?" Eclipso motioned at the pencil-sized gator still swaying to a reggae version of the Beatles' "Good Day, Sunshine."

To Stephen's continuing disgruntlement, Bonsai worked an affirming-looking nod of his long snout into his dance.

"But my reason for barging in at clearly not the most opportune time," Eclipso went on, "is to apprise you of a most significant development regarding our security breach. I, Eclipso Sunray Smith, have narrowed down the possible culprit, as it were, to three items of jewelry among you. Three suspects. Doesn't mean the wearer of the offending piece necessarily knew she wore a tracking device. I want to believe she had no idea her ornamentation was providing the hoaxers with useful, timely info as to your whereabouts. Anyway, step one will be to identify the particular jewelry at fault. Step two, we question its wearer, to discover what she did and did not know. Hopefully she knew nothing; I don't relish the prospect of having to remove any of you from our quest."

"Okay," said Stephen. "Who are we talking about? With which pieces of jewelry?"

"I'll have Samuel collect them on your return aboard Cloud Nine. For starters, there's your copper bracelet, Ms. Laura Gómez."

Laura reflexively cupped her hand over the gift from her boyfriend, Tom, as she anxiously asked, "You will return it to me afterwards?"

"As long as it's not the tracking device, Ms. Gómez, you can depend on that. But moving forward, there's your thermos bottle, Ms. McDowell."

"Not what I'd call jewelry," huffed Irene, holding it up for all to see.

"Yes, of course, a misnomer indeed. Not sure why I lumped that in with the other two."

Perhaps you remote-viewed Skip trying to use it as an engagement ring, Irene thought to herself while she said, "Where I'm concerned, you can do what you want with it. Melt it down for all I care."

"That's more than fair, Ms. McDowell. Anyway, finally, there's your distinctive Welsh pendant featuring two intertwined dragons, Dr. Quiñones. Most apropos for your current venue. I should hope you would never want to see *that* melted down."

If Daniela had anything to do with helping the hoaxers sabotage the search, all the more reason it's over between us. Which it is, regardless! Roberta Quiñones raged to herself as she said, "No matter to me, one way or the other." She removed the necklace for the very last time, far as she was concerned, before going on, "After the determination is made, of whether it was used as a tracking device, would you like to have it, Ms. Jones?" She held it forward for Kay Jones to enjoy a closer look.

"Thinking on me feet, Augie Matias," Kay reacted, "perhaps you'd like to give it to your wife?"

"Vicky does love Celtic designs."

"That fine-looking young man there," said Eclipso before Augie, or Kay for that matter, could get in another word, "you must be David, who had the courage to come forward about your experience. I'm most envious!"

"If you mean me dinosaur sighting, sir," said David to the TV screen, "I am that David, and do feel like a most lucky bloke indeed. But who is he, please?" David pointed at Bonsai Gator on the screen.

Bonsai had finished dancing, the reggae-fied Beatles tune having concluded. But he remained standing erect on his hind legs, his wee little fore claws laced prayerfully together for contemplation of the TV screen his end.

"He's my constant companion, besides Mother, of course. His name is Bonsai Gator."

"Bonsai Gator?" giggled David as Bonsai struck a number of poses.

Bonsai could have been showing off some special outfit on a fashion show runway, Augie mused.

"Correct," nodded Eclipso. "He thought it was a good idea for me to follow up on reports such as yours. See whether we can confirm, once and for all, the survival of non-avian dinosaurs to the present day."

"Yes, that's right, isn't it," said David nonchalantly. "Birds are the great great great great, a million times the great grandchildren of Tyrannosaurus Rex types of dinosaurs, aren't they? They'd be eating us rather than pecking away at seeds, if they weren't so small."

"That's an impressive lot you already know about them, David," said Eclipso approvingly, leading to a celebratory bite of his humus-dipped pretzel.

"Bloody hell!" Nigel raged, suddenly stalking into view on

Eclipso's TV monitor. He bent forward much as Eclipso would have expected from a stalking T-Rex prowling the Welsh beach, and curious about the TV set. "Did I actually hear you tell our David here that your world's smallest and weirdest gator, who you call Bonsai *Gator*, 'thought it was a good idea'?!?!" finger quotation marks. "He 'thought it was a good idea' to go searchin' for dinosaurs still up and about?!? In other words, not for your usual fossilized dinosaur that's in even worse shape than me?!"

"You did hear me say exactly that, though I must note you appear very far removed from being fossilized."

"Well!" Nigel exclaimed, tottering before the TV screen like he might collapse any moment into a misshapen heap on the pebbly sand. *Requiring only a sudden volcanic eruption to cover him in lava, begin the fossilization process*, Irene mused to herself while Nigel went on, "How in Jesus's name do you know a sheep's fart what it thinks?!"

"We've spent enough time together for Bonsai to trust me with his thoughts."

To Stephen's eternal frustration, Bonsai Gator nodded in apparent agreement.

"Oh, I get it," said Nigel sarcastically. His persisting stagger incidentally lent Augie the impression of someone standing on board a small boat rocked by heavy seas. "The only reason me sheep don't share any good ideas with me, about expeditions we should undertake, is because we don't spend enough quality time together! Aside from the occasional shear! I suppose the whole bloody animal kingdom would share more of their thoughts with us, as well! If only we would just put in more hours with them, is it? And that horsefly to blame for such a swollen rash on me leg this past August, it was only tryin' to get me attention so we could share a tender moment together?!?! David, there's a good lad if you cover your ears while I curse like a sailor!"

"Best not tell him about our time travelers," Irene thought she could confide in Scott without anyone else hearing. But just as she opened her mouth, Nigel flustered himself silent, conflicted on which particular obscene epithet would best suit the occasion. The surf paused after its latest ebb, before mounting its next series of wavelets. Even the seagulls wheeling overhead went quiet briefly from their constant cawing. And so, every last word Irene spoke softly came out loud and clear.

Nigel staggered Irene's direction, head lowered like he might adopt one animal's behavior as a good idea, and charge like a bull. But he came to an abrupt halt instead, and muttered, "I'm goin' to pretend I didn't hear that." No sooner speaking than something else caught his attention on the TV screen. "Wait; what's that on your conference table?!?! *Ych a fi*, looks like a bloody swamp!!"

"It *is* a swamp, a small swamp to accommodate Bonsai Gator."

Bonsai Gator dropped down on all fours, the few steps to the swamp's edge. Then he craned his long snout back around to the camera, and nodded as though to say, *That's right.*

Stephen told himself that Bonsai must have sensed an insect flying past.

"Bonsai feels at home there. That, plus Beatles reggae, eases his long wait on our quest coming to fruition."

"I say, Nigel, who exactly are you talkin' to?" asked John Jones, stepping forward smartly with an open can of Toohey's in hand. "Some bloke inside that telly?"

Nigel turned John's way to garble, like his mouth was full of phlegm, "He calls himself Eclipso!"

"Eclipso?!?" John paused from taking another sip of beer. "Is he out of his mind? Who calls himself 'Eclipso'?!"

Nigel staggered so clumsily close beside John, John lifted his Toohey's high for fear of a spilling bump. Then Nigel vented, "The man keeps a bloody swamp on his desk! For the sake of the smallest alligator you've ever seen! Who dances to Beatles tunes! Correction, reggae versions of Beatles tunes! That's who calls himself Eclipso!! Burp!!"

As John Jones waved off the disgusting stench from Nigel's latest burp, Nigel turned seaward. Still appearing about to tip over any second, he shouted, his drool mixing with the sea spray, "IF YOU ARE OUT THERE, YOU BLOODY BRONTOSAURUS, PLEASE TAKE THIS WHOLE CRAZY LOT WITH YOU!!!" Reconsidering, though, he turned Robin's way, and added in as delicately polite a voice as he could muster, "But I hope you enjoy an evening full of romance, m'lady. Burp!" He made a gallantly sweeping gesture as though he'd removed the most elegant hat possible from his head. But realizing there was nothing on his head to remove, he stopped midway, and sent himself keeling face first onto the pebbly sand.

Chapter 5

"Mind you, Eclipso is still monitoring every sound we make. In case you're tempted to go potty-mouth on me," cautioned Augie. Nevertheless, he wished he could reach through the phone to give Vicky a bear hug and smooch. "But now that he has three suspects in custody, awaiting Sherman's determination which one-"

"Or ones."

"True; could be multiple," acknowledged Augie. "Anyway, things are loosening up. It's not just that I can finally chit-chat with you again. Eclipso has also approved resumption of filming our explorations for your sordid educational purposes."

"And torturing Diane Mueller, let's not forget that."

"Ah, yes, Wild E. Coyote still trying to catch you as Road Runner. Be that what it is, our stakeout later tonight isn't going to time well with any of your classes."

"Not even close," confirmed Vicky. "In fact, have to assist with dismissal soon. This place will be a ghost town when you're on the prowl."

"I'll be sure to transmit you only the most interesting segments tomorrow, i.e. those most liable to drive Mueller straight up a wall."

"You mean the segments where women try to pull down your pants?"

"Eclipso sells those for expedition fundraising purposes, my Queen Victoria."

"But that is wild about Irene especially. All three of them, really."

"Yeah, you'd think they'd leave my pants alone, 'specially since I'm already spoken for."

"No, Augie-Doggie! I mean that any one of them would

64

have wanted to sabotage the search. Who do you suspect?"

"I don't believe they had the faintest idea. They all insist that once Sherman confirms which item or items were embedded with a tracking device, look out. The gift giver will be in deep, deep doo-doo. Poor Laura said she'll be crushed if the bracelet Tom gave her was the culprit."

"Would that mean you were back on the meat market?" Stephen asked Laura when she expressed dismay over the possibility her boyfriend sabotaged Eclipso's search.

"How he sweet-talks women," Irene asided to Scott and Augie. "I'm surprised they're not falling over each other to pinch his butt."

"I think they're falling over each other to stay out of his way," Augie asided right back.

"That teacher with the schoolboy who maybe saw a dinosaur," went on Vicky presently, "and saw something, herself...is she unattached?"

"She's been unattached since childbirth. At least that's what Stephen thought was a clever thing to say when she asked, um..."

"What's up, Augie? I can hear your ears turning red over the phone!"

"She has hit on me a few times. Although it seems to be for making one of the locals jealous."

"Oh?"

"I said I was married. To you." Augie couldn't feel more awkward.

"You didn't tell her about your other wives? Just me?"

"Didn't want to give her any false hope I might add her to my harem."

"And that's when she quoted Stephen Stills? 'If you're not with the one you love, love the one you're with'!" sang Vicky.

"I would have told her I am always with the one I love,

Vicky. Because you are always with me, in my heart."

"Well played, sir," Vicky slow-clapped over the phone; she was good at hiding how choked up she got. "I suppose it's like we're playing doctor. You showed me yours; time for me to show you mine."

"Huh?"

"That too-full-of-himself ESOL teacher I told you about, Mark Waltzer?"

"Yeah?"

"He's tried a couple of times to get me out for a cup of coffee."

"Ooo, a cup of coffee; that sounds pretty steamy, unless it's a Frappuccino," quipped Augie, relieved over Vicky confirming his intuition that something, or rather someone, was going on her end. She likely wouldn't have done that, were something *really* going on her end.

"Listen, there's a certain vibe a woman knows…"

"I believe you. Too bad we can't have Kay and Mark meet up somehow. Or can we? It's not like they're living on two different planets."

"Wouldn't want to do that to Kay. I sense Mark is just after another notch in his belt, like he's collecting butterflies. Worst hobby, ever!"

"I wouldn't be so sure Kay isn't doing the same thing."

"In other words, they'd be two trick-or-treaters raiding each other's bags?"

"Of course; why not mix in that metaphor as well? But I don't know. Maybe I give Kay too little credit, and she'd blow off your tempter."

"No real temptation for me."

"For which am eternally grateful. Okay, can we get back to talking about dinosaurs?" *What did she mean by: "No real temptation"? Am I overthinking it?*

Chapter 6

"A 'flatus emission detector,' you say?" Nigel Morgan asked Sherman Peabody.

The detector burdened Sherman on his slow progress down a gorse-strewn hillside.

Eclipso's away team, their time-traveling hangers-on, and Kelpyguard locals were all headed for the Pembrokeshire seashore below the Strumblehead lighthouse.

Sherman would have had his artificial intelligence entity, Charly, carry the detector for him. But Charly's efficiency function proved impossible to override, even with the empathy program activated. He would have made a spectacle of himself, magnetizing the detector to his chest so he could keep both arms free.

"We suspect that creatures from Papua, New Guinea to the Amazon River Basin might be surviving non-avian dinosaurs. And that they share a signature sound when they pass gas," Sherman elaborated while he balanced the detector against his chin.

"Let me get this straight," grumbled Nigel. "You'll be on more of a stink-out than a stake-out? Or should we call it a fart-out? Bloody hell!"

"Well," Sherman sighed with relief as he set down his special contraption on a convenient boulder near bottom of the footpath to the shore. "My only regret is that the flatus emission detector is not also useful for sniffing out such putridness as this booklet. Elwin Kneath handed it to me in the parking lot. Claimed he found it sticking out of a bushel of hay at his barn."

Sherman produced a sheaf of brown-edged parchment paper, bound together by frayed string, and entitled in all-caps: **A DINOSAUR AMONG US**

"Don't think for a tick I didn't overhear your most uncharitable characterization of what I went to considerable trouble to secure for you, sir!" Elwin stormed indignantly. "Certainly, you can't help but be impressed by the obvious antiquity of the paper employed for that document! And the deft artistry of the calligraphy! Not to mention, no small coincidence can it be, that the date printed inside is 691 A.D.? Around the same time Adomán of Iona wrote of Saint Columbus's fateful encounter with the Loch Ness Monster?"

"What impresses me the most," responded Sherman, unflappably, "is the blatant anachronism. Not to mention the spot of ink that came off on my hands while handling it."

"Anachronism, you say?!" blustered Elwin.

"The word, dinosaur, was not coined until 1841, I believe. Unless you're going to argue the author, Linew Theank, was another Nostradamus. And that it is no more than an incredible coincidence his name is an anagram of yours, Mr. Kneath."

"You must understand, sir," Elwin persisted with his bluster. "There really wasn't a whole lot of time to effectuate that artifact! Even given your delay of nocturnal surveillance, to explore the cave during daylight!" He pointed at the faux antique held limply in Sherman's hand to rant on, "Nevertheless, notwithstanding, you do have to concede the sheer artistry of the gold-embossed calligraphy, if nothing else."

"Another masterpiece, for sure," said Gerwyn Davies as he stepped forward with Robin Pugh following close behind. "But Mr. Peabody, I believe Robin has a question for you regarding tonight's proceedings."

"Well first a compliment, if you're going to put me forward like this, Gerwyn," said Robin, stepping up beside

Gerwyn. She briefly alighted her hand on his shoulder, yet not so briefly that he didn't feel obliged to pretend focus on a particular seagull gliding out to sea. And thanked the sunset for casting in shadow what had to be a deep blush. "This scent you sprayed on us, to mask our spoor from the object of your search: I rather fancy it. A wee bit of a heather fragrance; that's proper, that is."

"A far cry from the stench that had me holding my nose all the way through Brazil and Cameroon, Jesus PU Christ!" cursed Sergeant Fred Frankly.

"Just want to make sure I understood correctly," Robin continued. "For the vigil, we can choose where we disperse ourselves along the coastline, can we? So long as it's a secluded location where nobody will spot us?"

Click...whirr...Sherman's artificial intelligence entity, Charly, did a 360-degree head rotation, and robotically said, "Am uncertain which 'ourselves' you are referring to, Robin. But dispersing yourself along the coastline would require disassembling in ways that would be exceedingly painful and, indeed, fatal, given your biological nature. Most important of all," ...click...whirr... "the attention subsequently given to you would detract seriously from the search for a surviving non-avian dinosaur. In conclusion, don't do it." Click...whirr... "Allow me the honors, instead, as that has lots of potential for serious evidence gathering."

Sherman felt conflicted. He easily understood the benefit that could accrue from Charly dispersing himself. But he also feared such behavior would profoundly upset the locals; so much for any further pretense that Charly wasn't a robot. No matter. Before he could find the words to say, Charly snapped off his own right leg as effortlessly as were he unzipping a jacket.

"All parts of me are equipped for sensory data accumulation as well as independent mobility," Charly explained. "I will report regularly, Sherman, and reassemble down there on the beach an hour before dawn." Click...whirr... "That is, unless you direct me otherwise."

"I'm good, Charly. Just be careful."

"I will be careful not to impede the search, and take only those actions reasonably hypothesized to enhance it," Charly's head, all alone, assured Sherman. Then it turned away to follow the lower torso, upper torso, arms and legs. They rolled off between gorse bushes, for positions all along the coast.

Gerwyn and Robin stole puzzled glances at each other.

Nigel, ever tipsy as though standing on the deck of a rocking boat, slobbered, "I'm not bein' funny, right? That's the most bizarre thing I could ever hope to see, the rest of me life! Check that off the bloody list!"

"Um, Mr. Peabody," said Gerwyn most tentatively, "we assume your robot-"

"Artificial Intelligence Entity."

"Right. Your artificial intelligence entity will be solely focused on anything that could be a living dinosaur, or evidence thereof?"

"If your real question is, will he pay any attention to the amorous activities of two lovers, definitely not."

"Ych a fi, maybe me boys need to get up a canoodle patrol! Cheers, mates!" chortled John Jones. He held forth his latest can of Toohey's, like a battering ram to barge his way into the conversation, seemed to Augie.

"I hope you and your boys don't plan on popping open beer cans incessantly, and trashing the coastline with them into the bargain," Gerwyn addressed John most sternly.

"That's nothing a bloke ever plans; just happens naturally, doesn't it, mates? Cheers!"

"Cheers!" a chorus answered, while five hands shot up from behind a gorse bush on the hillside down to the shore.

Each hand clutched a popped-open can of Toohey's.

"Unless I miss my guess," Gerwyn reacted in a prickly voice that made clear he was not to be amused out of his concern, "your rowdy ways after sunset, not to mention your beer breath, might scare off any prehistoric reptile still roaming our Pembrokeshire coast. Remember, Mr. Peabody here took great pains to spray us with heather scent for the purpose of masking our odors."

"Gerwyn is quite right," nodded Sherman.

"That's in case you're wondering why a dinosaur never darkens the doorstep of what is your pub? Drunk In The Wool?" Stephen asked for the purpose of an accurately rendered snark.

"You gents could stand to benefit from following Nigel's example, and lay off the alcohol for a while," Gerwyn continued in lecture mode.

Still staggering about the beach in a seemingly stuporous haze, despite his sobriety, Nigel let out an especially profound belch.

"Careful there," Stephen cautioned Nigel. "Someone might mistake that for a dinosaur fart."

"*Ych a fi*, Gerwyn!" John Jones burst out irritably. "Maybe *you* could stand to benefit from me and me boys not givin' you any business for a while! Here I bought out half your canned stock! Which I planned to share, incidentally," he added as though that's what the onlookers from Eclipso's crew had foremost on their minds. "What else is there to do, hunkered down behind the gorse, awaitin' Godzilla's cousin?" He held up a plastic garbage bag stuffed full of six-packs. Augie mused to himself that John could have been showing off an animal carcass for a feast. "But from what you're tellin' me, might as well be a fart in a jam jar, for what we're allowed to do with it tonight! Which is apparently nothin'!"

"If you are going to crouch down behind the gorse with

us overnight, fine. But I'm going to ask that you and your associates also don these caps I've prepared." Sherman extricated a trio of them from his backpack, and held them forward. The top of each dark-green cap featured sewn-in needly sprigs of real gorse.

"So tell me," John Jones blustered, "will me big bag-o-beer here also need to be fitted with one of those gorse caps?"

"I should think you could leave your bag concealed behind that especially large gorse bush." Sherman pointed halfway back up the hill. "Of course, remember to take it with you whenever you leave."

John emptied the rest of his Toohey's down his throat, then unpleasantly found himself thinking better of just chucking the can. So many witnesses standing in for his conscience, he crumpled it in his hand, and awkwardly stuffed it inside his beige woolen sweater. Thereafter, he roughly swiped the caps from Sherman's hands, and grumbled, "Suppose you'd told me to wear a hot, steamin' pile of sheep's poo on me head! That is, if I wanted to catch a moonlit glimpse of a bloody Welsh dragon risin' from the sea! Well, I would have figured you were takin' me on a ride to Stupid Pig Land, I would! But seein' whereas some of you lot have already donned these cheeky gorse caps..."

"What if some of our 'lot' *had* placed a hot, steaming pile of sheep's poo on their heads?" Stephen inquired with a twinkle in his eye.

"For a guaranteed peek at a prehistoric monster, you mean?"

"*O fy duw*, John Jones!" one of John's crew popped up from behind the gorse to erupt. "You're actually hesitatin'! You're hintin' there's a chance-"

"No, man!" John shook his head emphatically. "No chance at all, what?! A fellow can't take even a flea's poo to collect his thoughts before he answers?!"

"Well maybe you be eatin' that flea's poo into the bargain! Shouldn't take any time at all! Should be automatic!"

"Wait, Peter," John waved the gorse caps at his friend frantically. "You're sayin', are you, there'd be no sheep's poo on your head, even for a million quid?"

"A million quid?"

"Ohhhhh," nodded John, back in chortle mode. "Now who's hesitatin'?"

"I don't think the promise of a blink-of-the-eye look at a mythical monster be quite the same as a million quid, mate!"

"Let's explore this further, shall we? Maybe you'd also be willin' to eat a small, meatball-sized portion of sheep's poo for the million quid?? Or does that require an even bigger pot?"

"I think we can sum it up this way," Stephen leapt in. "Any one of us is willing to wear a silly hat on our head in order to see a living dinosaur. But we will require a whole lot more than that before we let a sheep take a dump on our heads."

"One of those self-evident truths, no need to have engraved in stone," Gerwyn allowed, moving an amused Robin to modestly cover her mouth.

By then, John Jones was dragging his bag full of six-packs back up the hill, a forlorn Santa Claus where Augie was concerned. He halted long enough to look down at Gerwyn and grumble, "You do understand, don't you, Gerwyn? I'm not bein' funny about this! Since me and me boys will have to save these for later, it will be a good long while before we need to turn up at your establishment for reinforcements. Hope you don't go broke in the meantime."

"Some things are more important than the bottom line,

John," Gerwyn reacted, unable to resist stealing a glance Robin's way in the darkening twilight.

"Yeah? Well, I'm guessin' there's one bottom you don't say that about. Cheers, mates!" John hoisted his black plastic garbage bag as high as he could. And from behind the gorse, five empty beer cans were also lifted skywards, accompanied by a chorus of cavernously deep belches.

"Quiet down there now," Stephen advised them not-at-all seriously. "Don't want to keep chasing away the dinosaurs like we've been obviously doing up to now."

"David?!? Where are you, David?!?" suddenly called David's mother, Ethel, nearly on top of Augie and company to their surprise. Her commotion descending the gravelly dirt path to the shore was drowned out by the clankety-clank of John Jones dragging his garbage bag full of six-packs along the ground up a hiking trail. "Are you almost done?! It's getting dark!! Your father and I have been waiting it seems forever and a day at the parking lot!!"

"I told you, Ethel," remonstrated her husband Wilfrid hurrying to catch up to her. "It's a stake-out likely to last half the night or more, it is! Not some early evenin' football scrimmage!"

"Mum! Dad! Shh! No dinosaur will want to show himself while you are yelling like that!"

"That's right," said Stephen. "We've already scared off all the unicorns."

"I'm very sorry if there was any misunderstanding, Mrs. Taylor," said Augie Matias, hurrying to greet David's mom. "But we really are not expecting anything to, um, observe here until well after midnight."

"Or ever, if you're talking about a dinosaur romping about," Stephen couldn't help adding.

"Well, I don't see how that can be a thing for me son since his bedtime is nine."

"Mum!!"

"Don't you want to read me one of the comic books that nice man gave you, David?" Ethel asked her son. She crouched down to lovingly hold him. "They're about Native Americans in the American Southwest fighting off dinosaurs, right? I'd fancy hearing about that, meself!"

"They're made up, Mum! They're not real!" David lectured his mother, complete with emphatic arm gestures. "I do very much like *Turok*, kind sir," he then addressed Augie. "But here is my chance to see a dinosaur again, for real! Maybe it will be the same bloke with the snake's neck Ms. Jones and I saw here last week!"

While David argued his case to Augie, Irene nodded Ethel aside to whisper, "These night stake-outs often grow very tedious; I know from experience."

"I should think so, especially when nothing shows up."

To which remark by David's mom, Stephen nodded agreeably.

"That is often the case," Irene conceded. "Us adults are going to have trouble enough remaining alert as the evening wears on. Can't imagine your precious son won't have drifted off well before midnight. Of course, we'll only wake him if there's something really extraordinary..."

"In other words, David will have no problem getting his entire eight hours sleep, and more," drily said Stephen.

"Another thing that grows very tedious," reacted Irene, rolling her eyes.

"You mean my always being right when your supposed dinosaur evidence turns out to be a balloon, or whatever?"

"Not always."

"Yes, I almost forgot. There's the odd fart, torn pants, a golf ball that rolled back out from under a pile of rubble, and a macaw that could only have been agitated because he had the hots for an invisible, party-hopping

Ceratosaurus."

"I'll be here all night as well, Ethel," Kay Jones told David's mom, giving her a reassuring pat on the arm. "If your fine young lad, or anyone else here," she stole a glance at Augie, embedded with a sneaked peek Nigel's way, "needs a *cwtch* to stay warm, they can depend on me."

With a sigh of resignation, Ethel gave her son a hug and said, "My wee Welsh Dragon here, you be good to all these nice people, won't you? No breathin' fire on them?"

"Shh, Mum!" David put forefinger to his lips as he wriggled free of Ethel's hug, then gave Augie a tug on his windbreaker to ask, "Isn't it dark enough for the dinosaur to be waking up soon, Mister? Shouldn't we be making a quiet conceal of ourselves sooner rather than later?"

"Oh, that sounds proper, that does, Ethel, my dear little lamb," enthused Wilfrid. "You don't suppose we could-"

"Stop for fish-n-chips on the way home? Only if we leave right now!" Wilfrid's dear little lamb pushed him back so hard towards the hiking trail, she nearly knocked him totally off balance.

*

"You can speak a little louder, a wee bit louder as they say here, David," Augie advised his young stake-out companion. Surf echoing through the cave drowned out David's whispers that succeeded his tug on Augie's windbreaker. "Our dinosaur won't be able to hear us above those crashing waves out there, unless we shout."

"And not even then," Stephen's leaden voice cut through the seaside din. "That dinosaur doesn't have any ears. Or a nose, head or body, either, for that matter."

"What? You're saying there are two monsters out there, are you?" David asked Stephen in a loud-enough whisper. "The bloke I saw, and one that doesn't exist?"

"Couldn't have expressed it better myself," said Augie while Stephen found himself at a rare loss for words.

"Okay, not being funny here. I'm getting a bad case of the willies," complained David, bravely disciplining himself not to start a whiny cry about it, but rather keep his voice level calm. "How will we spot our dinosaur before he sticks his huge mouth out of the darkness, to bite me head off?"

"As luck has it, I was about to share these special goggles with you." Augie pulled two pairs from his backpack. "They're for night vision," he explained as he fitted David with one. "Even when it's dark, there's still some tiny amount of light, plus heat especially from living things. These are called night vision goggles. They magnify the light and heat to make things visible in the dark. Not perfect, but it's something."

"Oh, it's proper, it is!" enthused David looking all around. "Though I do wish it didn't make everything look so green! Wait! What's that?" He pointed anxiously towards the vertical stone Kay hid behind that resembled shale. It was a near replica of the one he and David hid behind, lodged right beside it. "It's moving about like a big crab, but *yucky dar!* Oh, I remember now," he giggled with relief. "That's a hand from the robot man, Charly, who spread himself across the coast like a pat of robot butter. You suppose the hand would fancy me shaking it?" he asked Augie pleadingly.

"Well, here's the thing," Augie responded gently. "I'm sure it would be grand fun, indeed, to shake a body-less hand. However, every last inch of Charly is programmed to do only one thing, rejecting all else."

"You mean, to search for a living dinosaur?"

"Exactly, David. Unless your hand contains information helpful to the search, Charly's hand is sure to slap it away, should you go for a handshake."

David turned his hands from side to side, desperate for something to be on them he knew wasn't there. An egg shell fragment from a freshly hatched Triceratops would have done splendidly. "I don't suppose me hands carry any dinosaur evidence," he lamented. "But I very much wish they did! Wait," he said abruptly. "Why *is* the hand crawling all over that rock? I don't see any dinosaur evidence there."

"Probably searching for clues," guessed Augie. "Maybe a scale scratched off the creature's skin, or a trace of dinosaur poop."

"Dinosaur poop, you say?" David giggled. "I should very much like to see that, I would."

"You can," announced Stephen, once again the deep voice of solemn, staid reality, Augie figured. "In a museum, fossilized, they're called coprolites."

"Sorry there, mate, but I fancy instead the fresh stinky poo from a living dinosaur, I do!" David declared with another giggle.

"I say, David, you can let your teacher have a wee go with these?" Kay Jones asked, already reaching to pull off his goggles. "Will return them to you in a flea's poo, I promise."

"Of course, Mum."

"Oh, wow, that does put a new light on things, now, doesn't it?" Kay ooed and ahhed looking all directions through the night vision goggles. "And there is obviously an especially strong heat source," she pointed towards Augie. "Although I am always ready to give anyone a good *cwtch*, that's Welsh for cuddle, who might be feeling the cold dark of this shoreside cave a wee bit too much."

"I'll keep that in mind," said Stephen.

"Your sweater looks more than sufficient for you," Kay reacted as in, *Zero chance.*

"David might need his goggles back," cautioned Augie. He sensed the young boy's renewed jitters, facing the surf-soaked darkness unaided by night vision.

"Oh, wow!" David enthused soon as he redonned the

goggles, Kay quick to oblige. "When I looked around before, I didn't see there's a cave inside the cave!"

"At high tide, you probably wouldn't notice it," said Augie. "It's almost entirely submerged then."

*

Early morning that same day, Augie and crew went out on their own for a private reconnoiter of the shoreline below Strumblehead Lighthouse. They wanted to familiarize themselves with the region before their all-night vigil. That's when they found the cave within the cave, pretty much underwater at high tide. They could see only the tippy top of one of the presumed vertical shale formations they found so convenient for crouching behind later on.

"The novelist, Ray Bradbury, wrote a short story about a sea-going dinosaur that attacks a lighthouse," Augie remarked.

"A fun fantasy, for sure," nodded Stephen. "But back to reality: For a beach purportedly visited by a sauropod dinosaur, there is a significant lack of any foot tracks. And you'd think they would be deep tracks, too, given how many tons such a beast weighed."

"Two points," said Sherman before Augie could open his mouth. "Pounding waves with the rising tide could certainly smooth out even deep tracks to shallow indentations. Exactly like these puddles we see scattered about here. And that's if they were not worn away entirely, inside of a few hours. Point two: From what our Welsh friends saw rise out of the fog, it's not clear that the creature came ashore at all. That it wasn't a relic sea reptile such as a Plesiosaur swimming close to the coastline. Though I have my own reason for discounting that possibility in favor of a terrestrial creature."

"Wait." Headache time again for Stephen, hand to head. "I'd say that where extreme unlikelihood is concerned, a sea-going reptile is marginally less impossible than a dinosaur that's managed to hide for so long in the presence of lighthouse keepers and coastal trail hikers. But impossible all the same, for the no small matter of the Irish Sea's frigid cold waters. Quite a stretch to believe a long-necked, elephant-bodied reptile could be splashing about out there," Stephen elaborated with smug satisfaction.

"Not necessarily," Sherman hastened to push back. "Plesiosaur fossils along the Australian coast have confirmed such beasts used to flourish in Antarctic seas, millions of years ago. But the only way they could have achieved such a feat, I am convinced, was by storing huge mounds of fat, like camels. That would have resulted in the classic hump shapes reported in some sea serpent sightings, including Loch Ness."

"Yet neither the teacher nor her student reported such humps on their creature," noted Roberta Quiñones.

"Which is exactly why I discount the sea serpent scenario," nodded Sherman.

"This bracing sea air," Augie exhaled after a satisfying inhale. He'd had enough of arguments for the time being. "Something about it causes me to savor more than suffer from the chill."

"Ah, yes," Stephen rhapsodized sarcastically, "the smell of dead fish in the early morning; nothing else quite like it."

"Or maybe it's from that dinosaur having traipsed through here," Irene proposed solely for the delight of irritating Stephen.

"Well, if that is the case," blustered Stephen, mission accomplished where irritating him was concerned, "the odor should be more densely pronounced, pungent as from some other large animal such as a hippo or a giraffe."

"That's also not necessarily," Sherman once more quickly rebutted. "No question that your line of reasoning is sound,

Mr. Feldman. But for my own part, I have been in the close presence of a fourteen-foot-long alligator in the Florida Everglades, on an adventure my sweetie pie insisted I undertake with her. We threw all caution to the wind where mosquito bites and errant meteorites were concerned. Anyway, I can honestly say the rose scents overpowered any odor that gator might have given off. If my eyes were not open, I could have easily been persuaded it wasn't there at all."

*

"Is it possible," asked David presently, having redonned the goggles Augie offered him, and pointing deeper into the surf-worn cave, "the prehistoric bloke I saw hides inside that cave inside this cave? And he only comes out when especially hungry? In those *Turok* comic books you gave me, Mr. Matias, dinosaurs use caves for their homes all the time."

"The people who drew those comics could have also had dinosaurs luxuriating in a jacuzzi while drinking chocolate milk shakes," snarked Stephen.

"Some grizzly bears use caves for their home, minus the milk shakes," Augie added to David's appreciative giggle. "Who knows? Maybe-"

"Excuse me, ladies and gents," interrupted Alistair Frump. He illuminated his path with an old-fashioned flashlight while he went on, "thought I better give you a heads-up before the evening wears on any further. Our resident skeptic here who keeps us on our toes, together with our fossil man extraordinaire Dr. Augustine Matias, I'm sure they both remember a certain something from our dino search in Papua, New Guinea. I sent a golf ball flying into a forest where we thought an Iguanodon or some such might be hiding. And something sent it flying right back out. Ditto from the ruins of a native shack in the Amazon rain forest. Well, I did some thinking-"

"And you realized that of all possible explanations, a dinosaur batting your golf ball back to you was the least likely; good," Stephen interjected.

"Ha ha ha…No," Alistair reacted tersely. "What occurred to me is that dogs, cats, not only us humans, are ever fascinated by spherical objects, balls of any size. They just love watching them roll hither and yon. Why wouldn't that also be true for dinosaurs?"

"Maybe it was; sadly, they went extinct millions of years before we could find out," Stephen snarked with great delight.

"On the off chance I'm not several millennia too late," said Alistair, not at all thrown off his stride, "should I suspect David's beastie is gracing us with its presence, I will use my seven iron, here, to hit a golf ball. Maybe then, you can be eyewitness to a dinosaur wielding its tail as a fairway wood! Yes, David?" Alistair called on the little boy, seeing him raise his hand like he was still inside a classroom.

"Me friend's family has a pet corgi that herds their sheep. Maybe she would be up for herding a dinosaur as well? No, forget that; she would probably chase after your golf ball instead, sir."

"He's so precious; I could just eat him up," Kay confided to Irene, crouched down beside her.

"Already aware of that. But what about David?" Irene quipped. She didn't require any night vision goggles to notice the gleam in Kay's eye, whenever it settled on the happily married paleontologist, especially with Nigel nowhere in sight.

"Okay, Alistair, think we've got it. If we see a golf ball on the loose, we are to leave it alone. And watch carefully for whether it rouses David's dinosaur like a pooch roused by a bouncing tennis ball."

"Exactly, Augie!"

"You better leave before your flashlight scares off the

creature. That's assuming it's as reclusive as the others we've tried to track."

"Yes, mythical beasts do tend to shy away from existing," snarked Stephen anew.

"There goes that legendary skeptical wit again!" Alistair playfully pointed Stephen's way. "Erupting as reliably as that geyser, Old Faithful!"

"Shh!" shushed David.

"Well! I've been put in my place," Alistair chortled quietly as he ducked back out of the shoreline cavern, to resume his vigil behind a stand of gorse alongside Scott, Roberta, and Laura.

David stood short enough behind the presumed vertical shale outcropping, flanked by two others in a row. He didn't need to crouch down like Augie and Kay either side of him. He was already well hidden from view by anything that might emerge from the cave within the cave.

The silent vigil, the all-night stake-out, had officially begun.

Not too many minutes later, David removed his goggles, and crouched down himself, intent on sitting against the outcropping. "Resting me eyes a wee bit, I am," he explained.

"Like we said, these stake-outs can become rather tiring," gently observed Augie.

"Oh, no, it's not that at all," protested the young lad in his high-pitched voice not yet breaking with adolescence. "I believe I might listen better for that special splash I heard before I first laid me eyes on the prehistoric bloke. That is to say, if I'm not also trying to see him into the bargain."

"Spoken like the star pupil you've always been in me classroom," said Kay. Then winking at Augie as in, *We both know he's too proud to admit he's exhausted, bless his wee little soul*, she added, "But come here, now; you don't want to be sitting on the wet sand, and getting your fine sweater all soaked against this slimy stone, do you? I can only imagine the huge fuss your Mum would kick up over that! My lap is open for business, it is," she concluded, patting her lap.

David did not resist, though saying as he welcomed the warmth, "What do you say, mates? Maybe a right proper idea if we do this in shifts? You two," he nodded at Irene and Stephen, "you keep your eyes on that cave, like me friend's corgi on the sheep. Meanwhile, Ms. Jones and Mr. Matias, here, can enjoy a quick snooze. Of course I be the common thread through it all, listening for that special splash."

"I'm glad you're here to add some needed structure to our search," said Irene, charmed. So charmed, in fact, she wouldn't think of laughing at the young boy for his face-saving pretensions.

"You're welcome, Mum. Me parents often say they're not sure how they ever went to bed at a reasonable hour without my help."

Augie and Kay played along. They figured it wouldn't take many minutes before David's intent listening turned into the sort of deep sleep that they wouldn't need to wake him from, until and unless a Welsh dinosaur did manifest. They had to be careful, though. The first time Augie thought the young lad finished drifting off, night goggles revealed him suddenly opening his eyes. He was checking that Augie remained seated still, trying to nap.

Not too much later, though, David was clearly on his way to Never-neverland, curled up like an oversized caterpillar in Kay's lap.

Peeking over top of the outcropping, Augie returned to the business at hand. He rotated his attention from the inside cave to the gently crashing surf, framed by the outer cave entrance. Then on to Irene and Stephen, ever watchful with their own night vision goggles.

There was also the puzzling behavior of Charly's isolated left hand. It persisted in a crab-like crawl across every square inch of rock outcropping. *How much longer before it realizes it's acquiring no useful data?*

And lastly, regarding the three outcroppings in a row, their similar angularities made Augie wonder. Did they comprise a spiritual site from the Neolithic era, like a mini-Stonehenge? Rather than a natural formation wrought of purely geologic processes? He had seen some pretty weird natural formations during fossil digs, and so...

...rotating his focus couldn't keep exhaustion from finally getting to Augie. After all, he'd been going nonstop ever since arriving in Wales. He even took time out to explore nearby cemeteries for deceased ancestors. Unlike David, though, he didn't pretend to close his eyes for listening more carefully. Rather, Augie strove to keep his eyes open by trying to identify certain stars, or the clouds that hid them. As well, he checked his watch frequently, and thought about Vicky, their Florida Keys summer trip with daughter Liz...

The moss-covered outcropping started to feel especially slimy. And Augie found himself standing up to inspect more closely the cave within a cave. Although, how was he scampering over there so easily while still crouched down?

A bluish glow emitted from deep inside the cavern. Augie was descending towards it, stopping only to...preen his feathers on his back? How was his neck long enough to do THAT?! And who bumped alongside-

Augie woke with a start. He only just managed to splay out his arms and hands before he would have toppled forward face first into rising, foamy surf, the outcropping gone.

"So very sorry, Mister!" cried David, standing beside Augie and shivering. "Afraid I wet meself!"

"Oh, heavens no, dearie!" Kay lifted him into her arms.

"We're all wet from a coastal gale kickin' up the surf somethin' fierce! Now you hang on tight while I hurry us out of here!"

Just then, a deep, prolonged moan issued from somewhere, until a crash of thunder echoed through the cave to deafening effect.

Thanks to an accompanying lightning flash, Augie, Irene and Stephen spotted Alistair's silhouette, frozen in his follow-through from swinging his seven iron.

Augie also caught a glimpse of something splashing an already raging surf before submerging.

The next lightning flash highlighted Alistair sloshing through the encroaching surf to join Augie and company on the footpath closer to the lighthouse.

For the briefest instant, Augie would have sworn that way down behind Alistair, out a considerable number of yards into the surf, he discerned three, grayish-green tips that— *No, those can't be the slate outcroppings we hid behind!*

By then, Roberta and Laura had fought the rainy wind gusts to set up a tarpaulin lean-to with its back to the elements, a most welcome shelter.

"Looked like you hit your golf ball, Alistair!" Augie shouted to be heard above the storm, while water dripping from his hair left him bleary-eyed.

"Whatever it was whipped its tail way up into the sky!" Alistair responded. "Unless it was seaweed made airborne by the wind! I don't think seaweed can moan, but what else…?!"

"C'mon!" Stephen scoffed. "When surf carves nooks and crannies into coastline rocks, it's not at all uncommon to hear all kinds of moans and groans from winds howling through!"

"Quiet everyone! Listen!" broke in Scott. "Is that someone crying for help?!"

The cries got louder and louder until it became clear they

were from Robin.

Everyone, even Kay with David back in her arms, braved spraying shower gusts to look out at Robin frantically waving at them while she stood knee-deep in surf.

"The monster!!" she cried. "The schoolboy was right!! It has a long neck on a whale-sized body! AND IT GRABBED ME POOR GERWYN IN ITS MOUTH!!! PICKED HIM CLEAR OFF THE GROUND, IT DID!!! HELP ME FIND HIM!!!"

By then, Irene and Roberta were to either side of Robin, bringing her ashore.

"Are you sure there wasn't a small tornado that lifted him into the air, alongside strands of seaweed?!?" Stephen proposed encouragingly. "And it dropped him into the sea near shore, or on the pebbly sand?! He might be okay! Just a little cut up!"

"I don't think so," disagreed Robin. But her uncertain tone together with her abrupt calm suggested to Augie that perhaps their resident skeptic had given her pause for hope. Hope that Augie fervently wished wouldn't turn out to be the cruelest possible tease.

"Okay, don't know if this helps or not!" Alistair stepped forward to focus Robin's attention on him. "When I launched my golf ball at- Well here's the thing. Just as the ball went flying, an especially big gust of wind from the storm, um, either it did blow a big seaweed strand skyward, or a monstrous creature whipped its tail about. Whichever, this big flash of lightning let me see the ball lodge into the base of the tail, or get stuck in the seaweed. So, look behind you, Miss, where I'm directing my flashlight. There is seaweed the size of a sea serpent stranded ashore, now that the surf is receding. Maybe there was no monster, after all."

"Sounds like we're liable to find your golf ball there, assuming the ocean didn't claim it," enthused Stephen. He delighted in hearing Alistair make the jump, however tentative, aboard the skeptic train.

"I would like to know what happened exactly to those outcroppings we hid behind," Augie blurted out. "Where did they go? During one lightning flash, I swear I glimpsed three stony-looking tips of something in a row, in the water, headed further out to sea. That couldn't be them, could it?"

"Storms have been known to dramatically reshape entire coastlines," Stephen pushed back. He would have none of what he feared Augie was suggesting.

"But we are talking about three very heavy slabs of slate," weighed in Irene, "if that's what they are. Can't imagine even a raging surf could have moved them that far, that fast."

"How do you know the seawater encroaching from the storm didn't turn the ground to quicksand, so they simply sank out of view?"

"*Ych a fi, sir!*" Kay shouted at Stephen, so harshly he cringed. "If it turned to quicksand where we were stationed, why didn't we get sucked below surface with them?! And then how did they wind up out there in that raging surf?!"

"This might sound totally nuts," Augie conceded. He felt bad for Robin; what he was about to suggest bode poorly for the fate of her boyfriend. At the same time, though, he figured it far better for her to receive unexpected joyous good news down the road, after assuming the worst. Better that, than have her hope cruelly dashed, allowed free rein. "What if those outcroppings are really the plates on back of a hibernating Stegosaurus? They reminded me of that. Did the storm awaken it? And Alistair saw its tail whipping about as it entered the sea?"

Augie watched the horror return to Robin's eyes, with fresh tears added to raindrops still running down her cheeks.

"Listen, people, I won't know for sure until I can download all the data back aboard Cloud Nine," boomed from a mike set into the helmet of Sherman Peabody's suit. "However, my flatus emission detector might have picked up noises comparable to our suspected saurian back on New Britain Island."

"You mean an amplified version of an iguana fart, correct? With lots of slurping-type noises?" Stephen asked irritably. As he saw it, the reasonable discourse train was quickly derailing. "Slurping-type noises are exactly what you'd expect from a storm as we've been experiencing," he insisted. "For my own part, I've been hearing gurgles. They're most likely from the surf ebbing, receding, out of all the nooks and crannies eroded into coral and other coastal features."

"A Stegosaurus, Mum?!" David said excitedly, suddenly wriggling free of Kay's arms to stand back on his own two feet. "We might have cozied up against one of its back plates? Oh, that is so proper, that is!"

"Of what would have to be a far larger specimen than any fossils suggest," cautioned Stephen with his usual voice of skeptical doom, Augie found to his continuing annoyance.

"It's also very different from my prehistoric chap, which was more like a Diplodocus. It had a big, fat body and a long snake's neck. There's hope, Mum, there is!" he shouted at Robin still ankle deep in the slowly receding surf, and bathed in moonlight breaking through the rapidly thinning clouds.

An occasional lightning flash and distant rumble were all that remained of the storm.

"Didn't you say the monster what might have grabbed Mr. Davies looked like mine?" David went on. "Because that type of dinosaur only eats plants. Maybe it picked up Mr. Davies by accident! Once it realized he wasn't a clump of seaweed, it dropped him on soft beach sand. Please, Mum, I don't want to see you cry anymore." Tugging on Augie's windbreaker, he added, "I quite fancy our hiking to where you last saw Mr. Davies. Maybe we find him too banged up to walk, but not too banged up for a hospital to heal him. That's the ticket!"

"You should consider, David, that hippos are plant eaters also," said Stephen. "But they don't hesitate to kill anyone trespassing on their territory."

"That's what I'm afraid of!" cried Robin, overcome by a new wave of grief thanks in no small part to Stephen's callously grim observation, Augie figured.

"But there are no known animals that size in this region of Wales, plant-eating or otherwise!" Stephen hastened to add, not insensible to Robin's reaction plus the fear in David's eyes. "I believe a mix of seaweed with tornadic winds, a microburst perhaps, best explains what Gerwyn experienced! The faster we find him, the better!"

"But what if you are bloody correct about a Stegosaurus, mate?" asked Nigel, suddenly lurching out of the shadows before Augie. "And that tosser with the golf club over there – he reminds me of a Scottish bloke I used to know. He described playin' the full eighteen holes during a two-foot blizzard in the highlands. What if he's correct about where his bloody golf ball landed, assumin' it's not tangled in those clumps of seaweed? You can bloody believe it or not, but I'll tell you what it sounds like he did. And there's precedent as well, there is! Burp!"

Nigel's latest burp sent him staggering. Elwin Kneath emerging from the shadows caught him just before he would have tumbled head first into needly gorse.

"I want to hear this," said Irene.

"I don't!" Stephen shouted as he hurried down to the shoreline, hoping to locate Gerwyn.

"THE REAL WORLD IS TOO MUCH FOR YOU!!" Nigel called

after Stephen. "I GOT THAT, MATE!!" Then to Alistair, while Elwin firmly held Nigel's shoulders to keep him on his feet, "What you described, well bloody hell if it doesn't sound like you launched yer golf ball straight away into a dinosaur's butthole! Or a dragon's, if that be the real source of all that lightnin' we saw flashin' the night into day!"

"You're too late, Mum!" David furiously batted Kay's hands away from covering his ears. "I heard every word he said!"

"And you heard every word your lad said, Kay!" shouted Nigel. "You might as well be insertin' the bathtub stopper after all the water has already made for the drain!"

"So out there," Alistair faced seaward with a bright glimmer in his moonlit eyes, "an oversized Stegosaurus might be swimming off with a golf ball up its ass? That really is totally monster!"

"I have to say," said time traveler Ali Magabu, stepping forward from his two fellow starship officers, "we have experienced truly amazing things on other, um, places," he edited himself, thinking better of opening a can of worms by saying the word, planets. "But this ranks near the top."

"And like I mentioned, there's precedent for it, too, there bloody well is!" ranted Nigel. He continued staggering about as he flailed his arms to emphasize his point. This posed a real challenge for Elwin to keep him from toppling over, hands on his shoulders or not.

"Jesus fossilized Christ, we might as well join the search for Robin's boyfriend!" time traveler Sergeant Fred Frankly advised Ali and his other colleague, Kevin Smith-Park. Fred hurried along the hiking path, nearly slipping on a patch of gravel moistened to ball-bearing slippery.

"It's a fact whether you bloody blokes want to hear it, or not!" Nigel called hoarsely after the three time travelers. "This isn't the first time a golf ball has been sent flyin' into some animal's business end!! No it's not!!"

"Really, now?!" asked John Jones skeptically as he carelessly tossed his beer can into the heather, one of his buddies quickly retrieving it. "Don't be daft, Nigel! I'm not sayin' that in the history of the universe, there won't be an occasion for a golf ball in flight to treat a butthole as a bull's eye! But that's one time only! In the history of the whole bloody universe! Burp! Which means the odds that any of us would be privileged to see it, well I'd be much more a-feared of lightnin' strikin' me three times, I would! Truth be told, Nigel, someone saw somethin' protruding from a cow's rear end, am I right? That they thought bore a resemblance to a golf ball what had been rollin' about in the dirt like a pig in a mud puddle?! But if they'd taken a wee bit more time to watch, would have seen it pop all the way out onto the ground, a cow's poo?!?"

Nigel waved his forefinger NO as he slobbered, "Nothin' could be further from the truth!! Belch! It was on the Southern-down Golf Club, year of our Lord 1973, a track that the great Harry Vardon had a hand in layin' down, by the by!"

"Oh, well, if Harry bloody Vardon helped design the course, it must have been primed for butthole target practice! Should have posted signs all over the place, there, warnin' farmers not to let their cattle roam across unless they're wearin' pants!"

"Shut yer mouth, John Jones, before I launch a golf ball into it for your carryin' around like you've got a spare butthole! Now listen, you ask any member of Southern-down! If they're honest, they'll tell you 'bout the time one of their own shanked an iron directly into a sheep's butt! And that they know it wasn't a poo they were mistakin' for a golf ball! Because that animal ran up onto a green, and deposited it not two feet from the cup, for a tap-in par!"

"Oh, so maybe we better be checkin' the Sheep's Shank

Links tomorrow mornin'! Make sure that Stegosaurus isn't helpin' one of our distinguished visitors to cheat at that idiotic sport! *Yucky dar!*" John spat out, like he was trying to get the taste of a butt-embedded golf ball off his lips, Augie mused.

Click…whirr…As the storm continued to recede into the distance, and the surf calmed considerably, these mechanical noises were plenty loud enough to call everyone's attention to Charly.

Charly stood mostly reassembled down by the shore, and said in his usual robotic monotone, "My left hand might have recorded where Alistair's golf ball was launched, whether towards a surviving non-avian dinosaur or these washed-ashore clumps of seaweed made air borne by the storm. But as you can see," he held up a tangle of wires and bent metal, with shredded latex hanging off like plastic seaweed, "the wind and rain pummeled it inoperable against coral rock."

"Did any part of you notice what happened to a certain fellow named Gerwyn?" Sherman asked urgently.

Click…whirr… "Gerwyn Davies." Click…whirr… "My right knee spotted him standing beside-" …click…whirr…

"-Robin Pugh, one-half mile down the shoreline from here. I was eavesdropping on them, in case they shared an observation pertinent to the search for surviving non-avian dinosaurs. But when their lips formed a tight seal, I could not hypothesize that being a method for secretly passing along useful information. And when she started to unbutton his shirt, I calculated the odds were astronomically large that that was for the sole purpose of sexual activity. That's when my right knee turned its attention away from them, to search elsewhere for useful information. Although the thunder storm blew up most pronouncedly soon thereafter. It was all my knee and other parts of me could do, to shut down protectively until the worst was over, when it would be safe to seek ourselves out for reassembly."

"But why didn't your left hand do that?" asked Sherman.

Click...whirr... "It must have been actively involved collecting what seemed pertinent data. Whether that can be accessed after its repair remains to be seen."

Just then, from down the shoreline everyone heard the shrillest scream, ever.

Running the rest of the way to the coastline, in the moonlight Augie easily discerned Robin collapsed in Irene's arms.

Irene motioned Augie's attention to a discarded, long-sleeve woolen shirt washed ashore. His night goggles didn't tell him much, but with his small penlight he saw clearly that the shirt was stained by lots of blood. So much blood, in fact, that whenever the surf touched it, the water got colored like hot water colored by a fresh tea bag.

Chapter 7

"I tell you, Officer Leung, I tried hard to imagine approaching this fifty-mile-diameter vessel. To actually be here, though, might as well be seeing crab and octopus join lobster to whistle on mountaintop!"

"Huh?"

"Sorry; I make reference to old Russian expression. But oh my God, as you Americans say when not cursing impolitely. That thing must be three times the size of Space Station 2 geodesic dome!"

Tanya Petrovsky piloted a tear-drop-shaped shuttle pod well ahead of the starship, Smoke and Mirrors, to visit the amazingly massive donut-shaped UFO. It had entrained the Smoke and Mirrors on an unwanted course through a wormhole. And so, Tanya and First Officer Buddy Leung were set on contacting its occupants at close range.

Getting there wasn't the simplest thing, though.

The shuttle pod could access too few photons inside the wormhole for light propulsion. Yes, wormholes didn't allow light to escape. But most unexpectedly, their interiors reduced nearly all drawn-in light to an unusable state of quantum uncertainty. Anyway, besides the lack of "functioning" photons, too little hydrogen for gas propulsion remained from the last refueling. The shuttle pod had to lean on its anti-gravity backup. But there wasn't much of that left, either. After reaching the gargantuan, donut-shaped object, there wouldn't be enough anti-gravity material to propel the shuttle pod back to the Smoke and Mirrors. But Buddy calculated it would suffice to hold the pod in a hovering state until the starship caught up.

"And you are certain, Buddy, this space vessel isn't from

hostile civilization like Tictoctic? That another alien species didn't thread camel through eye of needle to survive with war in its toolbox, and not destroy itself? We don't need to fear laser cannons are mixed in with all those light-propulsion mirrors? Like sprinkles on one of my Ali's heaven-sent cupcakes?"

"Extremely fluke circumstances prevailed on Tictoctic," said Buddy. "And remember, if not for intervention by the Nuah-Cherpels, the Tictoctickians were about to wipe themselves out, after all. Besides which, definitely no need to worry this time," he went on reassuringly. "I've scanned and rescanned every last one of those 'sprinkles,' and can confirm they are light propulsion and stabilization features, not a weapon among them."

"Okay, very good," sighed Tanya, finally allowing herself to feel relieved. "I'm scanning all conceivable frequencies for radio communication. Nothing yet."

"You're also scanning for any visual data they might transmit?"

"Nothing yet there either, Buddy. Meanwhile, I've charted course through middle of their donut hole, closely inspecting its entire surface. But if their entrance ports are anything like ours, they are sealed imperceptible until opened."

"Which the occupants won't be able to do if they're incapacitated, Tanya. And which we won't be able to do for them unless by some miracle, we figure out how to hack into a system likely incompatible with ours in every conceivable way."

"Nothing but static so far. Nothing that even sounds like a quiet fart, excuse my language, Buddy. But speaking of which, how accurate do you think that assessment is, by Ali's past-time friend, of the audio we received from monster donut?"

"We do know that Ali and company have fallen in with a

group searching for living dinosaurs. It's possible they've become like the guy with a hammer who believes everything is a nail. They're wishful-thinking every mysterious noise is a Triceratops passing gas, or some such. Moreover, our stumbling across dinosaurs from space would seem too crazy a coincidence. Nevertheless...like you said, the sheer immensity of that thing," Buddy nodded out the shuttle pod's transparent bubble dome at the donut-shaped object. Light from outside the wormhole cast it in silhouette, even though few photons were viable inside. "A hi-tech space ark for saving animals from extinction while their home planet civilization careens towards self-destruction? Not the craziest speculation by any means."

"But in addition to recorded extraterrestrial dinosaur farts, we are supposed to believe the dinosaur herders themselves speak to one another through noises made out their rears? Seriously, Buddy?"

"Maybe that's not from their business ends at all," said Buddy. "Maybe it's exactly like what I did with my hands, here."

"You mean, when you prepared that audio pictograph linking particular fart-like sounds with stick-figure depictions?"

Buddy responded with a couple of farty noises by pressing his hands together.

"In other words, maybe the creators of that monster donut vessel communicate with noises they make by pushing hand-like appendages together. Like you just did."

"We can't even be sure how they ingest food, if we're being honest about it," nodded Buddy.

"Air filtration of gnat-like creatures? Analogous to baleen filter-feed system of baleen whales for plankton? Not the type of mouth an extraterrestrial could open and close for speaking?"

"Who knows?" Buddy shrugged his shoulders. "For whatever reason, whoever's inside there is currently noncommunicative in any way, shape or form."

"Maybe they suffered major life support calamity," suggested Tanya. She nodded towards the immense extraterrestrial hull taking up more and more of their view, the closer they came. "For all we know, nothing is left alive inside. Space ark has become space tomb on autopilot."

"Although one would think that such a calamity involved an explosion of some sort. That would have left at least a burn mark somewhere on the exterior," remarked Buddy, puzzled. "But we still do need to assume the worst, meaning-"

All the sudden, one of the shuttle pod's console monitors lit up, and a line drawing slowly filled in, crossing the screen from left to right.

"If someone had bet me about this, I surely would have lost," said Buddy, intently watching the image's completion.

"I never bet, Buddy, which in this situation would have been good thing."

A toilet bowl, complete with a handle for flushing, was depicted at wash basin level. And a wash basin was drawn on the floor.

Before Buddy and Tanya could discuss any implications for the extraterrestrials' physiology, they noticed a door to the presumed bathroom. It was fitted with a doorknob closer to the floor than any doorknobs with which the two Earthlings were familiar. The other side of the door, a reptilian-looking snout- the transmission ended right there.

"That partial head is depicted at just below ceiling level," observed Buddy with dawning realization.

Buddy and Tanya turned each other's way, thinking the same thing.

"They're trapped in a bathroom," Tanya beat Buddy to

vocalizing, "with large extraterrestrial dinosaur-type creature trying to barge in from outside?"

"And they just ran out of power before they could finish making that clear? Oh!" Buddy ohhed in surprise. "You remember the communication we received back aboard the S & M, that also seemed incomplete?"

"Maybe they had to cut that short because extraterrestrial dinosaur broke into their command center? Then they fled to a bathroom where it took them this long to figure out how to get out new message?"

"But the well went dry, so to speak, just a bit too soon?"

"Or a beast attracted by flashing lights shorted the system while being electrocuted?"

"In other words, our extraterrestrial friends might be sitting in the dark now, in that bathroom, with no hope of escape, and no way for us to rescue them."

"Never say no hope, Officer Leung, after all the no hopes we have successfully turned into hope!" bristled Tanya. "Nyet!! For starters, as you Americans say, we see maybe if we can tap small part of our electrical reserves into one of their cupcake-sprinkle solar panels. No, that would not work, would it? If entire system has been shorted?"

"Especially assuming there's an electrical fire. We might only worsen matters. Although who knows? You'd think there's a redundancy system, plus water sprinklers to put out any such fire while a workaround supplies power to the bathroom."

"And crew from other part of vessel comes to the rescue."

"Unless this is a one or two-person operation," cautioned Buddy. "Maybe a space-age Noah wannabe hijacked the vessel away from its builder's original intent?"

On this suggestion, Tanya and Buddy shared a long look. To Tanya's shock, it ended with tears streaming down Buddy's face.

"Buddy Leung," Tanya said in a voice Buddy found a curious mix of sympathetic and admonishing. "In our worst, most imperiled moments before, never I see you like this!"

"I'm so used to riding my fears like a tamed horse," Buddy couldn't help sobbing. "Not them tossing me off like a bucking dragon."

"Isn't the expression, 'bucking bronco'?"

"Maybe under the circumstances it should be 'bucking bronto,' but not sure what got into me," Buddy confessed. He was already settling down, and even smiled through his tears over his whimsy substituting bronto as in Brontosaurus for bronco. "I've always been so confident about getting us out of deadly scrapes."

"I know!" Tanya exclaimed emphatically. "You're the applied physics genius who pulled time travel rabbit out of your hat crowded with so many other rabbits!"

"I guess the notion crept under my skin, that I was taking that ability too much for granted. And might soon find all of us in a situation where our luck runs out so that I never see my Cathy ever again, plus oh yes, the dying part."

"Fear, in other words," said Tanya, having just put the shuttle pod on autopilot orbit of the massive metallic donut so she could lend Buddy her full attention. "I remember old expression from your President Roosevelt, that we 'have nothing to fear but fear itself.' But I would rephrase that, to say we fear nothing, whether it is nothing after we die, or nothing more of a departed loved one, or bad guy turning us into nothing."

"Huh."

"I can finish, Buddy, okay? You have shared your physics with us for all these years. Now I share mine."

"Your physics?"

"Exactly. In the beginning, before so-called Big Bang even, I believe there was an unexpressed love."

"An unexpressed love?"

"That's what I said. The Nuah-Cherpels called it a sense of being that split into two because it was lonely. Everything proceeded from there. But I see it as having split into two to have someone to love. Just before the split happened, though, you know what I think it felt for the first time?"

"Fear?"

"Fear, exactly! Before that initial act of creation, there was no fear because there was nothing to fear losing. There was fear of nothing because nothing was all there was. If anything, there was fear that nothing was all that could be. There was fear, perhaps, that creation would prove impossible, that the very effort would settle that matter, for endless nothing. If the unexpressed love had surrendered to that fear, and not even tried..."

"There would still be nothing."

"Always you are quick study, Officer Leung! Anyway, that love was for something that did not yet exist: company! In my physics, fear is the inertia that the force of love overcomes to create. It's even present in our brains, how frontal cortex rides the more reptilian part of ourselves, the part that's still afraid. It makes sure we keep progressing towards greater and greater happiness for the whole."

"Not that that reptilian part doesn't still play a useful role. For example, it helps us avoid accidentally falling off a cliff to our doom," Buddy pushed back only the gentlest bit. "Well thank you, spasiba, Tanya. Looking at our present predicament that way does help."

"Good. If I am perfectly honest, actually," she leaned over to speak confidentially in Buddy's ear as though anyone else were around to speak confidentially in front of, "I feared you wouldn't appreciate my digression at all."

"Now that we have that little irony out of the way, I think we need to assume the worst," lamented Buddy, "about both what is going on inside that mammoth thing, and where it might be headed."

"You mean, if no one is left alive inside there for navigation once it leaves the wormhole?"

"Yep; in our history books looking back eighty years, it did not strike the Earth. But on this new time line, with all our history-changing interventions…"

"I assume the ark vessel, shall we call it," proposed Tanya, "exited wormhole near Earth on original time line. But there are no reports I know about, of such a large object cruising through solar system."

"In the early 1980s, though, nobody on Earth was equipped to have a real good look at this thing unless they lucked out with a close, satellite probe flyby. Unless missed altogether, it would have been written off as simply another asteroid making a visit from the Oort Cloud."

Buddy referred to a region outside the solar system, known to harbor several asteroids and other cosmic debris that hurtle regularly in and out of the solar system.

"Then is likely that Ark Vessel will again avoid collision with Earth, same as first run-through of history?"

"Likely, but far from certain," warned Buddy. "We need to accompany it out of the wormhole like a pilot fish riding a shark. What has me concerned, but keeping fear under heavy sedation," Buddy assured Tanya, "is the probability something has gone seriously awry aboard there. Maybe the same thing happened on that 'first run-through.' For all we know, it flew directly into the sun, the end of it. And will do so now, again, unless we can somehow…"

"But if 'seriously awry' is new, we don't know that it won't come under influence of Earth's gravitational pull. Then it could head for collision several times worse than from asteroid that took out the dinosaurs."

"Or almost all the dinosaurs, if our away team's new friends are on to anything."

"Then once we exit wormhole, calculations should tell us

whether we need to budge Ark Vessel's trajectory off course?"

"Exactly, Tanya. Even a small tweak of the ark vessel's flight path should be sufficient to keep it well away from Earth, or the sun. If we need to do that, it's a good thing the Smoke and Mirrors was entrained by..." He waved at the curved metallic surface filling the shuttle pod's bubble window view, softly illuminated by the shuttle pod's cockpit lights.

"I share secret with you, Officer Buddy Leung," Tanya lightly patted one of Buddy's hands to say. She smiled at him, a rare departure from her usual poker-faced demeanor. "Comforted me greatly to discuss fear with you, as that is constantly pounding at my own mental cage door, in regard to holding Ali in my arms, ever again."

Chapter 8

"Sorry, mates, I can't have you contaminatin' the evidence, even if you tell me there's a keg of Toohey's out there, sittin' at the bottom of the sea with me name on it," gruffly snorted Officer Rhys Williams, Chief Constable of the Kelpyguard Constabulary. He was addressing Augie, Scott, and Irene at the base of the cliff below Strumblehead Lighthouse. That's where the coastal hiking trail opened out onto the pebbly beach, and Augie and others encamped inside a cave the night before, hoping a young schoolboy's purported sauropod dinosaur would make an encore appearance.

Yellow crime scene tape stretched up and down the coastline, far as Augie could see. Chief Constable Williams and his assistant constable, the brusque, imposingly proportioned Angharad Gruffudd, spent hours securing the perimeter.

"You see that stony-looking tip of something out there?" Scott pointed into the surf, a good hundred-fifty yards offshore.

On each ebb of the North Irish Sea, said tip became clearly visible, but was totally submerged on each wave-crashing flow. Scott thought he might have caught a glimpse of a second, shorter tip nearby, but could not have sworn to it.

"If we go out to investigate," Scott continued, "how are we going to contaminate it, with surf constantly pounding against it? Especially if we wear plastic gloves? And besides, wouldn't fingerprints and the like already be washed away? What evidence of anything is going to remain there? Unless someone fired a bullet into it?"

"Oh!" Chief Constable Williams got in Scott's face by

standing on his tippy toes. And his puckered mouth quizzically bounced from side to side of his face as though, Augie mused, it was batted back and forth by ping-pong paddles. "What would you know about someone firin' a bullet?"

"I'm simply raising a hypothetical."

"They think that might be the tip of a Stegosaurus back plate," Stephen explained. No problem, barging in on most any conversation where he could speak mockingly of a fantastical possibility. He just wished he had as much guts to introduce himself to the assistant constable. He found her fetchingly buxom.

"To be fair," Augie hurried to add, "none of us are sure what it is. Do wonder, though, whether it could be the same object we took shelter behind in that cave last night, that appears to have up and left from there."

"'Up and left from there'? Stones that large and heavy? C'mon," scoffed Stephen. "I'm sure if you dig into that soil inside the cave, you'll find they're still there. They were buried by shifting sands, courtesy of that wild storm. Likewise, Scott, those stony tips you're glimpsing out to sea, they are probably ancient eroded coral beds."

"Well, I'm not spotting them now."

"In that case, your eyes were playing tricks on you."

"Unless they moved," Augie inserted.

"Seriously?"

"Sounds like you're talkin' good sense there, Mr.- What's your name, mate?" asked Assistant Constable Angharad Gruffudd.

"Um, Feldman, Stephen Feldman," Stephen responded bashfully for the first time Augie could ever recall.

"Well, Stephen Feldman, I've heard the Druids left carved stones and the like all across Wales. Maybe we can add the stones inside that cave to the list."

"Should you and I enter there to undress, I mean, remove

the dirt from, um..."

"I suppose that's the opposite of dressing a wound with a bandage, undressing a rock clothed by dirt," Irene couldn't help teasing Stephen, who couldn't help snatching admiring glimpses of Angharad's ample figure crowded into her police uniform. But her heart did go out to him, as she was reminded of Scott's puppy dog looks her own direction...when she wasn't giving him the same.

"It's yer bloody eyes, man!" raged John Jones, stumbling down off the hiking trail practically into Stephen's face. "They're just screamin' 'Tits ahoy!'"

"I need to find a restroom," Stephen mumbled, hurrying off.

"I've never heard a gorse bush called a restroom before! Cheers!" cried out John Jones, raising his beer can in ridiculing salute as Stephen fled from view.

"That cave is also a potential crime scene! There will be no rummagin' about it for the next Stonehenge, or a late mornin' cuddle!" blustered the chief constable. "But what's this about Stegosaurus plates that Mr. Feldman said you're talkin' about, Mr.-"

"Augie Matias."

"Well, Mr. Matias, what's that about? Valuable fossils someone might have committed murder to steal?"

"Speaking as a paleontologist who specializes in dinosaurs," answered Augie, "I do have to admit something notable about those objects we hid behind, inside that cave last night. They bore an uncanny resemblance to the morphology of Stegosaurus back plates. Although for their proportions, the Stegosaurus would have had to have been the size of a blue whale."

"But you're still talkin' fossils, right?"

"Mmm," Augie mmmed squeamishly. "Fossils are usually found set in rock. To have them sitting there like that, someone would have had to have gone to a whole lot of trouble, chiseling them out. As incredible as it might sound, I don't believe we can ignore the possibility that an incredibly large relic dinosaur was roused from its hibernation."

"A livin' Stegosaurus you say, mate?" Chief Constable Williams' puckered mouth resumed bouncing from left cheek to right and back again, like a ping pong ball where Augie was concerned. "And it woke up same as Rumpelstiltskin, did it? After millions of years rather than a mere century? To murder poor Gerwyn Davies into the bargain, just when he was finally connectin' with his true love?!"

"NO!!" screamed Robin tearfully, making fists seemingly to get a grip on herself. "The creature that took Gerwyn away in its evil serpent's mouth didn't look anything like a Stegosaurus!! It was more of a Diplodocus!!" On that, she buried her face in her hands, Irene quick to place a consoling arm round her shoulders.

"So, it was more of a Diplodocus than a Stegosaurus, you say?" the chief constable grumbled dubiously despite Robin's apparent grief. "Listen, lass, and the rest of you as well! I'm willin' to grant the possibility some barmy bloke placed a bloody large papier-maché dinosaur's head over himself, of the kind you might lug about in a street parade! And in the darkness peppered with lightnin' flashes, it looked like a Welsh dragon seekin' revenge for being consigned to a mascot on hats and wallets in Cardiff souvenir shops! Then he dragged Gerwyn off the coast to smash his bloody head against that coral rock you saw breakin' surface! You, there!" Chief Constable Williams pointed at Scott. "That I can believe! And am goin' to proceed with this investigation accordin'ly! For starters, poor lass," he turned to address Robin.

She lifted her head out of her hands, bleary-eyed from apparent grieving.

"I'll need to know any other lads besides Gerwyn who might have had an eye for you, 'specially if one was a stalker. But as for a real dinosaur committin' murder, that's worse than a null hypothesis, even! That's total bloody bullocks!!"

"Your coroner has Gerwyn's shredded, blood-stained shirt that washed ashore?" asked Scott, intent on defusing the chief constable's understandably angry reaction to a seeming impossibility.

"She's inspectin' every blessed wee bit of it, even as we speak, sir," nodded Chief Constable Williams. "And you're...?"

"Scott MacDonald, also part of the search for prehistoric creatures that might or might not have made it to the present day. I'm curious about your hypothesis, given there's no body in hand yet. You're guessing the human murderer left it out there in the Irish Sea? Hoping sharks and other sea life would feast on it before it could wash ashore? Literally consume all the evidence?"

Williams got his twitching pucker-mouth up in Scott's face to say, "Well haven't you given the body's disposal extra thought! Where were you last night, around the time the thunderstorm was at its most intense?"

"By then, I was huddled with Ms. Gómez and Dr. Quiñones under a lean-to." Scott pointed up the hill at Laura Gómez and Roberta Quiñones, waving hello from behind a low stand of purplish-pink heather.

"We had an eye on him the whole time!" asserted Laura, loudly enough to be heard down below.

"You're sure it was just an eye?" asked a gravelly-voiced Nigel, lurching into view from further up the hiking trail. "Didn't keep a couple of hands on him as well? Along with a pair of lips?"

Just then, an especially strong wind gust from off shore blew the chief constable's helmet-type hat clear off his head before he could grab hold. Fortunately, the cord he'd tied to it, attached to a collar round his neck, kept it dangling by his side, where he could easily retrieve it.

"Oh, I see your hat has taken you out on a leash for a bit of a stroll has it, Chief Constable?" wisecracked Nigel anew. "Hope it brought along one of those special plastic bags to pick up any – ahem! – important evidence you might deposit along the way!"

"Nigel Morgan, disrespectin' an officer of the law like that should carry a hefty fine, it should!" grumbled Rhys Williams at the unshaven fellow tottering down the hillside hiking trail towards the shore, like he might fall flat on his face any second.

"But officer! I'm simply worried about your well-bein'! No tellin' that any minute now, an even stronger wind will push your hat skyward for a little Mary Poppins action! Burp! Only with that leash round your neck, it will be Mary Poppins hangin' from an airborne noose!"

"You want me to take care of him, Chief Constable?" asked the assistant constable as she rolled up her sleeves, revealing impressively muscled arms.

Just then, Nigel stepped on pebbles that acted like so many ball bearings. And in his haste down the hill, he went flying flat on his back.

"That's okay, Officer Gruffudd," the chief constable finally responded to his assistant. "I think he just took care of himself."

"Wait! Wait, I say! Whoops!"

A singularly odd sight treated anyone who happened to look back up the hill. Two panted legs, feet in the air, speedily descended behind fields of heath, and were occasionally lost from view altogether behind gorse bushes. The feet were fitted with purple-themed tartan design socks and impeccably polished, dark-brown dress shoes. A bespectacled fellow followed behind, careful not to also take a tumble. Augie was sure he'd seen him recently, but couldn't quite place where.

At trail's end, onto the pebbly beach, the flailing-about legs were revealed belonging to Elwin Kneath, he of the most elegantly counterfeited free-dinner coupon. He gracefully segued back onto his feet, as though he intended to go sliding downhill on the seat of his pants all along.

Augie realized the fellow who hastened after Elwin was the one sitting with him at the pub, who ended up paying their bill.

"I fully expected to arrive here a good bit earlier," Elwin explained defensively, while his sidekick brushed gritty dirt and bits of heath brambles off his pants with such efficient speed, Augie suspected this wasn't the first or even second time he'd been employed for that purpose. "But under these especially humid circumstances, ink does take rather longer to dry."

With that, Elwin un-scrolled a tube of paper from inside his wool vest, and announced most formally, "Chief Constable Williams, this document establishes I've been deputized to play a major part getting to the bottom of the awful tragedy that has befallen our dear beloved Gerwyn Davies. I must say at the outset, no other theory of the case appears more viable than that a surviving member of the dinosaur family did spirit him away for an evening's gory repast."

"Let me have a look at that sheep's poo!" blustered the chief constable, swiping the purported document from Elwin's hands.

"Sheep's poo is it, Chief Constable?!" bristled Elwin. "With the elegance of its Gothic lettering, someone could be forgiven if they concluded it also establishes my credentials for removing an inflamed appendix at surgery!"

"Okay, who signed this?! Can't make head or tail out of it!" complained Chief Constable Williams. He directed Elwin's attention to the illegible scribble at the bottom of the curling page.

"Chief Constable Williams," said Elwin in a haughtily admonishing tone, "it is most typical, is it not, for a professional signature to prove totally illegible?"

"You got me there, mate. But I find this particular document most unfamiliar."

"That is precisely how I designed and autographed it, I'll have you know!"

"Wait, you signed off on your own certificate to serve as Constable's Deputy?!"

"If I didn't, who else was going to?!?" Elwin asked in an isn't-that-obvious? huff.

"I say, down there! I'm not too late to shed a wee bit of light on the situation, am I?" shouted a new voice from up the hiking trail, growing ever louder. "Well, maybe more than a wee bit, but not nearly so much as to be blinding!"

"Rupert Hamster Holmes!" exclaimed the chief constable as the trench-coated Rupert stepped down off the hiking trail to trudge his way across the pebbly sand towards him. "Don't tell me *you* know something about what happened here last night!"

"'Something' might be putting it too strongly. But my curiosity got the best of me last night, about why so many people made a pilgrimage down this way. Well maybe it was not that many people. And there was no sense of any religious ritual as far as pilgrimages go. And I'm not at all sure any part of my being is so good as to deserve labelling as 'the best.'"

"Good God, *ych a fi*, man!! Enough with the qualifications on top of qualifications, and out with it!! What do you know about the happenings here last night?!"

"Well, I suppose you could call what I thought I might have seen last night something that happened here, inasmuch as it appeared to present itself in this very location. In short-"

"Too late for that," Irene whispered to Scott, just loud enough for Scott to hear above the surf.

"-I believe I saw what gave every appearance of being a large reptile, like a dinosaur, if not actually a dinosaur. It had large, stony plates across its back. That is, unless it was simply so many clumps of seaweed and bush brambles sent flying by the stormy wind, suggestive of a dinosaur to the fertile imagination. Though by no means would I rate me own imagination as much more than infertile topsoil, with perhaps a few clumps of clay mixed in."

"You wouldn't have noticed anything that looked like a creature's rear end," started to ask Alistair, "with-"

"Good God, man!!" screamed the chief constable, beyond exasperated. "Until we establish physical evidence that such a beastie could really and truly be out there, we will have no talk of its rear end! Now tell me, Rupert, where were you when you believed you saw- - - whatever it was?"

"Where was I, last night? With lightning flashes providing the only useful glimmers of anything, what with the storm cloaking the near-full moon? That is a very good question, indeed. Deferring to those aforementioned glimmers, it would seem I was not so very far down this hill behind us to the shore. But neither did I find myself stationed so very far up it either, for all the other detail I- Well, maybe detail is too strong a word…"

"Elwin Kneath, your deputization to the Kelpyguard Constabulary is hereby officially recognized!" the chief constable impatiently declared. "Your first professional duty will be a full debriefing of Rupert Hamster Holmes! God willing, you'll get back to me before we toast in the new year! Now take him away to the Kelpyguard police station!"

For bringing Rupert Hamster Holmes back up the coastal hiking trail to the nearest parking lot, Elwin's sidekick undertook another task Augie sensed he'd undertaken before. He laid his trench coat on the ground for Rupert followed by Elwin to trample without fear of losing traction on any more ball-bearing-type pebbles. Then he retrieved it, only to set it down further ahead for trampling anew.

"Your new assistant deputy seems to have quite the penchant for boasting about his counterfeit documents," Irene remarked to Chief Constable Williams.

"Excuse me, um…"

"Irene McDowell."

"Listen well, Irene McDowell: As nice as it is to make yer acquaintance, you've got quite a lip on ya. I'm talkin' about what issues from yer mouth. Here's the thing: Before your circus came to town, we were pretty short on dinosaur sightings. And suspected murders have been almost unheard of, save for fifty years ago when me great uncle drowned in a vat of moonshine. Though I still suspect that was just an accident."

"Short on dinosaur sightings, but more than zero," interjected Augie. "Aside from your schoolboy's experience that brought us here to investigate, something else happened back in 1975. Well north of here near Anglesey, at Barmouth Harbor, five schoolgirls reported seeing a strange ten-foot-long creature on shore. It had a long neck and a plump body, and waddled its way back into the surf."

"No evidence whatsoever," Stephen weighed in with his usual voice-of-doom dismissiveness.

"Never heard that one," said the chief constable. "Maybe their parents let them start drinkin' too young. Anyway, back to you, Irene McDowell is it?" He consulted his notepad. "Where were you last night at the height of the thunderstorm?"

"I was with the schoolboy who reported the dinosaur, his teacher, and Augie Matias here. We hid behind those rock outcroppings or whatever they were inside the cave, before they sank out of sight, or moved off."

"I can confirm that," said Augie. "Irene crouched down behind the outcropping next over from mine."

"I was also there, behind one of the other outcrops. I can confirm Irene's presence before the storm revved up," said Stephen, adding emphatically, "But have to admit, I drifted off until seawater entered the cave from a combination of the storm and rising tide. Then to be perfectly honest, I lost track of her until we huddled under a tarp-covered lean-to, much later on. That's when the storm was waning, and Robin came screaming to help her find Gerwyn."

"But-"

"No need to cover for me, Augie," Irene waved off Augie Matias, at the same time giving Stephen a thanks-for-throwing-me-under-the-bus dirty look. "Apologies, Chief Constable, for not sharing a more precise, comprehensive account of my whereabouts for your investigation. Here's the detailed version: As the storm intensified, I stood out of my crouch to stretch my legs, and have a better look at the shoreline surf. I was especially concerned it might trap us inside the cave. That's when everything around me felt in motion. Thought I was having a bad case of vertigo. Maybe food poisoning from the fish and chips."

"Wouldn't be a problem if you'd had enough alcohol in your system to deal with the bacteria, burp!" burped Nigel, lurching into the picture just long enough to comment before Sergeant Frankly muscled him back to the sidelines.

"Actually, they were the best fish and chips I've ever eaten."

"You mean the fried haddock in the paper-thin beer batter at Drunk In The Wool?" asked Assistant Constable Angharad. "Oh, that's a proper fine dish, that is. Can't imagine it ever goin' bad."

"Perhaps I could take you there for an early lunch, Assistant Constable," suggested Stephen. "I assume they have catsup for the chips."

"And a squeeze'o'lemon for that heavenly haddock! And non-mashed peas steamed only the slightest wee bit. Have no idea where they get them so crispy fresh this time of the year," added Angharad.

"What?!" Nigel did a double take. "I'm not bein' funny, right? I didn't receive any peas at all there, mashed or otherwise, on me last order!"

"OH MY GOD, MAN!! ENOUGH ABOUT THE BLOODY FISH AND CHIPS!!!" Chief Constable Williams exploded. "ASSISTANT CONSTABLE, WE ARE INVESTIGATIN' A POSSIBLE MURDER, SURROUNDED BY A HERD OF LOONIES STILL LOOKIN' FOR A LIVING DINOSAUR!! NOT DEBATIN' HOW MANY ROSETTES TO AWARD THE DRUNK IN THE WOOL!!!" Then very softly to Irene, "Now as you were about to say, Ms. McDowell..."

"Gerwyn's fish and chips *were* the best in all Wales!" cried out Robin. "Never to be prepared by him, ever again! Please tell me, mum, that one of the last he served didn't poison you!"

"It didn't," Irene shook her head, worried the chief constable might blow another fuse. "I felt fine once I stood outside the cave to get fresher air. And knowing what I know now, about those three big stones vanishing, have to wonder about them, Chief Constable. Not quite ready to buy into the oversized waking-up Stegosaurus myself, yet. But maybe their migration, whatever the cause, is what made me dizzy."

"So, you stepped outside the cave for fresher air, you

say," said Chief Constable Rhys Williams, barely reigning in his impatience. "Can anyone else here confirm that?"

"You've got to believe us, mate," pleaded Alistair Frump. "Whatever any of us did or did not see, distracted by the storm, the surf, or..." He trailed off, giving his seven iron a brief look. "Irene McDowell is as decent as they come, Chief Constable. And things got so crazy out there, I had trouble following where my own golf ball flew, let alone where anyone else went! That's the truth!"

"Down on this rugged beach last night, you faced an angry Irish Sea all riled up by that fierce thunder bumper! That was the time and place you decided to practice hitting golf balls, did ya??! Unbelievable, man! Wait!" A glance Irene's way swung Rhys's attention back to her before Alistair could explain himself. "I need to examine something on your pants a wee bit more closely, Ms. McDowell."

The chief constable whipped out a big magnifying glass with a long handle, and he crouched down before Irene for a careful inspection of her light-brown capris. "The streaks on these pants just above the knees, they look like blood to me. What do you think, Officer Gruffudd?"

"Probably are blood stains," said Irene before Angharad Gruffudd could finish crouching down herself for a look.

"What explanation have you for this, that isn't a confession of murder?" the chief constable growled up at Irene from still crouched before her.

"Alistair Frump confirmed what we saw during a lightning flash last night, that he did hit a golf ball seaward. His stated goal – you're going to love this – was to play 'go fetch' with a relic dinosaur. And so, I came out here close to dawn this morning, to see whether I could find the ball."

"You can't blame her, Officer, for the dinosaur makin' off with me Gerwyn for a late-night snack!!" protested Robin in a tearfully whiny voice.

"I'm not blamin' anyone for anything yet, lass; you really must calm down," the chief constable lectured Robin. "I'm not questionin' that you believe you saw what you claim you saw! But sorry. I'd be less than honest, not to inform you in the strongest possible terms, that I've ruled out any such livin' dinosaur, or sea monster, or dragon even! And I'm still waitin' on poor Gerwyn's body! Expectin' to have our coastal guard trawl for it offshore soon, while me other officers comb the hillside. For now, I want to hear our American visitor's explanation for what she has admitted is blood on her pants! Ms. McDowell, please proceed! Despite my fear you're about to waste me time with more sheep's poo!"

"I don't do time wasting, Chief Constable," asserted Irene, holding her chin haughtily high. "Like I was starting to say, came here in the first morning light, looking for Alistair's golf ball amidst clumps of washed-ashore seaweed."

"Truth be known," interjected Alistair, "I did think some lightning flashes illuminated an enormous creature headed out to sea. But I can't be sure the tail I saw whipping about wasn't actually airborne seaweed, tossed by the waves."

"When I kicked at those seaweed clumps, hoping to reveal a golf ball, gorse brambles somehow got stuck up my pants. By the time I removed them, their needly thorns scraped my legs pretty badly."

"Gorse brambles were mixed in with the seaweed, you're sayin' there, Ms. McDowell?" asked the chief constable dubiously.

"I don't think it's the craziest thing in the world to suggest that that wild thunderstorm last night blew loose dead branches down to the shore, Chief Constable," insisted Scott.

"You've got that right, mate!" snorted Chief Constable

Williams. "The craziest thing in the world would be hittin' a golf ball into the surf during a wicked nasty thunder bumper, at the same time thinkin' you might be snatchin' a peek at a dinosaur there!"

"From our prior expeditions, I have reason to believe dinosaurs might be playful puppy dogs when it comes to balls tossed their way, Chief Constable," said Alistair, not backing down.

"Oh you do, do you? Well I have reason to believe that most if not all of you need to be fitted for straitjackets! Assistant Constable, go further down this shore, and check for gorse brambles mixed in with the seaweed. Meantime, Ms. McDowell, you'll be comin' back with me to the Kelpyguard station for further questions."

Irene rolled her eyes, but thought better of levelling any snark at the chief constable, simply saying, "As you wish."

"We'd like to come along as character witnesses," Scott reacted impulsively, moving to join Irene and Chief Constable Williams.

Augie, Sherman and the rest didn't require any prompting to follow suite.

"For the first time I can recall," said Sherman, "my flatus emission detector had great difficulty sorting out possible saurian flatus from other noise. Crashing surf accompanying the thunderstorm might have been the main problem. In any event, I will check on my artificial intelligence entity, Charly, left back aboard our mode of transportation. Maybe some part of him saw, and even recorded, something last night that could prove helpful to your investigation, Chief Constable."

On a pause from leading Irene back along the hiking trail to the parking lot, the chief constable gave Sherman a good, long look before he said, "Before you called attention to yourself, I didn't notice you wearin' that wet suit, plus an empty goldfish bowl on your head. What, were you plannin' to take a dive out there, tamper with crucial evidence before me coast guard chaps could get to it?"

"Very different atmosphere on the planet he's from," deadpanned Stephen.

"Not a wet suit, though perhaps it would also work to that end," conceded Sherman. "It is special insulation to guarantee no lightning would strike anywhere near me. As for the helmet: With the Draconid meteor shower ongoing, I found it a wise precaution against the one-in-three-billion chance of fatal micro-meteor impact. But," he added, giving Stephen a derisive sideways glance, "I'm not one to judge those unwilling to take such precautions."

Chief Constable Williams came to a dead halt. His puckered mouth shifted from one side of his face to the other, in tandem with his eyes shifting back and forth between Irene and Sherman as in, *Who should I detain and interrogate first?* "Tell me, Mr…"

"Peabody. Sherman Peabody."

"Okay, Mr. Peabody, when you use the term, 'saurian flatus,' do I understand you to mean you are searching for dinosaur farts?"

"Well, yes as a matter of fact, I am." *Nothing to apologize for.*

"As for character witnesses, Chief Constable," broke in John Jones, his open can of Toohey's held forward like a torch to light his drunken way, in Augie's estimation, "I'm the character witness you require, mate! I witnessed they're all a bunch of characters! Every last bloody one of them! Cheers! While you're at it, you're goin' to want to ask those three retirin' wallflowers over there about their time travel aboard a spaceship from the next century! Burp!" John Jones pointed towards Ali, Fred, and Kevin huddled together off to one side of the hiking trail.

"No. No-no. No-no-no," Rhys Williams shook his head. "I can't be handlin' so many bloody crazy suspects all at the same time. This is what I propose to do: I'm still goin' to start with Ms. McDowell back at the station. Meanwhile, the rest of you, the whole bloody lot, you can wait aboard your bloody spaceship, or however you got here in the first place. I'll get to each of you in due course."

"Actually, we arrived on a steam-powered, inhabitable drone," said Sherman in his usual professorial manner. "You see that square-ish cloud way up there above your head?"

"No, you're not goin' to tell me-"

"Its operation generates so much condensation of the surrounding air that it's usually lost from direct view."

"And when its rainbow headlight is turned on, you can follow that down to a bloody pot of gold, can you? Isn't that just perfect!"

Chapter 9

Crrrrackkk...BOOM!!

"Oh, jeez!" fourth grade student Anni Reyes sighed breathlessly. At first, the crash of thunder startled her. Ditto for the figure standing tall at a cave entrance, and cast in silhouette by lightning flashes. But then she realized the object he raised high over his head wasn't a long sword. It was just a golf club.

"Keep cool, kiddies," teacher Vicky Copplestone urged in hushed tones. "This is video from hours ago across the Atlantic Ocean in Wales, not live TV."

Vicky well knew that the last thing she wanted to have happen again was bound to anyway, sooner or later. A classroom ruckus would draw the curriculum adviser, Diane Mueller, back into her classroom, to take another stab at proving she was unfit for teaching at the elementary school level. Or at any level, for that matter. *Dare to dream!*

Hubbie Augie Matias judiciously edited down the video clips he transmitted to Vicky from "across the pond." He excluded anything that showed the Welsh beach below the Strumblehead lighthouse taped off as a potential crime scene. Neither Vicky nor Augie wanted to expose her young charges to something so potentially upsetting. Of course, that would also open the door for Diane's nasty agenda, for the umpteenth time.

"Ms. Copplestone, could you replay the last part?" student Erin Manley asked in her distinctive nasal voice that made her sound old beyond her years, to Vicky's amusement. "I noticed something else besides that nut job with the golf club."

"Okay," said Lucas Lambert as Vicky reversed the video

to the lightning flash at the cave entrance. "If there really is a dinosaur roaming that beach, why don't more people see it, Ms. Copplestone? You told us there's a walking trail along the coast."

"I don't have a good answer, Lucas," Vicky confessed, pausing the video where she was pretty sure Erin wanted. "Mr. Copplestone has the same question about these reports from other parts of the world he's explored."

"They might be very shy," interjected Anni. "The few times I ever see a lizard, it scurries into hiding before I can get a close look."

"Mr. Copplestone thinks that's one aspect."

"Yeah, but a forty-foot-long dinosaur is going to have a harder time scurrying into hiding than a three-inch-long lizard," Lucas pointed out dismissively. "I mean, how does something that big even hide in the first place?"

"That's a good question, Lucas," agreed Vicky. "Mr. Copplestone wonders whether dinosaurs hibernate for long periods, and only emerge from underground, or underwater even, to eat and have babies."

"Have babies? Ewww!" ewwwed Kurt Lansing.

"All living things have babies," chuckled Jack Feuillet. "That's a whole lot of 'ewww'!"

"I'm not having babies!" declared Kurt.

"You're not? Ewww!" ewwwed Jack to riotous laughter.

"Okay, guys," said Vicky in mildly admonishing, let's-settle-down mode. "Back to what my husband said about dinosaurs that might still be alive."

"Your husband? Ewww," Jack couldn't help adding.

With a resigned sigh, Vicky went on, "The average crocodile only eats about fifty meals a year, and mostly sleeps the rest of the time. And if necessary," she went on emphatically before one of her students could interrupt, "they can go for up to two or three years without eating anything. They enter a kind of hibernation. Mr.

Copplestone believes that if there are any surviving dinosaurs, they hibernate like that on a regular basis. They only come out into the open from deep caverns and the like to find their next meal, plus do the 'eww' thing. Although my husband also thinks they might be extraordinarily good at camouflage."

"That's how they survived the ice age after an asteroid struck the Earth sixty-five million years ago?" asked Lucas, intrigued.

"The same as several other reptiles such as turtles and snakes. They are able to sleep all winter long at the bottom of ponds, if need be."

"Well maybe the dinosaurs only come out to eat in bad weather, like during that thunderstorm," speculated Erin. "Usually, won't be many hikers then. And if they're not looking for a dinosaur, maybe they wouldn't notice anyway. Unless one kicked their ass with its tail!"

"Erin Manley, watch your language!" Vicky said admonishingly, though her amusement was plainly evident while many students giggled.

"If they only come out in the open during bad storms, maybe they're foul weather friends?" joked Jack.

"Not necessarily," responded Vicky, more focused on the point than on Jack's wit. "The young man and his teacher had their sighting under foggy conditions...Okay, while not stormy, it was still weather that easily conceals things."

"What was that guy doing with a golf club in a thunderstorm?" asked Anni before Vicky could finally replay the segment requested by Erin. "When he swung it skyward, looked like he was trying to get himself electrocuted!"

"That guy with the golf club," Vicky responded, "he's Alistair Frump. On earlier expeditions in Papua, New Guinea and along the border of Brazil with Venezuela, he hit his ball into the most unlikely spots, on purpose. And something, he doesn't know what, hit it back out. That happened in the same locations where other members of Mr. Copplestone's expedition thought they glimpsed dinosaur-type creatures. Could surviving dinosaurs enjoy playing with balls, the same as dogs and cats do? That's a question Alistair is trying to answer."

"Okay, maybe my pet dachshund is really a Triceratops in disguise," said Emme LeGrand. But the way she crossed her arms and rolled her eyes made crystal clear to Vicky she was being totally sarcastic as she went on, "Maggie must have a super-power camouflage ability."

"Maybe Alistair should throw a couple of golf balls her way, Emme. But let's review that part of the video Erin asked for," said Vicky, undaunted. "I've got it on slow motion for easy stopping at any point."

The most tantalizing few seconds were obscured by the weather. Something did whip out briefly from the left side of the cave entrance. And something else at the shoreline looked like more of a giant splash than a huge wave crashing ashore. But sheets of rain kept it all blurred, even during lightning flashes, except for Alistair and his seven iron.

Vicky and her students also noticed a deep moan during those frustrating run-throughs of the film clip. The room was divided on whether it issued from the storm or a large animal.

After the ninth review, Vicky played the rest, which was not a whole lot more. Once Augie stepped out of the cave, rainwater droplets covered his camcorder lens, making it impossible to discern anything, even during additional lighting flashes.

"They headed back to Cloud Nine to dry off, and returned for a better look in the early morning. That took place while we were still asleep," explained Vicky. She left out that someone screamed about a dinosaur killing her boyfriend, and that a blood-soaked, shredded shirt washed ashore.

"Do you have any video from their return to the beach this morning?" asked Lucas, anxious with curiosity.

"The only-" *Whoops!* Vicky caught herself before she would have said, *The only video clip I can show you.* That would have hinted at something kept secret. Instead, she went on, "Um, the only other clip my husband has sent so far is rather boring. Has mostly to do with searching for that golf ball, and tracks on the beach." She left out how Augie avoided filming any of the crime scene tape, or recording any of the interrogations by the chief constable.

"Can't be more boring than my social studies unit this afternoon," said Lucas. "Let's see it!"

"Okay, but you might need a pillow," Vicky warned playfully. "Feel free to fill your journal with thoughts on the Welsh dinosaur search so far, while the video plays to the lunch bell."

"This strange-looking object is a skate egg, sometimes referred to as a mermaid's purse," said Augie in voice-over. Close to the camera, he held a dark brown, somewhat rectangular object with four, long, pointed corners. "The skate, of course, is a kind of fish that looks like a stingray. So unfortunately, this is not a dinosaur egg. Let's toss it back into the sea, and hope it can still hatch successfully," Augie concluded for his wife's classroom audience...keeping crime scene tape well out of view.

Slam!

Diane Mueller swung the classroom door slamming against the wall, in her excitement over seeing the video about which she had made a certain assumption. To wit, "Ms. Copplestone, I can't believe you're exposing these students to the situation over there in Wales!"

"You mean, exposing them to a boring video? Not the first time a teacher has done that," quipped Vicky, genuinely perplexed.

"Well," bubbled Diane effusively, beyond amazed at how oblivious Vicky was to her irresponsibility. "YOU might think it's boring, that crime scene tape where someone has vanished under suspicious circumstances! And their bloody shirt left behind! But..." Diane paused. It finally sunk in that Vicky was giving her a horrified look whilst shaking her head urgently as in, *Stop talking!*

Earlier, Diane had her office TV on the world news when the BBC reported something about a quixotic dinosaur search in South Wales. It had turned into a murder investigation, with one of the searchers held for further questioning.

Moments later, Diane was click-click-clicking her high heels down the hall. She thrilled at the prospect of Vicky not knowing any better than to risk traumatizing fourth-grade boys and girls with a possible murder at the scene of her husband's insane dinosaur hunt.

Presently, Diane's heart beat a mile a moment with a floor-dropping-out-of-the-bottom-of-her-stomach *Oh-oh.*

The next part of the video Vicky was showing her class featured boots kicking at washed-ashore seaweed, and Augie saying, "If there's a golf ball here, I'm not finding it."

"Augie and I carefully culled only those portions of the video related to the dinosaur search, save for a sidebar about the sea skate egg," Vicky managed to explain despite her shock over what Diane just said. "Anni?"

"What is Ms. Mueller talking about?"

"I think she's talking about...murrrrrderrrrr," Jack concluded in a dramatically deep, affectedly gravelly voice that sent the class into hysterics.

Diane could only give Vicky a deer-in-the-headlights look until she finally asked, still in disbelieving shock, "You mean, they didn't, um..."

"They knew nothing until you, uh, said what you said."

With one, eyes-closed calming inhale and exhale, Diane turned to Vicky's students with the friendliest, most solicitous smile she could affect. In her nervousness-spawned, girlishly shrill, hi-pitched voice, she said, "Now boys and girls, I'm sure you will want to share with your parents all the fascinating details of the search by Ms. Copplestone's husband for - Oh, my! – a living, breathing dinosaur! And those fascinating details, only!" As several heads nodded earnestly, albeit also worriedly, she added, "There's no need to bother them with anything that might have been said here, not having to do with dinosaurs, is there?"

"Or sea skate eggs?" Vicky added.

"Or sea skate eggs, of course, Ms. Copplestone!" Diane gritted her teeth to maintain her ingratiating façade.

"Ms. Mueller, what are you afraid might happen to you if one of us *does* tell our parents about the crime investigation you mentioned?" Anni asked innocently.

Jack beat Diane to the response. "Murrrrderrrr!"

Chapter 10

As usual, Cloud Nine pilot Samuel Longbottom tuned in Eclipso's live transmission on the steam-powered drone's panoramic flat-screen TV. And Eclipso's search team found themselves greeted by Bonsai Gator dancing to a reggae version of a Beatles tune.

This time, Bonsai boogied to "Maxwell's Silver Hammer," about a serial killer. The pencil-sized alligator accompanied each "bang bang" in the refrain with two of his reptilian booty shakes.

"Since Irene is not here to snark, I'll snark for her," said Laura, "and wonder what Bonsai Gator's end-of-the-world boogie would look like."

"The same as most other moves he makes," drily proclaimed Stephen. "I think it's more of a bug-hunting strut than anything else."

"Quite amusing, really," inserted the soft-spoken Bernie Coleman, who was managing to keep an extra low profile on this leg of the dinosaur quest.

"But it really is expletive-deleted unbelievable," muttered Scott, "that Irene sits in a police station, being interrogated for murder!"

"At least the chief constable allowed me to search those seaweed clumps long enough to find broken-off gorse branches. They corroborate how she claims her legs got cut up," said Augie. "It just remains for lab tests to find any blood or skin on them that wasn't washed away."

"Unfortunately, if there are threads on any of the thorns from Gerwyn's shirt that Robin found washed ashore..." trailed off Sherman.

"You're suggesting Irene might have clawed Gerwyn to death with gorse?" asked Scott defensively. "Really??!!"

"I don't believe that for a second," said Sherman, reflexively holding up his hands to fend off a physical blow from Scott. He well knew, though, that such a fear belonged in the same irrational camp where he had his outfit equipped for unlikely calamities. For example, were the ground to suddenly open below his feet, helicopter blades would bloom like an opening parachute from his backpack, and lift him to safety. "I do worry, nevertheless. Discovery of blood-soaked shirt threads on those gorse thorns might stymy our search, and Irene's exoneration, far longer than we would wish."

"Which is not at all," Laura said pointedly.

"Exactly," Sherman nodded his chin into his neck. "Clear, dry weather is expected this evening. And with a full moon to boot, I was hoping we could get a much better look at exactly what's out there. Although as you've pointed out before, Augustine, these creatures' departures from hibernation might be few and far between. Unless they are in the process of migration, they might sleep for weeks, months, or even years on end between meals."

"We have to hope the storm last night prevented whatever was out there, if anything was out there, from getting its fill. In which case, it should return tonight," Augie suggested. "Incidentally, that assumes it is herbivorous. Rather than feast on that hapless barkeep, it carried him to his doom because of territorial instinct. Otherwise..."

"What terrible luck for us, and of course the barkeep," Harry Letterman concluded, embarrassed.

"I take our luck over Gerwyn's," Laura said pointedly. "By comparison, we might as well have won a million-dollar lottery."

"I agree completely," Harry nodded emphatically. "What I meant is, the one time we don't have to deal with hoaxers, one of us is caught up in a murder investigation. And crime scene tape prevents exploring underwater near the coastline, to see if a dinosaur is hiding there."

Harry's wife Harriet laced an arm round his, and looked up at him to say, "At least you don't have to worry about me trying to murder you, honeybun."

"Not necessarily true," said Stephen, rushing to add, "I mean, Harry, when you say we don't have to deal with hoaxers here."

"But there's no way they knew where we went this time, soon enough to plan anything," Harry protested. "Eclipso cut off their covert surveillance. The first they would have heard was from the local news."

"That's true as far as it goes," conceded Stephen. "But the United Kingdom is notorious for elaborate pranks on a wide-ranging basis. There's an entire culture of crop circle makers across the British Isles."

"Hold on, there," objected Sherman. And he'd bowed his chin down far enough into his neck to make it appear to Augie he was prepared to charge at Stephen, enraged-bull style. "I don't have a horse in that particular race. And yes, most definitely, several so-called crop circles are forged by humans. However, I do happen to know there are serious questions about a few of them, especially those accompanied by unidentified aerial phenomena. And it only takes one that's unexplained to have a mystery, even if the other 99.999% are bogus."

While Stephen made his usual dismissive eye roll, Roberta Quiñones burst out, "Again and again this happens! We come away with tantalizing clues, and not much else!" She turned towards Eclipso on the TV screen, seated as usual behind the reggae-dancing Bonsai Gator, and apparently contemplating his half-eaten, humus-dipped pretzel. "Eclipso, you've been so generous to us already, even without much to show for our efforts. Let me assure you I am fascinated beyond all reason by the prospect of definitively proving the survival to the present day of non-avian dinosaurs. I really am, despite personal consequences. Although, perhaps, there's benefit to the futility of another type of quest having been made plainly obvious." She cleared her throat to go on, "Maybe, just maybe, we are doomed to experience perpetual uncertainty no matter how many resources we throw at this. Maybe the non-avian dinosaur we seek is locked up with that proverbial cat in Shroedinger's Box. We never will be able to open it to see whether such a creature is dead, or still alive."

"That's especially interesting to me what you're saying, Dr. Quiñones," Scott found himself admitting. "It gets into questions of faith my brother has raised."

"The brother with the Bible museum," Stephen said in a I-hold-the-right-to-be-dismissive tone.

"Yes, he did help with its construction," Scott admitted. "Be that as it may, his take on this whole dinosaur question is that there's been enough circumstantial evidence already. He doesn't require anything further; his professed faith in non-avian dinosaur survival is as strong as in life after death."

"I think whatever happens to us after death has proven rather more difficult to investigate than dinosaur survival," dispassionately observed Sherman. "Tantalizing near-death experiences, children who describe past lives in remarkably minute detail, these things plus more are true. Nevertheless, it's not like anyone is regularly able to visit the afterlife. But we *can* muck about where people believe they've seen a living dinosaur.

"There is a scenario that might vindicate your concern, though, Dr. Quiñones," Sherman continued. "Which is to say, we might not be able to definitively answer yea or nay to the question of dinosaur survival, at least anytime soon. What if people are seeing dinosaurs on temporary forays through space-time rifts from millions of years ago? That would certainly account for the sparsity of sightings. And would maybe mean we are centuries away from grasping enough of the physics involved to make any serious progress."

"On a planet we explored several light-years away," interjected Sergeant Fred Frankly, "we experienced a stampede of dinosaur-like creatures that seemed to emerge out of thin air, and then return the way they came."

"The sergeant is truly correct," chimed in counselor Ali Magabu. "Our shipboard astrophysicist's best thinking on the subject is that a miniature black hole collided with the planet eons ago. But even he remains far from a full understanding."

"Of course he does," snarked Stephen dubiously.

"Just for the record," said Scott sharply, ignoring Stephen and hoping what he was about to say would get back to Irene. "I don't believe faith in something difficult to prove or disprove scientifically should ever mean you stop trying to better understand it. Yes, such a quest might lead you places you're afraid to go, because those places might undermine rather than reaffirm your faith. But so be it. What I've told my brother is, if he believes in a god that created us as we are supposed to be, fine. But then he must also accept that this ever-curious inquiring mind we are born with means we are meant to keep trying to understand more and more of the universe's inner workings. We should never stop learning and investigating, just to sit back and relax, self-satisfied with what we already know."

"Scott MacDonald, you've provided a most excellent lead-in to a crucial point I should like to make. It's regarding Roberta's fear our dinosaur search might never bring us to any kind of certainty."

While Eclipso set the stage for his crucial point, Bonsai Gator kept busy. He pretended to be struck to the ground by Maxwell's Silver Hammer coming "down upon his head," to conclude the song in grand fashion. And Eclipso's demur, mousey-haired mother hastened to open an old issue of a *Turok Son Of Stone* comic book to the first page, on a short dais set before him.

"Ah, here we go with another lesson from the gospel according to Turok," Stephen whispered to Laura, who brushed him away as in *Shut up and leave me alone*.

"In the hundredth issue of this comic book, *Turok Son Of Stone*, there's a story entitled 'Don't Give Up.' Turok's younger relative, Andar, proposes to make a cave inside Lost Valley their permanent home. That, rather than continue one fruitless effort after another to find a way out of Lost Valley. What Turok is not able to get across to Andar through mere words, Andar learns the hard way, through experience. For after all, Lost Valley is ever full of dangerous dinosaurs, plus equally dangerous cavemen who wallow in their ignorance, more often than not. Settling with life there, giving up the search for a way out, amounts to surrendering to a life of constant peril, bereft of hope. A faith in hopelessness, if you will.

"During recent U.S. history, we have a dramatic example of people who likewise could have settled for a life of constant peril, a Lost Valley of injustice."

"The descendants of slaves, including our Irene," Scott offered as an example, though wanting to call Irene *my Irene*.

"Not to mention people of non-heterosexual orientation," Roberta made a point of adding.

"Exactly!" thundered Eclipso with a triumphant jab of his latest humus-dipped pretzel. "Think of that famous speech made by the husband of presidential candidate Coretta Scott King, twenty years ago! He talked about seeing 'the promised land,' an exit from the Lost Valley of fear-stoked bigotry!"

"Last year, he even referred back to that," said Scott. "He said African Americans can make out the light at the end of the tunnel. But aren't there just yet, with a long gloomy hike still to go. He could have been Turok describing a possible exit from Lost Valley."

"Wait," Stephen held up a just-a-minute-there-not-so-fast hand. "I think you've got this all backwards. That is, if you're going to suggest that giving up on finding an extant dinosaur is like Turok giving up on finding an exit from a land full of them. Certainly, Dr. King wouldn't agree that living in a world where the dinosaurs are all extinct is anywhere near as bad as living in a Lost Valley of Ku Klux Klan members behaving like those ridiculous cavemen in *Turok* comic books. There's nothing notably perilous, in and of itself, about a non-dinosaur world. On the contrary. And in fact, isn't that what Turok and Andar are always trying to return to?"

Bonsai Gator reared back on his hind legs, standing impossibly upright for any other alligator Augie had ever known. He came close to the camera on Eclipso's end, and bore what Augie felt spookily was a scornful look.

Of course, Stephen told himself Bonsai's look had to be from closely, hungrily inspecting a crawling bug.

"Nothing notably perilous about a non-dinosaur world, perhaps," admitted Eclipso. "And yet, a world where we were not searching for surviving non-avian dinosaurs would certainly have proven more dangerous than otherwise. That is, for certain special people we have encountered along the way. Prince Englebert and Prince Angelbert, for example. They would still have been living in daily fear of persecution for their homosexual love in Cameroon, rather than preparing to open a clothes boutique in College Park, Maryland."

"And Maggie wouldn't be studying at Cambridge University," piled on Augie, "preparing to combat betelnut addiction in parts of Southeast Asia."

"The latest news from Belém is that our run-in with a surviving giant ground sloth has shut down cattle land development in one part of the Amazon rainforest. *And,* Adriana Souza and her husband have started up a tour company there that will educate everyone on the need to protect rainforest ecology," added Samuel Longbottom.

"We leave positivity in our wake, everywhere we go!" proudly boasted Eclipso, followed by a triumphant bite of his pretzel.

The same as always, incidentally, Augie puzzled over why that bite was followed by Eclipso's mother moving her jaws like a farm animal ruminating. The ultimate in motherly empathy for her child?

"And you can't do all those things without a dinosaur search in the mix?" Stephen asked drily.

"The point is, we would not have been doing any of those things *without* a dinosaur search in the mix."

"Excuse me, Eclipso," said Samuel, hand to ear. "Just receiving a call from Chief Constable Williams I'll put on speaker phone. Yes, Chief Constable? How might we assist you?"

"I have good news about Ms. McDowell," the policeman's gruff voice erupted from the speaker phone. "None of the blood on the shredded shirt matches her blood. And none of the blood from where she says she was scraped by gorse thorns matches the blood on the shirt, which was presumably shed by poor Gerwyn. So she's released. You can pick her up whenever suits you. Oh, and one other thing," he went on, cutting the cheers Samuel's end abruptly short. "It's about one of the gorse branches your Mr. Matias found mixed in with shoreline seaweed. Fiber on it did come from the shirt, and might suggest somethin', or nothin'. And the blood on the fiber matches the blood on the shirt. Again, nothin' to link Ms. McDowell to Gerwyn's disappearance. But I did have a thought about you crazy lot with your dinosaur search and your time travel. Might not be the worst idea to have you combin' the coastline again for a Stegosaur playin' hide and seek. No tellin' what other evidence you might find along the way that could help my investigation. What I'm sayin' is, if you still want to cross the crime scene tape for a full-moon continuation of your madness, you're on!"

The cheers Samuel's end resumed, louder than ever.

Chapter 11

"Impressive," remarked Jake Rumblehouse, leafing through a photo album that detailed the stages of construction for an enormous balsa wood Pteranodon. "You say that in the middle of falling apart, as it was designed to do, its machinery came flying home to you?"

"Three micro-jet aircraft," nodded Paul Smith, seated across a plexiglass coffee table from Jake in an executive suite thirty-two floors up a skyscraper in Los Angeles, California. "Let's imagine Augustine Matias's search team was miraculously able to locate the wreckage before it rotted away. They would have found absolutely no indication of how such a large contraption could have emerged airborne out of the Amazonian flood waters."

"What else have you guys hoaxed?" asked Jake as he slammed shut the photo album and handed it back to Paul.

"They were featured on those two other dinosaur-related episodes of your *Crypto-fake-ology* show," said Aaron Levy.

"Oh my God! You were also the guys behind that foot-track-making contraption left to rust offshore at New Britain Island? And the Brachiosaurus balloon fished out of the Sangha River in West Africa?"

"The balloon would have harmlessly biodegraded if left there long enough," Paul explained defensively. "And the last time we checked, that dino-track maker was already growing an impressively sized coral reef."

"Uh-huh," Jake nodded not a little warily. "Okay, before we go any further, what's in this for you? No bullshit!"

"No bullshit," Paul couldn't help bristling. "We have a benefactor who chooses to remain anonymous while

137

underwriting even our most expensively elaborate schemes."

"Hey, maybe I could get an anonymous benefactor to underwrite a nuclear submarine hull constructed out of toothpicks. But why go to all that trouble? Why build a flight-enabled balsa wood Pteranodon with a twenty-five-foot wingspan, simply to fool a bunch of eccentrics? And then rub their noses in it, having it come apart in mid-air before their very eyes? I don't get it."

Aaron and Paul gave each other significant looks as in, *Who should do the honors?* But Paul knew himself well, that he tended to be the hothead. So he nodded for Aaron to proceed.

"Whether or not the explorers we've pranked are searching in vain-"

"You mean," Jake interrupted, "whether or not any dinosaurs have survived to the present day."

"Exactly. Whether or not that's the case is somewhat beside the point."

"'somewhat beside the point'??" Jake leaned into repeating. "How do I know you guys aren't trying to ridicule that nut brigade off the board so you can have the biological find of the century all to yourselves?"

"Not for one second," Paul couldn't help bristling anew. "What Aaron means is, no doubt our scheme could help stave off an extinction most reputable scientists are certain already happened over sixty million years ago. But our plans would go forward, even were we one-thousand-percent certain no Triceratops is still grazing out there somewhere. You see, those remote regions of the Earth most often favored for prehistoric monster investigations also happen to be the very same areas most favored for ecology-destroying development."

Paul knew as well as his cooler-headed partner that they could never share the real reason for their actions, as crazy as it would sound. And as close as it shaded towards their cover-story motive. That would betray a sacred-feeling trust, a trust both partners found themselves willing to lie for.

"Of course, those mysterious confiscations of weapons round the world have defused wars, at least a few of which would likely have taken place on a large scale. As a result, the environment is in much better health than it otherwise might have been."

"Or might currently be in an alternate universe where such intervention is not taking place," Paul added, ever ready to emphasize the negative.

"But back to the universe we *can* do something about," Aaron said irritably, unable to help himself. "It's possible that the decreased pollution from our less violent world has had an unexpected added benefit. Certain mythical creatures such as the Loch Ness Monster might be thriving that otherwise would already have been poisoned to extinction. However, it's not as though we are totally free from such environmental degradation."

"Far from it; they're still burning coal like crazy in parts of China, India, and even this good old U.S. of A.," Paul added anew, emphasizing brutal specifics.

"Regretfully very real, what Paul says," Aaron admitted. "The Beatles might have summed it up best on that new recording, *Be Careful What You Wish For*. Yoko Ono sings on, 'From You,'

"'Don't depend on ghosts to do it all;
A wee bit of salvation's
Got to come from you.'

"Then the whole group comes in, harmonizing, 'It's got to come from you, oh yeah!'"

"So where is it coming from you next, exactly?"

"That's what brings us here," said Paul, straining not to sound impatient despite that being exactly how he felt. "By now, we expected our next hoaxing operation to already be well underway."

"Fodder for one of our future episodes," Jake put in terms important to himself.

"By all means," Paul allowed. "Only we were stymied until way too f-ing late."

"We are guessing they discovered, and disabled, our eavesdropping device disguised as a useful expedition item. We paid one of the explorers' boyfriends to gift it to her," Aaron went on.

"Paul, you said you were kept from learning where Don Quixote's crew would be mistaking windmills for dinosaurs, next, until 'too f-ing late,' as you put it. Does that mean you still did somehow manage to sleuth out the location?" Jake asked, intrigued in spite of himself.

"Dumb luck, really," Paul responded, handing over a Welsh newspaper, *The Candlewick Glow (lighting the way to truth)*. Circled in lime-green marker, lower righthand corner of the front page, was a small article entitled, *My Boyfriend Was Abducted By A Dinosaur*.

Jake's face lit up, all wariness of his two barging-in visitors put on hold, as he read what little there was to read. "This is great stuff," he effused, then quoted, "'The search for living dinosaurs by a group of Americans, including zoologist Dr. Roberta Quiñones from the University of Maryland, took a frightful turn. One of our locals, Robin Pugh, produced a bloody, shredded shirt of finest Welsh wool. She claimed it was all that remained of her boyfriend, a bartender at the Drunk In The Wool pub, after a ferocious prehistoric monster carried him out to sea in its snake-like jaws,'" Jake read aloud from the article. "I love it! My team has to go there, pronto, to investigate."

"But again," Aaron reminded the TV personality, "we learned about this only after Dr. Quiñones and company arrived there. Way too late for us to put on the kind of show that you documented on New Britain Island, the Sangha

River, and deep in the Amazon."

"Looks to me as though this Robin Pugh character is doing your work for you this time. Her story is simply unbelievable, even as a misinterpretation of something real," confidently asserted Jake.

"We're guessing you're correct," agreed Paul, "and there's soon to be more egg in the Eclipso crew's collective faces. But if they nevertheless decide to move on to the next report of something dinosaurian, our planet might not be so lucky. Especially given their apparently vast resources, including a fog-enshrouded flying vehicle the size of a football field!"

"'Our planet might not be so lucky'?!" Jake repeated, back to regarding Paul and Aaron most warily. "What the hell is *that* supposed to mean?!"

"What if their next destination yields tantalizing findings, untainted by any hoaxer muddying the waters? That could open the floodgates to environmental degradation, as everyone and his brother combs the region in question for the ultimate biological discovery."

"Ah, let me guess," Jake nodded knowingly as something occurred to him. "You learned of my association with the paleontologist of the group, Dr. Augustine Matias. You figured I still have an 'in' with him to receive advance word where they're headed. In exchange for sharing that info with you, you'll clue me in on your new hoax so my film crew can be there to record their humiliation as it happens, live? Well gee whiz, guys, hate to disappoint you..."

Paul waved his hand dismissively. "That's not it at all. We figured you two had a major falling out. Rather, assuming this latest search does end in another farce, as we're expecting even without our help, we propose to bait them into their next expedition."

"Bait them?" Jake repeated, back to gleefully intrigued.

"Do go on."

"We intend to stage something especially outrageous, sure to garner media attention," explained Aaron. "This will take place where Eclipso's crew would never dream of searching, otherwise."

"On other trips," went on Paul, extra animated, "they've always come away with an intriguing sliver of something that gives them continued hope that one fine day, they might come face-to-face with a surviving non-avian dinosaur. If they take our bait, however, they're virtually guaranteed to walk off with nothing but absolute, profound, public embarrassment, far worse than with any other hoaxes we've staged."

"And my crew would be there to film that, as it happens?" Jake asked, by turns excited and leery about what Aaron and Paul were up to.

"Exactly!"

"Where will this take place? With what kind of bait?"

"Not where you would expect," Aaron grinned broadly. "You'll love it!"

Chapter 12

"Before you start questioning me, Chief Constable," said Robin Pugh sitting across a plain table from Rhys Williams, her head modestly lowered, zero eye contact, "I'll have you know I've been offered legal representation, and rather fancy accepting it."

"Legal representation, you say?" Williams reacted gruffly. "Who might that be?"

Sitting in attendance were three of the dinosaur searchers. The chief constable knew them as Augie, Laura and Dr. Quiñones. He had grudgingly agreed there might be mutual benefit to joining forces with those American crazies, as he saw them. And there were also two of his local crazies, Nigel and the ever-inventive Elwin Kneath. *No lawyers here, far as I know.*

"No mights about it," said Elwin, rising from a bench along one wall to take a seat beside Robin. "Ms. Pugh's legal representation most definitely, assuredly derives from moi," he concluded with a flowery wave of his hands as he bowed his head.

"YOU??!! A lawyer?!?!" the constable growled in disbelief.

Elwin indignantly bristled, "I'll have you know, your honor, that I passed the bar with room to spare! Here's my barrister's certificate to prove it!" He pulled a rolled-up paper from inside his vest, and unfurled it like he was cracking a whip in the chief constable's face. Then far more gently he leaned over and, pointing at the document, said, "You certainly must appreciate the artistry that went into the Gothic lettering."

"The ink has already dried, has it?"

"There's no bar he's ever passed without first enterin' for

a pint!" burst out Nigel animatedly. He took Augie by surprise for how suddenly the fellow roused himself. "And betwixt his lips and the tankard, there's absolutely no room to spare, whatsoever!"

"Very well, Elwin," the constable waved aside the purported documentation. "Whether your representation of Ms. Pugh is legal or illegal, you need to know that the term, 'your honor,' is saved for a court judge."

Elwin did a doubletake, and asked, "Are you suggesting, Chief Constable, there is nothing honorable about you?"

Are you for real, man? the chief constable wanted to say. He batted that prospect back and forth, as reflected in his puckered lips once more shifting from side to side. What he finally settled on was, "Elwin Kneath, please don't tempt me to do somethin' so *dishonorable*, I'll require a lawyer, meself!

"Now back to you, Ms. Pugh. I understand we are to believe Gerwyn's sad fate in the jaws of a bloody impossible dinosaur is especially upsettin' for you, because you quite fancied the poor sod."

Robin's head still lowered, a tear coursed its way down her cheek.

"Yet I have testimony from a regular at Drunk In The Wool," the constable nevertheless proceeded, lifting a paper from his desk. "It's to the effect that you were constantly fendin' off his unwanted advances while you were waitressin'. Who's to say you didn't see this night-time dinosaur search on the Pembrokeshire coast as the perfect opportunity to lure him where nobody would see you offin' him? And then tossin' his body into the sea? On the promise he'd finally beguiled you into alone time with him, for a brilliant canoodle?"

"You don't have to answer that," Elwin advised Robin, her sudden fierce glare moving him to quickly add, "unless you want to."

After a deep breath to collect herself, Robin made eye contact with the chief constable to quietly admit, "It's true that at the outset, I only worked at Drunk In The Wool to bring in a wee bit o' cash on the side while I make a go at the acting circuit. And it's also true I was constantly having to rebuff Gerwyn's romantic advances. But he was never particularly overbearing about it," she shook her head emphatically. "And it only just recently dawned on me, 'Well he's not such a bad-looking chap, and he does have a rather gentle way about him.' If I might make a comparison, it's to chancing a dip at White Sands Bay. Even on the hottest summer afternoon, it can feel frightfully cold at first. After you splash around for a wee bit, though, you rather fancy it. You don't want to come ashore until your fingers shrivel up like raisins."

"In other words, he wore you down," Chief Constable Williams summarized, impatient to mount a different line of questioning.

"Like a piece of sand-paper, he wore away her resistance! So disgustin'! *Ych a fi!*" Nigel stuck out his tongue like he'd gotten a mouth full of sheep's poo, the chief constable imagined.

"My Gerwyn was the perfect gentleman!" Robin insisted tearfully. "Up until I finally said yes, he only pressed his case so far, and no farther! I'd rather say, Nigel, that yours is the voice that sounds like sand-paper! Rubbing me the wrong way, it is!"

"Well then, if that's all you've got to say to me, fair creature, I might as well sprawl out as usual!" blustered Nigel, pursuant to which he actually did flatten himself against the cold slate floor. "Don't even require a drink or ten! I cut out the middle man, and avoid knockin' me head on the ground from keelin' over, into the bargain!"

"Your honor," said Elwin turning to the constable, "I respectfully request you place a gag order on the plaintiff."

"We don't need to order any more gags from Nigel than he's already inflicted on us," growled the chief constable. He thought better of hauling Nigel up off the floor, at least for the time being. "And how many times do I have to tell you, Elwin, I'm not 'your honor,' and this isn't a trial! And Nigel is not a bloody plaintiff!"

"But you must admit he's been complaining a lot!"

Chief Constable Williams gave Elwin a riveting stare whilst playing ping pong with his puckered lips anew, bouncing them from side to side across his disgusted-looking visage. Then, "If you did pass the bar, Elwin Kneath, your paper must have been graded on the kind of curve that would have admitted a bloody penguin and a couple of turkeys as well!

"Back to you, though, Ms. Pugh," he said in an affectedly sweet voice. "You mentioned makin' a go at the actor's circuit. Well, my assistant constable turned up the interestin' detail that you recently starred in a Shakespeare production. A revival of one of his comedies, what was the title?"

"It was a rather irreverent spoof based on *As You Like It*," admitted Robin sheepishly.

"I ask that you share with us the title of the spoof, Ms. Pugh."

"Objection, your...not honor," broke in Elwin.

"Objection ignored! How many times do I have to tell you this is not a trial, you bloody idiot?! You are no more admitted to the bar than I'm the dinosaur the schoolboy and his teacher thought they saw the other morning! Ms. Pugh, please..."

"*Ass You Like It*."

"And a might proper ass it was, too," Nigel lifted his head off the floor to assert. "Robin was brilliant as Roseythin, though my favorite line came from Jaccuse, when he said,

'Do you not know I am a man? When I fart, I must stink!' Immortal words! Then there was-"

"Enough! My assistant told me all about it bein' a bastardized version! But it was still the play, was it not, Ms. Pugh, where someone said, 'All the world's a stage'?"

"The very same, Chief Constable."

"Well, Ms. Pugh, you would have us believe a livin' dinosaur made off with the man of your dreams between his jaws. And that it's the same man you used to not care for comin' on to you, but just recently grew to love. Given such a fantastical story, how are we *not* to suspect this fair corner of Pembrokeshire is *your* stage?"

"My love for Gerwyn is no act!" Robin cried out tearfully.

"A proper display of grief that is, Ms. Pugh," declared Nigel, from where he stayed reclined upon the station house floor of the Kelpyguard Constabulary. "Looks to me like a classic example of method actin', it does."

"What are you saying?" asked Robin in shocked disbelief. She gave Nigel a look that to Augie said she wanted to ask that drunkard, *What are you doing?* as in, *This isn't part of the script.* Good reason for wondering what they were both up to, where Augie was concerned.

"What I'm sayin', fair young lady," said Nigel, "is that maybe Gerwyn wanted to run off with the dinosaur, and you were terribly aggrieved. So terribly aggrieved, in fact, that you were able to recall that emotion just now to produce fake tears."

"But that's absurd! If she was upset over losing Gerwyn to a dinosaur, how are her tears fake about losing him?" asked Laura. "I thought method acting had to do with recalling a real event to reproduce sincere emotion in a fictional context."

"Exactly," Nigel smiled, winking at Robin.

"To believe my client murdered the missing person, you'd have to believe she was all about offing her true love,"

Elwin piled on.

"But if she believed her true love was about to run off with a dinosaur," growled Chief Constable Williams, "maybe she murdered him! Maybe she decided that if she can't have him, nobody can! Wait! Bloody hell! Now you've got me spewin' total nonsense not worth an ant's poo!"

"So little time together, after I grew to really appreciate Gerwyn! This separation is almost more than I can bear," panted Robin. She seemed on the verge of hyperventilation. "And know this," she addressed the chief constable most severely. "Say his affections were drawn another person's way. I care for his happiness so much, I would have learned to let him go! Murder would have been the thing after the last thing on my mind!"

"Ms. Pugh, what is that you said about 'separation'?" asked Chief Constable Williams with sudden animation, pouncing on that single word.

Robin gave the chief constable what Augie took to be a deer-in-the-headlights look, until she burst out tearfully, "Separation until the next life, if we can realistically hope for reincarnation!" With an explosive sob, she buried her face in her hands.

Augie found himself guiltily wondering whether the sob was for real, or she was trying to cover over busting out laughing.

"I hope you're happy with yourself," Elwin Kneath addressed Chief Constable Williams admonishingly, while unnecessarily straightening his already perfectly straight bow tie as though, Augie mused, he'd gotten rumpled from beating up someone.

"If we might interrupt," said Scott, ducking his head in the front door, followed close behind by Stephen.

"It's no interruption at all, sirs, when you might be savin' me from losin' me bloody mind!" vented Williams. "Let's hear it!"

"Yes, well..." Scott thought better of asking what the chief constable alluded to. "...Stephen and I have located another set of rock outcroppings, underneath gorse bushes on the hillside below the Strumblehead lighthouse. They might be like the ones we lost track of inside the shoreline cave."

"We better hurry before they crawl away," snarked Stephen.

"Sorry to barge in on you like this, Guv'nah," said Assistant Constable Angharad Gruffudd, pushing past Scott and Stephen into the police station. "I just checked into a report from the Sheep's Shank Links. There's something you're goin' to have to see!"

"Definitely!" agreed Stephen.

Chapter 13

The putting green for the par three twelfth hole at the Sheep's Shank Links sat on a flat-topped hill.

While Assistant Constable Gruffudd led the way up the hill's steep footpath, Augie paused for a look heavenwards.

Fluffy cumulus clouds dotted the azure blue sky, almost as numerous as the sheep that dotted the countryside below. The square-shape Cloud Nine hovered amidst them, lost from direct view inside its generated mists.

Augie fantasized the par three being a mini version of one of those vast mesa plateaus in southern Venezuela that inspired Sir Arthur Conan Doyle's *Lost World* novel. Beside one of which plateaus, incidentally, part of his crew thought they might well have had a run-in with a camouflaged theropod dinosaur during their Brazilian expedition. Anyway, Augie could easily imagine a horse-face-sized reptilian visage peering down at him over the twelfth green's edge.

What peered down instead was a bright-eyed Alistair. The only thing keeping him from breaking into an equally bright smile was the seriousness of the circumstances, what with a possible murder afoot. He shouted, "Hurry on up here, mates! You won't believe what happened!"

"You're right," said Stephen in his ever-somber deep voice. "I most likely won't believe what you *think* happened."

On reaching the green, Augie took a breath-catching moment to look northward at Garn Fawr and other structures of ancient volcanic origin. They loomed many times larger than the hill he presently stood upon, and blocked the North Irish Sea from view. Complex geologic processes created this epic vista, processes that started hundreds of millions of years ago, near Antarctica!

Augie could only wonder what else might be happening underground that would prove totally astounding. But what could be any wilder than the bizarre tableau he beheld next?

Center of the carefully manicured green, not three yards from the pin, egg-sized, dark-brown blobs formed a pile, obviously some animal's prolific excrement. And embedded atop them, like the crown jewel, was a golf ball.

"That's not just any golf ball," gushed Alistair. "That's the very same brand I struck with my seven iron last night! That made a beeline for a long reptilian tail during the lightning flash! I feared kicking up too big a fuss at the time, lest I be labeled a kook! But I could have sworn the ball lodged in the creature's – how can I put this delicately? – its business end!"

"Exactly as happened decades ago," Elwin insisted, snapping his fingers. "Some bloke chipped his ball into a sheep's rear end, and then the sheep proceeded to deposit that ball on a green, within tap-in range of the cup!"

"Well I'm not sayin' it's *not* sheep poo we have here," said Assistant Constable Gruffudd. "But in my experience, it's certainly on the larger end of the scale."

"We don't know for sure that ball was Alistair's," pointed out Stephen.

"Unless you're willin' to say that's the only one of its brand ever produced. Would require a whole lot of proof before you ever convinced me, it would!" Assistant Constable Gruffudd testily addressed Alistair.

Alistair cowered before her onslaught while Stephen sighed rapturously.

"Um, can't argue with you there, Constable."

152 | David Taylor

"*Assistant* Constable," haughtily corrected Angharad Gruffudd.

"Yes, Assistant Constable, of course," timidly accepted Alistair. "What I wanted to add, if I might..."

"Nobody here is going to tackle you to the ground for it," snapped Assistant Constable Gruffudd.

"For which I am most grateful. So, I direct everyone's attention away from the poo sundae with the golf ball cherry on top, to these depressions in the green. They appear to be large, three-toed foot tracks, do they not?"

Assistant Constable Gruffudd bent down, hands to knees, to more closely inspect two of the tracks. "I'm not bein' funny, right? I have to wonder how a creature with tracks this large, if tracks indeed they be, hasn't left deeper impressions than these. And how we don't see dramatic signs of such a beast havin' ascended this steep hill, right? Such as matted-down foliage?"

"Assistant Constable Gruffudd," gushed Stephen, "the brilliance of your assessment is only, well, say this was the dinosaur my associates are clearly hoping it was. One would think that, besides deeper foot tracks from its massive weight, there would also be a crease along the ground, between the tracks, where the creature dragged its tail." Stephen thought better of how he really wanted to conclude his remark: *The brilliance of your assessment is only eclipsed by the buxom massiveness of your beauty!*

"Hold on there! I object!" protested Elwin Kneath raising his hand high.

"Still in court are we, Elwin?" quipped Nigel. He staggered about the green so that Augie worried he might accidentally tumble right over the edge. "Made the dinosaur your new client?"

"Well at least the sheep know which end their poo is supposed to exit from, unlike yourself, Nigel!" vented Elwin. "What I'm about is that the ground atop this hundred-million-year-old volcanic poo, if I'm not mistaken, is notably firm." For emphasis, he stomped the green's fringe with his booted foot. "It might take a whale-sized beast to make the sort of impression you're suggesting, it might! And look at all those broken heather and gorse branches on the foot path to the green! More than a few over-plump golfers with too many cans of Toohey's under their belt would have been required to make that trail! But one modestly proportioned dinosaur would certainly have done the trick, it would!"

"So, are ya goin' to complain we're not fully appreciatin' the artistry of your latest forgery, are ya, Elwin Kneath?!?" Nigel got in Elwin's face to ask.

Elwin's mouth dropped wide open. Whether from real or feigned indignant shock, Augie wasn't sure.

Either way, Scott piped up, "The firmness of this hill top is certainly something to consider. As for the tail dragging, I call your attention to recent anatomical research into theropod dinosaurs, the meat-eaters such as Allosaurus and Tyrannosaurus Rex. That research concludes they held their tails horizontal, did not drag them along the ground. Unless they were ill, perhaps."

"Wait," Robin looked away from the mound of poo, wide-eyed with dawning realization, seemingly. "If this pile was pooped here by the dinosaur that devoured my-" She fell to her knees before the poo, and looked as though she required every last ounce of her willpower not to gather it up in her arms as she cried, "GERWYN!!!" Then she buried her hands in her face, sobbing inconsolably, supposedly.

Stephen needed to get something off his chest, shout it from the hilltops. Fearful of coming off cruel, though, he didn't want Robin to hear him. And so, he settled with harshly whispering to Augie, "There is no creature that could have eaten that much, less than eighteen hours earlier, and already be expelling the resultant waste product."

"Unbelievable that I might be losin' out to that pile of poo," Nigel staggered over beside Angharad to mutter, out of everyone else's earshot. "You can let Kay know I said that, can't you? The first chance ya get?"

"Now why should I-"

Before the assistant constable could finish her question, Nigel interrupted loudly enough for general consumption. Lurching from side to side, he vented, "What I want to know is why some bloody dinosaur would go to all the trouble of climbin' this hill, simply to dump its load!"

"And why not more regularly, assuming this is a first?" piled on Stephen, hoping to make a good impression on Angharad. "And also assuming that wasn't a sheep you launched your golf ball at down on the beach, Alistair. We've been told of at least one precedent for a sheep, um, shedding a golf ball onto a golf course after it got stuck in an, um, inconvenient location."

"If I might play devil's advocate," interjected Sherman Peabody while with an oversized plastic doggie bag in hand, he plowed past everyone for a closer look at the golf-ball-ornamented pile of suspect poo.

"By devil's advocate, you mean advancing the ridiculous notion this nauseating mess provides evidence for surviving non-avian dinosaurs," Stephen stated more than asked.

"This is true," Sherman acknowledged. "Suppose a relic Stegosaur, or okay, a relic ceratopsian since we've yet to unearth any Stegosaur fossils from the late Cretaceous-"

"As we've yet to unearth a verified non-avian dinosaur fossil, of any type, dated any time after the late Cretaceous," Stephen voice-of-doomed, delightedly.

"Or of other creatures such as the Coelacanth we know have survived to the present day from over one hundred million years ago," Augie hastened to add.

"Well worth remembering," nodded Sherman. "And so, suppose a relic Triceratops eats a big meal of seaweed. Then she crawls underground to hibernate for an amazing length of time. And she wakes up to eat her next meal, or to mate, etc. only once every four hundred years or so. Such a life trajectory would certainly have helped her past whatever time it took for the Earth to warm back up sixty-five million years ago. That is, after an asteroid sent so much sunlight-blocking debris into the upper atmosphere, the planet was plunged into the worst ice age, ever."

"Then she also takes a dump every four hundred years, mate?" Nigel asked while still staggering about. "Okay, why on this particular hill?"

"Of course, a golf course green would not have been here four hundred years ago," Sherman reflected aloud, not the least rattled by Nigel's question. "And if you travel back far enough, this topography would have been significantly different. The pooper's great ancestors, whatever the pooper is, might have easily congregated in large numbers here to do their business. This, as assuredly as the monarch butterfly migrates to a particular cluster of trees in Mexico every winter. The reason for that is also lost in the mists of time, incidentally."

"Bloody hell, it just occurs to me," said Nigel, coming to a sudden halt in his constant staggering about. "Maybe a dragon woke up from centuries-long slumber. It would have had no problem at all landin' on this hilltop green. That would explain the absence of any obvious trail up this hill, aside from those broken twigs. And if it continued to flap its wings while doin' its messy business, that would have kept it rather light on its feet, wouldn't it? Its foot track impressions wouldn't have been too deep, just as we have here?"

"I guess that's proof beyond a shadow of doubt," said Stephen ultra sarcastically.

"I might have launched my golf ball into a dragon's anus," Alistair waxed rhapsodically, looking off dreamy-eyed.

"Sorry to say, speaking historically," cautioned Sherman. "The tales of dragons in Wales were apparently woven as stand-ins for animosities between various peoples. They didn't stem from handed-down stories of actual beastly encounters, aside from the occasional rare snake. And we've not heard anyone report the recent creature being airborne, or sporting wings. What I suggest is that everyone take a deep breath, and wait for my lab analysis of this, um, specimen."

With that, Sherman turned his plastic bag inside out to grab hold of a good quantity of the poo, golf ball included. Then he tied it up for bringing back aboard Cloud Nine.

While Robin blew kisses at Sherman's departing bag of poop, Stephen came up beside Augie. At the top of the footpath down the par three hill, he quietly asked, "Might I have a few minutes with you, Augustine?"

Totally misconstruing what Stephen was about, Augie reacted, "For once, Stephen, I strongly agree with you. I'm not sure we're not wasting precious hours here, as intriguing as the school boy's report was initially."

"No. I mean, not no, good; I'm glad you see it that way. It's about something else. Someone else."

"Oh?" *What have we here?*

"You're happily married, am I correct?"

"Not as much time together as we would like, but yes, I hope Vicky is still as thrilled with me as I am with her."

"How did it all start?"

Recollection put a wistful smile on Augie's face. "We found ourselves side by side in this college chemistry class. Well..." Augie cut himself off to give Stephen a bemused look, and said, "How about we take the shortcut, and talk about you asking the assistant constable on a date?"

"Have I been that obvious?"

"Assuming you weren't making puppy dog eyes at the pile of mystery poo, I figured it out fast."

"Okay, guilty as charged. What do you suggest I do?"

"Well, with any luck at all, we're going to try the coastal stake-out once more this evening. That should be under much better weather conditions save for an occasional stiff breeze from the cold front that went through. You could ask her out for a nibble beforehand, on the pretext that I wanted you to join her for the second surveillance tonight. Assuming, of course, some new lead on Gerwyn's disappearance doesn't require her attention."

"For a nibble on her ear? Wouldn't that be too soon in our relationship?"

Oh boy. "I was talking about a nibble as in a bite to eat, supper, that sort of thing," clarified Augie while thinking to himself, *Can't believe I'm having to deal with this!*

"Ah, that makes sense. Assuming she says yes, what do I say to her while we're waiting for our order?"

Oh my God. "Maybe you can whisper sweet skeptical dismissals in her ear."

"Seriously."

"Okay, seriously: Why can't you simply admit you fancy her, as they say here, and would like to get to know her better? If there are no reciprocal feelings, no big deal. She'll respond she'd prefer to keep your relationship strictly professional, related to our dinosaur search and the potential murder investigation. Or she might say she already has someone else, which true or not would amount to the same thing: no interest in you."

"What if she responds positively, but expresses skepticism I'm really interested in her?"

"Stephen, any sensible person is going to approach a potential for love and romance cautiously," Augie counseled Stephen, amazed at the silly grin Stephen got on his face accompanied by his ears flushing deep crimson.

"Okay," the color suddenly drained from Stephen's ears until they went nearly albino pale. His silly grin flipped upside down for him to go on, "What if she fears I'm a murderer, possibly Gerwyn's murderer? And that I want to get her alone on the stake-out to claim my next victim?"

"I think she's seen enough of you in action, that – talk about skepticism! She'd be as doubtful as anyone, that you could ever be a murderer."

"You really think I come off as not the murdering type?" Stephen gushed hopefully.

"Don't let it go to your head. Look, I'll see if I can ask around about whether Angharad is already spoken for."

"That would be- Oh, I'm sorry, Scott. You need a word with Augie? I'll see you," Stephen winked at Augie, then hurried off.

Augie suspected Stephen didn't want to give Scott the chance to ask about anything he might have overheard.

"Augie, I hope this isn't coming out of the blue for you," Scott started in, making Augie want to scream, *Now what?!?!* "But, your being a happily married man and all, there's one of our teamies I've been struggling with, um, I've already made a fool of myself, accidentally spilling my guts to Charly..."

"This is about Irene, isn't it?"

"You've cut right to the bone, excavating the fossil in record time!"

"Well look, I wouldn't be surprised if she doesn't already suspect."

"Really?"

"Really." *Oh my God, another lovelorn dinosaur searcher!* "There's no reason you can't team up with her for our stake-out tonight. If you'd like, I can make the assignment. It should be a perfect opportunity, in the privacy of that seaside cave, or gorse bush, to-"

"But I don't think Chief Constable Williams will want her left alone yet with anyone, even though he's released her from custody."

"Is Augustine Matias up here?" breathlessly panted Kay the school teacher, rapidly ascending the par three hill.

"We can talk later," Scott assured Augie, making a quick, embarrassment-fueled exit while Augie said, "Sure," and under his breath, "I can hardly wait."

Taking a huff-and-puff moment to catch her breath while Nigel staggered about in the background, Kay finally said, "Got here fast as I could after school let out, I did. Everyone knows about that poo on the green, and those large three-toed tracks as from a large dinosaur! Brilliant!" she enthused, noticing the impressions near what was left of the poo after Sherman scooped away a sample. "I just wanted to ask," she went on, sparing a fleeting sideways glance at Nigel, "Do you need me? Um, that is, for anything? Anything at all?"

What, is there something instinctive about the fall, that has all the lonely hearts gathering potential sweetie pies to keep snuggly warm for the winter? The same as squirrels gather nuts to keep themselves fed? "Well, there was something I need to know about the assistant constable."

"Yes?" Kay reacted with a mix of puzzlement, and mild alarm.

"Uh, is she attached, going with someone? I'm asking for a friend, I assure you."

"Oh my God! Oh my God! Don't tell me!" exclaimed Kay in disbelief, and once more sparing a sideways glance Nigel's way. "I had no idea she was your type! And after you insisted you're happily married! That's poo from a diseased sheep, that is!"

"No it's not, and yes I am! And no she's not!" was all

Augie could think to say, responding to Kay's three remarks in no uncertain terms, and reverse order.

"I'm not being funny about it, okay, Augie?! If I didn't fear that poo might contain remnants of poor Gerwyn, I'd shove your bloody face in it, I would! 'Asking for a friend'; that's the oldest *porkie* in the book! I'm so tamping angry, I'd feed you to the dinosaur, meself, if I knew where it was hiding!"

Right when Kay stomped off, Nigel staggered into view. Before Augie could ask him to wait on whatever he had to say, he confessed, "If I wasn't such a tosser, I'd try consolin' poor but ravishin' Robin meself, I would! But I am! A tosser, that is!"

Nigel's lurching about just happened to block Augie making even incremental progress off the hill-top green, for him to continue, "That's where you come in, Mr. Matias! And a good Welsh last name that is, burp!"

"Baaaa!!!"

"Sorry to interrupt, Nigel; that sounds like a bleating sheep nearby," said Augie. "But I don't see any."

Nigel made a quick look around, as anxious as he was to resume his own bleating. He spotted a small oval of white fluff alone on a hillside near Strumblehead Lighthouse. Then he said, pointing, "Well there you go, mate; probably desperate for companionship, himself."

"From that far away, we're hearing it that loud?" Augie asked, stunned. Though gradually less so, the more he thought on it.

"I've heard whale calls carried on wind blowin' off the North Irish Sea. They must have been from ten, twenty miles out, soundin' like fog horns. And they were so loud, those bloody large blokes might as well have been groanin' right beside me! If I can get back to me wee bit of an ask, though. I couldn't help overhearin' you advise your mate, the one who doesn't believe anythin' exists that isn't slappin' him in the face. That is, advisin' him on affairs of the heart, how to go about strikin' the love match without burnin' off his manhood. And I was just wonderin'-"

"Help!?"

"Hold there, Nigel," interrupted Augie, raising a hand. "Mixed in with the surf, did you hear a cry for help that sounded a little tentative?"

Nigel froze mid stagger, to lend a more careful listen.

"Help, I say! Well, not actually 'help' as in: Someone's trying to push me off a cliff to my doom. That is, unless I'm lucky enough to miss the rocks completely, and hit nothing but sea, plus get me bearings fast enough to swim to shore before I drown! Rather, 'Help!' as in: A definite spot of bother, though to be truthful about it, not sure I'm suffering any more than a bad sprain, if that! So maybe 'Help!' is not the precise word I'm seeking. Perhaps the phrase, 'I am in desperate need of' - Well maybe not as desperate as were I sinking into quicksand..."

"YCH A FI, RUPERT HAMSTER HOLMES!!!" Nigel screamed beyond disgusted. "I'VE GOT A GOOD BEAD ON WHERE YOU'RE LOCATED!! SO IN EXCHANGE FOR YOUR SHUTTIN' YOUR FLY TRAP RIGHT NOW, WE WILL BE THERE TO RESCUE YOU ASAP!!"

Rupert went silent for the duration of Augie and Nigel making it all the way back down the par three hillside. But then Augie could have sworn he heard more from the fellow, carried ever-so-faintly on a stiff breeze. "Forgive me saying that 'rescue' puts too fine a point on it, perhaps. Though I most certainly don't want to detract any from a sense of urgency, well maybe not urgency..."

Augie turned Nigel's way to emphatically ask, "What was that you were wondering, Nigel?" *Please distract me!*

Chapter 14

On a gorse-and-heather-covered hillside that led down to the North Irish Sea, Augie beheld an unnerving sight. The head of Rupert Hamster Holmes appeared to lie on the ground, all by itself. But it exclaimed happily, "Well there you are, finally! Or rather I should amend that to say, 'There you are, rapidly transitioning to here'!"

Rupert's head was still attached to the rest of his body, and comfortably so, appearances to the contrary aside. That was, unless Rupert had become another artificial intelligence entity, like Charly, and could disassemble into several independently mobile pieces, head included, then reassemble none the worse for wear.

As Augie and company did indeed transition from "there" to "here," they could see Rupert stood up to his neck in a deep hole. That's what facilitated the gruesome illusion of decapitation.

"You're late," continued the relievedly talkative Rupert Hamster Holmes. "Well not so much late as a trifle bit delayed, given how much time it must have taken you to arrive here from wherever you were. Which is to say, I will be ever so thankful, absolutely no modification of that sentiment necessary, for whatever you can do to extricate me from this predicament I literally fell into. It happened from one moment to the next, on account of my full concentration, whilst roaming this beauteous Pembrokeshire countryside, on glimpsing any least saurian presence that might dare reveal itself from the North Irish Sea. Well maybe not full concentration, as the occasional seagull caw lifted my regard heavenwards, though-"

"Bloody hell, Rupert!" angrily interrupted Nigel, resisting an impulse to boot Rupert's head as though it were a soccer ball. "Did you not stoop down at all to take the full measure of your situation?"

"How so?"

"'How so?' You bend at your waist and knees to lower yourself! That's how bloody so!!"

"How much should I bend? A wee bit, or a wee bit more than a wee bit?"

"All the bloody way, you tosser!"

"Well that sounds- Isn't that rather extreme? And no need for insults, Mr. Morgan, sir."

Augie imagined if Nigel were a tea kettle, the whistle would be on full blast.

"You have to bend down all the bloody way, Mr. Holmes, sir!" Nigel snarled to mock the politeness his "Mr. Holmes, sir" suggested. "That is, if you've a mind to see what I'm talkin' about!"

"Well! I'll have you know that such precipitous action runs counter to every last fiber- Oh, how about this!"

Rupert found that when he bent all the way down, there was a big enough hole in the side of the hill for him to simply crawl out through, which he proceeded to do.

"My, my, my," Rupert chuckled while brushing bits of bramble and strands of cobweb off his pants and vest. "Of all the unexpected delights I've ever experienced! This most blessedly facile exit from a seemingly unmanageable predicament, where handling it all on my own was concerned, has to rate, if such things are to be rated, um...Excuse me, does anyone have a clue, or at least a suspicion, whether strong, weak, or something in between, where I was going with my previous sentence?"

"We'll get back to you on that," Irene snarked. She was among others besides Scott and Nigel drawn towards Rupert's cries for help.

Elwin, pondering the hole in the ground Rupert just exited, said, "I must admit to not having been aware of this particular sentry burrow. There are a couple of these further up the coast, also overlooking the sea. An Oxford group recently established they are among the oldest human structures in all the United Kingdom. They date back close to seven thousand years ago, even older than the Pentre Ifan stones."

"Bloody hell, Elwin!" Nigel cursed anew, staggering in between him and the burrow to look him right in the eye. "How do you know so much about a hole in the ground?!"

As he was often wont to do, Elwin produced an official-looking document from a pocket inside his dapper, dark-green-dyed woolen suit jacket. And he proudly announced, "I happen to be a founding representative, I'll have you know, of the World Archaeological Consortium, as it states here in most artistically rendered Gothic lettering!"

"I thought it was the World Archaeological Congress," interjected Stephen.

"Ah, yes, that; we have a bone to pick with them," haughtily reacted Elwin.

"We" being yourself, and the voice in your head, Stephen thought to himself while asking, "Would that bone to pick have to do with their being officially recognized, while you're not?"

"Is that a fossilized bone that needs pickin'? I thought you'd rather have had a nose to pick with the International Bodily Orifices Society, instead. Cheers, everyone! Burp!" John Jones concluded, lifting his latest can of Toohey's to the sunny blue sky.

"Check under this gorse bush here!" called out Scott, crouched beside the large, thorny plant blooming citrus orange all over. "But careful you don't shred your hands and arms on these razor-sharp thorns.

"Wow," wowed Augie merely from giving the gorse his attention, before he could get anywhere near it. "I can see from here that those could be like the beach cave stones, but buried up to their tippy tops."

"Let me see that this isn't another fart in a jam jar," grumbled Angharad Gruffudd. She made everyone part like the Red Sea for her to stomp past them, Scott mused.

"While I officiate," Elwin insisted, though backing away himself, lest the assistant constable bulldoze him.

"Mm-hm, mm-hm," Assistant Constable Gruffudd nodded knowingly from a semi-crouch. Then she rose back up to her full, imposing stature to announce, "Looks to me like an outcroppin' of the same blue stone the Druids hauled east to assemble Stonehenge, millennia ago. Erosion must have washed away enough soil to expose it, despite the gorse."

"Wow," Stephen sighed dreamily.

"Her default to conventional explanations is such a big turn-on for you-know-who," Irene whispered to Augie. "They could make beautiful debunking together."

Laura Gómez looked up from her copious note-taking to ask, "Is it possible that those millennia ago, the Druids or whoever noticed this outcropping? And posted what you called a sentry burrow to guard it until excavation? Yet never quite got around to that?"

"Augie," jumped in Roberta Quiñones, "did you happen to notice whether those stones that looked like oversized Stegosaurus plates in the shoreline cave might have been blue stone?"

"Way too dark to tell," Augie shook his head. "And they were very slimy. If they were blue stones, their blueness was covered over by moss and the like."

"What if there is a large creature with plates across its back, camouflaged as blue stone? And once or twice every few millennia or so, it unearths itself? For a feeding followed by a poop where the, uh, pile was discovered? Only to bury itself again, for several centuries more? And the sentry was posted here to send early warning of its next awakening?"

"Sure," nodded Stephen, going on sarcastically, "and what if pixies magically transformed their fairy dust into that pile of excrement on the hilltop green, to throw pixie hunters off their trail?" On a sidelong glance stolen at Angharad as he concluded, Stephen was delighted to see a broad grin break out.

Scott closed his eyes to shake off Stephen's usual deprecation before he asked, "Can we assign at least two people to this hillside tonight? To keep an eye on the coastal water for the schoolboy's creature-"

"And also make sure those stones underneath the gorse don't exhume themselves to go crawlin' off?!" John Jones scoffingly concluded Scott's question. "Egads, I usually require at least five shots of whiskey before I see somethin' like that! Cheers!"

This time, John Jones's can of Toohey's lifted high was lost from view, for he tripped over a ground bramble, and fell amidst a stand of heather.

Assistant Constable Gruffudd shrugged her shoulders as in: Nothing she hadn't already seen from John Jones on numerous prior occasions. Then she said, "I am well aware this is the agreed-upon tradeoff: We help you lot from out of town with your dinosaur search, and you help us with our murder investigation. But I'm not bein' funny about it, right? I think you're not only barkin' up the wrong tree here. I'm still not convinced the particular tree you want to bark up is anywhere out there in the first place."

Stephen nearly fainted in ecstasy.

"But okay, we help you out, you help us out, and maybe we both benefit. We find our murderer, or whoever has otherwise made Gerwyn unavailable to us since last night, and you find- Well again, I think you're chasin' after a fart in a jam jar, I do. Be that as it may, though, I understand you lot want to keep an eye on those blue stones continuin' to sit there twiddlin' their non-existent thumbs. It comes down to this: Are there also enough people to keep an eye on each other, to stymy the likely murderer, or kidnapper, out of anything more than revealin' himself, or herself?"

"I should be able to help in that regard," offered Sherman Peabody, trudging up the hill from the inland side. His artificial intelligence entity, Charly, followed stiffly behind, though wearing a very sporty-looking velvet-shaded windbreaker. "First, though, the latest on my lab analysis of the poo of undetermined origin."

"What I always knew this search was going to come down to: shit," Stephen cursed, emboldened by the presence of the most alluring kindred skeptic, Angharad.

"Not necessarily," said Sherman, making a rare chin lift off his neck to look Stephen in the eye. "Anyhow, the bad news is that at least so far, my content analysis suggests nothing special. There's the same sort of digested plant matter I found in the sample of known sheep poo so generously supplied to me by a local farmer. It's very true that there are also traces of partly digested seaweed. But my understanding is that it is not unknown for the occasional sheep to wander down to the coastline, and nibble at kelp washed ashore. On the other hand, who knows what happens in the dead of night? Assume our wished-for dinosaur does thrive here, most likely herbivorous if indeed it's the sauropod young David Taylor thought he saw. Or a relic Stegosaur with those large, narrow, stone-like things on its back, that seem to have migrated away from the coastal cave, that some of us hid behind until rising storm waters chased us back outside. Could it be that in the darkness, such a beast partakes of the vast Welsh hillside pastures?"

"Is there any good news, Sherman?" Augie asked

impatiently.

"Good news, potentially, yes," enthused Sherman, struck all over again by the hopeful prospect. "The very same finding of nothing other than partly digested plant matter in the mystery poo also means there is nothing discovered, at least so far, of a fleshy character. Meaning that whatever relieved itself on the hilltop green might not have eaten Gerwyn. If he was devoured by some fearsome creature, as Robin seems so sure she saw start to happen, maybe it was not by this whatever-it-was. Of course, not quite enough time might have elapsed yet for Gerwyn to have been fully digested."

"One thing I do have to say about Robin's report," admitted Augie. "It has me wondering why none of us, not even Robin, heard the blood-curdling scream you would expect from a monster reptile biting into someone."

"Like when a Great White Shark takes a chomp out of someone's leg, you mean. An experience I've been most fortunate to avoid up to now, burp!"

"Exactly, Nigel. With the local acoustics, we could hear Rupert Holmes calibrate how strongly to cry for assistance as clear as day, from much further away than Gerwyn would have been."

"But we are talking about smack in the middle of a wicked thunder bumper, mind you," pointed out Elwin Kneath. "At times, that storm made such a racket, it would have drowned out the seven horns of Jericho, it would!"

"So maybe it drowned out Gerwyn's blood-curdlin' screams. Egads!" exclaimed the ever-staggering-about Nigel Morgan. "Me thinks a plaque needs to be mounted here to commemorate the one time that Elwin Kneath made a valuable observation! About anything!"

"Mr., um-"

"Sherman Peabody."

"Mr. Peabody," proceeded Angharad Gruffudd, "did I

not hear you claim you could help us juggle keepin' an eye on all the many potential murder suspects this evening? The same time your lot watches that these blue stones don't suddenly magically crawl off?"

"I did indeed, Assistant Constable Gruffudd. Charly here, my artificial intelligence entity, I've reprogrammed him to look out for any murderous human activity at the same time he seeks evidence of non-avian dinosaur survival."

"Ah, so he is robotic. That's a far better prospect than continuin' to feel sorry for him comin' off as the stiffest, coldest human being I've ever encountered. However, I'm not bein' funny, right? As one entity, as you call him, how is he goin' to do better than any of the rest of us, at keepin' an eye on so many locations at the same time?"

"That's right. You were not here last night; it was rather your chief constable-"

"Who is askin' around our village as we speak, to discover what anyone else might know."

"Yes, good. Anyway, you didn't get to see Charly not only keep an eye out, but several other parts of him as well. Each is equipped with its own mobility, vision, hearing and recording device. They can spread far and wide up and down the coast. Charly, can you demonstrate?"

Click...whirr... "Yes I can."

"Very good."

A full half-minute elapsed, nothing happening save for a lone seagull cawing as it circled overhead.

Something dawned on Sherman, giving him a noticeable start. With impatient irritation, he said, "Charly, in reference to what we just discussed, please demonstrate."

Click...whirr... "Consider it done."

With that, Charly's head sank steadily groundward as his feet, ankles, legs, knees and the rest disassembled into a multitude of independently mobile units. Some remained more recognizable as their original parts than others such as the torso, which became so many identical cubes on wheels.

As Charly was fully clothed, most parts had to crawl scurrying out of his pant legs and shirt cuffs, leaving his outfit in a shapeless heap on the bramble-strewn soil.

"However long I live, I never imagined livin' long enough to witness a sight such as this! Heavens!" gasped the assistant constable.

This wasn't Augie's first time viewing the peculiar spectacle. Nevertheless, it unsettled him enough, he only grew aware of the soft whir from an approaching electric golf cart mere seconds before it climbed the hillside ridge over to the coastal face, crunching across low-lying heather.

The golf cart was clearly marked COURSE MARSHAL on its hood, and flew the Sheep's Shank Links flag featured atop every flag pin. Said flag depicted a golf club held by a sheep standing upright on its two hind legs.

"Ych a fi!" exclaimed the fellow driving the cart, of such ample girth that he took up the entire seat. "Did none of you lot hear that foursome back there complainin' after you?!"

"Now calm down, Oliver," Angharad advised the fellow in her usual husky voice backed by her imposing stature. "You're not goin' to want to be like a dog with two willies over the coastal breezes carryin' their racket the opposite direction from us! What would they have been complainin' for, anyway?"

"You bloody lot left some of the sheep poo on the green! Thanks to that, three of their four balls landed directly in it! Even worse, they think one of them might otherwise have rolled right up to the pin for an ace!"

"The person we spoke with at the clubhouse," explained Laura, "said it made no difference whether we took a sample for testing, or just left it all there. Once we were gone, your maintenance guy would clean up before he reopened that hole."

"There will be words with him, there will!" raged the course marshal. "In the meantime, what is this mess you scattered across the hillside?! Looks like some careless children left their toys layin' about, small enough for sheep to accidentally choke on when they're grazin'! You better pick it up, as I'm not goin' to be askin' maintenance to do that after they deal with the poo!"

"Time to reassemble, Charly," ordered Sherman.

Charly's two hundred autonomously mobile parts reconverged on the artificial intelligence entity's abandoned clothes. They returned crawling through pant legs and jacketed shirt arms back into place, rebuilding the entire robotic body to its full height. As they did so, the course marshal's eyes grew bigger and bigger, until he grumbled nervously, "Glad this is all sorted out. Hope none of me nieces or nephews ask for that for Christmas. If you'll excuse me, I need to go have a tidy word with the course maintenance supervisor. Need to give him what ho for not cleanin' up the twelfth green, soon as you lot left!"

By the time he finished what he had to say, the vastly proportioned fellow had turned his golf cart completely around, and was headed back over the hill ridge to the inland side.

"Too bad he didn't wait long enough for me to discuss the commercial potential of a relic plant-eating dinosaur making their twelfth green a bathroom migration site," lamented Alistair. "I might try to have a word with their maintenance guy, myself. Just hope the marshal doesn't go too hard on him."

"Extremely doubtful, that is!" slobbered John Jones, waving about his latest can of Toohey's seemingly to balance himself, keep from keeling over. "He *is* their maintenance guy. Cheers!"

"So why did he say- Oh never mind."

"Don't know about you two," Sergeant Fred Frankly muttered to fellow time travelers Ali Magabu and Kevin Smith-Park. "But far as I'm concerned, this would be a good time for our starship to carry us off, before it feels like we've skipped over entirely into the Twilight Zone. Getting way too crazy here."

Fred did not speak softly enough to evade staggering-about Nigel's ever-attentive ears. "Attention, everyone, you should have heard what this tosser just said!" Nigel vented. "And I quote, 'This would be a good time for our starship to carry us off'! Then he complained that we're the ones gettin' too crazy! Egads!! Anyone want to throw a crop circle into the mix while we're at it?!?"

Chapter 15

Nigel came into view, out from behind an especially large gorse bush on the hillside down to the Pembrokeshire coast near Strumblehead Lighthouse. He did not create quite the stir Augie would have expected from a roaming Stegosaurus making a likewise dramatic appearance. But still, his tartan suit jacket, a patchwork quilt of violets and pinks, clashed sharply with the blazing reds and yellows of fall foliage. His hair looked freshly washed, combed neatly down the middle, no longer tousled and greasy like every previous time Augie saw him stagger into view. And he didn't stagger into view, rather stepped spritely.

"Trying to impress the non-existent dinosaur?" Stephen snarked in a quiet aside to Sergeant Frankly.

Not so quietly, though, that John Jones couldn't hear him clearly. He subsequently bellowed, "Careful there, mate! Robin is not accustomed to bein' called a non-existent dinosaur! Cheers!"

Robin buried her face in her hands, and ran off with what impressed Augie as a very peculiar shrieky whimper. He had a fleeting impression he discounted out of hand, that it was actually more of a suppressed chuckle than reignited grief over the fate she claimed to have seen Gerwyn suffer. *How could I entertain such a ghastly thought?*

Nigel stomped over beside John Jones, and got in his face to growl, "I'm tellin' you this, Johnny Jones, I am! You're lucky I'm not a violent man!"

"Otherwise, you would have spilled me Toohey's all over meself, would you? On the way to my shovin' it up your smartly dressed arse? Cheers!" John Jones fearlessly drunkenly toasted Nigel with his beer.

"Well even though I'm not a violent man, think I could make an exception, you keep talkin' like that! Then you'd have a tough time shovin' your Toohey's anywhere, 'cause it was already scrunched so far up your nostrils, it was pokin' out your ears!"

"Careful there, mate!" cautioned John Jones, playfully holding up an arm in a self-defense he knew wasn't necessary. "That's some pretty fierce threat you're makin', what with a murderer about!"

"I don't have time for your sheep farts, Johnny! Robin has gone off all upset again, thanks to your insensitivity!" Nigel shouted as he followed after the woman who he appeared to have a special thing for, even while she still grieved the gruesome loss of Gerwyn.

"Sorry I'm so late; had an especially messy classroom to sort out," apologized Kay Jones. She hurried down the hill so soon after Nigel vanished past the gorse, felt to Augie like they were changing shifts. "Have I missed anything? Oh, what happened to our robot mate?"

Kay referenced Charly. He stood statuesquely still, missing his left arm below the elbow, plus his left ear.

"Some members of our team have already taken up monitoring posts down the coast," explained Augie. "And parts of Charly equipped with cameras and independent mobility accompanied them. They'll be watching for any real-life Welsh dragons, as well as any enterprising murderers."

"That's proper, that is," nodded the schoolteacher approvingly. Then looking around she added, "Did Nigel leave with them?"

"He chased after a very distraught Robin; I believe his heart went out to her," Elwin Kneath remarked.

"Along with Charly's left ear! It might have to serve as their chaperone! Cheers!" John Jones raised his newly-popped-open beer can for yet another toast. "But now that you're here, Ms. Jones, the dinosaur that was waitin' for you can come out into the open! Let's see you, you bloody Hide'n'seekasaurus, you! Belch!"

John Jones kept his can raised a bit too long. A seagull swooped down, grabbed it from his hand, and flew off, spilling Toohey's in his face as he ran after it to no avail.

Augie eyed the seagull's flight along the coast, stunned at the ease by which it made off with the beer can. He told himself he better guard well the chocolate chip scone burning a hole in his pocket since he bought it at the Kelpyguard Bakery (along with a bag of miniature Welsh cakes). That is, if he ate it during the next stakeout.

Onward, Augie noticed the full moon already visible if ghostly pale, rising off the east horizon inland. Nothing unusual, if very picturesque, about that. But just to one side, he saw what he would have described as equally ghostly swirls, as though a drain had impossibly opened into the heavenly firmament.

"Sherman?" Through a small microphone affixed to his windbreaker collar, Augie addressed Sherman Peabody.

Sherman presently remained alongside Samuel Longbottom plus Harry and Harriet Letterman, as well as a most reclusive Bernie Coleman, back aboard Cloud Nine. With that overhead view of the Pembrokeshire coastline for the stake-out, Sherman hoped to help direct fellow searchers down below. And also marshal Charly's many autonomous parts to converge wherever necessary.

"Beside the moon-"

"Sherman here, Augie, and presuming I mindread you correctly, no, the answer is no. That is not an odd cirrus formation beside the moon. In fact, a portion of its swirl looks lost from view *behind* the moon."

"Which means it's farther away from us than the moon," concluded Augie.

"A certain astrophysicist back aboard our starship could

likely have told us loads more about it," interjected Kevin Smith-Park, walking over beside Augie. Kevin was accompanied by fellow time traveler Fred Frankly, and Charly's independently mobile ankle. "But from what little I understand, I'd guess something large perturbed a local wormhole. Like ripples from a stone dropped in the water."

"Hot damn! Maybe the Smoke and Mirrors is about to emerge for our salvation from Crazytown?" enthused Fred.

"I think Buddy would tell us that whatever it is, it must be a good deal larger than the Smoke & Mirrors, to make that much of a visible disturbance."

"An extra-large flying giraffe to return you to the land of mind-reading trees and, doubtless, numerous pots of gold at the end of the rainbow? That's your salvation from 'Crazytown'?" snarked Stephen.

"Mr. Feldman," barged in Assistant Constable Gruffudd, "I'm not sure I want to know what THAT was all about. But I would appreciate your clear-headed companionship for what I must say is the strangest stake-out for a murderer I've ever known. I'm not bein' funny, right?"

"Before they're done, they'll think they've spotted a crop circle on the beach," Augie could hear Stephen saying to Angharad Gruffudd as the two trudged towards the shoreline.

Charly's right hand scurried after them like an especially large tarantula.

"Ha! That's a knee-slapper, that is!" Angharad laughed like she meant it, Augie sensed. *Stephen might not need my dating tips nor anyone else's, if she really finds him that entertaining.*

"Whether a perturbed wormhole or something else, I've lost sight of it," reported Sherman. "My more immediate concern is with a fog bank only a few miles offshore. Hopefully it will stay put for our second night of surveillance."

"Or hopefully it will not stay put," suggested Augie. "Remember the sighting young Mr. Taylor had, what brought us out here in the first place? That was on a foggy morning."

"True."

*

Stephen felt awkward, crouched down beside Assistant Constable Angharad Gruffudd, and hidden behind heather overlooking the Pembrokeshire coastline. They were both well aware that Charly's hand was stationed atop the heather. There, it kept a robotic eye and ear on their well-being, in addition to scrutinizing their surroundings for non-avian dinosaurs. But Stephen feared Charly's hand might let the whole world know, were he to let slip his feelings for Angharad. Consequently, he limited his communication to such mundane remarks as, "There's something about a bracing sea-air chill that doesn't feel as cold as inland chill."

"I've noticed that also, I have," Angharad agreed.

Stephen wondered whether she strained not to reveal in front of the hand that his feelings were reciprocated.

Awkward indeed. And an odd swirl in the twilight sky rendered Stephen lost for words. What could he say about it that would continue to impress Angharad with him as "clear-headed companionship"?

For endless-seeming moments where Angharad was concerned, a tense silence was broken only by the rhythmic, gently crashing surf and the odd seagull.

"It really is amazing," Stephen finally spoke up, "how easily our senses can be fooled. Just now, I would have sworn I saw something like a cosmic drain open beside the rising moon. But I know that can't be."

"Egad! I saw the same thing, and had the same thought as you! Makes me feel a wee bit better, actually, that even with your brilliant powers of observation, you're as flummoxed as I am. Or are you?" Angharad turned Stephen's way, worried she might have offended him.

"No, you're correct. Although I think we agree it has to be an optical illusion. Maybe cirrus clouds, upper atmosphere ice crystals, were blown about by swirling jet-stream currents in a certain special way."

"Or eye floaters? No, how stupid of me!" she laughed in a girlishly high-pitched voice new to Stephen. "How could we both have floaters in our eyes at the same time?"

"Hey, not stupid of you at all," earnestly pushed back Stephen, pained to hear Angharad deprecate herself. "That wouldn't be the strangest coincidence ever. And is certainly far more likely than an actual drain opening in outer space!"

"This is what I need you...um...here for, that is," she said, her eyes riveted on his. "It *could* be some other phenomenon altogether, couldn't it? A trick of the eye caused by the early moon in the sky, perhaps?"

The crashing surf grew loud enough, Stephen found himself feeling reckless. Counting on the seaside din to drown out his words for anyone who reviewed the recording from Charly's detached hand, he said, "Well one thing that is no trick of the eye, Angharad, is your beauty."

"What was that?" Gruffudd asked, since the surf made an especially loud racket just when Stephen got to the meat of his remark.

"Uhh, what did you think I said?"

"I'm not sure it's worth repeatin'." *Couldn't have possibly been what I thought I heard, glory be!*

Eyeing Charly's disembodied hand like it was a cobra about to strike, Stephen leaned towards Angharad Gruffudd. And up on his tippy toes so he could reach far enough, having to do that despite his own, lanky height, he whispered, "Acknowledgement of your beauty is definitely something well worth repeating, my dear."

Angharad reared her head away from Stephen to say, "Well is it, now?"

"Not so loud. Whether or not that's a dinosaur," he pointed down towards the shoreline, "you might scare it away before we get a good look."

"Say what?"

Stephen's ruse worked. The camera embedded in detached hand's thumb turned seaward.

Stephen whipped off his windbreaker, and tossed it over the artificially intelligent body part, covering the camera lens. Quickly thereafter, he gave Angharad a peck on her cheek...and hoped the crew aboard Cloud Nine would never know what they were missing. Driftwood mistaken for a sea serpent, etcetera... Certainly there was enough of that for them not to bother with one of Charly's widely dispersed cameras suddenly blacking out.

"I'm not bein' funny, right? What did you go and do that for, Mr. Feldman?"

"I'm happy you remember my last name. But I'd be even happier if you called me Stephen. And know that I want you, every square inch of you."

Hands to her waist, Angharad arched her left eyebrow to say, "Well do you, now? I'm mighty skeptical of that, and will require far more than a wee bit of corroborative evidence, I will!"

With that, she lifted Stephen in her arms so he could plant his lips on hers.

*

Augie found Kay's distracted demeanor most puzzling, though also gratefully relieving. When she jumped at the chance to be by his side for the second night's dinosaur vigil on the Pembrokeshire coast, there was no good way to argue a third should join them, Laura for example. They were not spread thin enough as it was, if they were to keep an unbroken watch on so many miles of shoreline. But Augie dreaded being all alone with Kay behind gorse. Or, as it turned out, beside the gorse-covered, mostly-buried blue-stone formation he was only ninety-nine percent sure wasn't part of a Stegosaur-type dinosaur in hibernation for millennia. He feared he might have to fend her off. True, not many hours earlier, she seemed super upset with him, had stormed off mistakenly believing he had the hots for Assistant Constable Gruffudd. *But someone might have set her straight in the meantime.*

While awaiting the full sunset, Augie prattled on nervously about the golf-ball-embedded pile of mysterious poo found on an elevated par three green at the Sheep's Shank Links. Happily, though, Kay Morgan looked all around like she was impatiently expecting a bus.

"I better be quiet now, with nightfall here," concluded Augie. "Hopefully the full moon will highlight anything of interest, and that fog bank will stay put out there."

"Let's hope," responded Kay vaguely, leaving him to wonder whether she was referring to the moon and the fog bank…or just wishing he'd shut up. *Maybe she still thinks I'm ready to dump my wife for the assistant constable, after all. But she's setting aside her personal animosity to get to the bottom of what has really happened to Gerwyn.*

Whatever, there was enough moonlight to make out the fog bank offshore. It stretched like a fluffy gray wall from horizon to horizon.

Kay seemed satisfied to have a long silence prevail between her and Augie as they waited for something absolutely incredible to make its presence known. A long, serpentine neck lifting out of the sea would have done wonderfully, where Augie was concerned.

Instead, he found himself focused on a thick strand of washed-ashore seaweed lying beside a driftwood log with branch stubs worn down to sharp spikes. Both sat so close to the surf, the encroaching tide gradually made them float, more and more. Would the tide come in far enough to carry them back out to sea?

Adding to this intrigue was a curious, what Augie supposed was an optical illusion. The driftwood as much as the seaweed undulated like a snake, even the portion still firmly grounded on dry land.

"Oh, crappadoodledo, here's the fog," lamented Augie; the first wisps of condensed water vapor were drifting in amidst the seeming seaweed and driftwood.

That's when the seaweed undulated so much, Augie wondered, *How did it do that?* It swept skyward, then slapped the restless sea with a splash distinct from the din of crashing surf.

The driftwood undulated off the water's surface as well, and slapped against the skyward-sweeping seaweed like they were the tails of two beasts engaged in combat.

As the encroaching fog bank obscured that bizarre spectacle, Augie would have sworn he saw three stony plates break the water's surface, just out past the driftwood.

Something about how the seaweed and driftwood undulated, impossibly so in the driftwood's case. I've seen it before, but where? Augie wondered, vexed. And he uneasily noticed the trudge of someone or something approaching. This, even as the fog thickened so much, the moon overhead was lost from view. *Don't tell me I'm going to be the monster's next meal! Well at least Kay isn't using this as an excuse to cling to me.*

To Augie's exhaled relief, Chief Constable Rhys Williams emerged from the dense fog.

"*Ych a fi* with this damnable fog, I say!" Williams complained. "Sorry, Mr. Matias. I understand your fancy robot dissolved into a mechanical herd of surveillance mice spread up and down this coastline. But I don't see that they will be able to give early warning now. Makes no bloody difference whether Gerwyn's murderer or kidnapper is a human, which I'm sure of, or your prehistoric survivor. How to detect anything in this murky mist? Afraid we need to call off the stake-out, at least until the fog-"

A deafening roar was punctuated by chirps as from a bird with its throat hooked up to an electric guitar amplifier, Augie imagined.

Chief Constable Williams found himself stunned silent, fearing wondrously what also worried Augie. *That can't be a beast's roar, can it?*

The roar, whatever its source, resolved into a thunderous CRASH, welcomed by Augie as an indication of maybe nothing more than noisy surf, after all.

No sooner welcomed, though, than the ground quaked.

Augie wondered whether he was really losing it, for he espied something impossibly enormous through the foggy mists. Whatever it was sank slowly below water, seaweed and driftwood alike enclosed by its pond-sized maw.

Augie wanted to note how sulfurous fishy the fog smelled, compared to when it first rolled in. But before he could let out a peep, there were two additional roars, but of a more raspy, less deafening nature. They came from not far down the coast. And somehow, they reminded Augie of Nigel's voice, even when he was sober. They were followed by a woman's shrill scream that ended in a loud crunch, nauseously sickening for what it implied. Curiously, though, it sounded to Augie very amplified, complete with electronic feedback.

Nevertheless, Augie and company found themselves paralyzed by shock and fear. Which company included the freshly arrived Irene, Scott, Laura and the time travelers.

Chief Constable Williams felt most relieved to see those familiar if curious characters. They lent a safety-in-numbers vibe. Yet he still fretted over a hubbub of scurrying low to the ground, to the point he turned on his flashlight.

The chief constable's flashlight revealed a motley crew of disembodied feet, ankles, an elbow, upper and lower legs and arms, as well as cubical units from Charly's torso. They were racing like a herd of so many panic-stricken farm animals in the direction from where the screams, roars, and crunchy munches issued.

"We need to stay together for venturin' through this confoundin'ly thick and fetid fog," the chief constable commanded. Then into his walkie-talkie, "Assistant Constable Gruffudd, can you report in? Assistant Constable Gruffudd? *Ych a fi*, where ARE you, Gruffudd?" he vented.

That's when Elwin Kneath materialized out of the mists, from the direction of the terrorizing racket. "Oh, good, this is where you are," he sighed in apparent relief. "The shrillness of that woman's blood-curdling scream, the visceral quality of that munching noise...And all of that after something took such ponderously heavy steps, the very earth shook...There can be no question as to the authenticity of what we heard."

What, are you jealous you didn't counterfeit it yourself, like that dinner coupon? Irene so wanted to snark. She didn't, in respect for the gruesomeness of a situation where someone might have been heard crying out in the awful throes of being munched to death.

Before anyone could follow up Elwin's remarks, Rupert Hamster Holmes emerged from the fog bank next, higher up the coast-facing hill. "Ah, well at least you lot are safe, or maybe not so much safe as at least temporarily spared from not being safe," he prattled on. "Especially after hearing what sounded like someone or something biting into bone, or maybe it was crunching twigs underfoot. Twigs underfoot could well simulate bone-munching for

184 | David Taylor

impressionable ears, prone to make the dreaded worse out of all they hear. Whatever it was, thereafter I felt pursued. Or maybe it was merely another bloke like ourselves, coincidentally travelling my same direction without having any least intention of following me. Indeed, I am reminded of an especially damp and dreary evening in downtown Kelpyguard when I stayed out rather later than-"

"Sh!" crisply ordered Chief Constable Williams as the assorted lot headed down the coast, Rupert running to keep up. "Do you hear that?"

Everyone paused mid-step for a more careful listen. They were rewarded by the sound of heavy panting. Some ghastly creature taking labored breaths as it raced across the heather-covered seaside wilderness? That's what Augie wondered nervously.

"Hold on; what do we have here?" Chief Constable Williams grumbled wearily. His flashlight revealed a constable's badge and a navy-blue jacket, strewn across a patch of gorse. But before he could fully process what he was seeing, the intensifying pants accompanied by noises of trampled underbrush suggested the whatever-it-was loomed menacingly closer. Top priority became for everyone to duck down out of sight behind the gorse and heather, the flashlight shut off.

Rupert and Elwin, though, tried to duck down behind each other, until Elwin stumbled on pebbles like ball bearings beneath his shoes. That sent him toppling backwards, and Rupert along with him going head over heels down the hillside trail.

To Augie, they sounded like a dislodged boulder caught in a landslide. He hoped they wouldn't avalanche themselves into the open maw of some impossibly large beast as he thought he glimpsed off shore.

But thanks to the fog bank's brief dissipation, a terrifying moonlit silhouette quickly eclipsed any concern for Rupert and Elwin.

Augie's heart skipped a beat, multiple times. What he saw looked for all the world like legs dangling limp from a reptilian monster's enormous mouth.

Is this finally it?! Scott wondered breathlessly, squat beside Augie. *Oh my God! Of all the dinosaurs to have possibly survived that major extinction event sixty-five million years ago! I never thought any of the meat-eating theropods had a chance, as reliant as they were on plentiful plant-eating dinosaurs!*

The awful silhouette dropped out of sight, yet the ominous-seeming commotion grew ever louder.

Chief Constable Williams made a snap judgement to turn his flashlight back on. Maybe the prehistoric monster would mistake the bright lens for a rival's eye, and be scared off. That is, assuming it didn't want to take a chance on a fellow dinosaur wrenching its gruesomely seized prey out from between its massive jaws.

Augie wondered whether Sherman and company back aboard Cloud Nine saw what was approaching, enhanced by infrared lens. And if they did, why they weren't giving him a heads-up.

Closer, closer, ever closer came the panting and trudging...

...until Angharad Gruffudd and Stephen Feldman, both totally buck naked, were in full view. Angharad carried Stephen slung over her right shoulder. His legs dangled forward like he might as well have been a big unwieldy bag of mulch, far as Augie was concerned. *In silhouette, oh my God, Angharad was the meat-eating dinosaur from whose hungry maw Stephen's legs dangled!*

"I'd ask you two whether you felt the earth move, but am guessing you would have mistaken that for something else," Irene couldn't help snarking loud enough for the whole world to hear.

"This isn't what it looks like!" moaned Stephen as in, he feared there was no reasonable way to deny it was exactly what it looked like. Hanging down behind Angharad's back, he yanked at his pants and shirt draped across the gorse, tearing them in the process.

"If you bloody blokes had an ounce of decency, you'd avert your eyes yesterday!" cried Angharad well beyond embarrassed. "And turn off that flashlight into the bargain, you would!" she concluded while finally pulling her uniform off the gorse without too many audible tears in the fabric.

"Oh, not what it looks like, is it?" came John Jones's voice out of the darkness, his location not immediately obvious to Augie. "What, did the bloody dinosaur strip off all your clothes for its personal amusement, then make you go search for them? Burp! Cheers!"

Augie could be sure that somewhere in the darkness, the perpetually drunken fellow was saluting the hapless lovers with his latest can of Toohey's.

"*Ych a fi*, Assistant Constable!" Chief Constable Williams shouted after Angharad, who made a hasty retreat with Stephen still slung over her shoulder. "There will be words with you later, there will!"

"A few too many full moons out here tonight, I'd say! Burp!"

"Don't know about you guys," Laura came over beside Augie, Irene and Scott to unload. "But I've been pinching myself to wake up from what I saw. Please give me an alternate explanation, Stephen-style."

"I've already drawn blood pinching myself," quipped Irene. "But I predict that Stephen, as our skeptic in residence, will argue that his getting it on with the assistant constable was a more probable event than running across a surviving non-avian dinosaur."

"Maybe that was the point," said Augie.

"Why Augustine Matias," said Irene in a tone calculated to make his ears glow in the dark, "if I didn't know better, I'd say you were having a ha-ha at Stephen's expense."

"Help!" tearfully cried who Augie guiltily recognized as Nigel, sobbing out of a darkness still enchanted by moonlit crashing surf. Guiltily, because he felt he should have known better than to joke around.   Only minutes earlier, they'd heard a woman's scream, accompanied by a roar, then an awful crunch. "Did you bloody lot not hear Robin scream her last breath in the grip of jaws that must have been the size of a big bale of hay?! Though I confess to not bein' able to make them out clearly in all that bloody fog!!" Nigel continued to grieve. His moonlit staggering about was apparently due to extreme emotional upset this time, rather than drunkenness.

"I was very favorably impressed by the notion that what we heard was exactly what we would expect to hear, carried on sea breezes from a latter-day Allosaurus treating someone as a spot of sushi, bone and all."

"'Very favorably impressed,' you say, Elwin?" angrily reacted Nigel. He easily recognized Elwin's voice, what with Elwin himself lost from view in the shadows, despite the moonlight. "Bloody f-n' hell, do you want me to extend your compliments to that prehistoric devil incarnate for a job well done? Hold it! Wo! Pray tell what this underwear is doing here!" Nigel had lifted Stephen's pair of briefs to Chief Constable Williams's flashlight. To steady himself from staggering about, he inadvertently settled his hand on that article of clothing where it was left draped atop the heather. Otherwise, he would have keeled over.

The dinosaur might have snuck up their pant legs like an unwelcome scorpion, if Stephen and the assistant constable didn't shed each other's clothing, Irene surprised herself at having to consciously resist snarking aloud. That she conjured it to mind in the first place, despite the horrific circumstances...In her defense, she told herself there did seem something ridiculously unreal about the whole situation, something undeserving of serious regard.

"Over here!" shouted time traveler Fred Frankly from all the way down the hill on the pebbly shore, as the last wisps of fog fled the scene further inland like so many phantom sheep, Augie imagined.

"Don't touch anything that could be crime scene evidence!" warningly instructed Chief Constable Williams.

Meanwhile, everyone else joined the Kelpyguard law officer on a tumultuous descent to the shoreline.

Unless Angharad or Stephen was the murderer, at least you don't have to worry about them having touched anything other than themselves, Irene found herself thinking mischievously yet again. *I might as well be having trouble not laughing at someone's funeral.*

Meanwhile from high above, inside Cloud Nine, Sherman directed his artificial intelligence entity, Charly, to reassemble himself on the downhill trek.

Charly grew taller and taller, thereby clearing a wide swath what with people either side of him spooked by the spectacle.

"This is the bloody spot where somethin' snatched up my Robin in its whale-sized jaws, or what I'm imaginin' were whale-sized jaws! Could have been our mythical Welsh dragon, for all I knew in the damnable darkness, um..." Nigel followed Augie's eyes to the moon overhead. "...despite that moon, due to- Oh, right, the dense fog that moved in!" he concluded most spritely as though it just occurred to him, to his grateful relief.

Most peculiar, far as Augie was concerned. *Something else is going on here.*

Nigel bent at the knees to pick up a lone, blood-stained sneaker from the pebbly sand. But then he appeared to think better of that. Augie wondered: Did he remember the chief constable ordering them not to touch any potential crime scene evidence? Whatever was up with Nigel, he said in what struck Augie as feigned tearfulness, "I TOLD her we shouldn't wander too close to the shoreline! After all that's happened, and despite one of the robot's bloody parts – think it was an ear attached to a piece of skull. Looked like a crawlin' conch shell, it did. Despite it taggin' along to film everything, I warned her! But always the adventurer..." His voice broke in either genuine grief or a fine bit of acting; Augie couldn't tell which.

"You're certain that's her shoe?" asked Fred, unsure what to think.

"Must have fallen off as she was hoisted away," Nigel shook his head.

"Looks like it's blood-stained," noted Fred, shining his flashlight on it. "And those gelatinous clumps, also blood-soaked: What the hell might those be, Jesus Dragon-heart Christ?!"

"Maybe cartilage, like from a shark losing teeth when it, uh..." Zoologist Dr. Roberta Quiñones didn't have the heart to complete her sentence with Nigel nearby, in case he really did love Robin all that much.

"Most impressively realistic, I must say," Elwin Kneath raved. "Especially that cartilage detail, if indeed that's what it is. Far more of what I would expect to find at the scene of a marauding dinosaur, though the remnants of last night's attack are not to be denigrated."

"Oh, so you'd like to praise the bloody monster for actin' more like itself tonight than last night, would you, Elwin Kneath?!?!" raged Nigel. He made a point of staggering over, into the dapperly dressed fellow's face. "Maybe with a wee bit more practice, it will be ready to take its show to the West End, do you think?!?!" he concluded tearfully. Pursuant to which he spun full around, and fell to his knees before the lone shoe, bowing his head low like he was come before some sacred shrine, Augie imagined.

"What are you doing, Nigel?" asked Kay, down beside him to gently place a comforting arm round his shoulders,

Which he violently shook off, crying, "What does it look like I'm doin', Kay?! I'm grievin' to the high heavens, I am! If not for the chief constable's idiot orders, still searchin' for a human murderer he's never goin' to find, I'd take up that shoe in me arms, I would, and kiss it all over!! Isn't it obvious?!" he turned and looked straight into Kay's bulging eyes to ask. "I'm in love!!"

This struck Augie as rather odd. Why lean on the present tense rather than the past, to declare his love for someone presumed dead? And look into someone else's eyes while doing so?

"Nigel's puppy dog eyes for Robin, his exploiting every opportunity to be at her side..."

"Nearly as impressive as your restaurant coupon, Elwin! Cheers!" interrupted John Jones. Once again, he emerged from the shadows into the moonlight with a can of Toohey's lifted high.

"That is truly a mean thing to say, sir," bristled Ali Magabu as Kay rushed away, seeming to Augie authentically, unquestionably distressed.

"So maybe it's time for you to return aboard your spaceship, mate?" John Jones staggered closer to the time traveler to say. "Take a trip through that swirly thingie we saw beside the moon before the fog-o-saurus moved in? Burp!" His burp appeared to lift him up, then collapse him into a formless heap on the pebbly shore.

"I think the school marm gave up on using you to make Nigel jealous," Irene whispered to Augie. "Beyond that, though, I'm not sure of anything. Maybe we've been wasting our time here with a variety-pack box of loony chocolates."

"Wo!" Augie exclaimed, just when he was about to agree with Irene, while Scott inserted himself to not miss a word between them. "Can you guys take a close look at the sand?" he asked. "See if you notice anything; I missed it at first with the ground so pebbly."

Scott went from noticing one, deep, dinner-plate-sized depression to realizing there were several others. Seen clearly in the moonlight, they headed all the way into the water, and became ever shallower before his eyes as the ebbing and flowing surf moved more pebbly sand to fill them.

"Look," said Irene pointing shoreward towards the very same cave she and Augie staked out two nights earlier. "They either led into, or came out of there."

"But they stop at the entrance," observed Scott, puzzled, though he could hear Stephen's voice in his head, deadpanning, *That's where the forgers tired of making foot tracks.*

"That would be where our Welsh dragon took to the air," said Irene with a straight face.

Augie noticed Nigel and Elwin exchange brief looks between themselves and the large depressions in the pebbly sand. Those looks appeared filled with genuine astonishment, at least on Nigel's part. Which seemed especially curious if he really believed he was in the fog-obscured presence of his true love being munched to death by a monstrous beast.

"Wait!" Scott held up a cautioning hand while he bent down to take a closer look at the beach on the threshold of the cave. "There are marks here as though some unbelievably large broom wiped the sand clean of the depressions."

"The creature's tail dragged along the ground, swinging from side to side," Augie thought aloud. *Maybe dinosaurs don't always keep their tails elevated?* He recalled something from earlier, in the moonlight before the foggy maritime layer moved in. Long strands of intertwined seaweed waved hypnotically through the air, reminding him of...*So vexing that I can't remember!*

Click...whirr...clicked and whirred Charly back to a semblance of life. "The alternating location of those depressions in the sand are consistent with the gait of a four-legged sauropod dinosaur twenty-five feet long."

For each photo Charly took of the depressions, his eyes flashed to illuminate them.

"The sauropod dinosaur Charly spoke of typically had a long neck, a bulky torso, and a long tail," Augie explained to Nigel. "The long neck with a bulky torso is what young Mr. Taylor and his teacher described. Does that jive with what you saw of the creature that seized Robin?" Augie asked Nigel, despite his head spinning. Between suggestions of a sauropod dinosaur, a Stegosaurus-type dinosaur...*How many different dinosaurs are roaming the Welsh coast, actually?*

"No, me dinosaur rode a surfboard out to sea so it wouldn't leave a stinkin' mark!" Nigel spat out with bitter sarcasm. "What do YOU think, mate?"

"Oh, that's right. Sorry," Augie apologized. "You did say it was too dark, in the fog, to see exactly what it was."

Click...whirr... "There is no fossil evidence, to date, of a dinosaur ever riding on a surfboard, or even having been capable of producing one."

"Well just keep diggin', you bloody robot!" raged Nigel circling Charly with his usual stagger, like a barking dog nervously circling a stranger.

Click...whirr... "Decades of digging have turned up no evidence dinosaurs ever made tools of even the most rudimentary sort, let alone a surf board. Therefore, any further digging with that specific goal in mind comes under the heading of..." ...click...whirr... "...a waste of time."

"Over here!" Augie shouted louder than he otherwise might have, if he hadn't grown irritated with the back and forth between Charly and Nigel. "This gorse branch washed ashore," he pointed with his flashlight, "looks also dipped in blood! Like the gorse branch found washed ashore not far from here this morning! Sherman?" he spoke more loudly into the mike attached to his windbreaker. "Any results yet from your analysis of the shredded shirt and other stuff?"

"Remember to leave that gorse for the evidence bag, Mr. Matias!" cautioned Chief Constable Williams.

"Do you have an evidence bag large enough for those crab burrows a.k.a. dinosaur tracks? Burp!" John Jones lifted his head off the ground just long enough to slobber, before drunkenly swinging it back down again. It landed with a THUNK against the pebbly sand, loud enough to hear even above the surf's din.

This, while Augie noticed Nigel and Elwin share a knowing look. *Knowing what?*

"The blood on the shirt, it is human blood matching the blood on the gorse bramble," Sherman reported over Augie's speaker phone for all to hear. "Type O, the same as Gerwyn's blood from the birth registry in Kelpyguard. But of course, he's likely not the only bloke out here with Type O blood."

"Truly unfortunate our DNA analysis kit was lost in a West African swamp," Ali Magabu lamented. "I'm sure we could have located a DNA sample on Gerwyn's shirt to confirm the blood was his."

"You lost your leprechaun detector in that swamp also, did ya?" Thunk!

"We're just not used to dealin' with murders here," Chief Constable Williams shook his head regretfully. With gloved hand, he carefully bagged the gorse branch, avoiding any of its steely strong needles piercing through the latex to draw his own blood. "We are plentiful with murder mysteries of every possible sort on the tele, we are. So plentiful, in fact, we avoid the real thing because people have more than had their fill. At least that's my supposition."

"But surviving non-avian dinosaurs would not typically watch any TV, now would they?" Elwin asked in a lecturing tone.

Click...whirr...but Sherman disabled Charly by remote before he could comment, to Augie's great relief.

Augie went on to ask, "Can you tell us, Sherman, whether you, Harry, Harriet or Samuel saw anything from up above to corroborate what Nigel experienced?"

"That's the really frustrating thing, Augustine. Seconds before the roar, screams, and...um...such," Sherman stumbled. He was well aware of Nigel listening in, and didn't want to cause him any more distress than he might already be experiencing. As a result, Sherman steered clear of mentioning that awful munchy crunchy sound what seemed to cut off the screams. "Right before that, fog materialized all around where we saw Nigel and Robin wandering the shoreline, the fog bank itself yet to roll in. So we saw nothing."

"Nothing," Augie repeated, unable to hide his disappointment.

"Nearby, though, we did notice a large clump of seaweed oddly swirling about. Will definitely bear additional review of the video."

"There you go. The beast's exhalations condensed into the mist that enveloped them, quite obviously," declared Elwin as though the matter was entirely settled. "Really had nothing to do with the fog bank, did it?"

"And you couldn't discern much of the creature, Nigel, enveloped in its fog, or the fog?" Irene asked in a dubious tone she couldn't help.

"That's my story, and I'm stickin' to it!" Nigel insisted tearfully. Albeit, the tearful bit seemed to Augie strangely tacked on at the end, forced.

"I say, there, are you talking about loud exhalations?!" called out Rupert Hamster Holmes from the irregularly moonlit darkness. "Well, maybe not so loud as evidencing a certain air of desperation..."

"You mean like this?" Irene whispered in Scott's ear, with a sigh of resignation to more nonsense from Mr. Holmes.

"I'm not sure anyone heard the particular exhalation you're talking about, Rupert," said Elwin. "They are discussing an exhalation of an untowardly voluminous quality, from a creature with uncommonly large lungs. Propelled into this already juiced atmosphere, the condensation might well have been enough to conceal its predatory behavior even from those standing closest to it."

"Oh, well, the exhalations we heard, and by 'we' I mean Elwin and meself, they were perhaps more of a rhythmic panting. And they were succeeded by someone of the feminine persuasion, I believe, calling out, and I quote verbatim, 'Oh, Stephen!' Under these circumstances of an actual living dinosaur on the prowl, I thought she might be calling for help. Or maybe not so much calling for help as having her breath taken away by the impetus for her alarm."

"No, you idiot!" raged Nigel. "She was havin' sex!"

"Sex with a dinosaur? On the very frontier of bestiality? Before leaping to such an preposterously perverse conclusion, shouldn't serious consideration be given to the possibility the lady in question was cradling some delightfully petite creature in her arms? And she was calling over this Stephen chap to have a fun look-see at it in the ample moonlight?"

"Yes! That's it!" raged Nigel, back to staggering so unsteadily, Augie gave him a wide berth for fear of him toppling over. "Assistant Constable Gruffudd was rockin' to sleep a baby T-Rex! They are the cutest twee things when they're too small to bite your head off, or swallow a sheep whole like it's a raw oyster!" Suddenly aware of the looks he was receiving, and fearful some might think he was rather enjoying himself too much, Nigel abruptly shifted gears and tearfully bellowed, "Can't any of you bloody blokes see I'm grievin' here?!?!"

"So Gerwyn accompanied Robin on the first stake-out, and he disappeared with his blood-soaked torn shirt left behind. Then Robin accompanied Nigel the second night, and SHE disappeared with a blood-stained shoe and blood-soaked cartilage left behind," observed Augie. "Too soon to draw a conclusion?"

"No, it's not," said Rupert in the simplest declarative sentence any local had heard from him in recent memory. "The conclusion is obvious, or rather plain for all to draw, well maybe not all, but most certainly a majority. Anyway, clearly, if you don't want to experience a fate similar to Gerwyn's and Robin's, if not actually identical, mark my words well. You don't want to be the first-named of a couple going on the next coastal stake-out."

"Here I thought the obvious conclusion was that you're better off getting caught dashing across the heather in your birthday suit, like Adam and Eve," Irene snarked in Scott's reddening ear. She bolted before he could turn her way.

Great; after that, how can I possibly tell her how I feel?

"I don't think that's what Mr. Matias was suggesting," said Fred, stifling himself from adding, *you bozo!*, for Rupert's benefit before going on, "My takeaway is that for any future night-time surveillance, you need more than two people per group." *Which I hopefully won't be here for, safely reunited with Cecilia and our two young runts back aboard the Smoke and Mirrors.*

"Will have to think hard on whether I can even allow that, takin' the risk of a third victim. Not sure it's worth it, so you offbeat out-of-towners with your robot that disassembles then reassembles at will can keep chasin' your phantom dinosaurs," cautioned Chief Constable Williams. "But as for you, Nigel Morgan, we need to talk at the station in far more detail regarding Robin's fate. Easier to believe there's been a web of murderous jealousy afoot than a Welsh dragon on the literally bloody loose!"

"But the tracks in the sand, you heard the artificial intelligence entity! Their placement is consistent with a quadruped sauropod dinosaur twenty-five feet long!" protested Elwin. "Toss in the blood-stained shoe, the loud roar, that awful crunch that cut off a woman's scream, and the blood-soaked cartilage beside the foot tracks, and the real conclusion writes itself."

"It writes itself because a work of fiction is all it is!" growled the chief constable. "A work of bloody fiction you are most welcome to write yourself, like one of your ridiculous counterfeit meal coupons!"

"I never said it was a dragon, Chief Constable!" pushed back Nigel, careful to make certain his every word was uttered tearfully. "Truth be told, didn't have a good enough look at the monster to even insist it was a dinosaur! All I'm sayin' is that it wasn't no human attacker, unless enough of them joined forces inside the craziest costume ever!"

"You can describe all that and more back at the station, Nigel! Let's go!" Chief Constable Williams concluded, grabbing Nigel by the elbow.

Elwin shouted after the departing constable with Nigel in tow, "This was a so-much-better, um...evidenced attack by a surviving non-avian dinosaur than anyone experienced the night before!"

"What a strange way of describing it," remarked Roberta

to Laura and Irene.

"Last night's attack must have been done by an amateur dinosaur, not really used to what it was born into," quietly snarked Irene, met with suppressed snickers. "While tonight's attack had more the mark of a seasoned professional."

Assuming the three women's noises were sympathetic to his point, Elwin approached them to say, exasperated, "You would think Nigel's profession of love for Robin, together with the grieving spectacle he displayed, would have been far more than enough to get him off the proverbial hook!"

Chapter 16

"Yes, Erin?" Vicky Copplestone walked over beside fourth-grader Erin Manley to ask quietly, seeing she'd raised her hand.

"Ms. Copplestone, what if I don't like any of the choices for answering a question?"

Despite Vicky's protestations, curriculum adviser Diane Mueller went ahead with her plan. She had the fourth-grade teachers administer a test developed by the fifth-grade teachers. It was meant to prove the interdisciplinary unit inspired by the dinosaur quest was leaving Vicky's students behind academically. Especially with Augie's current expedition on hiatus due to a murder investigation, Diane considered the way fair and clear to insist on this experiment.

Yet here Vicky's class was, not five minutes into the test, and one of her star pupils was already throwing a shoe. "Can you point to the question in question?" Vicky whispered while sensing several figurative rabbit ears going up among other students.

Erin directed Vicky's attention to an analogy item:

_____ is to _____ what _____ is to _____.

1.)A dozen eggs is to a pair of ducks what
  a)twelve donuts are to a flock of geese.
  b)36 candy corns are to six trick-or-treaters.
  c)twenty-four cartons of milk are to three grocery bags.
  d)48 acorns are to a dozen trees.

"None of these answers look any good to you?"
"They're all wrong!" Erin insisted, shouting her whisper.
"But can't you select the least-wrong?"

With a huff to contain herself, Erin answered, "I think I know what they *want* me to answer, but it's bull dookey!"

"Okay," said Vicky wearily, sensing from nearby snickers that things might be about to get out of hand. "We better continue this in the hallway. No. Scratch that." Something snapped for Vicky. If the powers that be wanted to fire her, fine. So be it. *Enough is enough!* "Everyone," she said to get her entire class's attention, "if you'll put your pencils down, I'd like to give a full airing to Erin's complaint."

"Yes!" enthused Jack. He slapped his pencil on the desk with gusto while Lucas did a cat stretch. Lucas became intent on stealing a few winks before he had to resume neatly filling in little ovals all up and down his score sheet.

"We're looking at question four, people," said Erin, bringing a smile to Vicky's face the way she took charge. "'A dozen eggs is to a pair of ducks'...anyone? How many eggs is that per duck?" Grinning mischievously at Vicky hovering over her, she added, "You didn't want me to just give them the answer, did you?"

"Lucas?" Vicky called on Lucas despite his being one of the few students not raising a hand.

"Six," groaned Lucas, when he really wanted to answer, *Leave me alone.* Although, he did proceed to flop his sweater over his head.

"Correct! Six!" confirmed Erin before Vicky could say, *That's right, Lucas. Now get that sweater off your head!* "Which answer do you think we're supposed to choose? Emme?" Erin selected from many raised hands. To Vicky's proud amusement, she continued to dominate the proceedings.

Lucas cast his sweater aside voluntarily, curious to check out the multiple-choice item himself. He hadn't gotten to it yet.

"Okay, well," Emme sighed melodramatically, "we don't know exactly how many geese are supposed to be in a flock. But probably won't be more than a donut or two for each goose. Which I doubt they'll want to eat anyway." Emme paused for her fellow students to finish snickering. Then she proceeded, "And three grocery bags for twenty-four cartons of milk, that's eight cartons for each bag, not six. And who puts eight cartons of milk in a paper bag? That's too many! Even if you could, the weight would tear the bag apart!" she exclaimed with a disapproving head shake, received by more laughter. "So, what about forty-eight acorns to a dozen trees? Seriously?? That's only four acorns a tree. They must be very small trees, because any acorn trees I know drop hundreds of them! We're left with choice 'b': thirty-six candy corns for six trick-or-treaters. Six candy corns for each trick-or-treater, that's the same number as the eggs for each duck. I don't see a problem with that, Erin. Oh, and you're welcome, everybody, for my sharing the correct answer! Now some of you won't score zero after all."

Emme stood and took a red-faced bow to riotous applause that Vicky found herself hoping would suck Diane Mueller into her classroom, to fire her once and for all, on account of so willfully violating testing protocol.

No telltale click-click-click of Diane's high-heeled shoes grew ever louder outside her classroom door, though. Instead, Vicky heard Jack complain, "Only six candy corns? Worst Halloween, ever! I'll starve!"

"Best Halloween, ever," giggled Emme. "Candy corns suck!"

"To be honest with you, Erin, I don't get it," said Vicky once the additional laughter subsided. "What's wrong with answer 'b'? I thought Emme made a persuasive case."

"The problem is: Ducks lay eggs, but trick-or-treaters don't lay candy corns!"

"Maybe they lay them twenty-four hours after they eat them, in the toilet," quipped Jack.

"Which gets to my suggestion for a better answer!" Erin shouted to be heard over the raucous laughs that Jack's remark set off.

"Okay, everyone, let's cool it for Erin's suggestion."

"Thank you, Ms. Copplestone. How about this: Thirty-six poops from six trick-or-treaters?"

The laughter and applause were even more raucous than what ensued from Jack's grossness. And Vicky thought she finally heard those familiar click-click-clicks down the hallway. But she soon realized that her imagination was filling them in based on prior experience. For once, her class teetering on the edge of out-of-control didn't draw Diane there like a magnet. And whether or not it did, that made no difference. Such was Vicky's damn-the-personal-consequences intent. Once the ruckus ran out of steam, she said, "Given what Erin most persuasively argued, I'd like to propose options for how you continue the test. Option one: Take it as directed. When none of the answers seem correct to you, choose the one that is the least wrong."

"Yeah, right," snarked Maria, accompanied by grumbles of, "No way," from other students.

"Option two," Vicky went on loudly, "take the test as directed."

"Say what?!?!"

"BUT, again suppose none of the answers seem correct, or correct enough. On a separate sheet of paper, copy the question, with your suggested answer beside it. Jack?"

"Ms. Copplestone, what if I want to write a whole new set of answer choices for a question?"

Vicky hesitated, thinking, *That should get me fired, most definitely. But my heart is so NOT into putting these children through this activity the way I was ordered to.* "Sure, Jack; why not? But please write as neatly as possible."

"Yes!"

"And don't take the cheap way out, using 'none of the above'!"

"Yes!" "Alright!" "Wow!" accompanied hi-fives and fist-pumps galore as students crowded Vicky's school supplies table for blank paper.

Chapter 17

"Well, Nigel, I have a different theory of the case from Elwin," Chief Constable Rhys Williams finally spoke up, after impatiently drumming his fingers on his desk. He had been waiting for Nigel to offer up something, anything other than a monster, regarding the disappearance of Robin Pugh the night after Gerwyn Davies vanished.

Elwin Kneath insisted a prehistoric beast savaged both Robin and Gerwyn. He pushed that narrative far harder than did the out-of-towners intent on discovering just such a creature.

But Chief Constable Williams would have bet everything he owned that the real culprit was human. All else was a ridiculous distraction, perhaps intentionally so by the murderer.

However, Williams couldn't yet one hundred percent rule out the possibility he was dealing with a situation for the history books. That was in fairness to the school lad who set off the whole circus, as he saw it, in the first place.

Meantime, the robot christened Charly found neither foot tracks nor dinosaurs off the Pembrokeshire coast, after he transformed himself into a miniature submarine. Yet he did bring back curious video of a crease in the seabed that looked recent. Moreover, many bits of crushed sea shell and coral floated nearby, like a bomb had gone off and sprayed them all directions.

Did a fault line open and close the previous night, causing a tremor mistaken for an enormous creature's ponderous steps? Or did a dinosaur really lumber along the shore?

And what about the whole bizarre business with this guy named Eclipso? Who watched the interrogation of Nigel on a two-way tele set up in the Kelpyguard Constabulary? And kept a pencil-sized alligator by his side named Bonsai?

Bonsai stood unbelievably erect on its two hind legs, and danced to a reggae instrumental version of the Beatles' acapella tune, "Because." That created such a distraction, the chief constable insisted the sound be muted. *But in a world with a gator such as that, what other bloody unfathomable wonders might exist?*

"This is not a court trial by any means, I'll remind you, Nigel," Chief Constable Williams went on, careful to avoid even the teensiest peek at Bonsai Gator doing its own special boogie-woogie.

For that matter, the chief constable also averted his eyes from anywhere near Assistant Constable Gruffudd. She stood with arms folded in back of the room, far from where he did allow himself the occasional glance at Stephen Feldman.

Stephen sat in quiet counsel with paleontologist Augustine Matias, who had family roots in the area. *Just as well I can't make out what their chin-wag is about.*

"You're keeping your distance from Angharad, I see," Augie said under his breath to Stephen.

"The problem is, she's provided insufficient evidence she wants me for anything more than my sexy body."

"Wo," Augie couldn't help reacting loudly enough to feel compelled to tell Williams, "Sorry." Then quietly again, he went on, "You certainly seemed carried away by her, quite literally."

"How so?"

"The, um, condition our flashlights found you both in, emerging from that dense fog..."

"What?" Stephen's whole face crumpled into a look of disgusted astonishment before he said, "I think that besides sheep, they still have red deer stag roaming parts of Wales."

"I didn't notice either you or Angharad with antlers."

"Especially at night, the mind can play some really crazy tricks on you when you're hoping to see something."

"I wasn't hoping to see THAT! Shh! Let's hear what they're saying."

"I have a report from a regular patron of Drunk In The Wool," Chief Constable Williams was going on, ignoring any side chatter. "Three days ago, Nigel, you said, and I quote, 'I'd kill her if that's what it took.' Can you explain?"

"My blessed God!" Nigel lifted his slumped-over head to shout. "That regular patron must be hard of hearin' if he missed the crucial word, 'for'!"

"'For'?"

"Oh!" Alistair Frump stirred from his slouch in a back chair. "Did I hear someone yell, 'Fore!'? Who's tee shot flew wildly astray?"

"No, man!" Nigel turned Alistair's way irritably. "What I said was, 'I'd kill *for* her!' Not that I'd kill her!"

"Kill for her, why?" Williams asked dubiously.

"I didn't mean that literally. It was about securing a certain special stamp for her."

"A stamp," Williams repeated, even more dubiously.

"Um, it was issued, I believe," Nigel hemmed and hawed. He ran his eyes across the ceiling as though what to say next might be written there, Augie mused. "In 1901. Yes, that's right. 1901. Or rather, maybe I should say, was almost issued."

"Almost issued," Chief Constable Williams repeated, no less dubiously.

"It celebrated our special breed of pooch, the corgi. The artist's rendering featured that wee furry fellow enjoyin' a bit of a lip lock with a red Welsh dragon. Only, the postmaster at the time was very stuck up, no pun intended. Decided the picture was too outrageous, would cause a major smelly dog, it would, if ever actually sold," Nigel continued ever more animatedly.

Augie couldn't help suspecting Nigel made up the whole thing, energized by the inventiveness he brought to bear.

"By then, however, well wouldn't you know the first run had come off the printers. The postmaster went on a major search and destroy mission to stop any distribution whatsoever. But legend has it he wasn't entirely successful. Around a half-dozen stamps ended up in top-secret collections the owners demurred from sharin' with anyone. They feared a covert ultra-nationalist squad intent on not only destroyin' the stamps, but killin' off their owners as well. That way, nobody would ever learn of what those fascist crazies regarded as the ultimate sacrilege against Welsh honor."

"How come I've never heard a flea's poo about any of this before? Belch!" belched John Jones, standing up unsteadily the rear of the constabulary.

"Nearly all the people who *do* know about it are afraid to breathe a word to anyone," Nigel answered without hesitation. "I be takin' a big risk, meself, speakin' of it like this. As I was sayin', though, got wind of someone tellin' someone else they found one of the stamps in a shoebox in their attic. That's when I spoke of killin' for it, to give Robin."

Kay stormed out of the constabulary, her feet sounding to Augie like they must have been fitted with ten-pound bricks.

Chief Constable Williams said, "So Robin was a stamp collector, was she?"

"Wasn't somethin' she liked to share with anyone, not even our local postmaster."

Nigel added the postmaster bit, Augie figured, to pre-empt the chief constable making any inquiry that particular direction. Moreover, Augie could easily imagine Stephen deadpanning, if he wasn't so preoccupied with

Angharad, *People usually don't like to share an interest they don't have in the first place.*

"But she was willin' to share it with you," noted the chief constable, still dubious if not anywhere near as certain as Augie of Nigel's detailed story being totally bogus.

"Which is exactly why I felt love-bound to make sure her entire stamp collection would be part and parcel of the memorial crypt we will be buryin' on her behalf."

"A crypt, even though there's no body to fill it yet, you say?" asked Chief Constable Williams, this time more astonished than dubious.

"Like one of those Egyptian pharaohs buried beside all his earthly possessions to take to the next world, is it?" interjected John Jones. "Here's the problem with that, Nigel: If her body's not included, don't think that's goin' to work, belch! As for me, I plan on emptyin' out any cans of Toohey's before ever they can be placed beside me, inside me crypt. Don't think I'll be requirin' them when I cease to exist! Burp!" John Jones concluded not only with his signature noise. As well, he wiped dribbled beer off his chin with his shirt sleeve. His way of bringing the subject to a definitive close, Augie figured.

"I be comin' to terms with the sad likelihood, I am," Nigel said, disregarding John Jones, "that my dear Robin was consumed by some survivin' prehistoric nightmare. There will be no recoverin' her remains, 'ceptin' were another deposit to be made on the Sheep's Shank Links, which I'd as soon not have to face."

"Regardin' that blasphemous stamp, Nigel, I suppose you haven't had any luck latchin' on to one for Robin's memorial crypt?"

"To be honest with you, Chief Constable, even if I had, I wouldn't breathe a word to anyone. Not even yourself. Could set off tomb raiders like no-one's ever seen since the openin' of the pyramids."

"Sorry there, mate. My assistant constable will be servin' a warrant to search Robin's memorial crypt, make sure you're not depositin' a pile of sheep's poo in me face about her stamp collection. And incidentally, let me ask one more question on that particular subject," he continued while Augie wondered about Elwin Kneath's timing.

Elwin suddenly rose noisily from a chair in the back of the room, and rushed out a side door.

"There's goin' to be one of those memorial crypts for Gerwyn into the bargain as well, is there?"

"A very lightweight crypt, at that," nodded Nigel. "Gerwyn never was a collector, of anything. Didn't read any books he didn't promptly return to the library. Never listened to any music he couldn't tune into on the radio. And as for the small assortment of clothes he couldn't help but collect, well! Only last year, he confided in me that he believed the afterlife was going to be like a big nudist colony! Because of that, he didn't even want his corpse suited up, let alone any additional attire buried beside him."

Chief Constable Williams gave Nigel a long, hard stare Augie read as, *You've got to be kidding me*, before he finally cut loose with, "Here's what *I* think happened, Nigel! Can't be denied, your recent obsession with Robin. I believe that obsession was so, err, obsessive, you drank yourself into the decision that Gerwyn had to be taken out of the equation. And what better way to bump him off than to exploit a nut-job dinosaur search? You convinced yourself that with Gerwyn gone, Robin might finally notice you. Maybe she'd get infatuated, watchin' you stagger about like you were walkin' across the deck of a sailboat caught in a mighty tempest. But it didn't turn out that way, did it, mate? We could all see how desperately she yearned for Gerwyn's miraculous return. On that second stake-out last night, she continued to blow you off. And that drove you so mad, so over the bloomin' edge of sanity, you couldn't stand it anymore, could you? My God, man! Suppose you had waited out her grievin' process for even a month or two? And meanwhile sobered yourself up enough so a soul wouldn't go dizzy watchin' you lurch about? Maybe Robin would eventually have given you a wee bit of consideration in the romance department. But instead, well you knew the out-of-town circus troop had their cloud ship watchin' from overhead. And that their bloody weird robot took itself apart to keep a video eye on everything and everyone all up and down the coast. Even with a thick fog blanket movin' in, it wasn't goin' to be near as easy to rid the world of Robin as you did Gerwyn two nights ago, under cloak of that naturally concealin' storm. And so, I believe you set off a smoke canister, wantin' us to imagine it was the flesh-hungry monster's condensatin' breath to hide what gruesomeness you really had goin' on! And don't think for a moment I won't have me crew searchin' the whole coastline for that canister!"

"Where did I hide the bodies, Chief Constable?!" Nigel cried tearfully, anew. "Had I tossed them out to sea, the bloody tide would have washed them right back in to shore! More importantly, it's distressin'ly disappointin', it is, that you think so little of me, you're willin' to believe I'd commit multiple murders over me love not bein' reciprocated!"

"Sorry, Nigel. But it's either that, or actually buyin' a huge mound of whale poo! That after coexistin' with us, undetected here for centuries, some prehistoric monster was suddenly pickin' us off one by one! That's the next level of crazy!"

"Unless, Chief Constable," Sherman Peabody raised his forefinger to interject, "what we are experiencing here is a most remarkable biorhythm that requires millennia to play out, rather than hours or days."

"What do you mean, sir?" the chief constable asked gruffly.

"I mean, your typical Florida alligator might spend days sleeping off a meal before it goes back on the prowl. But perhaps a surviving relative of the Tyrannosaurus Rex takes hundreds of even thousands of years for his after-dinner nap. And just suppose our particular monster, assuming it's of the saurian rather than the human kind, wants dessert. I should like to see us 'out-of-towners' have one final moonlit vigil this very evening. Three's the charm and all that."

"Okay, let's say you come up with nothin' more concrete, again, than a trail of deep puddles across the beach, or some such," stipulated Chief Constable Williams. "Can I have an absolute promise? If tonight goes no better for you evidence-wise than the first two nights, can we call that strike three and you're out of here? Except for any of you we might need to detain for further questionin' in our murder inquiry?"

"I say, guv'nah, isn't an absolute promise a wee bit too final?" protested Rupert Hamster Holmes seated up front. "How about, rather than strike three and they're out, strike three and they will give an expeditious departure their most serious consideration? Taking into account a multitude of factors? At least some of which might not have occurred to us yet?"

"Speaking personally," said Stephen, careful to keep his eyes averted from any direction where they might land on Angharad, "I think we've already seen all there is to see here, even if we skip tonight."

"In his case," Irene whispered to Laura seated the opposite side of her from Scott, "I think we've seen far more than any of us ever bargained for."

"What was that?" asked Angharad severely as Laura strained not to bust out laughing.

"I was just saying I'd recommend a midnight stroll of the Pembrokeshire coast for anyone who wanted an especially picturesque view of a full moon," audaciously lied Irene. And under cloak of numerous approving mumbles that ensued among the locals, she added for Laura and Scott's benefit, "or moons."

"Excuse me, everyone," growled Rhys Williams, just shy of a full-out shout, "I would like our out-of-towners, as represented by..." he motioned Sherman's way.

"Sherman Peabody."

"Sherman Peabody, yes, I'd like him to have an opportunity to answer my question. Suppose I agree to a third night of dinosaur-searchin' madness amidst a major crime scene. Will that secure his circus troop's rapid departure, should they come away from it as inconclusively empty as their first two nights left them? Mr. Peabody?"

"Thank you, Chief Constable."

"I'm sorry, Angharad, you should be on your way already for that search warrant to rummage about Robin's memorial crypt."

"Oh, sorry, Chief Constable; I'll get right on it."

While the assistant constable ducked out a side door, Irene couldn't help whispering to Laura and Scott, "I wonder if she'll get right on it like she got right on Stephen."

"Surprised Stephen doesn't join her; wonder if they've had a falling out," remarked Laura.

"That would have happened anyway, once Stephen finished."

"Irene, that is beyond nasty!" Laura slapped Irene's shoulder at the same time it took all her willpower to keep from giggling.

"And maybe he feels he's seen all there is to see of her, as well," Irene nevertheless added incorrigibly, to both Laura and Scott's mirth-suppressing distress. Neither one wanted to make a scene with their amusement. Plus, they did feel sorry for Stephen if so soon after he found romance, it ended.

"Okay, Mr. Peabody, will you please continue."

"Of course. What my colleagues and I have devised is a rather complex plan to obtain more concrete results, come earthquakes, storms, surprise fog banks, and or who knows what else. This time, one of us, unaccompanied, would roam the same part of the coastline where Gerwyn and Robin disappeared. He would be the bait, quite frankly."

"Don't be daft, man!" complained John Jones. "Have a sheep be the bait, instead!"

"And risk wasting good Welsh wool? Not goin' to hear of it!" insisted Nigel. "But I also don't like the idea that one of you out-of-towners could leave us feelin' guilted into erectin' a statue in your honor. What if our resident bloodthirsty dinosaur makes a flippin' martyr of you? Somethin' happens to me, though, won't much mind 'cause then at least I have a chance, sooner rather than later, of joinin' me beloved Robin in the afterlife!"

"Well whoever we make the bait," went on Sherman diplomatically, "we have a plan to virtually guarantee their safety from the reptilian beast, if reptilian beast indeed it is."

"What, when Mr. T-Rex is about to bite off someone's head, you're goin' to dangle a prime cut of lamb in its butt-ugly face and say, 'Yoo-hoo! Look over here, mate!' Cheers!" John Jones saluted everyone with a freshly popped-open can of Toohey's.

"Not at all," Sherman shook his head as though the question came from a dead serious place. "As we speak, our cloud craft, as you call it, Chief Constable, hovers low to the ground. Its fog hides us digging a deep hole for inserting an underground shelter. That shelter will include a trap-door slide our sitting-duck bait can access at the push of a button. We have special excavation equipment for this purpose, brought over aboard a second cloud craft."

"How absolutely absurd!" Nigel slobbered in Sherman's face, having staggered over before him. "You're sayin' that when the dinosaur attacks, rather than catch it in a trap, you're goin' to cage its prey instead?"

"Its prey will slide safely to rest on a most commodious bean bag chair. There, he or she can heat up a large cup of marshmallow-stuffed hot cocoa, and indulge a tray piled high with traditional Welsh cakes our Cloud Nine navigator Samuel Longbottom is preparing while we speak. All of that inside a pleasantly lit room including TV video to the outside, for a front row seat on whatever happens next."

"What about the fearsome monster that probably ate me Robin?!?" tearfully raged Nigel, though Augie again found himself feeling there was an acted quality to the emotional aspect. "You bloody blokes will also build a giant swing set and slide for it to play on while you obtain all your photographic evidence?! C'mon! You heard Elwin Kneath before he left! The bloody cartilage! Those puddles that evidenced the stride of a stonkin' beast twenty-five feet long! The shredded shirt soaked in Gerwyn's blood type! Those stones inside the cave that looked like Stegosaurus spinal plates, which mysteriously vanished...That should be more than enough evidence to convict the prehistoric rotter!"

"I hear you grievin' somethin' fierce, Nigel. But how about stiflin' yourself long enough to hear that 'whatever happens next' part Mr. Peabody hasn't shared with us yet?" grouched Chief Constable Williams.

Meanwhile, Scott reflected on Nigel's argument they shouldn't require any further proof a dinosaur or dinosaurs were romping about. His brother said the same thing. And in his case, Scott sensed fear that further investigation might prove relic non-avian dinosaurs weren't so extant after all, thereby threatening a whole belief system. But Nigel seemed intent on getting the out-of-towners to leave before they discovered...what, exactly? *This couldn't have anything to do with that bizarre story about the stamp depicting a romantically entangled dragon and dog, could it?*

"Thank you again, Chief Constable," Sherman Peabody said appreciatively, then continued, "Let's look at what happens when our bait, whoever that might be, presses the panic button due to being confronted by either our hoped-for dinosaur, or your proposed human monster. A trap door safely slides him or her into our special underground cubicle amply equipped with snack delights. And soon as the trap door automatically reseals, knock-out gas issues from nozzles hidden amidst nearby gorse and heather. Whether reptilian or human, within seconds our quarry should faint into an hours-long slumber. That will allow us plenty of time to photograph, take a biopsy, and electronically tag if it's the stuff of our dinosaur quest. Or to handcuff for arrest and booking if we are dealing rather with a serial killer. Although, those two scenarios are not necessarily mutually exclusive. Far from it, in fact."

"In other words, Mr. Peabody, you're suggestin' there could be a human murderer afoot as well as a bloody prehistoric reptile what doesn't realize it's already extinct?" asked Chief Constable Williams most gruffly, as usual. "Well, I say bollocks to the latter scenario, your supposed evidence be damned!"

"An enticing picture you painted of that underground cubicle, Sherman. Chief Constable, you might raise funds for your constabulary by selling raffle tickets to pick the guinea pig," quipped Stephen.

"There will be no raffle tickets," firmly stated Chief

Constable Williams with a no-nonsense hand swipe. "Here's the deal! Either Nigel is the bait, where I can keep an eye on him durin' your third exercise in futility, Mr. Peabody! Or there will be no such exercise at all! Instead, I'll crime-tape the entire bloody coastline from here to St. David!"

"That seems rather extreme," gently fussed Rupert Hamster Holmes. "Might you really want to say: If Nigel is not the guinea pig - and I rather think there's a not-inconsequential chance that is not the best-chosen term for him, if also far from the worst - I will have to seriously consider weighing the possibility-"

"No."

"Okay, well how about, probably most likely 'no,' but-"

"No buts, Rupert!"

"I say, guv'nah!" exclaimed Rupert, utterly taken aback by the chief constable's decisive forcefulness. "Even were Gerwyn and Robin to suddenly, miraculously reappear, all safe and sound?"

Chief Constable Williams heaved a sigh of resignation, conceding, "Yes, of course, their miraculous reappearance, all safe and sound, would cause me to reconsider."

"Then let's have a further chin wag about it, or should it rather be termed a chin hop? Speaking for me own chin, it doesn't so much move from side to side as up and down. When I talk, that is. Which is why I never properly understood the expression. Although 'hop' probably isn't a fair description of what the talk-engaged chin does either; don't want to imply any likeness to a kangaroo on the move..."

As people one by one made their way for the exits, Augie imagined Rupert's endless monologue as a perverse sort of recessional hymn at the end of a church service, inspiring ministers and acolytes alike to file out of the building as fast as their feet could carry them.

Chapter 18

"I'm not bein' funny, right, Father?" Assistant Constable Gruffudd advised Father Hawkin. She was visually sweeping the cramped interior of Robin Pugh's crypt, a former rental trailer. "This is three steps past nuts, no offense to you."

"No offense taken, my dear assistant constable," the diminutive Father Albert Hawkin shook his head, hands prayerfully entwined at his waist.

"Have you ever had anyone prepare a memorial like this before the body was even located?" asked Angharad Gruffudd while taking in a chest of drawers, Robin's favorite throw-rug, and a bookshelf full of her novels and travelogues.

"Not in my twenty-seven years serving the Lord," the Anglican minister responded emphatically. "And now we have two, if you include the one for our beloved Gerwyn. But it must be noted what is probably already obvious: There is insufficient churchyard space for their burial, or to leave them here as makeshift mausoleums. Rather, after the service tomorrow, the town council has granted permission to install them permanently along the Pembrokeshire coast. In coming months, volunteers will paint over the commercial ads on their exteriors, to blend in both trailers with God's good acres. Maybe they'll even depict a sheep or two."

The assistant constable ducked down into the trailer, and pulled open the chest drawers until she happened upon a stamp collector's book.

Father Hawkin prattled on about his discomfort with Robin, or at least her memory, being immersed in such an abundance of material goods. "Is she to be like an

Egyptian pharaoh, trying to take her bits and bobs beyond the grave?" At the same time, though, he didn't want to be judgmental, in light of the profound grief people were experiencing.

No matter to Assistant Constable Gruffudd. Paging through the stamp book, she came across the stamp Nigel described. Exquisitely detailed for its tiny dimensions, it depicted a corgi kissing the iconic Welsh-flag dragon smack on the mouth.

After she carefully removed the stamp for a closer look, a realization left Assistant Constable Gruffudd shaking her head in an odd mix of disgust and amusement. Then she hurriedly put the whole thing back where she found it. *Elwin Kneath up to his old tricks again, he is!*

"I thank you for your time, Father. Now I better be returnin' meself to the coast afore the sun sets. Our out-of-towners insist on one last dinosaur-searchin' vigil to finish workin' that entire absurd notion out of their system. Like a fart in a jam jar, if you'll excuse me language."

"Go in peace, child, and may there be no more awful disappearances of our town folk tonight." Father Hawkin patted Angharad gently on her back as she returned to her squad car.

"We're makin' extra certain there will be no more victims tonight, I assure you," Gruffudd boasted to the church minister.

That's when a THUMP sounded like it came from Gerwyn's oversized memorial crypt. But the assistant constable dismissed out of hand any thought of an additional inspection before leaving.

It's not as though I believe in ghosts or any of that nonsense, Angharad told herself as entering her squad car. *But I don't need any more woo-woo playin' with me head! Plenty bad enough, this ache in me heart for Stephen when I'm sure all he sees in me is testosterone-*

driven!

*

Augie, Alistair and Scott encamped at an extensive gorse bush close to the Pembrokeshire shoreline. This afforded them excellent views of both the pebbly beach and guinea pig Nigel further uphill, while keeping concealed. Yes, someone or something could sneak up behind them. But that's what the third person was along for. To watch the other's backs.

Sherman speculated that surviving dinosaurs were endowed with fellow reptiles' general skittishness, even when they were of the towering large variety. Such creatures would favor going after someone who stood alone, a twosome at most. They would definitely steer clear of such trios as Irene, Laura and Roberta, or Fred, Ali and Kevin.

The only exception to people grouping in threes, apart of course from Nigel, was Stephen. He wanted to be off on his own, to forestall embarrassing questions. Sherman supplied multiple pieces of disassembled Charly for a hi-tech surveillance moat around him.

"I wish Sherman, or any of the rest of us, for that matter, had thought of this earlier," said Augie regretfully while eyeing Nigel through his infrared binoculars. "Stephen would mock me, but I'm feeling a can't-put-my-finger-on-it emptiness out here now, compared to the last two nights."

"Elvis-osaurus has left the building?" quipped Alistair. Then more seriously, "Yeah, have to admit the same. And where Jurassic Links is concerned, say we do put a memorial plaque beside that par three green. And dedicate it to the suspected dinosaur poop embedded with my golf ball. I don't think that's going to have the same cache as would a large reptilian specter rising on a serpentine neck out of some swamp. Along the Sangha

River, perhaps."

"Where are you on this, Scott?" Augie asked to bring Scott into the conversation. Even in the waning daylight, he could see his esteemed colleague looking off into space, eyes fixed on neither the shoreline nor Nigel anxiously pacing from side to side like the sitting duck he was. "Scott? Penny for your thoughts?"

"Oh!" Scott flinched. "I was just feeling bad for Stephen and that assistant police officer. Angharad was her name?"

"Yep," nodded Augie.

"Appears they don't trust each other, in the wake of letting go their inhibitions. Such a shame."

"Stephen confided to me he doubted Angharad was into anything more than the, uh, physical side of their relationship," Augie whispered, fearful a rogue breeze could carry his words within hearing range of Stephen. "If she's feeling the same way, what with their skeptical temperaments being so similar..."

"To be perfectly honest, Scott, I'm talking brutal truth," said Alistair, tempering his usually joyful tone with a dash of severity, "I believe who you're really feeling sorry for is yourself. You're not letting go your own inhibitions enough to approach Irene. C'mon, mate! Just boogie on over, and admit you've got the hots for her!"

"How do you presume to know I'm feeling anything at all in that department?" bristled Scott. He looked aghast while dusk muted the redness of his fully flushed face.

"Seriously, mate?" reacted Alistair with an are-you-kidding-me grin. "I wouldn't be surprised if even our robot Charly has noticed your puppy-dog eyes for her."

"Maybe you didn't see when I tried confessing to her on the bus from Eclipso's place. I ended up talking to Charly instead. She probably thought I was a total idiot!"

"Irene is one of the sharpest tacks I've ever met," Alistair noted. "Surely, she knew Charly wasn't your intended target. And that's assuming she knew anything at all; didn't she exit the bathroom *after* you stuck your foot in your mouth? Either way, I'll bet you all the sheep in Wales she suspects you've got a thing for her, and has been waiting on you to make another move ever since."

"And when I do," nodded Scott, "she will snark me so ruthlessly, I'll want to curl into a fetal position."

"Steady on there, mate! You don't know that at all!" Alistair pushed back.

After a sigh of resignation, Scott asked, "Okay, what would I say to her this time? I thought we were supposed to be looking for a surviving non-avian dinosaur! Not engaging in soap opera about someone's love life! Namely my own!"

"Tell her exactly what you said the last time, when you thought she was seated in front of you on the bus," earnestly counseled Alistair.

Meanwhile, Augie thought to himself, *I can add Scott's complaint about us being here for a dinosaur search, not someone's love life, to the growing list of improbable remarks I've heard, ever since joining Eclipso's quest.*

In reaction to Alistair's encouragement, Scott surprised himself reflecting yet again on his brother, Donald. Donald wanted him to cut his dinosaur search short. He wanted him to declare success even before he got involved with Eclipso, by drawing certainty from, at best, inconclusive evidence. Scott couldn't help suspect Donald was afraid of further investigation. Afraid that might prove non-avian dinosaurs did not survive to the present day, after all. And thereby cause him a crisis of faith regarding many tenets of his chosen religion. Well here Scott wanted to believe his feelings for Irene were reciprocated, also based on tenuous evidence. And feared that probing further might prove those feelings were as non-existent as a surviving

Stegosaurus. But didn't he also fear his feelings *were* reciprocated? Then how to handle his family, after they learned he's in love with a hard-nosed student of myths and legends? Who obviously was more open-minded than Stephen to amazing possibilities? And yet who nevertheless expressed deep concern about the Bible museum promoting misinformation? While that museum also ended up being his brother's salvation from drug addiction, during its construction? Not to mention his economic well-being? *Still in all, it's important to learn the truth, important for my brother and other relatives, and important for me! And if any of them are queasy about my being with an African American woman, if there's any such bigotry right under my own nose, well I need to know that too! That cannot stand in the way of – gulp! – our happiness!*

"Guess what, Alistair?"

"Chicken butt?"

"Not *this* butt," Scott laughed in a whisper, ever concerned they not scare off a reclusively skittish prehistoric monster. "I'm going to go for it! ASAP!"

"There's no time better than the present, mate!" rejoiced Alistair, if likewise keeping to a whisper. "And while you made your statement of decisive intent, I happened to notice something serendipitously helpful to your cause through these infrared goggles. I thought Irene, Roberta and Laura were supposed to stick together. But up that rounded ridge, over there," he pointed, "Irene appears to have separated off from the pack. She may have noticed something, and wanted the others to hold back while she investigates. Hurry! A private moment like this might be harder to get once we return to Cloud Nine."

By the time Alistair finished, Scott was already on his way, wading through heather.

*

"Wait up, Irene!" Roberta Quiñones whispered harshly to be heard at a distance, but hopefully not draw the attention of some blood-thirsty prehistoric beast on the prowl. *Although truth be told, would we really be wandering about here, even in groups of three, if we seriously believed there was an actual danger of that?* "You don't want to leave us so far behind!"

"Unless she's arranged a rendezvous with Scott," joked journalist Laura Gómez.

"That's it, uh-huh," snapped Irene, in a pause from her stealthy pursuit of suspicious noises. This, while grateful the dusk was so far along that even with the rising moon, no danger anyone could tell how much she was blushing. "He's one of those animal spirit shamans who can transform into a wild beast at night."

"'A wild beast at night'! Does that work for you?" Laura couldn't resist asking.

Whatever giggles that might have erupted were nipped in the bud by sudden, ample rustles just up ahead of Irene, accompanied by distinct huffing and puffing.

Had something monstrously large been roused?

Looks were exchanged all around by Irene with Roberta and Laura, for what none of them needed to say. Far as they knew, the only other people out there that evening were hunkered down in particular locations up and down the shoreline. Many were assigned to keep a special eye on Nigel. But maybe the noise that caught Irene's attention was from an unexpected group of people. A coastal hiking party, perhaps. *Although, what would they be doing on the move so late into the evening? Or...*

*

Stephen Feldman felt extra secure from any prospective murderer, thanks to Charly's camera-equipped body parts encircling him. The Lettermans constantly monitored those parts' video feeds, back aboard Cloud Nine hovering over the Pembrokeshire coastline. And so, Stephen did not give another thought to the laughable prospect of a nasty Stegosaurus on the loose. Instead, he kept his infrared binoculars focused on sitting duck Nigel, as well as Nigel's immediate surroundings. Not to scope out a marauding dinosaur, for sure. But rather, to help the Kelpyguard constabulary solve the disappearance of Robin and Gerwyn. Maybe solve their murders into the bargain, as well as prevent a third. Once again, Eclipso's quixotic expedition would make some minimally worthwhile contribution to humanity, despite its ridiculous goal.

Previous expeditions resulted in a young woman from New Guinea attending college in the U.K., and two princes from Cameroon escaping persecution for their homosexuality. Last Stephen heard, the princes were about to open an African-themed clothes boutique in a college town in Maryland. And most recently, Eclipso's dinosaur search along the Amazon helped stave off rainforest devastation.

Then there was Angharad. Dear, voluptuously proportioned Angharad, Stephen found himself thinking, or rather lusting. Stephen regretted that in the wake of their evening of unbridled passion, they couldn't bring themselves to face each other again. Yes, they had gone from the heights of ecstasy to the depths of total public humiliation. *Oh, well.* About their intimate encounter, Stephen kept telling himself that true intellectual honesty required admitting the physical was all there really was, ultimately.

And yet, he also found he couldn't help asking himself, *Why do I have to keep telling myself this?*

"Ah, there's something guaranteed to put the team's gullible hearts aflutter," Stephen softly said to himself. He actually felt relieved he picked up on something with his infrared binoculars, anything to take his mind off

Angharad.

What had Stephen's attention was a large boulder. It sat to one side of the sitting-duck platform atop a monster-proofed shelter, wherein Nigel might avail himself of hot-chocolate delights. Stephen was sure it had to have been there all along. But it didn't receive any attention because of intense, if worthless, focus on spotting a row of Stegosaurus plates plowing through heather and gorse.

Stephen could easily imagine Augie insisting the boulder *wasn't* there before. That maybe it was yet another dinosaur camouflaged as part of the local geology. "The daytime overhead surveillance video from Cloud Nine should firmly establish that big rock's whereabouts earlier," Stephen no sooner whispered to himself than he noticed movement out the corner of his eye. It was up along the ridge line, well above where a jittery-acting Nigel paced from side to side.

Inspection of the ridge line through his binoculars established for Stephen there was indeed movement. A half dozen sheep paraded in a curiously straight row, one after the other. Their distinctive shapes were set off in silhouette by what Stephen guessed was the glow of streetlights from Kelpyguard.

"What in the world?!" Stephen couldn't help exclaiming, realizing the lead sheep appeared to be walking backwards. And that something cylindrically shaped hung from its forward-facing rear.

"Not too disgusting, is it?" Stephen playfully asked Charly's right knee and left foot, as he realized they were also focused on the odd procession along the ridge line.

Stephen expected any second the cylindrical, presumed sheep poo to drop out of said forward-facing rear, only to be surprised again. One of the supposed sheep's rear legs lifted off the ground at an impossible-seeming angle, and removed the cylindrical whatever from the rear end.

Whereupon, a puff of smoke blew out said rear. And then the cylindrical whatever was reinserted there, something Stephen never expected to see an animal do with its poop.

Humans rather than wolves in sheep's clothing, Stephen concluded, shaking his head disgustedly. No sooner that, though, than he froze dead still. From back behind him, he heard a familiar voice say, "I know this isn't the best time or place for what I have to say. But during our travels, it's occurred to me there is no best time or place. It will be awkward wherever, um, what I'm trying to tell you," the person went on as Stephen's eyes opened wider and wider, threatening to pop from their sockets, "is that I've developed strong feelings for you, romantic feelings. Can't say they weren't kindled the very first time you spoke to me at that book store in Louisville. You justifiably put me on the spot about the role of racism in some aspects of cryptozoology."

"I didn't know you cared," quipped a mischievously grinning Stephen as he turned to face Scott.

Scott couldn't have been much more shocked had Stephen turned out to be a Stegosaurus wearing one of Samuel Longbottom's cardigan wool sweaters.

*

"Will you pocket your bloody damn cigar, Barnaby, and pick up the pace a wee bit?" anxiously complained John Jones from two "sheep" behind Barnaby. "I'm not even sure, from what I can see back here, that you haven't put your costume on backwards. More's to the point, I'm hearin' somethin' especially loud tramplin' that heather not far behind us!" he continued to whisper harshly.

"I'm of a mind, meself, to ditch me own outfit and run for me bloody life, if that ruckus gets any closer!" also harshly whispered Howard from right behind John Jones. "Don't want me legacy to be that when all is said and done, got meself devoured by a prehistoric monster while disguised as a bloody lamb! Still don't understand why you made us chuck those gorse caps Sherman gave us!"

*

"Holy sheep poo!" Laura whispered excitedly to Irene and Roberta beside her. "Sounds like something enormous huffing and puffing up ahead of us, and I think we're all slouching towards Nigel!"

"Better hurry so we can warn him," advised Irene, "although..." she trailed off, not wanting to elaborate in case she was wrong. Especially if she was wrong to suspect they weren't actually tracking a relic dinosaur.

*

"That's it, mates; bloody hell, that monster is picking up speed! RUN!!" screamed John Jones, standing up to fling aside his sheep costume.

*

"I don't know what to say," Scott shame-facedly admitted to Stephen. "But given your, um..."

"ROOOAAARRRR!!!!" came deafening loud from Nigel's direction, followed by a chaos of other noises.

A hoarse, blood-curdling scream that Scott feared came from Nigel; something very heavy-sounding crashing through underbrush, perhaps tumbling out of control downhill; a chorus of cries that abruptly went totally silent...

"What the Hellasaurus Hex is going on?!?!" shouted Sergeant Fred Frankly.

Through their infrared binoculars, both Stephen and Scott, plus Augie and Alistair running up beside them, couldn't see a thing. Where Nigel had been restlessly pacing back and forth as a sitting duck, everything was obscured by billowing smoke.

As said smoke rapidly cleared, though, Stephen and company spotted several people scattered about, lying perfectly still where they collapsed. Some were draped over others, with discarded sheep costumes part of the mess.

Chapter 19

Augie's gang couldn't rush over fast enough to where Nigel acted as bait. By the time they arrived, the smoke had pretty much dissipated, revealing a curious aftermath.

Scott was cradling Irene's head in his lap. Spurred by what he saw through his infrared binoculars, he had sprinted well ahead of Augie.

Elwin Kneath was administering beer-to-mouth resuscitation to John Jones.

Rupert Hamster Holmes was wandering about aimlessly, wringing his hands guiltily regarding the several other semi-conscious bodies scattered across the ground. *I should be helping, same as those other two fine gentlemen are doing. But if I favor one, I neglect the rest. Yet if I don't favor one, well what good have I been? Although there is the matter that I'm not knocking people senseless with stones so they remain unconscious. And I am on the alert. Or maybe not so much on the alert as more positively disposed to noticing danger. For example, some predatory seagull might swoop down any second to peck at someone's face, mistaking it for a Welsh cake with eyes in place of currants. That's the ticket! Perhaps!*

Assistant Constable Angharad Gruffudd was hands on knees to ponder something more closely on an especially steep coastward incline. The full moon clearly revealed a trail gouged through the heather and gorse, as far downhill as she could see until lost in inky darkness. After shining a flashlight into that seeming abyss, she shouted back behind her, "Looks like we've got blood!"

"That's not Nigel's blood! It can't be!" Kay Morgan shouted as she rushed into plain view, thanks to tripod floodlights brought to bear by the chief constable.

Augie reckoned Kay was more in denial than actually privy to any information relevant to Nigel's status.

Nevertheless, when Chief Constable Williams asked, "What makes you so sure that's not Nigel's blood, Kay?" she didn't miss a beat answering, "I gave it a close look with me own penlight. I'm telling you, there was none of his usual drool! So I've been searching round here ever since, I have!" she concluded tearfully, burying her face in her hands and grieving, "Oh God!"

"Your fingers are lookin' pretty cut up, they are. I'm not bein' funny about it!" noted Williams.

Behind him, Augie could see Sherman Peabody leap from a rope ladder. It hung down from low-hovering Cloud Nine, that drone's steam-powered hiss blending with the din of coastal surf.

Just then noticing streaks of blood all over her hands, Kay said, "This must have happened when I pushed aside gorse branches for a better look after hearing a terrible roar!"

"Nigel's drool is really so prolific, Kay?" Chief Constable Williams just had to ask.

"Disgusting I suppose," Kay tearfully nodded. "But you never know how much you miss something...until it's gone!" she concluded, bawling inconsolably.

"Next time me better half complains about me thunderous snorin'... Good Lord God!" the chief constable exclaimed, smacking himself upside the forehead. "Just occurs to me, there's that shelter you buried under our feet here, Mr. Peabody! It's soundproof, didn't you say?"

"I did say indeed," confirmed Sherman Peabody while using a hand-held gadget to direct together Charly's head and torso pieces, at least, for a readout from the flatus emission detector.

"For all we know," went on Williams, "while we've been frettin' over Nigel's fate, he's tucked away safely below us, enjoyin' an early evening hot chocolate with a homemade Welsh cake!"

"So why were the rest of us stuck out here, faintin' from some strange-smellin' gas?" angrily asked John Jones, tossing aside the already-emptied can of Toohey's that revived him. "What, did a bloody dinosaur fart us to sleep? Or what??"

"It was the 'or what' part," delicately answered Sherman. "Presumably, Nigel pushed the panic button I gave him. Then the shelter opened just long enough to drop him smoothly down the slide inside, before sealing shut again. And finally, the sealing-shut bit automatically released the knockout gas."

"Panic button?!" John Jones repeated, staggering about naked without a fresh can of Toohey's in hand. "You mean this bloody thing that stubbed me foot when we came tumblin' down the hill?!? Trippin' over each other into the bargain?!? Figurin' some stonkin' dinosaur was after us?!?" He pulled a card-deck-sized box from his pants pocket, and held it forward. Its purple plastic button really shimmered in the floodlight.

Meanwhile, as Laura and Roberta struggled back up onto their feet, they noticed Scott giving Irene the VIP treatment. "What do you think, Roberta?" Laura asked. "Did Scott flip a coin, and Irene just randomly came up the winner?"

"That was exactly my dilemma. Well maybe not so much exactly, but at least approximately with 'exactly' certainly in the running," interjected Rupert Hamster Holmes. "To wit, which of you fair maidens was I to assist first, without playing favorites? And by golly if you, young lady, didn't propose the perfect solution. Flipping a coin! Had that only occurred to me sooner, surely one of you would have been availed of my services, guaranteed! Or maybe not so much guaranteed as-"

"That was a bullet dodged," Laura whispered to Roberta

under cover of Chief Constable Williams raging loudly, "When it comes right down to it, I said it before and I'll say it again! For all we know, Nigel is this very moment safely tucked away down below us! Mr. Peabody, I assume we can open your shelter simply by pushin' the panic button?"

"Not so simply," Sherman shook his head. "Didn't want to run any risk, in case the panic button remained topside while Nigel slid to safe refuge. Our hoped-for dinosaur could have accidentally stepped on it upon reviving from the gas, or upon arriving after the gas dissipated."

"But you *can* open it, I trust?"

"Which I'm doing this very instant," announced Sherman, holding a wand-like stick like he was dousing for water, Augie imagined.

John Jones and crew scrambled to avoid falling in when the shelter opened. But they were the first to peer over the edge, down past the slide to the shelter's bottom, lit up automatically by motion sensors near the top.

"Such a waste, this is," complained John Jones as with a fearful gasp, Kay realized along with everyone else that the shelter was empty of Nigel or anybody else. "That jar of pastel-colored marshmallows, just sittin' there beggin' for a cuppa hot chocolate! And that pile of Welsh cakes collectin' dust! *Ych a fi!*"

"The entire brutal matter is tragically clear," adjudged Elwin Kneath. "When the terrible monster, likely a surviving theropod dinosaur, lifted Nigel to its gaping maw, well here is what must have happened. Before pouncing, it sprayed a cloaking mist either from its nostrils, like a dragon, or from its nether region. And then it loomed out of that mist, shocking Nigel too much for him to gather his wits enough to push the panic button. Instead, he dropped it to the ground, well away from the shelter, as the fearsome creature made off with him down that incline where you see the underbrush has clearly been crushed flat by something most weighty. Then John Jones accidentally stepped on the panic button, concealed by the monster's lingering foggy exhalations, or emissions from its nether region. Nobody stood in the right place for the slide, as it were. But plenty were within close-enough range of the knock-out gas..."

"I would be a big fan of your narrative, Elwin," said Sherman with his eyes buried in readouts unrolled from Charly's torso, extruded cylindrically through his faux belly button. "That is, if my flatus emission detector didn't come up empty regarding suspected giant reptilian farts, if I might be so crude. The previous two nights it should be noted, though, were a whole different matter."

"I ask the lot of you," reacted Elwin with what struck Augie as no little amount of irritation. "Which is more persuasive? A supposed fart detector not noticing anything? Or that tremendous roar we all heard, in addition to the blood, in addition to this matted-down trail?"

"Wait," Stephen held up a go-no-further hand. "Just occurs to me what's missing. Through my infrared binoculars, I spotted a large boulder."

"Yes, you're right," said Sherman, for one of only a few times lifting his chin from his neck. "I spotted that from above, aboard Cloud Nine."

"Someone, maybe even Nigel, must have dislodged it to create the trail of matted-down heather and gorse on the hillside. If so, we will find it near bottom, almost to the shoreline, no dinosaur involved."

"We will explore that possibility ASAP," said Chief Constable Williams in no uncertain terms. "I want to make sure Nigel's dead body isn't underneath the boulder you're reportin'."

"Yes indeed," Elwin nodded while open-mouthed Kay shook her head in horror at the prospect. "A creature the likes of a large theropod dinosaur would have been necessary to budge such an enormous, weighty object, and send it on a downhill tumble. That fearsome beast could well have been intent on knocking out Nigel in exactly such a manner, before biting into him as though he were a most delectable Welsh cake."

"Not necessarily," pushed back Stephen.

"If you're saying he wouldn't have tasted anything like a Welsh cake, you do have a point," conceded Elwin, beyond oblivious to the stunned-silent, incredulous horror by which Kay was meeting his remarks.

"I'm not talking about that, Elwin. I'm talking about the entire dinosaur thing," corrected Stephen testily. "I don't see any depression in the ground here where that boulder could have been embedded. To dislodge it from being embedded, you are correct, would have required superhuman strength. But if it was not embedded, there are any number of ways it might have been started on its downhill descent, no dinosaur or superman required."

"Name one."

"Very well," Stephen responded still in testy mode. "Someone could have used a crowbar. And by the by, the constables should be combing the area for hidden speakers. Roars, munches, those noises and more might have been broadcast from them."

"Sheer, unadulterated, not worth a sheep's fart," bristled Elwin, tugging on his wool vest as though his very dignity was threatened. Although Augie did notice his eyes dart from side to side, as though he were thinking, *Hope I remembered to clean up after meself.*

"Wait down there, I say! Before you proceed any further!" came a familiar voice from uphill, if not particularly welcome where Chief Constable Williams was concerned.

Whereupon Rupert Hamster Holmes appeared in all his stiffly attired glory as though he'd just arrived. In actuality, he'd circled around to there from fretting over having done nothing for Roberta or Laura after he discovered them sprawled out on the ground, fast asleep from the knock-out gas triggered by the infamous panic button.

"I have something to report," Rupert continued, though he might have hemmed and hawed on whether that was the very best word to describe what he was doing, given half a chance. "Something that might prove significant, which is to say that it might instead prove of no significance whatso-"

"Can you dive right into the meat of it for a bloody change, Rupert?!" interrupted John Jones. "There be Welsh cakes collectin' dust down inside there!" He pointed at the throw-rug-sized opening in the ground, wherein motion-detector-activated light competed with Chief Constable Williams's tripod-stationed floodlight.

"Oh, my, well that does sound urgent, though urgent not so much in the sense of impending doom as- Dive right in, yes," Rupert abruptly changed course. He saw John Jones wave a broken-off heather bramble his way in a most threatening manner. "I was roaming, perusing if you will, inland trails several steps removed from our fair Pembrokeshire coast. What inspired me was the beast, if beast it was, leaving its calling card on a par three green at the Sheep's Shank Links. Though it was not the kind of calling card one would ever consider carrying around in one's wallet, unless stored securely inside one of those waterproof plastic baggies. And even then-"

"Me tummy be growlin' somethin' fierce for those Welsh cakes, plus them wee pastel-shaded marshmallows floatin' atop a steamin' mug of hot chocolate!"

Augie reckoned John Jones looked even more ridiculous than usual, striking such a threatening pose with his heather bramble over the prospect of "wee pastel-shaded marshmallows."

"Very well," Rupert reacted reluctantly. "Coastwards up the ridgeline, I saw - Well not so much saw as sensed something, some entity, of incredible length, on the move. Put five or six men in a row, then have them crawl one after the other on their knees. That might give you some notion of the thing's proportions. It was headed at a good pace, well not anywhere approaching that of a competitive marathon runner-"

"Maybe I have not made myself clear! Those Welsh cakes sprinkled with sugar, sparklin' as from the lightest dustin' of snow, there might be one with your name on it, Rupert old boy!" enthused John Jones, trying a different tack to encourage Rupert to be more concise.

"Oh, in that case, then, I must cut to the quick, clear away all the chaff, bring us in for a smooth landing on the bottom line, though maybe not so smooth as-"

"There'll be a thorny whack of one of these gorse branches on your bottom line, mate, if you don't get to the heart of it, your very next words!" growled John Jones, back in threat mode.

"Fine! Okay! Against every fiber of my being, I will take a belly flop leap into the main event! Cast in silhouette by the moonlit horizon, along a line of deep heather, six humps slowly lifted to view! They had to have stretched a good twenty-five, thirty feet from end to end! Humps what reminded me of reports from Scotland of the Loch Ness Monster! And yet, my eyes perceived them to be furry, wooly, as of our plentiful sheep! But which couldn't have been sheep because they moved as one! Which raises a certain prospect. Sightings of living dinosaurs seem, to date, to be the stuff of myth and legend. Moreover, their fossil bones certainly don't offer much where their skin was involved. So, who's to say for sure that the Brachiosaur and his companions weren't indeed a furry lot? But what's even stranger," Rupert went on without missing a beat, leaving

238 | David Taylor

John Jones open-mouth stymied from interrupting, "is that this monstrous entity, this maybe dinosaur, appeared to make its not-so-merry way, where we're concerned, backwards! Such an extraordinary event to witness! Such a humbling experience, I should add! And what's more, the creature passed gas, quietly!

"But how did I ascertain that happened if it was silent, you might well be justified inquiring? Well, it was more than the stench that so rudely barged in on me nostrils. Without that 'more,' in fact, one might be well justified arguing it issued, as it were, from a sheep. Or from more than one sheep, collectively, in what would have had to have been perfect coordination. Or maybe even a fellow puffing on an unusually pungent cigar. But here's the rub. Here's the detail that also informed me of the creature's rearward motion! From the very front of that line of humps, I saw the humid sea air condense the farted gas into visibility, as a puff of smoke! Even in nothing more than moonlight, not to minimize the brightness of the full moon! Wait! Wait, I say! It couldn't be that I only saw a small part! It couldn't be that the main event was so voluminous, it enshrouded poor Nigel in flatus mists, as I overheard you discussing on my hasty trek here?!?"

"You idiot!!" John Jones spat out, though staggering about too far away for his saliva to reach the intended destination. "You just described me and me mates, dressed in sheep's clothing to keep an eye on things without ourselves drawin' attention! Six blokes crawlin' one after the other on their hands and knees, who for all their trouble might just as well have been with the mission of sniffin' each other's behinds! What's more, that weren't no prehistoric monster passin' gas! That was Fergus puffin' on one of his damned putrid cigars; sorry there, mate!" he turned Fergus's way to add. "I'm goin' to stop right there, because those Welsh cakes plus those multi-colored marshmallows are callin' out to me somethin' fierce! Weeee!!!" John Jones cried as with a running leap through the entrance to the underground enclosure, he landed flying down the slide to the tasty repast awaiting below.

Chapter 20

Few were the funeral services Augie Matias had ever attended. Nevertheless, he brimmed full of confidence they could have numbered in the thousands, taken up as some bizarre hobby. Yet still, he would have been impressed by the oddity of what transpired at St. Mary's Anglican Church in Kelpyguard, Wales.

Sure, the service got off to a traditional enough start with the processional hymn, "All Things Bright And Beautiful" ("All things bright and beautiful, all creatures great and small, all things wise and wonderful, the good Lord made them all."). And a Welsh favorite, "Ar Hyd y Nos" ("All Through The Night") was scheduled for the closing recessional. But Stephen was already snidely whispering beside Augie, "Yes, there's nothing so wonderful as a murderer on the loose."

Far more importantly, where oddity was concerned, were the two rental trailers converted into oversized crypts for Gerwyn and Robin. Gerwyn's trailer would also honor the memory of Nigel in a future service, were a few more days to elapse without finding his body, either.

Both crypts expressed the town's oversized grief, whether due to a murderous human or a bloodthirsty prehistoric monster. And since they were too large for the procession down the aisle between church pews, the service was held outdoors, back of the church beside a cemetery. The crypts would reside there temporarily, until the expected follow-up service for Nigel. Then they would be ensconced permanently atop an ancient volcanic mound overlooking the North Irish Sea.

Pall bearers included Scott, such locals as Assistant Constable Angharad Gruffudd, and Samuel Longbottom (he trusted the Lettermans to keep Cloud Nine hovering steadily overhead like a lone, fluffy cumulus). They pulled along the crypts on trailer wheels, reminding Augie of a scene in the movie, The Ten Commandments, when slaves pulled along immense stones to build a pyramid. Minus the slave master's whip, of course.

Augie noticed Scott and Angharad steal longing looks at Irene and Stephen. And that whenever that happened, Irene and Stephen feigned attention elsewhere.

In any event, the so-called out-of-towners took up the back rows of unfolded chairs, while local town folk took up the rest.

At first glance, John Jones appeared unaccompanied by his usual can of Toohey's. But he kept his head buried in a hymn book, no singing issuing from his lips. Rather, at regular intervals he lifted the hymnal high, and tipped it slanting towards his greedily opened mouth.

Meanwhile, Rupert Hamster Holmes paged anxiously back and forth in his own hymnal, unsure which page he should turn to.

Poor little David Taylor appeared extremely uncomfortable, stuffed into a full suit and tie he'd clearly outgrown. He stood beside his mother holding her hymn book low for him to follow along. Augie's heart went out to him. He figured David was dragged there against his will. Doubtless, he'd rather be roaming the coastline again, for another glimpse, a better glimpse, of his dinosaur.

David did notice something, though, that brought a gleam to his eye. Bonsai Gator.

Eclipso Sunray Smith attended remotely, sitting behind Bonsai at his swamp-embedded desk. His mother stood stoically still behind him as he divided his attention between the service and a humus-dipped pretzel stick.

For David, however, Bonsai Gator was the main attraction, by far, on the two-way video screen set off to the left of the makeshift outdoor altar. As the choir slowly processed forward, David had to crane his neck awkwardly to keep an eye on Bonsai. He was fiercely determined on that score, since he'd never seen such a small alligator before. Let alone a gator of any size standing perfectly upright on its hind legs, and swaying gracefully from side to side, reminding Augie of a hula dancer.

Oh my God! Augie abruptly found himself marveling. *That's it! That's the similarity shown by the impossibly blown-about seaweed and driftwood! It was to the bushes and trees waving about in that video from the final episode of* Cryptomonster Hunt!! *And how the mango tree swayed when I was back on New Britain Island with Eclipso's team! The same mango tree where I saw that behemoth duck bill poke through, not visible on the camcorder video later! Maybe it is there, but our eyes are hypnotized into not seeing it?!?! Thanks to the dinosaur's camouflage ability forged by millions of additional years of evolution?!?! Wonder if Charly can spot it?*

What snapped Augie out of his reverie over a possible epiphany was noticing David sway like Bonsai in time to the hymn, no matter the lack of any reggae rhythm.

David managed to mimic Bonsai despite the effort it took to keep an eye on the little reptile, and how constrained he felt by his outfit. Augie was convinced the young lad wanted to leave behind his Sunday suit like an outgrown cicada larva shell left empty, stuck to a tree trunk.

David's mimicry of Bonsai didn't last very long, though. His mom forced him to stand perfectly still for the final verse of the hymn.

Which concluded, punctuated by a perfectly timed belch by John Jones.

Choir to his side, the side opposite from the TV featuring Bonsai Gator, Reverend Hawkin solemnly said, "Let us pray."

"Stop!" shouted Chief Constable Rhys Williams. He stormed into the church's courtyard from the back of the building, and lifted one arm high.

"Maybe not so much 'stop' as a temporary pause?" Rupert Hamster Holmes broke the hushed silence to gently propose in his meekest, most feeble voice.

Everyone else in attendance directed looks so severe Rupert's direction, he feared some enterprising bloke might deliver a punch to his nose. He hunched his shoulders flinchingly, and sat down while many others remained standing. "I will consider the constable's order also applies to meself."

"Assistant Constable Gruffudd, if you will assist me, I'm afraid I must make an arrest," sternly announced the chief constable.

"My goodness gracious, Chief Constable Williams!" breathlessly spoke Father Hawkin. "We are in the middle of a double funeral, on the burial grounds of a house of worship! Can't your legal action wait until the service concludes?"

"How the relevant facts of the matter interconnect, Father, had that only occurred to me sooner, I might have saved Nigel's life," responded Chief Constable Williams unyieldingly. "Three souls lost to this fair earth! I don't want to chance losing a fourth by waiting any longer than absolutely necessary in the pursuit of justice!"

Where she sat the second row back from the front, Kay Morgan burst into tears. "Nigel!" she cried.

"Might as well be grievin' for your own proper self, Kay. Because you're the one we need to arrest, under suspicion for the murder of Gerwyn, Robin, and Nigel! Assistant Constable Gruffudd, if you will..."

"You do not have to say anything," Angharad started reciting the standard police caution as she firmly pulled

Kay to her feet, and brought her hands together for handcuffing. "But it may harm your defense if you do not mention when questioned, something which you later rely on in court."

To multiple astonished gasps, Kay tearfully cried, "What possible motive could I have had for offing the man I love??"

"You act so innocent, Ms. Morgan," scoffed Chief Constable Williams while Angharad brought Kay out from amidst the unfolded chairs. "Such a well-respected school teacher, well I have to say that the word, disappointment, doesn't even begin to describe how I'm feelin' about this, if I'm goin' to be honest about it!"

"But surely, Chief Constable, there must be some mistake," protested Father Hawkin still in breathless mode. "In addition to a lack of conceivable motive, what possible evidence could you have?"

"How about we start with her blood type sprinkled amidst Nigel's blood type on the very ground where he was left a guinea pig by our unicorn-seeking out-of-towners?!"

"We said nothing about unicorns," Sherman mumbled to himself, chin pushed to double-chin effect into his neck. That coincided with an especially quiet moment, when all breezes calmed to a halt. He was easily heard far and wide so that the chief constable erupted, "Unicorns, dragons, survivin' dinosaurs, it's all the same value as a sheep's fart! Oh, that's right, isn't it?! You daft blokes have some special contraption you believe actually teases out the unique character of each 'flatus emission'!! To prove some prehistoric rotter is still on the loose!!" he concluded derisively.

"Of course you would have found me drops of blood there!" grievingly explained Kay. "As I already admitted, after getting meself all cut up on the gorse! In a panic I was, from hearing that awful roar followed by my Nigel's death cry! I had to go searching for him there, fast as me legs would take me!"

"Oh, so in other words, you're sayin' you returned to the scene of the crime like any typical wrong doer!" Chief Constable Williams pointed a forefinger Kay's way as in *Gotcha!*

"Yes, that's it!" Kay nodded ferociously, her anger overtaking her grief. "I returned to the scene of the crime within minutes of committing it! Peeking down the hill at me handiwork, I was! Singlehandedly, like Hercules, I kicked that boulder over the edge with me superhuman foot, like it was merely another one of those wee pebbles covering the beach! Better watch out that I don't leave St. Mary's a pile of rubble!!"

"I do find myself compelled to point out something, Chief Constable," Sherman Peabody rose from his seat near the back to say, albeit with his chin still firmly scrunched into his neck. "You've gone from accusing Robin, to implicating Nigel, and now on a third try, arresting a revered school teacher."

"You might call it a Rube Goldberg machine murder," Chief Constable Williams retorted with steady confidence. "My mistake was continually misapprehendin' a mid-point in the sequence was the original foot-kick that got the ball rollin', as it were!"

"Rube Goldberg machine? What the hell – sorry, Father – be that? Burp!" John Jones asked boisterously, lifting his head from his beer-stained hymnal.

"I can explain," said time traveler Sergeant Fred Frankly popping out of his seat. "Some idiot kicks a ball down an incline, the ball bumps into a bull, the bull rages after someone carrying a bucket of water across a field, he starts running until he trips over a rake and lets the bucket fly, and the bucket lands upside down on my head, nearly drowning me. Then I scream at the top of my lungs, 'WHAT

THE FRIED FISH?!?!?!'" Fred added quietly aside to Father Hawkin, "Hope you appreciate what I just did there, Father."

"I think me own example from the real world will prove much better, it will," growled Chief Constable Williams. He was not at all pleased with how ridiculous the out-of-towner made his suggestion sound before he even laid it out. "We start, Kay, with your obsessive love for Nigel."

"God help me to ever understand what I saw in that drunken sod. But can't deny it's true!" Kay concluded tearfully.

"Here's the bloody thing of it, what I believe turned your heart as dark as the inside of a cow's stomach. Accordin' to most of our town folk I interviewed, Nigel was at least open to the idea of a bit of a fling with you, Kay. All the sudden, however, his attentions seemed really set on Robin Pugh. But you could see, clear as sheep grazin' on the hillside, that Robin's heart was set on Gerwyn!"

"No, I didn't see that at all!" Kay shook her head emphatically NO. "Seemed to me she blew him off, whenever he asked whether she'd fancy fish 'n' chips with him after work. Made it all the more surprising when she grieved so much over his disappearance, even granted his blood-stained shredded shirt!"

"Bollocks! You knew secretly she was just playin' at hard to get! But you thought maybe Nigel was as unaware of that as you want me to believe you were! In your twisted mind, you wanted Gerwyn gone for good, his corpse sent out to sea by you for the sharks to finish him off. And his bloody shirt? Torn up by the kitchen knife you trusted the surf to bury in sand forever? You made sure it got good and wet in seawater to wash away your fingerprints, just in case. And you figured correctly that Gerwyn's disappearance would flush Robin's passion for him out into the open. Your next figurin' didn't turn out so well, though, did it? You believed Nigel would realize Robin's affections were too far gone on her beloved lost Gerwyn to give him the time of day. And then his heart would certainly be ripe for your pluckin'! But I repeat, didn't work out that way, now did it?

"And if I might back up a second, what a gift from – well whether or not in the good Father's presence, we're not goin' to be wantin' to call it a gift from heaven now, are we? But how...convenient! Ah, there's the right word! How convenient was young David's monstrous beastie sighting! Playin' along to gain it a measure of credibility, you gambled that would draw here a bunch of crazed barmies like those Nessie watchers up north in Scotland. They would provide the perfect cover for whatever number of people you needed to off, to push Nigel into your waitin' arms. They would do that, they would, by insistin' a bloody dinosaur was what did in your victims! Concluded by the murder of Nigel himself, if he wouldn't finally succumb to your charms! Whether to his death or your romance, that was the bucket of water in someone's face at the end of your Rube Goldberg contraption, it was!"

"I wasn't 'playin' along'!" Kay pushed back in no uncertain terms. "I saw what me young charge saw! Sure, at the end of the day maybe it was something more regular, like a large seal. But if so, it had to have been a seal with a neck the length of a boa constrictor! With a head to match!"

"Uh huh," Chief Constable Williams nodded dubiously. "Let's go back to that first night of the out-of-towners' dinosaur vigil, Ms. Morgan. Young David Taylor told me he fell asleep in your arms."

"True as true can be, Chief Constable," Kay Morgan confirmed, however warily.

"Ah, but the wee lad also told me that when he woke

up, he found himself on his lonesome, wet through and through from the storm!"

"Truth be known, Chief Constable, I was exhausted, meself, from a ripe full day in me classroom. Drifted off to Snoozyland as well, I did. That's when David must have rolled off me lap onto the wet ground."

"And the next thing you know, the tide rollin' in on stormy surf soaked you awake? And you found your lap empty, did you?"

"Exactly, Chief Constable! In a panic I was, to find the wee lad, and gather him back up in me arms, fast as the good Lord would take me! Relieved doesn't begin to describe how I felt, seeing him nearby, pouring out his dinosaur-sized heart to Dr. Matias!"

"A very convenient narrative that is, Ms. Morgan!" harrumphed the chief constable in unbridled disgust. "Too bad nobody around you can confirm you didn't sneak off for your foul deed! And then sneak back into the cave, just in time to pretend you never left!"

"But me teacher is no murderer!" insisted David. His face broke into a sob that he buried in his mother's woolen sweater while Kay gave him a regard by turns pained and pitying.

"I wish that were true, lad," Williams nodded sympathetically. "The best we can say for Kay Morgan is that she made a bid to cut short the Rube Goldberg sequence of events, leave out a murder or two. What I mean is, she tried to make Nigel jealous by fawnin' all over the out-of-towner with local ancestry, Mr. Matias in other words."

"I readily admit that, Chief Constable. But being willing to make someone jealous isn't quite the same as being willing to commit murder, is it now?" Kay asked rhetorically. "Sorry there, Augustine. I never really fancied hopping in the sack with a married man, especially one whose attentions are torn between me, and some blooming dinosaur."

"But the dinosaur means nothing to me!" protested Augie mock melodramatically. "I'll break off looking for it! I promise!" *Vicky will love hearing about this…to the extent she doesn't actually worry I'd be at all seriously susceptible to Kay's charms…*

Kay gave Augie a what-the-hell? look that left him feeling guilty over his flippant outburst. After all, even if she wasn't the murderer, something truly horrific had occurred, whether of human or saurian origin. Unless Gerwyn, Robin, and Nigel were simply in hiding.

"But Nigel could care less about your attention to Mr. Matias, could he?" Chief Constable Williams pushed onward. "And so, as much as you really didn't want to off Robin, your main competition in your twisted mind, you concluded you had no choice, didn't you?"

"Oh, I get it!" Kay nodded furiously. "The second night of dinosaur searching played right into me literally bloody hands, it did, providing cover for me second murder! This is on the far frontier of bonkers, it is! The proverbial fart in the jam jar!"

"Only it isn't!" insisted the chief constable. "I'm not bein' funny, right? Our out-of-towners spooked each other silly! With the fog rollin' in, they imagined every wave crashin' ashore was a stonkin' Stegosaurus frolickin' on the beach. Under cover of that, well I'm not sure yet exactly how you did it. Which is why I'm holdin' you under suspicion of murder, and not yet for murder. But we'll soon be checkin' your cutlery to see if any knives be missin'!"

"Knives are always missing, what with me neighbors constantly borrowing and losing them! That proves nothing!"

"I think you doth protest too much on that count, as they say! And I also think there was no end to the lengths you went, to point the blame away from anyone human, to the out-of-towners' prehistoric monster! There's an important piece of evidence you hoped would become the magician's proverbial distraction from your murderous sleight of hand!"

"I say, guv'nah," Elwin Kneath whispered to Rupert seated beside him. "Now he's mixing metaphors. So which is it? A Rube Goldberg contraption, or a magic trick?"

"What I'm talkin' about," went on Chief Constable Williams, undaunted by Elwin's quiet mockery, "is that pile of poo, sheep's poo we can be sure, unless their imagined dinosaur eats the exact same pasture grasses as our best prized lambs. It was left on a green at the Sheep's Shank Links, and topped with a golf ball rather than a cherry. You must have overheard one of the out-of-towners say he might well have launched a golf ball directly into some giant creature's business end!"

"I do have to admit – sorry there, Kay," Alistair added for the simmering mad teacher as he stood up. "Wandering the beach down directly below the Strumblehead lighthouse, I finally found my golf ball washed ashore, washed clean by the surf. The golf ball cherry atop a sheep poo sundae had to have come from elsewhere. Please, try to hold down the applause; it's going to my head," he mumbled as he returned to sitting, met by nonplussed reactions.

"Well, nothing I've heard is more than pig's poo, far as pinning any of the murders on me, if murders indeed they were. With still no bodies yet, there must be a chance..." Kay trailed off tearfully.

"How about the sheep poo your school's headmaster told Assistant Constable Gruffudd you tracked down the hall into your classroom yesterday? Does that suffice?"

"Several points, Chief Constable! One, I took it on meself, personally, to mop that up once I realized what happened! Two, anyone knows this who has lived around here long enough. Whenever you stray off a sidewalk, it's not exactly the easiest thing in the world to avoid stepping into a pile of- I think Father Hawkin will appreciate if I avoid repeating such foul language on the Lord's grounds."

"My dear child," Father Hawkin waved a scoffing hand to say, "given what's already been spoken here, plus all the actual obscenities done to people the world over, I really don't believe the Lord gives a shit."

Several gasps erupted from scandalized parishioners.

"Okay," said Chief Constable Williams, "can anyone attest to your whereabouts two nights ago, Ms. Jones? When you reportedly did not return for the second dinosaur vigil?"

"If only me tele could talk..."

"I submit that's when, after offin' Robin, you made a detour to gather a triple-scoop-sized amount of the sheep's poo, if we are to go with the ice cream analogy."

"Well how about that!" burst out another congregant. "I was wonderin' why me small herd made a chorale of baas for no evident reason two nights ago, that died down by the time I went for a look-see!"

"Once this is over, Gareth, I can return the whole stinkin' lot to you from our evidence room, if you require it for your fertilizin' needs."

"Cheers, Chief Constable, much obliged. But maybe I should sue Kay for interest on that unscheduled loan."

"I can supply the interest, mate, if you insist," said John Jones standing to unzip his pants.

"Zip it, J.J.! On both ends! Now like I was sayin', it became clear to you, Kay Jones, didn't it? That contrary to all expectations, Nigel's thing for Robin only intensified, if anything, on her untimely demise."

"Not at all what I expected, I'll be the first to admit, Chief Constable!"

"Ah-HA! Sounds like a confession to me, if we consider

the long form of your statement, which goes: 'Not at all what I expected after I offed Robin, and flirted with Mr. Matias'!"

"Don't be daft, Chief Constable!! My full statement really goes: Not at all what I expected, after Robin vanished under ominous circumstances I can no more shine a light on than anyone else. It's confounding for me, not to mention heartbreaking, how Nigel could go from no particular expressed interest in Robin that I could see, to mourn her disappearance as much as he might the death of his own beloved mum!"

"Well, here's what I believe was really knockin' about your head like a ball down a gutter in one of those Rube Goldberg machines. If you couldn't have Nigel for yourself, you weren't goin' to let anyone else have him, either! Not even a ghost! And the only way to do that was to off him!"

"This is well beyond ridiculous! Assuming you're correct, where did I pile all those dead bodies?"

"Tell us that, Kay, and I'll ask for your life imprisonment instead of goin' for the death penalty! Assistant Constable Gruffudd, take her back to the constabulary, and lock her up!"

"I don't even get to attend this funeral service?!?"

"I have to step in," announced Augie, rising from his seat. "Can't let you do this to someone who is clearly innocent."

"Oh, Dr. Matias!" Kay swooned.

"Your own special pile of sheep poo you're itchin' to step into, are you?" asked John Jones. He lifted his hymnal for another cloaked swig of his Toohey's before staggering out into the central aisle between rows of unfolded chairs. "Well follow me off the churchyard, and I'm sure we can locate one soon enough, cheers!" He raised the hymnal high.

"I think something is going on here very different from what you described, Chief Constable."

"Is that right?" Williams asked testily. "You solve complex crime puzzles on the side, do you, when you're not diggin' up old fossils, or chasin' dinosaur-shaped shadows? What, you're the new Monsieur Poirot, are you?"

"Actually," retorted Augie, "the identification of exactly which dinosaur bone has been unearthed is always a complex puzzle. The history of paleontology is strewn with fossil identification errors. The most famous involved Apatosaurus bones misidentified as an entirely different sauropod called Brontosaurus. Although it's a pity the name, 'thunder lizard,' as the Latin translates, had to be jettisoned."

"From my collection of arcane trivia," Ali Magabu raised a tentative forefinger to interject, "you'll be happy to learn, Augie, what happened back in 2015, I believe. New analysis established those fossils represented a different sauropod after all. Its wider neck could not be lifted quite so high as an Apatosaurus neck. Brontosaurus was thereby resurrected into the prehistory books."

"'Back in 2015' did you say, sir?!" Chief Constable Williams growled at Ali. "What, did you arrive here in some bloody time machine?! Sorry, Father," he added about the "bloody" part.

"Not the biggest poo in the pasture, shall we say, Constable," Father Hawkin shook his head.

"It's a long story perhaps best left for a less urgent time, if you want to know," Ali added.

"I don't want to know."

"I've chummed around with a lump of clay who used to chum around with a Brontosaurus bone," John Jones bellowed, ever staggering from side to side. The same as Nigel, like he stood on the deck of a rocking-about boat, Augie imagined. "Said it made a deep impression on him, cheers!" he saluted everyone with a half-open prayer book that obviously held a can of something.

"Okay, before we go totally off the rails, let's have the paleontologist tell us what he thinks is really happenin' here!"

"I appreciate your indulgence, Chief Constable," Augie nodded, then promptly went on, "I'll start with your original suspect, Robin. Clearly, she wanted us to believe she grieved over Gerwyn's loss as far more than simply the loss of an endearing work associate at the local pub. But I remember very distinctly her rebuffing his asking her out. And with her amateur acting work I heard about, it's not like she wouldn't be capable of feigning grief believably.

"Which brings us to Nigel, after her disappearance. He went to dramatic lengths, himself, to have us believe Robin was his own true love. And yet Kay found that completely surprising, not to mention totally disappointing. Previously, she thought she had a realistic crack at him, herself."

"A butt crack was that?" John Jones asked, pursuant to which a parishioner seated beside him pulled him sideways sprawled to the ground, letting out a welp.

"What it all comes down to," Augie continued, too enthused about laying out his case to be sidetracked by some drunken interruption, "is that certain people wanted us to think there was no alternative. A dinosaur, or some such monster like a fabled Welsh dragon, was responsible for their disappearance. Apart from Kay, that is. Her lovelorn grief strikes me as being the real deal, authentic through and through. This leads to the perplexing question-"

"But a dinosaur must indeed have attacked them, and carried their wretched half-chewed corpses out to sea!" Elwin Kneath insisted passionately. "That's the only explanation that truly fits! That makes any sense! Consider: The monstrous roars! The impossibly moved boulder! The depressions in the sand as from giant, reptilian foot tracks! And that giant pile of poo on the twelfth green at Sheep's

Shank! Regardless of wherever that second golf ball came from! And as for the likeness of the dinosaur poo to sheep's poo, why wouldn't poo from a Stegosaur grazing on seaweed look near identical to poo from a sheep grazing on grass?!"

"Not to mention those suddenly vanished stones that looked like oversized Stegosaurus back plates!" chimed in John Jones lifting his head off the ground.

With a deer-in-the-headlights look, Elwin remarked, "That was spooky, truth be told."

"Everything fits the attacking dinosaur scenario, doesn't it, Mr. Kneath?" rhetorically asked Augie. "Some might say: as elegantly as your counterfeit coupon submitted at the Drunk In The Wool should have earned you a free meal!"

On this, where Augie was concerned, Elwin Kneath's lips moved with the quiet desperation of a landed fish's mouth gasping for water.

"Ah-HA!!" exulted Chief Constable Williams, on taking in Elwin's guilt-ridden reaction. "Well God bless you out-of-towners for solvin' the case after all! Even if one of you thinks you arrived here from the future! Assistant Constable Gruffudd, remove the shackles from Kay, with our apologies, and handcuff Elwin Kneath!"

"I say, Chief Constable, wouldn't you rather impart to the assistant constable: If you please, Assistant Constable Gruffudd, seriously consider the possibility of handcu-"

"Shut your trap, Rupert Hamster Holmes! Before I seriously consider the possibility of havin' you arrested for indecent public prevarication!"

"Well!" said Rupert in a huff, rising from his chair. "I have never- or maybe I should say- Oh, almost forgot the time when..." and he subduedly retook his seat.

"Let me understand this correctly, Chief Constable," Elwin Kneath said haughtily, though he rose from his chair to be handcuffed, offering no resistance. "You more easily believe I committed murder as some sort of serial killer, than that rather, a dinosaur is the demonic creature visiting death on our fair realm?"

"Without question!"

"If I was gay, I'd kiss you smack on the lips, Chief Constable," gushed Stephen.

"And that's proper, that is, that you're not!" gruffly reacted Rhys Williams.

Angharad Gruffudd thought better of giving Stephen a longing look while holding Elwin handcuffed. Instead, she went out of her way to turn her back on him.

"Here is how I see it, thanks again to Mr. Matias's help. It paints a very sordid picture indeed. You had to remove suspicion, Elwin Kneath, from any of the other possible suspects. In your sick mind, you believed we would be forced to admit the disappearances were due to none other than the cavernous maw of a prehistoric beast! The same as you believed the management of Drunk In The Wool would feel compelled to honor your counterfeit coupon as the real thing, and give you fish 'n' chips for free! Anyway, how better to remove suspicion of a human murderer than to have every potential suspect act desperately, obsessively in love with their victim?"

"So you think Robin and Nigel played along?" asked Augie. "And Kay wasn't brought into the plan, because of her sincere thing for Nigel?"

"Much obliged for your explanation, Mr. Matias!" said the chief constable zestfully. "Helps me understand it better, meself!"

"But one part doesn't make any sense, Chief Constable," said Augie. "Why would they participate in a scheme leading to their own demise? Were they so intent on others believing a dinosaur was on the rampage, they were willing to sacrifice their own lives?"

"We need an answer here!" Constable Williams

thundered. "And Elwin is it! Not goin' to wait around for you out-of-town crazies to ride your time machine into the past for a different answer! Also not goin' to let Elwin off the hook, just because we don't yet understand how every last detail fits! Angharad, take him away!! Off to the holdin' cell he goes!!"

Before the assistant constable could follow through on her superior's harshly intoned order, one of the two crypt-converted rental trailers started rocking violently from side to side, and the other joined in.

"Whatever ghosts or zombies are cooped up inside those crypts, I really feel for them," muttered time traveler Fred Frankly. "I also want to get the f-n' hell - Sorry, Father, I should have said jalapeño hell – out of here. But until our starship comes into harbor..."

Both crypt entrances were finally jolted wide open, and Nigel spilled onto the ground from one while Robin and Gerwyn spilled out of the other. To gasps and cries of "Oh my God!" the three rose to their feet. And most notably where Augie was concerned, there was a bandage on every forehead.

"So," drooled John Jones in front of Augie, "you out-of-towners couldn't let them rest in peace, could you?! And as for you bloody blokes just raised from the dead," he drooled some more, spinning around to face Nigel and company. Then nearly falling over, Augie mused, like a spinning top that lost too much steam to still remain perfectly upright, he went on, "Cheers! On behalf of me blood pressure, burp!, I especially appreciate your makeup job! If I didn't know better, I'd hardly believe you're down to skull faces!"

"Raised from the dead?" asked Rupert Hamster Holmes. "Or rather should we say, not so dead in the first place, if not completely- Well Gerwyn, especially, I expected your undershirt there to be soaked bloody, through and through, after seeing how shredded your...Perhaps St. Peter allowed you a fashion makeover?"

"NIGEL!?!?!" tearfully gushed Kay Morgan, running at him with arms outstretched, "You're alive!!"

"I say, a rather precipitous assumption there," protested Rupert as Kay reached Nigel, who fully welcomed her embrace despite their large audience. "Maybe not so much alive as, um..." He waited out Kay and Nigel's long, lingering lip-lock until finally he conceded, "Okay, alive."

"Sorry there, old chap," said Gerwyn clapping Elwin's back heartily. "We couldn't allow you to be hauled away for murders that didn't happen."

"So none of you are actually dead?" asked a bewildered Rhys Williams.

"Goin' to make it a whole lot harder to convict Elwin of murder now, isn't it, Constable? Cheers!" John Jones raised his prayer book for yet another irreverent toast.

"No need to hide your can of Toohey's inside the Lord's book on my account, John Jones," Father Hawkin shook his head. "In fact, I'd rather you not."

"What, Father, afraid your other parishioners will be disappointed when they don't find a brew inside theirs?"

"Don't tempt me to arrest the whole lot of you for wastin' me time!" growled Chief Constable Williams.

"Tempted, are you? Ooooo, we can't like the sound of that, can we, Father! Burp!" John Jones inserted.

Chief Constable Williams went on, "Elwin Kneath, I will have the assistant constable remove your handcuffs. But first, you need to explain exactly what this was all about!"

"A rather unnecessarily byzantine way to advertise luxury crypts, isn't it? Burp!" asked John Jones, then crossing himself added, "Forgive me, Father, for I have burped."

"My enablers were especially good sports, allowing me to cut into their foreheads for the blood required to stain a shirt and a shoe and so on," dispassionately explained

Elwin. "At least it wasn't as though I was nailing them to a cross."

"Praise the Lord for that, right, Father? Wouldn't want them to upstage the Big Guy, now would we?" irreverently inserted John Jones anew.

"To partially make up for their inconvenience," went on Elwin, "I stocked their crypts with certain most delightful goodies."

"That card-holdin' board for playin' solitaire whilst sippin' on a marshmallow-infested cuppa especially dark hot chocolate; would have wanted to be pretend-mauled by a nasty Stegosaurus far sooner, had I known...with you as me co-victim, Kay."

"Oh, Nigel!"

"Will never forget when I first heard about young David Taylor's dinosaur sighting, corroborated by his school teacher," proceeded Elwin as though Kay and Nigel might as well have been merely two birds chasing one another from tree to tree. "I said to meself, 'Unless and until that creature does the necessary legwork to make a real name for itself, we simply can't allow such an historic event to pass as though nothing happened. We need to engineer a follow-up worthy of *The Mabinogion*.'"

"The Mabi-what-the- Oh, sorry, again, Father," Fred censored himself.

"If only I could accompany you on your curious sojourn, child, to continue being your conscience when nobody else is looking."

"F-n' shame that, Father. Cheers!" John Jones toasted Father Hawkin with his beer-can-cloaking prayer book.

"Someone will correct me if I am wrong, no doubt," Sherman Peabody assured his woolen sweater vest, it seemed to Augie, the way he as usual scrunched his bowed-down chin into his neck. "But I believe *The Mabinogion* is an anthology stuffed full of Welsh legends and myths."

"Legends and myths, you say?" asked Stephen. "The schoolboy's report will make a worthy addition, indeed."

"Only if we totally discount the hard data from my flatus emission detector, especially two nights ago. As well as those loud roars heard all across coastal Pembrokeshire."

"Sorry there, mate," interjected Elwin. "Those loud roars came from me sound system tucked away in the heath at various locations. Ditto for the munchy crunchies. Though I did notice an unusually harsh chirping in the thick of that thunderstorm, the first night of your monster vigil."

"Okay," Sherman nodded into his neck, "but there are still- Well maybe we should hear about all your other, um, artistries for simulating a prehistoric monster's presence, to strike them off my evidence list."

"That would include the pile of poo on the twelfth green at the Sheep's Shank Links. A golf ball the same brand as Alistair's was easy to find at the nearest golf shop. Sorry, Gareth. Me own sheep pasture is too far away from the course for stealthy night transport. Be assured that atop what the constable returns from his evidence pile, I'll repay you plenty of interest from me own flock. You continue to keep your pants on, John Jones!

"Anyway, I am also responsible for that boulder rolling down the hill last night, to produce what was supposed to be a trail left by a dinosaur sledding on its epic rear end. And the haze was released from canisters secreted inside the heather. It was to keep anyone from seeing me use a crow bar to leverage the rock on its merry way, start it on its downward tumble. Only, too bad you noticed it there in the first place, Mr. Feldman."

"What about the depressions on the beach that looked like worn-down foot tracks? And those odd stones my crew couldn't locate after hiding behind them, the first night of our stake-out?" Sherman managed to ask without sounding, at least to Augie's ears, the least bit defensive.

"Not my doing, happily," answered Elwin. "Though I must express disappointment our Welsh dragon didn't leave behind more concrete evidence, thus saving me the bother."

"Random depressions in the sand, a couple of 'pffft's recorded by Sherman's flatus emission detector, some misplaced stones on what one can be sure is a constantly shifting shoreline..."

"And don't forget our film of seaweed tangles, swayed impossibly skyward by the wind," Sherman interrupted Steven before Stephen could conclude, *Is that all you got?*

"Maybe the lightning flashes didn't last long enough to see that your seaweed was water-bound into the face of a building wave? Yes, that could only have been a paranormally camouflaged dinosaur," Stephen remarked drily.

"So just what was your plan, Elwin? Keep havin' people pretend to be offed by your wished-for dinosaur? Packin' these oversized crypts with them until the rest of us are convinced there's a prehistoric monster on the loose?" Chief Constable Williams asked, letting his irritation all hang out.

"I did have three more 'victims' lined up," Elwin sighed. "And a few more were considering it, if I could have warm pasties delivered regularly to their crypts."

"That makes me afraid, and I'm not bein' funny about it, right, to ask who among this congregation *didn't* consider becomin' a fake sacrifice to your absurd cause, Elwin," Williams grumbled. All the uncomfortable squirming-about appalled him. "But I do have to ask: Suppose you finally succeeded. Suppose your machinations even convinced Assistant Constable Gruffudd that we had a deadly angry Stegosaurus on the loose. Then what for all your faux victims? I mean, they couldn't very well live out their remainin' days in those crypts, even if you kept the marshmallows, warm pasties, and freshly baked Welsh cakes delivered in abundance."

Elwin, Robin, Gerwyn, and Nigel exchanged puzzled looks until Elwin finally admitted, "Well don't you know, we didn't think it through that far."

"Excuse me, Angharad," said Stephen sidling over beside the assistant chief constable, finished un-handcuffing Elwin. "Is there any chance you would consider joining us on our dubious quest? We went to great lengths to assure a band of hoaxers wouldn't prank us yet again. But Mr. Kneath did a more than adequate job taking their place. So, I'm guessing we will be leaving here soon for heaven knows where. How about it? Think of all the sweet debunking we could do together."

As it sank in what he was really asking, Angharad gave Stephen her full, undivided attention, by turns pitying and longing. And she lost no time answering, "If I did accompany you, Stephen, I'd run the risk of starting to believe in love. That, in turn, would be a slippery slope to seriously wondering whether those three blokes over there," she nodded at the time travelers bunched beside each other, "really did arrive from the distant future. And actually considering the possibility a surviving dinosaur – it would have to be families of them roaming the Pembrokeshire coast."

"I know," Stephen nodded, teary-eyed. "We wouldn't want any of those things to happen, losing our sharp mental edge," Stephen shook his head, tears slowly streaming down his cheeks. "Skeptical forever?"

"Skeptical forever!"

"I say, new chum," Gerwyn affably slapped Sherman on the back, "good on you for knowing of our beloved *Mabinogion*. The few mentions of dragons therein, any possible relation to these dinosaurs you out-of-towners are set on proving still roam the earth?"

"Our resident folklore researcher here, Irene McDowell, is probably far better equipped to address that issue. Irene?" Sherman motioned her way.

"Sure, Sherman," Irene answered, as she did catch the gist of Gerwyn's question. "That would be the tale of Lludd and Llefelys. My take is that by the time it was written, whatever basis in real reptilian monsters was already long lost in the mists of prehistory. The red and white dragons, as described, seem little more than symbolic stand-ins for tensions between ancestral Welsh and English. The only detail that leaves me going 'Huh' concerns the dragon's nocturnal scream carried across the countryside to terrifying effect. One time hiking a trail along the north California coast, I heard a low moan that I later learned most likely carried from miles offshore, from a humpback whale."

"I've noticed this is a tactic typical of cryptozoologists, UFO fanatics, etc. straining to establish credibility," Stephen found himself mumbling to Gerwyn; Angharad had already moved herself a far enough distance away from him to avoid once more falling under his jaded, cynical spell. "They'll concede a certain amount of useless crap is, indeed, useless crap, to argue that certain other just-as-useless crap is the real deal."

Gerwyn wanted to ask, *Isn't that a wee bit of an uncharitable assessment, mate?* But before he could, a low whine rapidly intensified to a deafeningly shrill shriek, coming from the coast. Augie would have likened it to an eagle's cry put through a rock concert amplifier. The ambience left in its passing reminded him of the faint echo from a pipe organ on completion of the final sustained note.

Angharad and Stephen dared not make any further eye contact, lest they rush back into each other's arms, while

Reverend Hawkin said, "If we can turn to, 'Ar Hyd y Nos,' 'All Through The Night' in your hymnal, for a joyous recessional from the funeral that turned out not to be a funeral..."

Chapter 21

"Ah, you're here early, Vicky. We might as well proceed. Marsha should arrive soon, along with legal counsel, of course," said Diane Mueller. She motioned Vicky Copplestone to a chair directly across from hers at a plain rectangular table inside the conference room.

"Of course," agreed Vicky. She could see the delight in Diane's eyes, no matter how hard Diane tried to convey a deadly serious, gravely concerned persona. *She must be suppressing a happy dance over the jitters she thinks she's giving me, casually referring to legal counsel.* But no matter. Vicky kept herself cool and calm, thinking about the driving range afterwards. *Who knows? If I'm kicked out early enough, might have time for nine holes before I pick up Liz from soccer practice. Then maybe we can go for a waffle cone to celebrate my liberation.*

"Let's start with this," went on the curriculum adviser. From the floor, she lifted onto the table a big, unruly pile of papers. Vicky could tell they included the "Gotcha" test, shuffled together with pages from her students. "I have a theory, Ms. Copplestone. Having failed to get yourself fired any other way, you told your fourth graders something to the effect of: 'Here's the test I'm supposed to administer. Your job is to make a mockery of it.' How am I doing?"

"That's not how it went at all," Vicky found herself responding with surprising calm. This was the benefit, she figured, of having abandoned any hope the meeting could end well. "May I explain?"

"Be my guest," Diane motioned. *The floor is yours.*

"One of my students-"

"And which student would that be?" Diane smirked as in, Vicky wondered, *Does she think I'm making this up?*

"Erin Manley."

"Ah," Diane nodded. *You're doubling down on your lie, are you?*

"She convinced me that one of the analogy items could have been better conceived. She even offered an alternative that actually made more sense, even if it was crassly worded. Had to do with eggs and ducks. Would you happen to have read that one yet?"

"I was not about to waste my time wading through so much gibberish, once I realized what it was."

"Well in many cases, 'so much gibberish' included deep-dive thinking," Vicky bristled, complete with finger quotation marks. "I believed it was more important to encourage that, than to strictly follow test protocol."

"'Deep-dive thinking,' hmm," hmmed Diane, thumbing through the pile. "How's this for 'deep-dive thinking' from Jack Feuillet?" she asked, pulling forth two sheets.

"He wrote far more there than he's written for me the past two weeks."

"Okay, but did you actually take the time to read what he produced?"

"I felt rushed to turn in the stack, so- Hey, I thought you weren't going to waste your time with 'so much gibberish.'"

"That's not exactly what I said," Diane retorted in a condescending voice Vicky found beyond ridiculous.

Vicky clearly recalled Diane's precise phrasing, but figured she'd be wasting her time pushing back without a tape to rerun. So, she met the false assertion with firm quiet.

Diane taken off her stride by her nemesis *not* pushing back, she found herself going on awkwardly, "It was hard to avoid noticing. Here's the original item: 'Penguins live in the wild on every continent in the southern hemisphere. From this statement, we can conclude,' and choice 'c' sounds perfectly reasonable, 'Penguins don't live in the wild in Canada.' But this is what Jack wrote:

"'(a) Since I am in the northern hemisphere, the penguin up my ass must have been put there by someone mistaking it for a zoo.

'(b) We can't conclude anything, because the statement doesn't say penguins live in the wild ONLY in the southern hemisphere.

'(c) Who cares? Let's party!'"

"Honestly, choices 'b' and 'c' sound better to me than what I agree with you is the choice the test writers were going for. Jack is correct. That sentence about where penguins live doesn't say they are *only* found in the wild in the southern hemisphere. What an astute observation that shows very careful reading! Which I thought was the whole drive behind this activity in the first place."

"It doesn't say penguins *are* found in the northern hemisphere!" Diane bristled defensively, leaning forward in her chair.

"Also true, but Jack is still correct."

"The bottom line: This is a flagrant violation of test protocol. So flagrant, I didn't need anyone else's heads-up to figure that out. But Emme LeGrand's mother was concerned enough to call me about Emme's experience."

Earlier in the semester, Vicky would have asked why Emme's mom didn't call her first, instead of going over her head to the curriculum adviser. However, Vicky quickly came to understand that Ms. LeGrand wanted her daughter to be in the interdisciplinary studies class not so much for the dinosaur search. Rather, Emme was to be an informant. This wasn't the first or even second time Ms. LeGrand reported to Diane a purported concern from Emme over something that transpired in Ms. Copplestone's class.

"So, what did Emme tell her mom, this time?"

"Emme described students making up their own answers

while she stuck to the original directions. Ms. LeGrand is worried Emme will be downgraded for not joining your rewrite gang."

"Nothing could be further from the truth," asserted Vicky with an emphatic head shake. "I'm not supposed to be scoring those tests, and neither are any of the other fourth grade teachers. You know that. Moreover, I'm guessing the scorers are instructed to downgrade my students who went ahead with the testing violations I allowed, if not trash their papers altogether. Not, not allowed. Make that, encouraged. I encouraged those violations. Proudly!"

Diane was about to share Emme's nightmares after the whole thing concerning, as Jack called it, "Murrrrderrrr." *Which wouldn't have been a thing, had Diane not unwittingly spilled the beans.* Before she could, however, there was an insistent ring from the phone situated center of the conference table.

"Huh," Diane murmured in a not-displeased tone, pushing a button on the phone. Vicky sensed the curriculum specialist considered this interruption an extra added bonus as she spritely answered, "Diane Mueller here. Who might this be?"

"Hi, Diane. Bill Yokeshire. Listen, sorry for barging in like this..."

"Oh, not at all."

"What you reported about Ms. Copplestone, that's a grave offense requiring immediate attention."

Vicky well knew Bill Yokeshire was the county school superintendent. But instead of meeting his ominous words with anger or any other stressful emotions, she found herself feeling uncommonly relieved. Soon, finally, this whole ugly business with an inflexible education system was no longer going to be her problem.

"Vicky is here with me to discuss exactly that, Mr. Superintendent."

I'm sure she would have called him Bill under other circumstances; she wants to rub in how deadly serious this is. Whatever!

"Ms. Copplestone, telling students they can blow off the directions for a standardized assessment to make up their own answers...Well short of sexual abuse, I don't think teacher behavior can be more seriously unprofessional than that. The consequences that must be imposed...But first, Diane, I need to clear up a minor detail, I'm sure."

"Of course," Diane responded warily, resettling herself in her chair with what Vicky took to be a bit of a squirm.

"I was looking at the master fourth grade schedule, wasn't it?"

"Um, yes."

"I'm not seeing the particular assessment you described."

"That's because, um, you see, to identify best practices for student achievement, we had our fifth-grade teachers prepare a formative assessment on reading comprehension to give the fourth grade."

"Then this was something in-house, not an official standardized assessment."

"We thought having the fifth-grade teachers prepare it, the fourth-grade teachers wouldn't have any idea-"

"Wait. The fourth-grade teachers had no input?"

"We thought-"

"Ms. Mueller," the superintendent interrupted her again, while Vicky was thinking she'd love to put Diane on the spot herself, and ask who that "we" was aside from Diane herself, "I think all the research is pretty clear on this point: In-house assessments provide the most useful data when they're prepared by the very same people who deliver the instruction. Then the official standardized assessments are meant to give some rough idea how schools in one part of the nation, or state, or county, are doing compared to schools in another part. Okay, this test formulated by fifth-grade teachers, exclusively, was given to the entire fourth grade?"

"Um, we wanted to drill down on just how well Ms. Copplestone's unconventional approach to interdisciplinary studies met student needs."

"Sorry to speak so bluntly, Ms. Mueller, but I really do hope this entire exercise wasn't for the sole purpose of casting aspersions on what you term Vicky Copplestone's 'unconventional approach'!"

"Heavens no!" Diane shrilly, almost tearfully denied the accusation.

Superintendent Yorkshire's sigh was audible over the speakerphone, before he said, "Vicky Copplestone, what do you have to say for yourself?"

"Thank you for asking, Dr. Yokeshire."

"Call me Bill; that Dr. thing is too stuffy."

"Thank you, Bill. What led to my admitted violation of the assessment protocol was a point one student made about an analogy item. Far as she was concerned, none of the answers fit closely enough, even as a lesser of evils. That is, if you thought the comparisons all the way through. I made a snap judgment that encouraging her deeper thinking was more in the class's best interest. I mean, rather than shutting her down with the usual 'just try to do your best' crap."

Diane visibly flinched like she received an electric shock, Vicky reckoned, on hearing the word "crap."

"I could wade into the observer's dilemma regarding behavioral research," Vicky went on.

"That won't be necessary, Vicky. The student you referenced would be Erin Manley, by any chance?"

"That's the one."

"Her parents called my office earlier to applaud your going off the rails to encourage their daughter. They-"

"I think it's worth noting that one parent called *me* to complain about everyone doing their own thing in Ms. Copplestone's class. They could make up their own answers like there's no right or wrong! She said that caused her daughter to feel *very* uncomfortable!" Diane bulldozed through defensively.

"Were there specific consequences, Vicky, imposed on any of your students? I mean, who decided to simply continue penciling in the answer bubbles, rather than writing out alternatives?"

"No. In fact," it dawned on Vicky as she spoke, "those students finished much earlier than the others. They had extra time to finish homework for another class, or read anything they wanted to their heart's content..."

"Diane," the superintendent's sternness erupted from the speakerphone, "the design of such an assessment as you described requires rigorous vetting by several stakeholders, including professional test designers. It should never be undertaken on the fly, especially for grinding axes as I suspect is the case here. Any results obtained from this ill-conceived venture, teachers are free to take from them what they can. But there will be no consequences for any one teacher as a result, do you understand?"

"I do."

"And as for you, Vicky, I applaud your unbending effort to keep your students' best interests at the forefront. But even if you feel all alone on a particular issue, two things I ask."

"I'm all ears, um, Bill."

"Thing one, certainly keep up your, I'll call it pedagogical courage. Thing two, however: Your colleagues aren't exactly unreasoning demons. If you smell a rat, as it sounds like you did with this 'gotcha' assessment, please share your concern early. Don't allow things to fester like this."

"That sounds like good advice," said Vicky while thinking,

This puts the onus on me. And ironically, I find myself backing down on sharing that concern with the very person who is encouraging me to let it rip!

Just then, principal Marsha Klondike rushed into the conference room with legal counsel by her side.

Legal counsel carried papers Vicky figured she was supposed to sign for easing her out of the school system.

"Sorry, Diane; he-" Marsha nodded at the lawyer "-hit some traffic on the Rockville Pike."

"One accident and it turns into a parking lot," legal counsel added as he took a seat. He studiously avoided eye contact with Vicky, who he guessed was the one to be axed.

"Is that you, Marsha?" Bill Yokeshire's voice once again crackled from the speaker phone.

"Bill? You wanted to address this situation directly?"

"I did. You can have our attack dog stand down."

"Oh?" Marsha looked around at Diane and Vicky. "Are we talking probation?"

"I don't envision that being necessary for Diane."

"For *Diane?*"

"I'm sure she will be happy to fill you in, while I strongly urge allowing Vicky Copplestone to resume what I suspect is her very busy schedule."

Good grief! Vicky thought to herself while headed back to her classroom. *I can't get myself fired, even when I try!*

Chapter 22

Ooo, a fog so thick, I can't see where the ground rises from the frozen river's edge, nor any of the spruce and pine up the hills, marveled eleven-year-old Amak Ashoona. She'd pushed aside the caribou skin flap of her father's ice fishing house dome for a peek outdoors. *Would it be too much to ask that it remain so thick, we're stuck here until Monday? Then I won't have to return to school until Tuesday! Going to take me at least that long to finish reading the collected works of Jane Austen. And fishing with my Cha'* (referring to her father) *is a whole lot more fun than overhearing the other girls tease me for bringing books everywhere I go.* "Maybe she's practicing for carrying twins" *got old the thirtieth time around. And I like Ahnah, but her parents are so strict, she's afraid to look anywhere but straight ahead. A bull moose might be about to trample her, and she'll never know what hit her. Ah, well,* Amak finally sighed in resignation. *Zero visibility fog has never stopped Cha' from going wherever he needed to go before. It's not likely to stop him now. What we need, instead, is an epic blizzard.*

"Din dąy (What are you doing), Amak?" asked Amak's father, Tulugaak, impatiently.

"Okay, I call you Cha'," Amak said with a huff as she let the skin flap fall back into place. "But, what, aren't there only nineteen people left around here who still speak fluent Hän? Not even including yourself?"

"I'm working to become number twenty, and working on you to become number twenty-one, in memory of your mother, Aurora."

"Okay, if you must know, I'm praying for the biggest blizzard, ever, to shut down school all next week."

"You did understand!" enthused Tulugaak, his heart

going out to his daughter. The mere mention of his beloved wife still brought Amak to tears that she fought off bravely to answer his question, no translation asked for.

Aurora passed on from shockingly unexpected heart disease, six months earlier.

"How about helping me pull in this net?" Tulugaak gave it a small tug on the end tied to a stake beside the fishing hole cut into the ice.

Amak raised her eyebrows to agree to the request, one of several nonverbal gestures common along the Yukon River some fifty miles east of Dawson. But she added, "I need to pee-pee first," motioning towards the door to the outhouse sealed into one curved side of the fish-house dome.

Amak's father raised his own eyebrows right back. And he added, with another tug on the net that didn't appear to be accomplishing anything, "By the time you finish your business, hopefully I'll have this freed from wherever it's stuck. It might be driftwood suspended in the slush."

No sooner did Amak shut the outhouse door latch than Tulugaak gave the net a much firmer tug, and found himself astonished by a strong tug right back.

Amak's father wasn't sure what happened next. It was all a blur, whether his daughter's blood-curdling cry, "CHA'!!!" came before or after a loud sloshy sound also from the outhouse, that concluded with a loud clunk on the floor. Plus, the entire outhouse suddenly rocked about chaotically, despite his having staked it secure into the frozen tributary. While that rocking continued, he shouted, "Open the door, Amak!"

"I can't!"

The lock was on his daughter's side so that she certainly ought to have been able to open the door. No matter. Tulugaak kicked it in.

He found Amak cowering and shivering underneath the

sink to the left of the door. Satisfied she was safe, if terrified, he focused on the putrid mess straight ahead, that he almost stepped into. Especially stenchy contents spilled from the shredded-apart outhouse container bag. The toilet lid was torn off its mooring, what must have made the loud clunk. And what looked like an unusually large fish scale sat in a brackish film of slushy cold water.

As Tulugaak pulled his daughter out of there, the chaotic rocking-about settled down, though not entirely. Before he could speak to Amak, something underwater, directly underneath them, clearly gave the fishing net two more fierce tugs. The second tug not only pulled the end of the net line into the fishing hole. It also took the pole to which it was tied. The net stretched a good fifty yards to another hole in the ice where the other end was tied to a second pole.

While Tulugaak gently, soothingly rubbed Amak's back, her clinging to him for dear life, he asked, "What happened in there?"

"Thank goodness it came before I could sit, you know," she spoke with no little embarrassment, averting her eyes. But then she looked up at her father, her face only inches from his, and said, "Cha', you must believe me when I tell you. It was the head of a dinosaur, a Tyrannosaurus. And yet with a peacock's crest like I've seen in my biology textbook!"

Tulugaak turned aside, pained to eye-watering effect by how much Amak sounded like and even looked like his late wife. He was as much upset by that as finding what she described impossible to believe...if anyone else but her had said it. Because also like his beloved wife, she was a no-nonsense sort, other than pining away for school closings.

"There's more," Amak went on, her account oddly settling her down. "Rather than sink back down through the toilet hole, it faded away."

"Ah," Tulugaak nodded. He had an easier time coping with the notion of something phantasmal, ghost-like. Better that than something totally, physically, solidly real. Especially as he had never experienced anything this utterly strange before. Although, he'd certainly heard enough comparably bizarre stories from fellow Canadians. He was always left thinking dubiously they were more for entertainment purposes, more to help get through especially harsh, poorly lit times of the year. That is, when they were not hallucinations brought on by over-exertion out in the arctic cold. But his hard-headed daughter coming up with such a story? Arguably the most bizarre tale of all, posing a dinosaur living in such frigid conditions? Weren't they creatures of the tropics, in addition to the no small detail that they went extinct millions of years ago?

Just then, before Tulugaak or his daughter could say another word, their ice-fishing dome, still staked secure, began rocking about again, if not nearly as violently as before. Then they heard an ear-piercing cracking-apart of thick ice that ended in an explosion of splashes. They could easily imagine an enormously powerful beast breaking through a frozen-over part of the Yukon River tributary.

Much as father and daughter, both, wanted to peek outside, see exactly what was going on, primal fear immobilized them. Instead, they clung tightly to each other.

What they heard next, the sounds were so familiar they knew exactly what was being impacted, if not by what agency. Something, presumably the creature Amak saw poke its head up through the outhouse hole, was gathering in the fishing net. And Tulugaak was sure a large pike caught up in that net was what he heard flopping about on the ice.

Then there was frantic tearing at the net, accompanied

by low hissing of reptilian frustration until at last, a deafening loud, screeching CHIRP!! echoed away down the river valley.

Tulugaak peeked outside while more tributary ice cracked into another slushy splash. He was in time to see a long tail, like an alligator's tail, he guesstimated a full twenty feet long. It slid rapidly out of sight, down through the watery slush.

I must tell the world about this creature, surely as endangered as my grandparents' language...and maybe more likely to help with that language's survival than any museum-run or school-run programs and exhibits!

Chapter 23

"Ah, I see familiar faces from- Shall we call it the aborted funeral?" asked Eclipso on one-half of a split-screen aboard the steam-powered drone, Cloud Nine. He gestured with his humus-dipped pretzel at the group Augie and company also had a good look at, in the other half of their split-screen.

If Augie didn't know better, he would have sworn he saw Eclipso's mother wipe away a small tear, standing ever-stoically behind him in her flower-print calico dress.

"Maybe not so much aborted as postponed until the lives of Nigel, Robin and Gerwyn run their full course, since..." Rupert Hamster Holmes paused to hunch his shoulders, cringing at how severely Nigel, Kay, Gerwyn, and Robin stared him down. Then he finished timidly, "Aborted describes it quite adequately, as it turns out."

"Mr. Sunray Smith, sir, we wanted to thank you and your Alistair Frump in particular, for concocting a plan-"

"Maybe not so much concocting as- Well, right, okay then, concocting it is," Rupert finished by mumbling quietly.

"For concocting a plan, as I was saying," Elwin Kneath continued a bit huffily, "that has the potential for reviving this entire region while still preserving the old traditions; everything from woolen clothes-making to choral music."

"More of a brainstorming session with the locals," inserted Alistair faux modestly, "since I doubt the Jurassic Links concept can survive on the promise of rare dinosaur poop-dumps soiling their golf-course greens."

"Which as it turned out was delivered by Elwin, but we still love you anyway, right?" said Kay before returning arm-in-arm to Nigel's side, lest he grow jealous.

"And what is this plan? Yes, Bonsai Gator, I see you are more than ready to boogie to 'We Can Work It Out.' But that celebration can certainly wait until we know why we are celebrating."

Holymamoomoo, Augie marveled. *Eclipso can tell which reggae-fied Beatles tune Bonsai Gator wants to dance to, simply by his wavy foreleg motions? Those all look like some variation on hula-hula to me, one no different from the rest.*

"We've heard from other parts of the U.K., about staged murder mysteries while people dine, whether inside a castle or on a special train ride," said Nigel. For once, he stood perfectly, soberly still rather than staggering all over the place. "Well as your good mate Alistair put it, we might not have dinosaurs droppin' by for droppin' somethin' impolite on a regular enough basis for the equivalent to a whale-watchin' tour. But sure as sure can be, we have plenty of counterfeitin' resources, thanks to Elwin, plus the actin' talent as displayed by Robin, Gerwyn, and yours truly." Nigel took a bow coupled with a flowery arm gesture. "We can repeatedly perform our 'Murder Most Saurian' spectacle, complete with the surprise ending, requirin' a funeral to be called off! The money to be made from tourists, it's enough for even John Jones to moderate his beer intake so he doesn't botch his lines! On behalf of all of us, I say a big fat 'Diolch!.' That's Welsh for thank you, the size of a Brontosaurus poo if there is still such a thing. And we wish you well findin' enough livin' dinosaurs somewhere, Alistair, that people will pay good money to watch them dumpin' loads on your Jurassic Links golf course!"

"Diolch!" Nigel's partners-in-fun all waved happily into the video camera. Pursuant to which Nigel added, "Well I guess we better let you get on your way in that giant cloud contraption I see floatin' overhead. As we say here, 'Hwyl fawr'!"

"Hwyl fawr!" the others repeated, waving skywards at Cloud Nine racing westward into an orange sunset.

*

"Well then, most esteemed quest team, nothing much else to report? Simply more tantalizing bits leading essentially nowhere?" asked Eclipso in what Augie sensed for the very first time was a hint of real exasperation.

"I wouldn't say that," Harry Letterman shook his head, taking everyone but his wife, Harriet, by surprise. "We might have found a pattern."

"A pattern?" Eclipso perked up enough to repeat.

Bonsai Gator stopped mid-sway in his dance to a Beatles reggae-fied song that hadn't been replayed for him yet. He was clearly if impossibly intrigued, where Augie was concerned.

"No insult intended," Stephen Feldman prefaced his remark. "But as brilliant as you might be, Harry-"

"And Harriet," Harry added. "We came up with this together."

"And Harriet," Stephen nodded with more frustration than he wanted evident. "I think your special condition, the Down Syndrome, predisposes you to finding patterns that don't actually exist."

Irene looked Stephen's direction, jaw-dropping shocked by his remark.

But Harry cooly reacted, "Stephen, I know you hurt from missing Angharad. I could feel that when we saw she didn't join the others to say goodbye. Hurt makes us say hurtful things. So my response to you is: I'm sorry the same love of skepticism that brought you two together now keeps you two apart."

"Skepticism that your relationship could last," Harriet joined in, nodding. "It's like our dinosaur search. You're afraid you'll be disappointed if we prove no non-avian dinosaurs still survive. That's why you put up this wall of not believing it's possible. And you're also afraid of love, afraid that if she doesn't love you back, how much that will hurt."

"Exactly!" Harry hi-fived Harriet, albeit somberly for how much he sincerely felt for Stephen.

"What is this pattern you two think you've uncovered?" asked Eclipso, while Stephen shook his head, flustered.

"We really don't want to say yet," answered Harriet. "Except to point out that over a very short time, in four different locations, we've had unusual experiences with possible dinosaurs. Previously, though, they were regularly reported years apart, not all within the same time frame."

"That's discounting the hoaxes," Harry chimed in.

"The pattern is one of no proof, beyond a fart here in the land of countless sheep, a missing stone there in the land of mysterious stones left scattered about by the prehistoric peoples of the U.K.," Stephen strongly pushed back, having overcome his discomfort over the Letterman couple's wildly in-depth psychoanalysis. "Reports of 'possible dinosaurs' spread years apart: That's exactly the frequency you'd expect for mistaken identifications fueled by wishful thinking. The sort of robust populations you'd require for non-avian dinosaur survival to the present day would generate far more sightings."

"Unless- I really have been set to wondering about the possibility of an extreme hibernation pattern," Augie interjected.

That led to a seemingly inquisitive head tilt by pencil-sized Bonsai Gator on the video screen, and Stephen rolling his eyes yet again. He was beyond frustrated by what he figured Augie and company were making of Bonsai's head motion.

"I know this isn't the first time some of us have wondered whether our quarry enters a deep stasis for years, if not centuries or millenia, between meals," elaborated Augie. "Although maybe like cicadas, different dinos are on different schedules."

"Which would make Harriet and Harry's analysis all the more potentially significant," suggested Sherman, his downward-cast chin ever-scrunched into his neck.

"Far as separating the proverbial wheat from the chafe, must have been some special addendum to Murphy's Law in effect," stewed Irene. "The one expedition we evaded the hoaxers, we were amply pranked by the locals. Though I do wish them good fortune rerunning Elwin Kneath's crazy scheme for profit. Plus keeping some of them from having to join the local Alcoholics Anonymous chapter. Your input on that, Alistair, good stuff. And as for *you*," she abruptly turned Scott's direction.

Scott was seated at the table on the navigation bridge where the Lettermans laid out numerous sprawling thumbtacked maps.

"Next time you need to spill your guts, you'll want to make absolutely certain whose back you're addressing," she concluded with a sly grin, as touched as amused by how Scott avoided eye contact with her, pretending total focus on one of Harriet's maps.

"Ah, yes, those pesky hoaxers," nodded Eclipso, his mother nodding along behind him in perfect sync. "As you know, we narrowed it down to three, the hi-tech surveillance suspects of which I am sure their owners had no prior knowledge. Well now, I'm relieved to report having determined the guilty party, if you will. With special thanks for Sherman's assistance."

*

"You remember what I told you, about Eclipso confiscating certain items, including that dragon necklace? One of which he had reason to believe was giving away our whereabouts to someone intent on bombarding our search with hoaxed dinosaur presences?" Roberta asked Daniela. She used this question to fend off Daniela going in for a hug while their two dachshunds ran circles round their townhouse foyer, pee-dribbling excited over Roberta's return.

"Oh my God!" Daniela suddenly backed off from Roberta to exclaim. "You thought I had the necklace bugged! Hoping if that idiotic expedition got sabotaged enough, you'd come running home! Like it wasn't going to collapse under the weight of its own absurdity sooner or later anyhow! Just how sick-"

"No-"

"Okay, that's it. Queenie, Prince Charles, we need to get the hell out of here!" Daniela turned every which way, frantically wondering where to start first.

Roberta thought to herself, *Well this is as expected; she's looking for an excuse to deep-six us...and on that we might agree.* "No, you stay," she insisted, picking up her suitcase to turn around and leave. "I'm sure Princes Angelbert and Englebert can put me up until...not certain when Eclipso-"

"God damn Eclipso! Couldn't care less! GET OUT!!!"

*

"Sorry I'm late, gir- errrrr, Irene," Skip corrected himself mid-stream as he sat across from Irene at a Spanish tapas restaurant in Frederick, Maryland. He almost recalled too late how she hated being called 'girl.' "That candy shop on the corner, you wouldn't believe how long the checkout line was. But here, a little something..." He pushed a small bow-tie-ribboned box of truffles across the table.

Normally, Irene might have snarked, *Yes, it's too bad there was no possible way you could have allowed for the time that might take, and gotten here earlier. No, wait...* Instead, she pushed the box right back at Skip like it was her winning move in some bizarre board game, he couldn't help thinking. And she asked, "That thermos you gave me before my first trip, where exactly did you get it from?"

"That's okay if you lost it," *or trashed it*, Skip also couldn't help imagining ruefully. "I'm sure I can find you another one just like it."

"I'm not asking for another one. I want to know how you got *that* one."

"Can I bring you folks something to drink while you, um, until you have a chance to crack open the menu?" the waiter intruded tentatively. He was clearly bothered seeing both menus left untouched beside Irene and Skip.

"I'll have whatever she's having."

"Tap water will be fine," Irene responded, her eyes not budging from severely staring down Skip.

"Make that two." Skip held up two fingers while screaming inside his head, *Skiiiiip!! You idiot!!! You don't say that about tap water like it's a gin and tonic!!* Then fiddling nervously with the truffle box Irene pushed back to him, he asked, "You sure you don't want to sample just one? They're homemade, I think... Okay, there were these two guys," he finally admitted, seeing whereas Irene wasn't going to let him off the hook of her piercing, unrelenting stare-down until...

"What about two guys? Did you know them?"

"Never saw them before. They read my interview with you in the *Gazette*, and contacted the news room to get in touch with me!" Skip continued defensively.

"Then what?" Irene persisted, feeling like she could use an industrial-sized hook on a thick, strong rope to pull answers from Skip's mouth.

"We met at that Italian place next door, and they asked me to have you bring the thermos on any future expeditions for your folklore research. They wanted feedback on how well some special insulation worked to keep liquids warm or cold, wherever you went," elaborated Skip in a tone that to Irene's ears remained guilt-ridden defensive.

"What were their names? I mean, who were they? And did they ever get back in touch with you for my feedback? Why didn't they approach me directly?"

"Far as their names go, um, we really didn't get into that. But here was the funny thing," Skip proceeded quickly to head off Irene ripping into him about how they "really didn't get into" their names. "After handing over that thermos, they never got back to me for your feedback, like they said they would."

"And you didn't think to tell me any of this when you- Wait, did they pay you to have me test their friggin' thermos?"

"I think so," Skip responded haltingly, cowering like he expected a pounding blow Irene had to work hard to restrain herself from delivering.

"You *think* so?! You mean you're not sure?! How much are you not sure they paid you?!"

"Uh, um, it might have been a few thousand dollars?"

"You're asking *me*?!?! Just how many was a few thousand dollars?!?" Irene roared as the waiter made an abrupt U-turn away from asking whether she and Skip looked at the menu yet.

"Um," Skip actually counted on his fingers like he didn't already know, "I suppose it was around seven thousand..."

"Seven thousand dollars?!" Irene this time limited herself to the harshest possible whisper. She didn't want the restaurant management to throw them both out the door...at least not yet. "Good God, Skip! Did you ever think to wonder, to ask why my using their freakin' thermos would be worth that much to them?!?"

"Um, I wasn't paid to wonder about that," Skip responded from a curled-up fetal position, his side of the booth. But as Irene continued to stare him down like a bull about to charge, he did work up the courage to ask, "Was there something wrong with the, um, product?"

"Only that someone – maybe those two crumbs who paid you off – used it to eavesdrop on us, so they could sabotage our search with multiple elaborate hoaxes. We weren't sure what if anything was real evidence, amidst all the pranking. And now I'm going to need a good, long break from you. I wish you every success on your future endeavors, but..."

"In other words, you're more optimistic about finding a living dinosaur somewhere out there than about finding, um, us," Skip summed up with soft-spoken resignation.

"Enjoy your chocolates."

"Well watch out for yourself. Talk about hidden monsters, you and I know the KKK-"

"If I need a bodyguard, I'll hire one."

Even though he was already out the front door to the tapas place, Irene could still hear him screaming at himself, "Skiiiiiip!!"

Chapter 24

"Mm mm mm," Jake Rumblehouse mm-mm-mmed. He couldn't stop marveling at, shaking his head over, the most elaborate drawing-board plan for a Bigfoot costume he'd ever seen. And he'd seen more than a few. "How can anyone, even musclebound, maneuver this contraption?" he asked Paul Smith seated beside him, and Aaron Levy seated across from him. They were on his chartered business jet headed north to drop off the hoaxing team and their equipment before Jake's television crew reached their final destination. "My God, it makes one of those astronaut suits for walking on the moon look like a tank-top by comparison!"

"The suit's proportions are indeed faithful to claimed Bigfoot proportions. Without its electronically enhanced pulley system, the strongest person in the world would have an impossible time operating it. But as it is, I could even run around in it without much difficulty," Aaron Levy patiently elaborated for the umpteenth time. He hoped to forestall the reality show host bailing out at the last minute on his important role in their most elaborate hoax, yet.

"Okay, I know I'm repeating myself," Jake set aside the schemata to say. "But I need you guys to talk me down off the cliff once more. This particular staging of a cryptozoological encounter is like nothing I've ever heard or seen *anyone* claim to have experienced before. It's so daring, so wild, isn't it going to arouse suspicion from the proverbial git-go? Especially among your seasoned, maybe even jaded explorers working for Eclipso?"

"No," Paul Smith shook his head defensively. "Exactly because it is so out-there, Eclipso's gang will overthink it. They'll decide nobody would try to fake such a thing because it's so ridiculous! What they're bracing for or hoping for, even, I'm sure, is more of the usual. Three-toed foot tracks, a strange roar, a whipping-about crocodilian tail sliding rapidly out of sight underwater while sonar shows something monstrous cruising by underneath their cigarette boat, that sort of thing."

"What we will have the locals witness...Once Eclipso's team takes the bait, they're certain to never know what hit them," Aaron chimed in as Jake Rumblehouse's charter jet came in for a landing, pontoons deployed, on a semi-frozen stretch of the Yukon River, several miles east of Dawson City, Canada.

www.ingramcontent.com/pod-product-compliance
Lightning Source LLC
Chambersburg PA
CBHW021957010726
47494CB00003B/776